A VISION OF ENCHANTMENT

Reluctantly, Lirrel lifted her head and opened her eyes to the vision. The evening mist cloaked her in darkness and she tensed as the thickened air held her in its grasp. . . .

A figure appeared on the crescent beach. It was a woman in an Islander's red skirt, and over her head a black shawl whipped in the wind, hiding the woman's face as she ran. The woman stopped and faced the restless waves.

"Turn around," Lirrel whispered, straining to see the woman in the vision. "Please, turn around for me." Lirrel stepped forward, a hand outstretched as if to touch the woman's shoulder.

But her foot found only air. Lirrel yelped as she teetered dangerously on the edge of the pier. The vision shredded apart as a cold spray of water struck her. Instead of the island, Lirrel saw the dark water splashing up to meet her. . . .

Also by Midori Snyder

New Moon
Sadar's Keep

BELDAN'S FIRE

Midori Snyder

A TOM DOHERTY ASSOCIATES BOOK
NEW YORK

This is a work of fiction. All the characters and events portrayed in this book are fictitious, and any resemblance to real people or events is purely coincidental.

BELDAN'S FIRE

Edited by Terri Windling

Cover art by Dennis Nolan

A Tor Book
Published by Tom Doherty Associates, Inc.
175 Fifth Avenue
New York, N.Y. 10010

Tor ® is a registered trademark of Tom Doherty Associates, Inc.

ISBN: 0-812-50913-7

First edition: January 1993

Printed in the United States of America

0 9 8 7 6 5 4 3 2 1

For Terri, my "step" sister.

"Evil customs of the past shall be broken off and everything based on the just law of nature."

—The Charter Oaths

"None of us lives as our own master and none of us dies as our own master."

—Romans 14:7-9

Prologue

"**M**adam, the watch is nearly over," Firstwatch Gonmer said discreetly to the woman walking at her side, her breath condensing into steam in the cold night air as she spoke.

"I'm not ready to return," the Fire Queen Zorah answered. Her gaze pierced the shadows of the old city's street and her eyes glowed a brilliant green in the stray light of a window.

"My duty, madam," the Firstwatch murmured, suppressing her impatience.

The Fire Queen stopped walking and faced Gonmer. "Of course," she said evenly. "Return as you wish."

"But madam, I shall not leave you unattended." The small of Gonmer's back ached from the long night following Zorah's aimless ramble through the streets of Beldan. Her feet were cold and the fingers of her sword hand stiff from the damp air. The serving maids had complained to Gonmer that the Queen rarely slept at night, stealing moments of troubled rest only in the daylight. And after the last two nights of walking, Gonmer believed them. The Fire Queen fled from sleep, seeking distraction in the movement and noise of the city's streets. More than once,

Gonmer had raised the alarm to call the Guard when Flocks of
beggars had tried to roust them in darkened alleys. But Zorah
had seemed less agitated by the scuffling than by whatever it was
that privately haunted her dreams.

"Your page may stay, if it makes you feel better," Zorah said.
Two drunken watermen came spilling out of the Barge determined to brawl in front of them. Zorah's mouth lifted to a thin-
lipped smile. She was amused by the clumsy fighters as they
staggered like Ghazali bears, their ponderous blows missing their
targets.

Gonmer looked at her page, Lais, who was swaying on her
feet with fatigue. Whore's shit, Gonmer swore furiously. Half
asleep the girl was worthless as a guard. She'd get her throat cut
long before she even saw an attack coming. Two nights in a row
she'd had little or no sleep; why couldn't the Queen see the cost
of her madness? Gonmer stole a glance at the Queen.

Zorah had changed since the spring's Firefaire. Once Gonmer
had believed, like all Orans, that the Fire Queen was immortal,
inviolate from time's scourge. She was beautiful, with skin as
white and smooth as Silean marble. Her fiery hair, the sign of
her fire element, wreathed her face with a crown of burnished
red gold. But when the victory at Sadar's Keep fell to the New
Moon army, something unexpected had happened. Time had
caught her in its cruel grip and Zorah had aged in a single night
from a young woman into middle age. Still beautiful, but without the keen edge of youth, her power had diminished like a
flame torn by the wind.

They now looked of an age, Gonmer thought, studying the
recent lines added to Zorah's face. But that was only an appearance. The middle-aged face did not reveal the truth, but the hard
green eyes did. Zorah was at least two hundred years old. She
had reigned since the Burning, when the destruction of the
Queens' quarter knot had left her Oran's only Queen, possessed
of the old magic. At Zorah's request the Silean armies had come
to quell the civil war and restore peace. In the two centuries that
followed, the Sileans had remained, not only as soldiers, but
increasingly as landowners, merchants, traders, and administra-
tors to every aspect of Zorah's regime. Gonmer, as captain of

Beldan's Firstwatch, and Lais, her page were all that remained of the old regime. Only an Oran woman could hold the position of Firstwatch and Gonmer believed Zorah clung to it to rankle the otherwise male Silean Guard that patrolled the city. A dubious honor, Gonmer thought sourly every time she saw the leering faces of the Silean Guard she commanded. Always a battle to teach them respect.

"Oy." Gonmer dug a sharp elbow into Lais's side. The girl gasped, roused brusquely out of somnolence.

"Z'blood, where are we?" she mumbled.

"Blessing Street."

Lais whispered an obscenity beneath her breath.

"The thirdwatch is nearly ended. I need to get back and release the firstwatch to their duties," Gonmer said quickly. "I heard the lighterman cry the hour a while ago."

"And the Queen?" Lais asked, looking around sleepily.

"Over there," Gonmer said with a nod of her head. "She wants to continue. You're to accompany"—Gonmer paused as Lais groaned softly—"you're to accompany her until she's ready to return. This is duty, Lais. The honor of the Firstwatch is at stake."

Lais rubbed her face briskly and drew a deep breath of cold air. She shivered lightly. "Aye, Firstwatch," she replied glumly.

Gonmer took off the silver whistle she wore around her neck and passed it to Lais. "Should you need it," she said gravely. "But remember, if you call the Guard be prepared to give orders. Otherwise handle it yourself. Either way, hesitation will prove your undoing." Gonmer stopped herself from giving the ten other pieces of advice she would have liked to pound into the girl's head. Now was not the time.

"Yeah, I'll be careful," Lais said, taking the short, two-holed whistle and quickly settling the chain around her neck. She stifled a yawn.

Gonmer scowled. She hated leaving them this way but she was going to have to trust the girl to her duty; one day Firstwatch would be Lais's responsibility. Gonmer saluted the Queen and headed toward the direction of the Keep. She could see its black bulk rising on the hill above the city. A few pale stars winked between the crenellated walls of the towers. The sound of drunken laughter raised her hackles.

Gonmer gave a final glance over her shoulder, seeing Lais fall into step beside the Queen. A chill tapped a warning on her spine and Gonmer knew suddenly that Faul Verran, the Firstwatch before her, must have felt the same. The chill was age, catching up with her at last. Immortal as the Fire Queen seemed to be, she would not tolerate aging in her servants. Sooner or later, she would take a close look at Gonmer's face and decide she was too old for the duty of Firstwatch. Decide that the gray hairs and the deepening lines etched across her brow were unacceptable. Experience would count for nothing. Neither would loyalty. Gonmer would be ordered to leave, as Faul had been. But how could she leave the position of Firstwatch? Gonmer wondered miserably. How could she ever leave the only life that mattered to her? Gonmer drew a deep breath and eased the worried furrow that stretched across her brow. One day she would face that problem, but not yet. She was too important just now, too needed, she reminded herself.

Beldan was still in turmoil after the massacre and earthquakes at Firefaire. On the heels of the disastrous spring had followed a long summer of drought. There were serious threats from the countryside. The rebel army, the New Moon, held Sadar's Keep after their victory over the Silean troops. More recently the New Moon had attacked trading cities on the Hamader River, cutting off food supplies to the city. As winter loomed, Beldan prepared for a siege. A new Silean Regent had arrived with two hundred ships and Beldan was occupied by Silean soldiers. In their black-and-gray uniforms they crowded the streets like flocks of ravens. It was rumored that more Silean ships were on the way, to wage a war in the countryside. Yes, Gonmer thought bitterly, she would keep her position as Firstwatch for now. She was a trusted servant in times of betrayal. Despite the suffering of her city, Gonmer gave a tight, satisfied smile.

The Fire Queen Zorah turned left and then left again, paying scant attention to Lais. In the narrow back alleys the darkness was almost absolute, and few sounds could be heard. Once Lais stared upward, needing a glimpse of the sky to reassure herself that they had not wandered into the ancient catacombs beneath the city. The girl clenched her fists, remembering how after the quakes at Firecircle fissures had split the old seams and the dead of centuries past had been tossed to the surface to join the newly slain.

But Zorah traveled with certainty, reaching out from time to time to touch the cold walls. Tiny fragments of plaster crumbled beneath her fingertips. Water dripped from low-slung eaves with a desolate sound. Lais stepped into a black puddle, stifling a cry as the icy water penetrated her thin boots and soaked her feet. Someone scurried past her in the dark, a shoulder shoved against hers, smelling of smoke and urine. Lais recoiled, her back hitting the rough surface of a wall. She crouched in the darkness, her heart rapping as she prepared for an attack. But none came, and as she waited she realized she had lost her sense of direction. Which way had she come? Which way should she turn? Damn this stinking dark!

Lais licked her lips, chapped from the cold fall air, and then cursed herself for hesitating. She couldn't hear the Queen's footsteps. Her hand gripped the whistle around her neck.

"Madam?" she called out quietly, peering into the dark.

"I'm waiting," came the Queen's curt reply.

Lais jumped, shocked to hear the voice so close. But having spoken, Zorah was walking once again, the loose stones grinding beneath her heels. Lais hurried to follow the sound.

Zorah walked with a steady gait and Lais caught up with her, grateful even for the Queen's prickly company in the darkness.

"What do you think of the Sileans?" Zorah asked. "Think they will succeed against the New Moon?"

Lais was surprised by the question. "Madam?" she replied.

Zorah gave an annoyed laugh. "Surely you must have an opinion, an assessment of the situation. That's your duty. To know what I don't know, to see in Beldan what I can't. Come now, don't babble." Zorah's voice bristled with impatience. "Give me your opinion."

Lais swallowed quickly, gathering her thoughts for a suitable answer. "Well, I don't think much of the new Regent—"

Zorah's laughter cut the darkness. "He's a pretty boy though, is Regent Ilario, with his beautiful black eyes. They always send the handsome ones, thinking it will soften my disposition. What's wrong with him?"

"He doesn't know anything about Oran and from what I've seen, still less of soldiering. I've watched him at practice. He's clumsy with a sword and blames his personal guard for his own mistakes. He's dangerous, but only because he is stupid."

Zorah nodded. "I agree. The man believes he will win against the New Moon, marching out in straight lines on an open field. But New Moon is more cunning than that, and Ilario has no experience with fighting in the woods, or skirmishes in village streets."

"I have heard—" Lais started tentatively and then paused.

"What?" Zorah demanded. "What have you heard?"

"There is another, General Re Silve, coming with more troops."

"Yes," Zorah agreed. "There is to be a winter campaign to free the cities on the Hamader River so that Beldan will not perish for want of food. And, more importantly, so that the Silean trade can continue uninterrupted," Zorah continued sarcastically. "You can guess which is of greater value to the Sileans."

"The thirdwatch were talking about him. They said General Silve was a brilliant commander, good at military strategy, and ruthless."

They passed beneath a torch, the weak flame illuminated Zorah's face. It still shocked Lais to see how the Queen had aged. Her profile was proud, her lips curved in a frown. The fiery red hair rusted in the pale light. Then they slipped into shadow again and the sight of her face was gone.

"Why do you think Silve wasn't sent as Regent instead of Ilario Re Anguar?" Zorah asked.

Lais shrugged. "The Guards said that General Silve is ugly. Face like a bull and a great mane of gnarled hair he'll neither cut nor style. One said a disease made him misshapen, but another said it was evil that poisoned his face."

"So," Zorah said, "the Silean parliament gives me the pretty-

pretty to keep me amused in Beldan while they send a beast to ravage my country." Zorah gave a pained sigh.

"Madam, whose side do you serve?" Lais asked, confused. "You despise the Sileans, and yet—"

"Yet I permit them to wage war in my country?" Zorah finished. "I serve no side but my own. No master but my own will. And you, who are soon to be Firstwatch, serve no one but *me*."

"Yes, madam," Lais answered quickly. The darkness hid the anger on the Queen's face, but not the menace in her voice.

"Oran exists because of me. And when the New Moon wage civil war they are attacking me, my flesh. They deserve their fate, even at the hands of those Silean bastards."

The Queen smoldered with anger and in the dark Lais smelled the coppery reek of the Fire Queen's hair. She swore silently to herself for the boldness that had made her ask such a question.

The sound of Zorah's footsteps ground to a halt and Lais tensed.

"Did you know that my sister Huld still lives?" Zorah said softly.

"Madam?" Lais replied, astonished by the confidence.

"Oh, yes. Much diminished in power. She is an earth element but she survives as something other than a woman; a field or a tree in Avadares, I can't be certain. But it is she inciting the New Moon to rebel, it is she urging the farmers to take up swords instead of plows. As it was in the Burning, Huld splits Oran apart as she tries to drive me into the Chaos."

Out of the dark, the Queen's hand gripped Lais's shoulder tightly.

"Huld will not succeed," Zorah said in a cold voice. "I will remain forever. The New Moon and the Sileans may destroy each other, but I will remain."

Zorah released her hold on Lais. "What do you hear of the Queens' quarter knot?" she asked in a strained voice.

Lais rubbed her shoulder, still feeling the bruising fingertips on her skin. She answered carefully.

"No more than yourself, I'm sure, madam."

"Not the answer I wanted. Do better," came the hard reply.

Lais tried again. "I've heard that the New Moon boasts of three of the elements needed to make a Queens' quarter knot. A child of fire—"

"Jobber," Zorah answered knowingly. "The girl who approached me at Firecircle. There isn't much of her story I don't know."

"A child of air."

"The Ghazali, Lirrel. I know her too," Zorah said flatly. "It was her flute that stopped the flow of Oran magic and did this to me."

Lais wondered at Zorah's words. She knew nothing of Oran magic, save that to be born with it was a certain trip to the gallows. After the Burning, Zorah had created a Guild of Orans whose only talent was to see the aura that all children born with the old magic carried in a halo of colored light. The Readers had been vigorous in their task of purging Oran of their children. And yet, Lais knew, some had slipped the noose. Stories had filtered back to Beldan that at Sadar's Keep there had been Oran magic. Lais now understood the fear that haunted the Queen's sleep. Four girls, four elements, could intertwine their power into a Queens' quarter knot and establish a new generation of magic in Oran without Zorah.

"There is also a child of earth," Lais said.

"Yes, Shedwyn. A farmer's child, and a daughter of Huld. She has weaknesses that Huld did not," Zorah said evenly. "And the fourth child? The child of water?"

Lais shook her head. "I haven't heard. Does she exist?"

Zorah laughed loudly. "Of course she does," she answered savagely. "I can almost taste the saltwater in her blood. The New Moon will find her."

"And then?" Lais asked.

"And then they will come to Beldan, to me. And I shall use their fledgling knot to free Oran of Huld's curse. And after that I won't need the Silean armies anymore, nor the Readers."

Lais was stunned by Zorah's words. She wanted to ask about her own future as Firstwatch but when she held out a hand she discovered Zorah was gone. She could hear the echo of her footfall growing fainter in the alley.

Swearing, Lais chased after her. Her breathing was shallow, puffs of cold steam trailing in her wake as she hurried. Smoke thickened in the air, and with the smoke came the cloying perfume of scent sticks mingled with the stench of burning flesh. Lais reared back, recognizing it, frantically wiping away the soft, sticky ash that swirled and landed on her face. She covered her mouth with her hand, not wanting to breathe in any of it.

The Death House occupied the center of a small square, surrounded by an orange haze. Scroggles it was called by those on the street, and not a place where one went strolling. For Beldan's poor, Scroggles was a final stop in a weary life. Too poor to pay the funeral tax that would permit a pauper's corpse to be interred, or even cremated in a single ceremony, the dead were left at the Death House door; hasty shrouds were stitched over the bodies that lay stacked and waiting for their turn upon the pyres. There were none to grieve; no grief was possible in this briefest of ceremonies where no words of consolation were spoken. For a penny, a person might purchase a scent stick, its bittersweet smell dissipating in a thin stream of blue smoke.

Lais stopped the Queen with a hand on her arm.

"Madam, please," she said.

But the Queen shrugged off the hand and moved away, her face expectant.

Zorah came to the first row of corpses, laid out awaiting their shrouds. Lais knew she should remain at the Queen's side, but she didn't want to approach the dead any closer. The stink was overpowering and her eyes watered from the scratchy smoke.

Zorah knelt and examined the first corpse. Lais saw the Queen's terrified face, limned by the orange blaze of the funeral pyres, as the corpse stared back in frozen silence.

What is she doing here? Lais asked herself. Z'Blood, what am I doing here? The Firstwatch doesn't question duty, doesn't startle with fear at dark things that brush in the night, she scolded herself. The Firstwatch was a follower of the sword. The path to the sword lies in death, she could hear Gonmer telling her. *Death.*

Maybe that was what the Queen was doing here. Facing death. Lais edged near the Queen slowly. Could she do that? Look at death's face and not tremble? It would make her stronger, harden her.

The Queen walked between the bodies, stopping to study them. Lais followed her through the narrow paths between the stiffened corpses spread out on the cold stones, their wide-eyed stares glaring back at her.

"Oy!" called a man from within Scroggles. He emerged from the open doors, his shoulders wrapped with a thin cloak of smoke. "Oy there, have you come to leave yer dead?" Soot lined the slab face, his eyes black in the deep-set wrinkles. He gave a racking cough, and spit, the yellow gob landing neatly between two corpses. The gorge rose in Lais's throat.

Zorah was silent, her lips pressed to a thin line, the fine nostrils flared. She came toward him, her hair gathering the light and blazing like melting copper.

The old man saw the halo of flame and took a step back, his mouth slack with surprise.

"How burns the fire, lighterman?" Zorah asked. Small yellow flames flickered in her green eyes, signaling her agitation.

"Hot enough to burn them quick and clean," the lighterman answered with a proud tilt of his head. "I'm good at my work, madam. I stack the wood just so"—he gestured with his broad hands—"so that the fire never snags nor cools. Oy, I know the fire all right." The old man inhaled deeply, sucking in the thick, sooty air with familiarity. A cough bubbled in his chest and he hacked it free. He turned politely from the Queen and spat on the funeral pyre.

Lais saw him fumble in the pockets of his old black coat, which was several sizes too small for him. She took a quick step closer, fearing some danger to the Queen. But the lighterman pulled out a twist of dried grass. It was a straw effigy of the Queen such as was made for Firefaire to commit to the great Bonfire for luck.

"Will you bless the straw, my Queen?" he asked in his harsh, gravelly voice and held out the tiny effigy to her.

The Fire Queen took the effigy and turned it round and round in her palm, the flames in her eyes growing brighter. She gave a dry laugh. "Fire's Luck to you, lighterman," she proclaimed and tossed the effigy into the funeral pyre.

Lais watched it catch and burn quickly, the pale yellow straw crackling before turning black. A small curl of smoke twisted up to the night sky. Then it was gone. The lighterman sighed and then coughed again.

"That's bad luck gone at last," he said between coughs. "Room for the new luck of the year. Even if it is a bit late in coming."

Zorah made no reply but moved away from the corpses, heading for the alleys once more. In the shadowed streets, Zorah's fiery hair crackled with angry sparks. "It will be day soon. I shall return now to the Keep," she said to Lais. Then she began to walk quickly, her stride lengthening with every step.

Behind her Lais struggled to keep pace, breathing in the coppery scent of Zorah's hair and shielding her face from the scattering sparks.

Chapter One

"*How many are there?*" *Jobber whispered as she crouched* in her hiding place among the trees. Gnarled oaks grew in dense stands, their black branches and russet leaves woven together. Intermingled were slender poplars, their silver leaves fluttering in the faint breeze. A muddy road threaded a gap between the trees. Jobber watched two lines of Silean horsemen riding alongside a horse-drawn cart. The cart, heavily laden with sacks of wheat, lumbered on the uneven road, the wheels groaning. As the horses bobbed their heads, the bridles clinked loudly in the still air.

Jobber's head darted around the trunk of her tree, the better to see the trading party. She counted the black-and-gray uniforms of the Silean horsemen, noting that there were others riding with them, wearing long cloaks of deep blue. The dried bushes rustled at her movements.

"Sit still," Faul commanded.

"How many?" Jobber repeated.

"Too many."

Jobber glanced along the ragged line of trees. Scattered among the bushes she could see the hunched figures of the New Moon, their faces trained to the road as they watched the slow-moving trading party enter the forest. A few she knew by name. Wester, a man with blue-black creases in his skin from years of working in the northern mines, held an ax in his capable hands. He smiled broadly at Jobber and gave her a wink. Next to him was Tarbon, a boy not much older than Jobber herself. He had fled the mines with Wester, and though his skin was not marked with the coal he was stoop shouldered as if he still avoided the low ceilings of the mine tunnels. But Jobber knew he had a good eye and that he had learned to pull the longbow with speed and accuracy. Beyond the waiting pair were two vaggers, their robes hitched up to their calves so they could move freely in the woods. In their brown robes, their faces mottled with the circular tattoos of their profession, they blended in with the trees. Jobber had to stare hard to see them. Only the small white fletch of their arrows emerging from the quivers proclaimed their hiding place.

Beside her, Jobber heard Faul grind her teeth. Faul's face was a mask of concentration, her pale cheeks flushed with excitement and her eyes slate-colored as she studied the advancing trading party. The graying hair that normally brushed her shoulders was braided back and out of the way. Though her shoulders were relaxed, one hand held the hilt of her sword and her legs were tensed, like a cat waiting to pounce.

The trading party was almost through the narrow pass. A small black carriage with red-painted wheels brought up the rear. Alongside and behind the carriage rode another pack of Guards. At least thirty, Jobber counted roughly, and then swore. Faul was right. Too many. Along with the twenty or so that passed in front and in all likelihood another twenty or thirty patrolling behind, the New Moon would have to be quicker than usual. Eyeing the carriage, Jobber thought it had to be someone with a lot of brass to buy that many butcherboys as guards. But then most Silean traders were known to be well-off.

It was market day in the town of Asturas. Once Asturas had been an Oran village called Merridown, a small village notable only in that the cold mountain streams joined there to mark the source of the Hamader River. The river bisected the old village and flowed out swiftly to the western Plains. Harvest fairs, bride dances, and pony races were once held in the late months of the year. But no longer. After the Burning, two hundred years ago, Merridown was granted to Silean merchants, who changed first the name and then the town. Asturas was a trading town, where grain was bought and sold and then loaded on the flat barges that would take it away down the Hamader River to the Queen's city of Beldan and beyond. The town had profited from the trade and boasted a tree-lined village square and two-storied wood-and-plaster buildings that housed the Silean merchants. There was a Silean religious house, and as the clerics strolled, their long, blue frocks brushed patterns into the dust of new streets. There were artisans whose labor became important as the demands of the town grew. Smithies stabled and shod the hooves of Silean horses; saddlers and leather workers mended the carriages and saddles of tradesmen; a mint house produced coin with the faces of the Silean Regents on the silvers and the Queen emblazoned on the gold. The copper pieces showed a sheaf of wheat. Coopers came to build the barrels that held Oran brandy, and journeymen weavers and tailors dressed the wealthier inhabitants of the town. Watermen and dockloaders trawled the river, keeping the barges moving down toward their destinations. There were travelers' inns, a stockade, and a gallows.

Though the town was wealthier than before, it could also boast of poverty. Oran farm laborers dispossessed of land, odd jobbers without hiring contracts, and other wandering poor settled miserably in the remnants of the old Oran village on the fringes of town. Their houses of rough stone were scraped together to keep out the worst of the winter wind. Mostly it was the women who found work, in the laundries or as domestics in the houses of the Silean merchants. Others with some skill did piecework at the linen looms. The rooms in which they wove were built over the river, the rushing sound of the water mingling with the steady thump of the beaters. The linen wove tighter when kept moist, so they endured a constant dampness from the river that eventually settled rheumatically in their bones. Oran men sought work where it was possible, as threshers and harvesters, making only enough coin in good seasons to keep themselves alive with bread. In the winter months they lined the docks, hoping for work loading the barges.

The town was an important target for the New Moon. The roads that led into Asturas were traveled by Silean landowners bringing their sacks of grain and baled wool to the market or returning with their payments in coin or cloth. The town was close enough to Sadar's Keep to make limited forays possible and the New Moon could count on hiding in the stone hovels of the old village. Since they had won against the Regent Silwa's army at the Plains of Sadar, the New Moon had kept up a steady stream of attacks against the Silean merchants in Asturas. And now that the New Moon was growing in number, they were raiding the other trading towns farther down the river.

Jobber chewed her fingernail and cast a worried glance at Faul. Faul hadn't moved since the trading party entered the woods. This was the first time Jobber had come out from the Keep since the Uprising at Sadar. She had forgotten the difficulty of waiting and was impatient for the fight to begin. Jobber looked across the road and saw only the trees. But she knew that among the dark trunks were hidden another twenty fighters, led by Treys, one of the old generals of Huld's army. Treys would be counting the steps as the Sileans approached, waiting for the right moment to sound the call to attack. She imagined she could hear the tension gathering in the bows, the quivers hitched high on the shoulders, arrows readied for the reach of a hand.

Jobber inhaled and touched the leather cap on her head. Then she exhaled slowly, calming her nerves. She frowned, hating the feel of the old cap. But in the muted brown and black woods the brilliance of her red hair would blaze like a fire. It had been a long time since she had worn a cap to hide her hair. In Beldan, growing up on the streets, she had needed it to hide her identity as a girl, and as a child of power. She scratched impatiently at the cap, the strings beneath her chin tight. Z'blood, how did she ever stand the feel of it before?

"Hie up," Faul hissed and Jobber drew herself up in anticipation. "They're almost through. Now look, Jobber," Faul warned, "I let you come because you complained of being stuck at the Keep. But stay out of the way, do you hear?"

"Yeah, Faul, I hear."

"Keep your head down, and if it looks bad, go for the horses and don't wait."

"Yeah, yeah," Jobber breathed.

A finch whistled between the branches and Jobber knew it was Treys signaling them to begin. Jobber clutched the sword at her side awkwardly. Faul had insisted that she learn to carry it, but Jobber hated the sword. And though it was a Fire Sword, skillfully crafted and possessed of Oran magic, it felt clumsy in her hands. She couldn't move with Faul's deadly precision, the sword an extension not only of her hand and arm but her intent. Faul had but to think the strike and the blade was there. Jobber's talents lay elsewhere. She was a Beldan street fighter trained to use her hands and her feet. Her body was her weapon. But it wasn't only her lack of skill with a sword that worried Jobber. The Fire Sword demanded more than skill, it demanded self-control. At Sadar's Keep, Jobber had lost control and the Fire Sword had surged with magic, transforming her into a column of flame. Jobber removed her hand from the sword's hilt, afraid of her racing heart.

Treys appeared suddenly from behind a tree. Standing straight among the oaks, he freed an arrow. With a swift thud it hit a Silean horseman riding beside the loaded cart. The man's hands flew from the reins as the force of the arrow jolted him backward. He lost his seat, his body falling to the side. A second horse balked at the scent of fresh blood. It whinnied shrilly and pranced away from the fallen man. The Guard on the frightened horse shouted to the other Guards as he drew the reins in tightly to keep the panicked horse under control.

More arrows buzzed angrily from between the trees and a loud cry went up among the New Moon. Faul sprang away from the bushes, her tall, slim frame cutting a path through the trees. The steel of her blade flashed as she freed her sword from its black scabbard. Jobber stood behind the tree, the better to watch the fight. Her body tensed as the blue-cloaked Sileans withdrew crossbows. They fired a round of thick-headed bolts at the New Moon scrambling through the trees.

"Z'blood," Jobber cried, seeing Wester hit in the chest by a bolt. He roared with pain, his face upturned to the trees. Tarbon raised his longbow and fired two arrows in quick succession at the crossbowmen. The first arrow found its mark in the Silean's throat. He dropped the crossbow, clutching his throat, his mouth gasping for air. Blood flowed from between the gloved fingers as he gripped the arrow in his neck. The second arrow went wide of the mark, hitting a horse in the withers. The horse reared up on its back hooves, pawing the air with fury.

Jobber bent low as she hurried through the trees toward Wester. The black leather fletch of the Silean bolt rose above the bushes. She parted the dried leaves and swore as she saw Wester's slack face. He was already dead. His eyes were half closed, his lips parted as a small trickle of blood etched the blue creases of his cheek. One fist curled around a handful of dead leaves, while the other hand still gripped the ax.

The sound of a Silean horn blared above the trees. Resting crows cawed loudly in answer before they flapped their wings and flew out of the woods. Jobber looked down the narrow valley of the road and saw Faul running toward the Guard blowing the horn.

Faul edged between the line of stamping horses, her sword raised in defense until she reached the Guard with the horn. She swung her sword upward in a sharp arc, slicing away the arm that held the horn to the Guard's lips. As the sword reached its pinnacle, she twisted it downward, bringing the blade edge across the man's lap and thigh, severing his leg. Blood sprayed over her head and shoulders and her face was speckled bright red.

Faul shifted her weight, slipping the sword from her right to her left hand. She snapped the blade's edge outward to strike another Guard on her left. The Guard brought his sword down toward hers and the swords screeched as they met. Faul turned her wrist outward and laid her sword flat against the Silean's weapon. She pressed her sword down, forcing his down as well. But as the Guard fought to lift his weapon, she quickly released the pressure. The man fumbled his grip, and Faul jabbed the point of her sword into his throat. She flicked the blade sideways, drawing it out along his jawbone. Faul didn't wait to see the man collapse over his horse, but darted through the line of horses leading to the cart.

The New Moon was pressing its attack, for the alarm had been sounded and soon there would be more Guards. Jobber saw the two vaggers using their long staffs to knock mounted Sileans from their horses. She shouted an unheard warning as a Guard rode up behind one of the vaggers, sword drawn. With a fierce thrust, the Guard stabbed the vagger in the back. But even as the Guard withdrew his weapon from the vagger's body, a white-fletched arrow shot through his shoulder, toppling him from his horse.

Treys was shooting the Silean Guards surrounding the loaded cart, trying to scatter them away. Tarbon reached the cart just as Treys' arrow pierced the driver in the side. As Tarbon clambered onto the cart he pushed the dying Guard aside and took the reins. With a yell, he slapped the reins hard over the horses' backs. They reared in the harness and then bolted down the dirt road.

Jobber knew that Tarbon would drive the horses farther up the old road to where the New Moon waited with fresh horses. They would quickly unload the sacks of grain from the cart onto separate horses, and then they'd disperse in different directions, riding into the Avadares Mountains.

A woman's scream startled Jobber. She turned and spotted the terrified face of a Silean noblewoman at the window of the carriage. A dying Guard clung to the carriage door, his head leaning against its side. Blood smeared the sides of the carriage as he slid beneath the wheels. The hulking frame standing over him, Jobber recognized, was that of Moar, an Oran farmer from the western Plains who now wielded his sickle in battle instead of harvest.

With the grain cart gone, the New Moon would fall back quickly, not wishing to engage the Sileans any more than was necessary. Already Jobber could hear the blasting horn of a nearby patrol. They would be here soon. Jobber raised herself cautiously from her hiding place and prepared to make for the ravine where the horses were waiting. A shout stopped her, and glancing behind she saw the remaining vagger trapped between two Sileans who had dismounted from their horses. They beat the vagger about the head and then shoved the staggering figure into the carriage. The screaming noblewoman began kicking the prone body.

Jobber searched for Faul and saw her fighting with another Guard. Those who could had extricated themselves from the battle and were fleeing into the woods.

"Whore's shit," Jobber swore, and knowing that Faul would probably kill her later if the Sileans didn't do it first, she tore through the bushes toward the carriage.

It was one thing to die in battle; it was another to be taken prisoner by the Sileans. Jobber had seen the bodies afterward, hanging from trees, mutilated and then burned. The Sileans held a special contempt for the vaggers, who preached the old faith and traveled the roads keeping Oran traditions alive. They believed in theft, especially from the Sileans, arguing that it was the Sileans who were thieves, stealing food out of Oran mouths. Jobber knew the vagger would be tortured in hopes of obtaining information. She also knew that the vagger would say nothing and that soon the torture would be merely to pleasure the rage of the Sileans.

Jobber reached the carriage, pulling the Fire Sword free from its scabbard. With a two-handed grasp, she slashed out sideways. Along the edge of the blade the red-gold pattern of waves sparkled. She caught the first Guard in the side and with a sharp thrust tugged the blade upward. The Guard turned away from the unconscious vagger and bellowed with surprise, seeing blood gushing from his side.

Jobber grunted, the sword heavy as the man's body crumpled over it. *Follow through,* she could hear Faul instructing in her head, *don't leave the blade halfway in the body!* Jobber jerked the sword out and faced the other Guard.

"Frigging bastard," the man spat. He lunged, his sword circling the air near her head. Jobber fell back, her sword raised in defense. She deflected the attack, the Guard's sword shearing upward over her head. But she overextended her defense, her arm raised too high, exposing her middle. The Guard saw the opening and countered with a second thrust toward Jobber's ribs.

"Z'blood!" Jobber shouted as his sword tore her shirt and nicked her skin. She leapt sideways, out of the way of the lunging sword. With a burst of impatience, Jobber threw the Fire Sword down and raised her fists. Freed of the sword's weight, she felt centered again, her body moving as a unit, with no extra appendages to manage. She saw the Guard's surprise and hesitation. Jobber knew he thought it was stupid of her to throw away her weapon.

With her fists crossed at the wrists, Jobber sprang forward, catching the handguard of his weapon between her fists. As she forced his sword upward, she thrust her body under his arm and turned, wedging her back into his armpit. Rotating her fists outward again, she snared the Guard's hand. Before he could resist, she contracted her body, pulling his sword arm down hard and smashing his straightened elbow against the crest of her shoulder bone. The Guard cried out, and as he sagged in pain Jobber turned, ramming her knee into his downturned face. His cheekbone splintered and he groaned thickly. Jobber let him fall heavily to the ground and turned to help the wounded vagger lying at the bottom of the carriage.

She pulled the vagger upright, and saw that it was a woman, her hair cropped close to the scalp. Blood trailed down the sides of her face and her eyes were dazed.

"Come on," Jobber urged, "raise it." The woman swallowed and awareness flickered on her slack features. She stirred under Jobber's grasp and tried feebly to stand.

Jobber had almost succeeded in wrenching the vagger out of the carriage when the noblewoman, who had been huddled at the back of the carriage, flung herself at Jobber. Her fists pommeled Jobber's head and shoulders.

"Get off," Jobber growled, grabbing one of the flailing hands. The woman's face was white with rage, foam glistening on the curled lips. Her black hair lay tangled down her back. She reached out to claw Jobber's face and as Jobber ducked her head, the woman snatched off the leather cap instead.

Jobber's red hair spilled out over her shoulders and the carriage was filled with the pungent reek of burning copper. The fiery hair sprayed a shower of yellow sparks across the woman's silk skirts, and a fine smoke puffed from the burning holes. The woman recoiled against the cushions in alarm and began screaming.

"Shut up!" Jobber yelled and, cocking one fist, punched the woman hard on the chin. The screams ended as the woman's eyes rolled upward and she slumped over the carriage seat.

Jobber returned to the task of freeing the vagger. Another hand reached in to help. Jobber looked up and saw Faul's blood-stained face.

"I told you to stay out of the way," Faul snapped angrily, jerking the vagger's shoulders through the narrow carriage door.

"Couldn't leave her for the butcherboys," Jobber grunted as they hoisted the injured woman down, draping her limp arms over their shoulders.

A Silean horn announced the approach of the patrol. Jobber and Faul hurried away from the carriage, dragging the groaning vagger between them as her feet stumbled over the ground.

As they reached the line of bushes Faul halted. "The Fire Sword. Where's your sword?" she demanded.

Jobber turned and saw it lying on the road near the carriage.

"Get it," Faul said savagely.

"But Faul," Jobber protested. She could see the Silean patrol riding just beyond the edge of the woods.

"Get it NOW," Faul commanded. "And run."

Jobber let go of the vagger and tore back to the carriage. She reached the sword as the Silean Guard entered the forest. A twang made her duck, and a leather-fletched bolt shot past her ear. "Z'blood," she swore, snatching the Fire Sword from the ground and escaping into the bushes. Another bolt followed but Jobber dove behind a tree, hearing the splintering of bark.

Jobber ran hard up the sides of the ravine, branches snapping crisply as she shoved through the dense cover. Twigs snagged in her freed hair and the faint scent of wood smoke enveloped her as they smoldered in the heat of her hair. Another bolt pierced the woods near her and she realized that her red hair made her a perfect target.

It was too late to change that. Speed was more important than a concealed flight. If she could just get to the top of this hill a

horse would be waiting for her. Jobber tripped over a tree root
and as she fell face first through the bushes another bolt cracked
in the branches above her.

"Frigging lousy shots," she hissed gratefully. She lifted herself off the ground and continued scrambling up the steep slope
of the hill. Her chest heaved with the effort and her legs ached
from the upward run. The Fire Sword's scabbard tangled in a
thicket until she wrenched it free with a curse. "Frigging get
me scaffered, you will," she complained to the sword. "Either
by those butcherboys back there for having you, or Faul for not
having you."

Jobber heard her name called and glanced up hopefully. A
small break between the trees showed the crest of the hill and
the blue sky rising beyond it. Faul beckoned, waving her arm
furiously.

"Come on—hurry!" Faul urged.

With a renewed effort, Jobber tore through the dried bushes.
Panting noisily, she reached the tree line and stumbled out of
the underbrush into a grassy clearing where Faul waited on
horseback, holding the sagging vagger upright in the saddle before her. A second horse pranced nervously beside Faul's. Jobber held up the sword to show the older woman that she had
retrieved it and then bent over to catch her breath.

Faul tossed down the reins of a second horse and wearily
Jobber hoisted herself onto its back.

"Now go," Faul ordered, and gave her horse a kick.

Jobber's horse flattened its ears and galloped after Faul across
a wide-open plain that skirted the foothills of the Avadares
Mountains. Jobber clutched the reins with one hand, bending
low over the neck of the horse. She held the Fire Sword tightly
in the other hand so that it would not slip from her grasp. As
they raced toward the mountains, Jobber's red hair streamed behind her and the cold wind dried the sweat off her neck.

They rode the horses hard into the hills, but they didn't ride
for long. Once in the foothills of Avadares they knew that the
Sileans would not follow. There were too many quirks to the
trails, too many places where Sileans had tumbled over sudden
cliffs, or disappeared in the woods. Avadares with its ancient

pines gathered among fallen rocks of pink and gray granite was the Earth Queen Huld's final domain and it remained a hostile territory to the Sileans.

Faul slowed her horse, his flanks stained with lather and foam collecting at the corners of the bit. The vagger woman groaned in Faul's arms, her face ashen.

"Get down," Faul said to Jobber and waited until the girl had slid from the horse's back before she dismounted herself. Faul leaned the vagger forward onto the horse's withers and laid her dangling arms loosely around the neck of the horse so that she'd not fall. With one hand resting on the woman's thigh, Faul continued walking the horse, speaking gently as she quieted the overextended animal.

Then Faul faced Jobber angrily. "I wouldn't have had to ride him as fast if you had done what I had asked in the first place. If the horse dies it will be your fault."

"If I'd done what you asked, Faul, that vagger would now be on her way to a slow killing. Which would you rather have?" Jobber retorted.

"You were right to help the woman," Faul said, pushing stray hair back from her face. She was tired, her expression more disappointed than angry. "You were wrong to forget the Fire Sword."

The girl was silent, thinking of the moment when she had dropped the sword onto the ground. Jobber longed to be freed of its weight. Freed of the training, the preparation for a final confrontation with the Fire Queen. Freed of the responsibility not just to Beldan but all of Oran, which pinned its hopes on her imperfect skill.

"Look, I'm sorry, Faul," Jobber said. "I just ain't no good with a sword."

"Then we will train harder, until you don't know the difference between your arm and the sword. Like it or not, Jobber, you will learn to use the sword, because there is no other way."

Jobber groaned. She knew what lay in store for her. Faul was determined, and when Faul set her mind to a thing it either broke or bent to her will.

Jobber bent down and picked up a granite stone lying on the

trail. She stared at the tiny flecks of mica sparkling in the late-afternoon sun. Then she lobbed it high into the air, watching its brief flight and wishing herself as easily freed.

Shedwyn lay on her back, staring into the shadows of the vaulted ceiling of the common room. A slice of the moon shone through the narrow windows near the top of the stone wall. She heard soft rustling noises as other people turned or coughed in their sleep. Only when she stared straight up, Shedwyn found, could she think without distraction, for when she looked around her and saw the dark figures huddled in sleep on their pallets she felt overwhelmed. Daily, more and more Orans came to Sadar's Keep seeking refuge from the Silean militias, from hunger, and from the winter that was fast approaching in the mountains.

Shedwyn's pulse quickened with anxiety. Too many depended on her. The true daughter of Huld the farmers and laborers called her. She was to them the promise of the earth long denied them by the Fire Queen. The women stopped their work to touch her hand reverently as Shedwyn went about the daily chores of the Keep. In their pleading faces Shedwyn saw the trust and faith they had put in her. She would stand for them in the months to come, when the New Moon entered Beldan against the Sileans and the Queen.

Shedwyn hugged her arms over her chest and sighed. But she was not invincible. And at the moment not even brave. Fear had settled into her heart and she could not shake its grip.

Shedwyn drew her hand over her brow, her face hot and flushed despite the cool night. The day had gone badly from the start. With the first light she had begun vomiting, her stomach gripping painfully. She had washed her face with cold water, praying it was over before she went into the kitchens to help in the baking. But there it got worse. The smell of the women crowded in the kitchens, the odor of sour mash in the making of ale, even the yeast bubbling in crocks was overpowering. She had managed to leave the kitchens and vomit in the privies without being seen. But the queasiness stayed with her and her mouth was tainted with a bitter taste.

Then she had been present when Jobber and Faul returned. She had helped Jobber wash the wounds on the vagger's head, the metallic smell of blood making her light-headed and struggling not to faint.

"Wester's dead," Jobber had told her. "I saw him scaffered. Frigging butcherboys."

Shedwyn had known the man well. He was always in the kitchens, odd-jobbing as he mended pans, gathered wood, or carved spoons. Though he was coarse looking, he could sing in a sweet tenor the miners' songs that praised the cool slate of the tunnels. If Tarbon was with him they sang together, their voices blending into a sad harmony.

"I'll miss him," Shedwyn had said, tears burning her eyes.

"Yeah, me as well," Jobber had answered quietly.

The rest of the day had fared no better. Shedwyn had dragged herself from task to task, her body sluggish. Every time she sat she'd wanted to sleep. She had snapped at the children playing in the corridors and barked out orders to the women in the kitchens. But later, at the evening meal, as Naima sang to her nursing infant, the tears had welled up again in Shedwyn's eyes. She'd fled the table as they started streaming down her cheeks, finding a private corner beneath the spiraled stairs where, to her own bewilderment, she'd sobbed into her apron.

Now she was exhausted, her eyes swollen and gritty from the outburst of tears. But every time she closed her eyes to sleep a hundred worries nagged at her. Her hands clenched at her sides as she tried to find answers.

"Shedwyn, what are you thinking?" Eneas whispered at her side. He had gone to sleep earlier, his back to her, annoyed because she had been so silent. But now he turned and touched her lightly on the cheek. "What is it?" he asked.

It was the gentleness of his voice that caused new tears to brim in her eyes.

"Shedwyn," Eneas said and leaned up on one elbow to stare at her in the darkness. His hand slid from her cheek down her neck to her breast and he felt the sobs that she choked back. "Sweetness," he murmured and gathered her in his arms, laying her head on his chest.

Shedwyn smelled the odor of his skin, a mixture of sweat and the dusty fragrance of lavender. He had been born into a Silean estate and Shedwyn had thought the scent of lavender that followed him was from his linen shirts, stored by Oran maids with small bags of lavender. But he had fled his father's estates and come with her to Sadar. He had fought for the New Moon in the Uprising and now, a whole season later, his shirts no longer linen but plain wool, he still smelled of lavender. Shedwyn looked up into his face and stroked his long blond hair. In the moonlight it was the color of silvery flax. The beard on his face was darker and made the square jaw more pronounced. His large nose that was once straight tilted slightly where it had been broken by the laborer Farnon.

"What worries you?" Eneas asked again.

Shedwyn drew a slow breath and spoke in a low whisper. "Everything."

"Tell me."

"The spring."

Eneas hugged her tighter around the shoulders. "The spring offensive will go well for us. You know Lirrel will find the fourth girl for the knot. And the rest is up to the careful planning of Treys, Faul, and the others. They've not let us down yet."

"Aye," Shedwyn said. "But that's not it."

"Me, then?" Eneas asked and brushed his lips against her forehead. "Do you worry for me?"

Shedwyn gave an exasperated laugh that caught in her throat. "Always, Eneas. Always. I worry that you'll be killed. Did you know Wester was killed today?"

"I heard. He was a good man and he believed in what he was doing. I don't want to die, and I'll try my best not to. But I will fight, as Wester did, for those things that matter most in my life."

"Me?"

"Yes, you."

"Aye." Shedwyn nodded, knowing that would be his answer. "But you go south this time. It's more dangerous."

"I'm going south to find those estates in the Soring Marsh that are open to the New Moon and gather an army. Then we will head east to the Sairas River where the Sileans have little influence. With luck, there will be no real battles to fight until spring.''

Shedwyn fell silent, listening to Eneas's heartbeat.

''Shedwyn,'' Eneas said and lifted her face to meet his eyes. ''There is more you are not saying.''

Shedwyn smiled thinly. ''You've been learning from the air elements. You know my mind too easily.''

Eneas chuckled softly. ''I didn't think there were secrets to be kept between us. And besides, your mouth makes a certain pout—a very kissable pout,'' he added bending to kiss her lower lip, ''but a pout all the same when you are holding something back. Go on then, what is it?''

''I am with child,'' Shedwyn said. She heard the sharp intake of his breath and his arms tightened around her.

''Are you sure?''

Shedwyn laughed despite her worry. For a man who claimed to know her so well, he should have at least understood this was not a thing she would make a mistake about.

Eneas sputtered and shook his head. ''I don't mean that, I mean of course you're sure.''

''Aye, very sure,'' Shedwyn said more softly.

Eneas drew her close to his chest. He placed his mouth over hers and kissed her deeply. His body was warm as his arms wrapped snugly around her. His hand stroked her side, the fingers playing over the rippled bones of her ribs and then moving upward to cup her breast. She moaned lightly as he squeezed her swollen breast. He leaned back to stare at her. He smiled, and in the moonlight his teeth were white.

''It's good news,'' he said.

''But at a bad time,'' Shedwyn answered, her fear returning. ''The baby will come in late spring, just as we march for Beldan.''

Eneas put a finger to her lips. ''Babies come anywhere. Even in battle tents. I'll see to it that you are safe.''

''But Eneas, I don't know what will happen when the knot challenges the Queen. I don't know if I will be strong enough to fight with the others. That's what frightens me.''

"Have you told Treys?"

"No." She shook her head vehemently. "And you'll not either," she said firmly.

"But Shedwyn, they must know."

"Everyone will know soon enough, Eneas. It's not a thing that can be hidden. But I want time." Shedwyn paused, thinking. "I need time to sort out a path for myself and our baby," she explained. "Please, Eneas, promise you won't say anything."

"All right. As long as you rest and don't worry too much. I am here for you, Shedwyn." He kissed her creased forehead. "And I will do whatever needs to be done to make you and our baby safe."

Shedwyn relaxed in the comforting warmth of his embrace and allowed herself to be convinced. She closed her eyes, inhaling the lavender scent of Eneas's skin.

"What do you think?" Eneas whispered.

"A girl," Shedwyn answered sleepily, understanding his question. She glanced up and saw Eneas staring into the vaulted ceiling, his expression puzzled. She sighed and closed her eyes, soothed by the nearness of Eneas's body. Exhaustion settled over her and as she drifted slowly to sleep, she smiled hearing Eneas whispering a litany of girls' names to the shadows above.

Chapter Two

Lirrel waited at the edge of a rickety pier, the wooden boards creaking as the waves lapped in with the tide. She closed her pearl-colored eyes and leaned her small frame into the wind, buoyed by the rushing air. The wind swept back her black hair, revealing her oval face, her skin browned from the journey. She could taste the salty tang in the ocean sprays that splashed her face. She dug into her pocket, her hand closing around the slim shaft of her flute. She wanted to play it, wanted to hear its soothing voice. Instead she waited, listening to the whispered voices that hovered in the air. She could sense the subtle shift in the wind, the almost perceptible thickening of the air that announced a vision.

Lirrel didn't want to see another vision. She wanted to play her flute and let the music drown out the voices that called to her. Lately the visions had been frightening and without hope. She had seen the coming battles and now knew they would be worse than anyone had anticipated. The New Moon would make their stand, but the cost in Oran lives would be great. The visions always began with a thudding roar of wind like the rhythmic beating of huge wings. Black shadows spilled over bare wheat fields, sucking the chaff into dusty clouds. Flames erupted, and in the swirling smoke Lirrel saw the chaff had become dying soldiers, tumbling over the fields like dead leaves.

Lirrel's hand closed more tightly around her flute. She could play her flute and banish the terrifying vision before it began. Then Lirrel sighed and her chin drooped to her chest. No, she couldn't do that. She was Ghazali, a peacekeeper. She must confront the sorrows of life as well as its joys. It was her responsibility, her duty to see the visions, and then to seek a path for all of them that would lead to peace again. She must not ignore the visions. They were scraps of cloth, the bright and dark, that stitched together her future and the future of Oran.

Reluctantly, Lirrel lifted her head and opened her eyes to the vision. The evening mist cloaked her in darkness and she tensed as the thickened air held her in its grasp.

And then the sky seemed to clear, no longer evening but the faint glow of dawn's light. At the horizon a line of thick gray clouds scudded along the edge of the sea. In the gap between sea and clouds, the sun rose, its orange rays slanting over the water before it disappeared again in the bank of clouds. Lirrel saw the tiny black speck of an island where it huddled beneath the lowering clouds. The brief sunlight brightened the crescent arch of a beach, its sand shimmering like a new moon against the black cliffs that rose behind it. Lirrel heard the lilting music of someone's thoughts drifting on the currents of the wind. A figure appeared on the crescent beach. It was a woman in an Islander's red skirt, and over her head a black shawl whipped in the wind, hiding the woman's face as she ran. The woman stopped and faced the restless waves.

"Turn around," Lirrel whispered, straining to see the woman in the vision. "Please, turn around for me." Lirrel stepped forward, a hand outstretched as if to touch the woman's shoulder.

But her foot found only air. Lirrel yelped as she teetered dangerously on the edge of the pier. The vision shredded apart as a cold spray of water struck her. Instead of the island, Lirrel saw the dark water splashing up to meet her.

A wiry arm grabbed her by the waist and roughly jerked her

away from the edge. She stumbled backward, falling on the pier, the boards bouncing as she landed. Stunned, Lirrel shook her head in surprise, gradually becoming aware that she was lying on top of her rescuer. She looked down, seeing first her black dress pushed up above her knees and then the arm still gripping her waist. The wind was cold on her thighs, but the arm at her waist was warm.

"*Faien saad*, Dagar," Lirrel murmured, giving thanks to her rescuer as she tried to roll herself off his lap without losing her dignity entirely.

"*Laille fasir*," Dagar replied, giving her a helpful push with his hands.

Lirrel winced at Dagar's sprawling accent as he spoke in Ghazali. Then she chided herself for her snobbery. Ghazali was a difficult language to master and Dagar had worked hard to twist his tongue around the half-swallowed words. "Like frogs gulping," he had once told her in dismay. Lirrel smoothed down the front of her black dress, covering her exposed legs.

Standing beside her, Dagar brushed off the dried remains of fish scales that clung to his trousers. He smiled, waiting for her to speak.

"I had a vision," she said and his smile faded. "No," she said quickly, shaking her head at his concerned face. "The vision was good. *Ahal*, it was very good," she breathed softly into the wind. "That is until I tried to step into it." Lirrel laughed.

Dagar pushed back the stiff bristles of his short black hair and whistled with relief. Beneath the prominent brow his dark eyes sparkled with the reflection of evening stars. Though he stood not much taller than Lirrel, he took her firmly by the arm and led her down the pier toward the lights of a tavern farther up the shore.

"Tell me," Dagar said.

Lirrel tilted her head, a smile playing on her mouth. "I will riddle it to you."

"Lirrel, you know I'm terrible at riddles," Dagar complained.

"Try," she encouraged.

"All right," Dagar said, "but only if you guess mine."

"Done," Lirrel said smartly. "I riddle it to you that I tremble with a breath of air, but oh, my friends, across my back a weight I bear."

Dagar cupped his chin, his brow furrowed as he thought. Lirrel watched him, pleased by his company. Over the months they had traveled together she had found him a good companion. It had been comforting to talk with someone who understood her fears. Dagar was no stranger to violence. They had met at the village of Cairns where he was the sole survivor of a Silean massacre. Standing amid the devastation of his village he had refused to accept hate and vengeance as a natural response to the dead lying around him. Instead he had chosen to follow Lirrel to Sadar's Keep and there, with quiet but determined steps, he had sought the path of a Ghazali peacekeeper. With Lirrel as a teacher he was learning the language, so that he might one day be able to sing the songs of healing.

He jerked his head up as the answer brightened his face.

"I will not tell you otherwise, the answer is water! Water!" he shouted. "Blow on it and it trembles, but it bears on its back the weight of ships." He captured Lirrel by the shoulders. "You saw her then, didn't you?" he asked eagerly. "You saw the fourth girl."

"Almost," Lirrel said, recalling the cloaked woman on the crescent beach. "She's here in the Islands. But more importantly, I 'heard' her. Like Shedwyn and Jobber, I can hear her thoughts as distinct as a phrase of music."

Dagar took her arm and began to walk quickly. "Come on. Alwir needs to hear this."

"Where is he?"

"He's at that tavern up there trying to barter for our meal with his fiddle. Can't say as the Islanders are looking too friendly though."

"I've told him before," Lirrel said, a little breathless as she struggled to keep pace with Dagar. "Beldan fiddle does not lead to an Islander's heart."

"Then we'd better hurry, or we'll be without supper again."

"Wait, what about your riddle?" Lirrel asked, tugging at Dagar's arm to make him slow down. A painful stitch knitted her side.

"Oh," he answered and slowed his step. He smiled shyly. "I riddle it to you: I am a clearing in a dense forest."

Lirrel frowned, her expression skeptical. "Dagar, I know the answer to almost all Ghazali riddles because you learn them as you learn the question. But I've never heard this one."

"I made it up," Dagar said smugly.

"That's unfair."

"Not really."

"It's not the tradition," Lirrel insisted.

"Lirrel, unless new things go into it from time to time, traditions wither," Dagar argued.

"Yes, but—"

"Yes, but, the truth is you don't like to be wrong," Dagar teased. "The teacher bested by the student. It's all right, Lirrel. Look at me—I'm always getting it wrong. But that doesn't stop me from trying. If you believe that your past always has the right answer, what will you do when faced with a new puzzle? You must create a new answer."

"Ahal," Lirrel said in good-natured defeat. "It's bad enough that I won't have an answer to your riddle, but you must teach me my own lessons." Lirrel fell silent, trying to guess Dagar's riddle. She knew she could pluck the answer from his thoughts. But Dagar knew that, too, and Lirrel had learned in the months they had traveled together that Dagar could hear the truth like a good musician knows a well-made tune. She smiled sadly and shrugged. "I don't know. Tell me."

"A clearing in a dense forest," Dagar repeated. "I will not tell you otherwise, it is a goat's knees."

"A goat's knees!" Lirrel shouted, incredulous.

"Aye," Dagar said. "Goats have no hair at their knees. They're shiny and very bald, though the rest of the leg, well, it's hairy."

Lirrel groaned. "I should have guessed that a herdboy like you might be missing your goats after all this time on the road."

"Come on," Dagar urged. "Let's give Alwir the news. The

sooner we find the fourth girl the sooner we'll be home to the ones we miss."

"I'd never think to miss a goat's knees," Lirrel muttered as she hurried up the shore with Dagar, who grinned triumphantly at her side.

Antoni Re Desturo, the Advisor to the Silean Regent, leaned back wearily in his chair and called his secretary, Re Estave.

"How many are left waiting to see me?" Antoni asked.

"Three more, your lordship," Re Estave answered. He was a tall, gaunt man, and he rustled a sheaf of papers importantly in his fingers. A neatly trimmed beard mocked the awkward set of his bony features, hiding a chin too small for the wide forehead.

Antoni rubbed a spot at the base of his thumb and stared, annoyed, at his papers. Not for the first time since the death of Regent Silwa Re Familia had he questioned his desire for this position. After Silwa was killed at the Uprising at Sadar, Antoni had managed most of the affairs of state for the Queen. Now he was trapped managing them for the newly arrived Regent, whose interests in Oran lay elsewhere. The new Regent, Ilario Re Anguar, was a vain, strutting cock and his arrogance and stupidity jarred Antoni's nerves. At least Silwa had had commonsensical intelligence and a good military mind. So far Ilario's contribution to the troubled court had been a few new dance steps and the bulging belly of one of the Queen's maids. The one thousand Silean soldiers and officers that had come with him did their damage, rattling their swords in brawls as they patrolled Beldan's streets.

"Who's left to be seen?"

"Re Varras, from Goltha. He wants an increase in the work obligations for his mines."

Antoni pursed his lips with annoyance. "I've told him before, if his farmers spend their time in the mines, there will be no one left to plow the fields."

"Perhaps he's given up on farming, because of the drought?" the secretary ventured.

"Yes. But if he plans to pay for his food goods, then he will lose whatever wealth he has made in the mines. Who else?'' Antoni asked.

''Re Fortina.''

''Bureaucrat,'' Antoni snorted. ''What doesn't he understand now?''

Re Estave glanced at the petition in his hand, quickly scanning the paper. ''The new land acts. He says he needs a clearer understanding of their exact purpose so he can know how to instruct the local sheriffs.''

''He doesn't have to understand them. Merely implement them.''

''With all respect, your lordship,'' Re Estave said, ''the new acts are ambiguous in their interpretation. While there are a good fifty offenses listed here, they are so loosely stated that any local sheriff—''

''Can add to the list of hanging offenses?''

''Yes,'' answered the secretary.

Antoni smiled unpleasantly. ''That's the beauty of it,'' he insisted. ''We are on the brink of rebellion. Oran peasants must be handled firmly. The new land acts give us another weapon. Capital offenses for crimes against Silean property.''

''But under these acts one can just as easily be hanged for breaking a tree on a Silean estate as for the poaching of deer!''

''Indeed. And I expect that before the year is out, we shall see just how creative our local sheriffs have been. Now who's the last?''

The secretary returned his glance to the papers in his hands. ''Ah, Re Aston.''

''The Reader?'' Antoni asked sharply. ''What does he want?''

''He wouldn't say.''

Antoni stroked his mustache. He didn't like Readers. They were the only Orans permitted at the Queen's court. That they were Orans was reason enough to mistrust them, but Antoni had other reasons for despising them. Reasons he kept private.

''His son is Alwir Re Aston, who was sentenced to be hanged at Firecircle,'' the secretary continued, lightly scratching his head as if to jog the information.

Antoni remembered the thin young man, his face sweating

with fear, but his voice strong and clear when he spoke. He was a traitor to the Readers Guild and an unlikely soldier for the New Moon. Yet his speech had been passionate, and had swayed the crowd, inciting them to riot.

"Send in Re Aston," Antoni said.

"But sir, the others will be outraged at being made to wait."

Antoni was silent, one finger tapping the surface of his desk.

"Re Aston is Oran, and as Silean nobles they won't take the slight well," Re Estave tried again.

Antoni settled himself in his chair and arranged his robes about him. He was familiar with the insult of awaiting Oran pleasure. He served the Queen, didn't he? Let them taste its bitterness. It will encourage their hostility, and perhaps Re Fortina won't find the land acts so difficult to interpret, he thought.

"Show in Re Aston," Antoni ordered. As Re Estave left, Antoni concentrated on calming his quickened pulse. He bent his stiffened neck, freeing the rigid column of his spine. With effort, he relaxed his shoulders and laid both hands on the surface of his desk. The elegant polished nails gleamed against the dark wood.

The secretary returned his pursed lips showing his disapproval as he ushered Ener Re Aston into the room.

"Re Aston," Antoni said evenly as the gray-haired man approached. Elderly but still strong, Re Aston carried himself erect. Beneath the wide shoulders a paunch thickened his waist. It was hard for Antoni to see the similarity between this man and the gangly youth who had stood before the gallows. Except for the glint of arrogance in the blue eyes.

"Re Desturo," Ener said, inclining his head. "Thank you for this audience." He sat in the chair opposite Antoni.

"Why are you here?" Antoni asked. Though his expression remained calm his heart began to race anew.

"I have come on a matter that concerns the Readers Guild."

"Indeed," Antoni sneered.

"We are concerned as to our future. Given the recent events—"

"You mean the rebellion at Sadar," Antoni said sharply. "Your countrymen are troublesome."

"That's why I am here."

"Your son fights for the New Moon, does he not?"

"Yes, Advisor, I have heard that. But Alwir is no longer my son," Ener said.

"Then you're not here to foolishly plead for amnesty?"

"No," he answered vehemently. "The man that was my son is dead to me. I have come to bargain for the lives of loyal Reader families."

"Loyal to whom?" Antoni asked, one eyebrow arched.

"Loyal to the Queen," Ener said. "And of course to Silea," he added hastily. "We owe you a debt."

"And how do you propose to honor your debt?" Antoni asked.

"The news in Market Square is that the New Moon boasts of a Queens' quarter knot."

Antoni tapped his fingers on the desk top. "I've heard the rumor too," he said. "But how much truth is really in it?"

"Enough to make it worth considering. For two hundred years the Queen had not aged a day, but with the downfall of Sadar's Keep she changed in one night to a woman of middle age. I don't know how they accomplished it, but the New Moon has magic and it is strong." Ener shifted uncomfortably in his seat.

"If they are so strong already, why haven't they challenged the Queen?"

"Because the knot is incomplete," Ener explained.

"The girl with the red hair at Firecircle?" Antoni asked, thinking aloud.

Ener nodded. "Yes, a fire element, from Beldan's streets. A Ghazali girl is the air element and an Oran laborer the earth element."

"Then all that is missing is water?" Antoni asked, his fingers drumming more loudly on the table.

"Yes."

Antoni's fingers stopped abruptly in midair. A pleasant shiver coursed his spine as an idea formed in his mind. He returned his hand slowly to the desk top.

"I'm interested. What are you proposing, Re Aston?"

Ener coughed lightly to clear his throat. "There are many in Beldan who have joined the New Moon."

"I am well aware of that," Antoni said coldly.

"It won't be difficult to place one of ours among their ranks. If there is a Queens' quarter knot, they will come to Beldan to face the Queen. We will provide the Queen and you with that information before such a time comes."

Antoni knitted his hands before his face in thought.

"And why would you do this thing?" Antoni asked.

Ener frowned, confused by the question. "Because we are loyal," he repeated.

"And because you fear your Queen cannot protect you."

Ener was silent for a moment. When he spoke again, his words were careful.

"There is no love among the Oran people for the Readers. Our task has been a painful one, like that of a battle surgeon cutting away diseased flesh. And it is hardest when the flesh is as innocent looking as a child. If a Queens' quarter knot is formed, it may destroy the Queen. I believe that she is already weakening. If the new knot succeeds then the Readers, like the Sileans, will be at the mercy of the New Moon."

"What would happen if Oran was without a Queens' quarter knot, and without the Fire Queen Zorah?"

"I can understand that has long been a Silean desire," Ener answered, his back stiffening with pride. "But you must know, Advisor, that without the Queen, without someone capable of holding the elemental threads together, Oran would cease to exist. It would be returned to the Chaos out of which it was formed."

"Are you certain that isn't Oran superstition? Silea has had no problem existing, even conquering this piece of the world. And we are not infected with magic."

"You command the lives of every Oran, myself included. You make the laws and set the trade. But Silea has not conquered Oran. It will never control the magic elements that bind the soil of our island. Perhaps the Mother Amaterasoran and her child Oran chose not to give Sileans magic as it was . . . unnecessary."

"Meaning?"

Ener raised his chin with a hint of defiance. "Meaning that

Silea is accomplished in war. That could be considered a dangerous enough power by itself.''

"Oran is Silea's stepchild. It has become Silea's duty to raise Oran out of its backward culture. And sometimes we must do it with a harsh hand."

Ener held his tongue, though a red flush invaded his neck and face.

"What, then, is your price for loyalty?" Antoni asked.

"We shall expose the members of the knot when they come to Beldan. In return, Reader families request a charter to run the linen trade along the Hamader River from Asturas to here in Beldan."

Antoni gave a low whistle. "A goodly enterprise. And a high price. But you will be in conflict with Silean interests."

"Not when the terms of trade are set by you, Advisor, to favor Silean needs. We ask only a share of the trading profits, sufficient to maintain our families."

"And why should Readers seek a new trade? You already have a Guild," Antoni argued.

Ener paused again before replying. "The time approaches, Advisor, when the Readers' sight will no longer be needed, when all Oran magic will belong again to the Queen. There are already some among us who have lost the ability to Read."

"Indeed," Antoni said softly. He pressed a finger to his lips.

"I tell you this in confidence, Advisor."

"Of course," Antoni said. He walked toward the hearth to warm his chilled hands over the fire. Ideas and possibilities shaped into a plan. He spoke, facing the fire. "These are my terms, Re Aston. I shall see that you receive your charter but I want more than information. I want the fourth girl. I will see to it that you have help, but the water element must be found and brought to me. Alive," he added, enunciating the word.

"That may be difficult, sir."

"Yes, I'm sure it will be. But I can use her to convince the Queen to accept some proposals the Silean government has wished to further. Either way, the fourth is a gambling piece, for the Readers and for me."

Ener protested, but Antoni held his hand up to silence him.

"First the girl, and then you will have your charter to run the trade on the river."

"We shall proceed, Advisor, as soon as I have received a written document confirming our agreement," Ener said sourly.

Antoni laughed drily. "Spoken like a Silean tradesman. Never commit to business until you first commit to paper. I'll have the terms drawn up today. My secretary shall see that you receive them before the thirdwatch."

Ener bowed, this time more deeply. "Good day, then, Advisor."

Antoni didn't answer but stared into the burning coals of the hearth. A water element. He would have her, the Readers would bring her to him like an offering. He turned away from the heat of the fire and stared out the window, seeing the thick gray fog that rose off the ocean and muffled the city. Have patience, he told his quickened pulse. With the spring, a child of Oran would be brought before him like a reluctant bride.

In the narrow alley the Upright Man walked with confidence, the heels of his black boots rapping the cobblestones. He moved purposefully, like a man who knows that he will not be bothered. Around his face he wore a black silk scarf that hid all his features except his eyes. They stared out from beneath the brim of a black hat, a faint red light shining in the ebony pupils. Street snitches and beggars doffed their hats to him as he swept past, though he gave them no notice in return.

He stopped at the door of a tavern known as the Mouth. Over the window was painted a wide-open mouth with a huge set of teeth. He shoved open the warped door and crossed the threshold.

The Upright Man waited in the doorway, surveying the crowded tavern. The small common room was packed with drinkers sitting elbow to elbow at the long wooden tables, while whores leaned over their shoulders, waiting for invitations. Four men near the wall played a noisy game of knucklebones, throwing the gambling bones down with a loud crack against the table. One cursed his defeat while another demanded his money. Close to the smoky hearth a skinny man with only a few teeth left in his head bawled with laughter at something said by a companion. His loose-limbed body shook and his head rolled in the direction of the door. He spotted the Upright Man and froze. The Upright Man smiled coldly as he saw the man quickly straighten himself and clear a seat for him. The gangly man motioned to the tavern keeper for a tankard, all the while keeping a fearful eye on the man in black.

The Upright Man walked toward the hearth, aware that the room had grown more quiet and that the drinkers edged away from him as if he radiated heat.

Two whores came to join him at the hearth. Chairs scraped along the ground as a circle around the hearth was widened to include the women. The Upright Man accepted his tankard of ale silently and then set it down beneath his chair. He would not drink with them, but they were obliged by his demands to buy him ale nonetheless.

"All respect, sir," the gangly man said, "but we ain't seen much of you these days." He drank a hasty draught of his ale, his knobbed throat bobbing as he swallowed.

"And what have you done, Bonesnip, in my absence?" the Upright Man replied coolly. "Frigging all, I'd say. I haven't seen any of the Flock working the streets. And I'd wager you've nothing but lice and shit beneath those rags. Scarcely of any value on the Silean trade, now is it?"

Bonesnip tried to meet the Upright Man's eyes, but his courage failed and he took refuge by gazing into his tankard. "Oy, sir, times is been hard, ain't they? The cheat ain't what it used to be. Half the Flocks have scattered to Beldan's tunnels, to join the New Moon, 'cause they at least promise 'em bread. I can't hold 'em anymore. Then there's the trade itself. Well, it's drying up. Z'blood, it's near impossible to get close to a good prig anymore, they've all got butcherboys in their back pockets looking out for them. Only ones as do any good these days is the whores. Least for now the Sileans still pay for it. If there's a siege of the city, Z'tits, they'll just take it," Bonesnip finished glumly.

"Oh aye, we've been very busy," one of the whores giggled.

The Upright Man turned to the whore who spoke. He knew her, a girl with the street name of Stickit. She was a heavyset girl with a face like an overcooked dumpling. Her lank brown hair was curled over her fleshy ears. She wore rouge on her cheeks, which set off the pasty color of her skin. Her blue dress was dirty, the bodice seams torn and strained around her huge waist. The Upright Man knew Stickit made more money from the snitch than the whoring, selling secrets to the highest bidders. She had sold out members of her old Flock, the Waterlings, to him years ago. She grinned, her dull blue eyes blinking nervously.

Next to her was another girl and the Upright Man gave her a more careful study. She was young, no more than fifteen or sixteen, her face a smooth oval of light brown skin. She had brushed her black hair back into a braided knot at the base of her neck. Her eyes were dark and had the poised appearance of a startled animal. Her figure was slim, her hands folded neatly in her lap. She didn't wear a dress but several lace bodices and petticoats layered together that gave the impression of a woman half undressed, even though very little of her body was actually revealed. The lace was a clean white against the brown shoulders. She smiled and the Upright Man found himself intrigued.

"Your name, girl," he demanded.

"The Petticoat," she said, her voice surprisingly husky for the slight figure.

"I ain't seen you before. Been here long?"

"Long enough, sir."

"Don't get smart," Bonesnip hissed at her. "That there is the Upright Man. He runs all the Flocks in Beldan, whores too if he feels like it. You mind yourself now. He ain't no fancy man."

The Petticoat raised her eyebrows but seemed otherwise undaunted. "I know who you are," she said. "Just ain't never met is all."

"Perhaps we will more often, in the future," the Upright Man replied.

The Petticoat bowed her head, on her face a knowing smile. "As you wish."

The Upright Man dug into his pocket and brought forth two gold coins, which he flipped one after the other to Bonesnip. Bonesnip snatched them neatly out of the air, open-mouthed in astonishment.

"Get two pitchers of ale for yourselves. Brandy for me," the Upright Man said.

Bonesnip scrambled over the people sitting behind him, hurrying to the tavern keeper to fill the Upright Man's order. The Upright Man smiled behind his scarf as he watched the tall snitch lick his lips at the cream-colored foam sloshing over the sides of the pitchers. Carrying the two pitchers in one hand and the tiny measure of golden brandy in the other, Bonesnip returned to the hearth, carefully threading his way through the crowded inn.

He handed the Upright Man his drink and then busily set to filling the tankards.

"Raise your glasses," the Upright Man said after they were filled. Everyone obeyed, lifting his tankard in the air. "A celebration."

"What are we drinking to?" Stickit asked, giggling again.

"The very slow death of my enemies," the Upright Man replied.

Their expressions faltered, gaiety splashed by chilling fear. But they drank, one by one tipping their heads back. It was then that the Upright Man lifted the bottom of his silk scarf and quickly downed his drink. When he replaced the scarf, he looked up and saw the Petticoat staring back at him.

The Upright Man narrowed his eyes. The faint red light of his pupils glowed. "Be wise, girl," he warned, "lest your boldness gives you cause to beware. I am not a man to brangle with and though you think yourself a pretty whore, it counts for little to me."

"I'm a silent creature, sir. One who well knows her place," the Petticoat said softly.

The Upright Man stood to take his leave.

"Oy, sir, I've something for you," Stickit whispered, tugging the hem of his cloak.

The Upright Man considered Stickit, his long fingers with polished nails tapping his thigh. "Outside," he said, and moved toward the door.

Stickit followed, nervously twiddling the ribbons of her bodice.

Once outside the Upright Man turned on the whore, and she backed away, alarmed.

"Give out," he said coldly, pulling his cloak tighter around his shoulders.

"Down at the Raven's Wing there's a whore named Trisse.

She's got a two-year-old. Got the old stuff, you know. Earth element, Trisse said. She'd sell him to you if you was to tell her it's so he can work the big houses. She'd like that. Been boasting on it, in fact, so don't let her give out no high price, claiming she's soft for the brat.''

"You'll be paid after I have the child," the Upright Man said, dismissing her.

"But when'll that be?" Stickit whined. "We ain't seen you much and—"

The Upright Man cut her short as he drew his sword and placed the point against her stomach. He prodded her gently and she squeaked. "I could scaffer you now and save myself the trouble of paying you later."

Stickit closed her mouth, tears glistening in her eyes. Slowly the Upright Man returned his sword to its scabbard. "Better," he said and left her rubbing her stomach as he headed down the alley.

As he walked, anticipation gathered in his gut. It had been a long time since he had taken power from a child. His lips felt dry beneath the silk scarf and with a bold gesture he let fall the mask. In the slanting light of a tavern window, Antoni Re Desturo smiled.

Two hundred years ago, Antoni's great-grandmother had been an Oran woman, part of the spoils of a battle. The child conceived had a Silean father but claimed the Oran birthright of magic. She had sent him away to Silea, where she hoped he would be safe, free from the accusing eyes of the Readers. When Antoni had been born, the youngest of three sons, there was no one who would tell him what he had inherited. Only a near drowning taught him that he could not be harmed by water, and it was a secret he kept to himself. Thinking back on his decision to come to Oran, Antoni was certain that his father knew. On the eve of his departure from Silea, his father had given him two ancient books on Oran history and Oran magic. Though he spoke no words of explanation, the gift had said much.

Antoni had come to Oran with a plan of his own. The Fire Queen could not cleanse magic from the blood of the Oran people. It was too much like plucking minnows out of a rushing stream. So she gifted the Readers with sight, that they would be the net by which Orans with the old power were caught and hanged. But Antoni had discovered yet another method. Water and magic flowed together in the blood. A simple cut, and all he had to do was drink. Water called to water and their blood poured into him, gifting him with the small feast of their magic.

The children were so easily trapped. They were the street brats, ragtags and snitches. Few claimed or cared for them, and those who did could be convinced that the Upright Man wanted them for a special Flock of thieves that plundered the Silean estates. Mothers sold them off for a few coins, content that their children were soon to be better off than they.

Antoni slowed his steps, hearing a scuffle in the darkened shadows of the alley. A man groaned and then swore thickly. Antoni replaced his scarf, a hand on the hilt of his sword. As he neared the shadows two youths dashed past him. One held a bloodied knife, while the other boy gripped a leather purse. They caught sight of the Upright Man and scattered in opposite directions. It was then that Antoni saw the other man, lying slumped against the wall of the alley. He wore the black-and-gray uniform of a Silean Guard. Antoni nudged him with his boot and the man toppled over into the dirty street.

Antoni stared at the uniform and then shrugged at the dead man. Tomorrow, in his office, he would be properly outraged. Three or four would be taken from the prisons and hanged in retaliation. But tonight he couldn't have cared less about another butcherboy lying dead in the street. Tonight the part of him that was Oran clamored for its own kind of revenge. He hated the Sileans almost as much as he hated the Readers.

He thought of Re Aston sitting in his office, pleading for the Readers. The stupid bastard. Even though Antoni had learned long ago to shield his aura from the Readers' gaze, he knew that fools like Re Aston never looked beyond the Silean garments he wore. The readers would bring him the very weapon he needed to destroy their Guild. He smiled thinking of the young girl, the water element. He would take her slowly, let every part of him be infused with the deep well of Oran magic. He would drown in the magic and then resurface, newly filled with the water of life. Oran would be his then. He would be the fourth element in the knot and he would take command of the Queens' quarter knot.

At the door to the Raven's Wing, Antoni saw a child playing in the dirt. He rolled small creatures of mud and set them down. The child hummed to himself, absorbed in his work. Antoni bent to look and saw the stubby figures moving clumsily around a circle. The child's hands were molding another figure that was already beginning to squirm between the pudgy fingers.

"What have you made there?" Antoni asked him, slipping the mask from his face so as not to frighten the child.

"A dog," came the distracted reply as the child released the mud dog to the ground. It was lopsided and lumbered with an uneven gait to join the other animals.

The child looked up, his rounded face streaked with dirt. His hair was a crown of yellow curls, and beneath the bangs two eyes regarded the Upright Man seriously. "Don't tell me ma you seen these. It's a secret."

"Come with me," said the Upright Man, taking the child by the hand. "I've something to show you."

The child tugged to free his hand, but the Upright Man held it firmly. "Me ma says not to go, but stay here and wait on her."

"I'm taking you to her," the Upright Man said smoothly. "She's got a surprise for you."

The child relented, his hand softening in the Upright Man's grip. "She does? What?" he demanded.

"Come and you'll see."

The child followed eagerly. Holding his hand the Upright Man could feel the child's excited pulse and remembered the warm taste of blood. Tonight he would drink, saluting the future and the real repast to come.

Chapter Three

In the gray dawn, Deveaux Re Silve slowly rode his black charger and reviewed his troops. He held the reins loosely, his careful eye taking in the polished weapons, the oiled gleam of their light armor, and the health of the animals. The journey by ship had been longer than he had planned, storms keeping them from a more timely landing. But as he surveyed his troops, he was well pleased. The horses looked rested and groomed, their heads bobbing in anticipation of the battle, their ears pricked forward to catch the sound of the horn. Astride their mounts his men waited, their expressions stern. There were no rough or inexperienced hotheads in the front lines. Only men Deveaux could trust. A few of them met his eyes and to those he inclined his head in greeting.

Not many of his soldiers were comfortable looking at his face. Deveaux's lips curled in a sardonic smile. The point of an incisor snagged on his lower lip. A disease at birth had left him strong in the limbs but his face grossly misshapen. His head was too wide at the forehead and his green eyes bulged, the gaze seemingly directed in two different directions. His nose was bulbous and round, the flesh red and chapped. His heavy lips barely closed over huge teeth that scattered like a broken fence in his mouth. In defiance of his hideous face, Deveaux kept his thick blond hair in a shaggy mane, into which he permitted talismans of good luck to be braided before battle.

He reached the end of the front line and turned his horse down the side of the column. He kicked his horse lightly and the animal began to trot, its pace increasing until Deveaux was cantering past the rows and rows of Silean soldiers awaiting battle orders. Behind his cavalry waited archers, the white-and-black fletches of their arrows rising above their shoulders. Mingled among them were the crossbowmen, shields mounted on their backs, the wooden crossbows in their hands. Quivered at their waists were the short wooden bolts with the black dyed-leather fletches. And behind them were his foot soldiers, each man armed with an ax or a bladed staff as was his preference.

Six thousand men spread across the grassy field, the dull yellow plain almost buried beneath the black and gray colors of their uniforms. Deveaux rode to the end of the ranks, shooting a brief glance at the supply wagons stationed at the back. Satisfied all was in readiness, Deveaux returned to the front lines.

He stared at the small town before them, watching the drab colors change as the morning sun rose to light the buildings and the stone fences. He smiled coldly at the quiet peace of the place. It was Doberan, an Oran town on the sea end of the Sairas River, and of no consequence, he thought, until now. After today, Doberan's name would not be mentioned among the Oran people without despair.

Deveaux leaned down to stroke his horse's proud neck. He felt calm, confident that although his reputation for brutality might spread to yet another country, he was strategically correct in his actions. Those bastards in the Silean parliament had thought to get rid of him by forcing him into this campaign. How well he knew that past campaigns in Oran had been expensive, ending the futures of those foolish enough to undertake them. Many a Silean nobleman found to be troublesome at home in the parliament was given the dubious honor of a post in Oran. And Deveaux knew he troubled the parliament. He was brilliant, ambitious and, despite the barbarism of his face, he had noble blood that entitled him to a position in the parliament. But they feared him. Deveaux knew they had appointed him to this campaign in hopes that he would destroy himself as others had before him. And if not that, there was always a chance he would remain in the Oran court and abandon his claims in Silea.

Deveaux had agreed to this campaign, but on his terms alone. The parliament grumbled at the expensive demands, but Deveaux would not back down. He judged it a measure of the intensity of their dislike that they gave in to his demands. Anything to see him away from the court. He refused to leave Silea until he had his soldiers' pay in trunks boarded on the ship—men confident of receiving duty pay maintained better discipline. Each man was to be well outfitted, and food had been billeted for the two months that they might wage a winter campaign in Oran. In addition to weapons, each man boasted of decent leather and wool to his back, hose and boots to his feet, and two blankets.

Deveaux had studied the maps of Oran and read the reports of Silwa's disastrous campaign against the New Moon at Sadar's Keep. It was rumored there had been magic, a sword that had built a column of fire and scattered the Silean armies in the field of battle. Deveaux's ambition prickled at the thought of a challenge. Magic swords. And why not one for him as well? Had he not grown up being taunted as an ogre's child? Weren't his face and his skill as a soldier a kind of dark magic? He would win one of these swords for himself.

To crush the revolt in Oran decisively, Deveaux judged he would have but a season. On foreign soil their supplies were limited, and he had little faith that the local Silean estates would assist his army. They must gain the upper hand immediately, weaken the morale of the rebellion and strengthen their own. To break the back of Oran resistance, they would kill as many Orans as possible. There would be no distinctions made between soldiers and the populace. All Orans, whether rebel soldiers, the aged, women, or even children, were to be seen as enemies.

The town of Doberan was at the end of the Sairas River. Farther north, the Sairas branched away from the Hamader River at a trading town called Gallen. Between Doberan and Gallen were Oran villages, clinging to the sandy banks of the Sairas River. The land had never been much for farming, so the Sileans had built their estates on the fertile land farther west. The river was narrow, opening out into the sea at a three-day ride from Beldan. To Deveaux, looking at it on the map, it was exactly what he wanted. He would tear his way up the Sairas River, obliterating the Oran villages as he created a new trade route to Gallen. The New Moon would not be able to defend both the Hamader and the Sairas rivers at the same time. Beldan might then be safe from siege. From Gallen he would go farther north, attacking the Oran villages along the banks of the Hamader River until he reached Asturas. He would see to it that the New Moon received no supplies from the trading towns all along the Hamader River to Beldan and along the Sairas River as well. Once in Asturas, he would rest his men until Ilario's army in Beldan could join forces with him to crush the New Moon's stronghold at Sadar. Given a winter cut-off from supply lines and two armies converging on their Keep, Deveaux was confident the New Moon would surrender quickly. Deveaux laughed softly. Even their magic swords would be of little use to them.

Deveaux raised his hand. Banners snapped crisply in the morning wind as the flagmen lifted the standards. Deveaux motioned toward the town and the army began to march, covering the field like a deadly fabric.

As they approached, Deveaux could see children standing on the stone walls, staring curiously at their approach. One child waved a red scarf in greeting.

Too easy, Deveaux thought, disappointed.

He signaled for the army to stop just outside of the town walls. By this time many of the townsfolk had gathered on the walls to stare at the huge army amassed at its gates. Women carried baskets in their arms. There were men as well, and here and there Deveaux saw the tall shaft of a pike. A slim figure in a brown robe caught his eye. The hood was pushed back and Deveaux saw it was a woman, her hair cut short. Across her back she carried a longbow and a quiver full of arrows. Deveaux raised his arm and the horns blared. An officer disengaged himself from the front line and rode to the town gates.

"By the command of General Deveaux Re Silve, you, the populace of Doberan, are required to lay down your weapons and surrender yourselves."

"Fools!" the woman in the brown robe shouted. "There is nothing for you to gain here. Go home."

The officer looked over at Deveaux.

"Again. Give it to them again," Deveaux said.

The officer repeated his demand that Doberan surrender to the Silean army.

The children rapidly disappeared from the walls. Deveaux frowned, seeing many of the women replaced by men carrying weapons. Not much of a resistance. But Deveaux wanted to keep his casualties to a minimum. Later it would be much harder.

Deveaux raised his chin to the new sun and howled. The piercing sound shattered the morning air. His troops replied, shouting and clamoring with their own battle cries. They hoisted their weapons high, the rattle like the roll of drums as they shook them.

The front line split open and two lines of archers appeared behind light shields. They raised their bows and began firing at the townsmen gathered on the walls. Many were hit, and the hard twang of arrows was joined by the chorus of their wounded cries.

But to Deveaux's annoyance, the volley was returned with Oran arrows. For the few archers they had, the aim was good. They chose their targets carefully, rather than wasting arrows on a barrage. Twenty of his men went down, green-and-yellow fletches stabbing their bodies like thick blades of new grass.

A second line of archers advanced, seeking to press their advantage. Deveaux saw the red scarf of a woman as she fled through a field on the west side of the village. Behind her a scraggly line of women and children followed, making for the ocean. Deveaux signaled his officers in the front lines and they broke apart into three columns, soldiers flowing around the village like a river. Deveaux nodded with satisfaction as his mounted horsemen rode down the fleeing women and children. No one from Doberan was to survive.

And then a wild shriek penetrated the clashing roar of battle. Deveaux jerked around in his saddle and saw the woman in the brown robe transform. Her hands reached above her head, her arms curving into high, arched wings. Her body expanded, growing huge and tall, the brown cloth of her robe shredding and then reforming into bands of silver and brown feathers. Her shorn head jutted forward on a long neck between her spreading wings. Her feet curled into hard shining talons. Stones tore loose from the wall as she leapt into the air. As Deveaux watched in stark astonishment, her human face disappeared behind the stout black beak of a vulture.

His archers retreated, terrified by the sudden transformation of the woman into a monstrous bird. Their ranks quavered, the line of archers breaking apart as the vulture rounded in the morning sky, blasting them with deafening screeches. She folded her wings and swooped. Her talons raked a soldier's back as he fled. He fell, tumbling and rolling over the dry plain, the flesh of his back parted to the spine. The vulture wheeled again, this time flexing her outstretched talons as she reached for a mounted officer. He slashed his sword frantically, trying to stab her in the belly. Her talons caught him first and, gripping him by the waist, she lifted him screaming off his horse. She flew in an upward spiral, the wind gusting with her beating wings. From up high, she straightened, drifting over the land. Then she opened her talons and released the man. She hovered, her wings spread to catch the updrafts as she watched the man falling back to earth, his arms windmilling in the empty air. The flat gold disks of her eyes caught the rays of the morning sun and glittered brightly. Soaring, she screeched again, and then turning sharply she dove toward the earth. The grass swayed beneath the frenzy of her wings as she flew low to the ground. She hurtled herself into the cavalry, clacking her beak as the panicked horses reared and bucked.

Around him on the field of battle, Deveaux's men fled in terror. He bellowed with outrage seeing the damage done in this first battle. Overhead the gigantic vulture continued to soar and dive, ripping his men from their horses. On the stone walls Oran archers killed and wounded his men, who were more intent on fleeing the monster.

Deveaux spurred his horse through the lines until he found a crossbowman, desperately trying to knock the heavy bolt into the machine, all the while staring at the sky.

"Give me the bow!" Deveaux roared.

Quickly the man handed it up to Deveaux, along with the quiver. Once freed of his weapon, the man retreated through the scattered lines of soldiers.

Deveaux wanted to shoot him first for the offense of fleeing, but instead he kicked his horse savagely and galloped to the crumbling front line. He rode into the clearing before the village gate. He raised himself up in the saddle and began to shout challenges at the soaring vulture. She rounded in the brightening sky to face him. The golden eyes fixed on him and she screeched in reply.

Deveaux's heart hammered violently but he held his hand steady as he aimed the crossbow. The bird's wings opened across the sky, the sun sparkling between the outstretched pinions. She tilted her chest upward, the black curved talons like iron sickles reaching down for him. Deveaux felt the rush of wind from her wings and fired the crossbow. The bolt caught her in the chest and her proud head jerked backward with the shock. She beat her wings frantically to lift herself up and away from Deveaux. He stole that moment to reload his crossbow, and before she could gain height he fired another bolt. It ripped through her wing and pierced her side.

She rolled in the wind and began to fall. She landed hard in the field, and a cloud of white feathers exploded into the air.

Deveaux kicked his horse and rode to where she lay. He approached cautiously, for though her chest plumage was thickly stained with blood, she floundered wildly, her beak gashing the soil. Deveaux loaded another bolt into the crossbow and shot her through the eye. The golden disk shattered like a mirror and she raked her head through the air, the screeches dying in her throat.

His horse quivered beneath him. Deveaux kicked its flanks

hard, forcing it closer to the dying creature. Deveaux dismounted and, ignoring the weak thrashing of her wings, came close to her. He drew his sword, preparing to thrust it into her breast. Standing with sword poised, Deveaux saw something between the shifting bands of brown-and-white feathers. It was a darkness, as if the vulture were no more than a hollow structure and contained within it the night's sky. In the darkness he saw the pinprick gleam of starlight. And as he thrust his blade deep into her chest, he heard the wind's shrill keening.

He stepped back startled, his sword dripping with blood. And as he did, the rest of his officers lunged forward and drove their swords into the already-dead vulture.

Deveaux wiped his blade clean before he resheathed it. Then he remounted his trembling horse and stared at the walls of Doberan. It was quiet, and he knew there would be no other surprises, that Doberan had given up its best and now was lost. He rode forward, calling orders to his soldiers to re-form their lines. Soldiers scurried to positions, his officers scrambling to their horses. Slowly the Silean standards were raised again.

When they were ready, Deveaux gave the command to attack. In a few short breaths the Silean army had spilled over the grassy plain and swarmed the gates of Doberan. He hardly needed to watch to know what they would do. They had been frightened by so unexpected an enemy. And yet magic or not, the creature had succumbed to death in battle like any other mortal soldier.

No longer interested in the battle for Doberan, Deveaux dismounted again and came close to study the fallen creature. He laid a hand on its beak, marveling at its cold metal hardness. He stared into the undamaged eye and was disappointed that the golden disk had faded into clouded blue. He walked the length of the vulture, ruffling the feathers and hoping to glimpse once more the darkness between the bands. But there was nothing in the mangled body that suggested the magic it had once contained. He leaned down to pluck a feather from the wing. Smiling grimly, he braided the shaft into a lock of his blood-stained hair.

Deveaux had been right. Oran would prove a costly battlefield. Already in this single fight he had lost more men than he should have against a miserable village. But there was a challenge here he could not deny, and briefly he hoped there were more beasts like this one yet to fight.

It was evening when an officer reported to Deveaux, who sat in his tent studying maps of Oran as he dined.

"Yes?" he asked, not bothering to look up.

"Sir, it's done."

"Everyone dead?"

"Everyone," the officer said, his voice husky.

Deveaux raised his glance to the officer. He was a young man, a new mustache barely covering his upper lip. Sweat beaded his pale forehead. Deveaux speared a small piece of meat from a plate by his elbow and chewed noisily. The officer averted his eyes.

"No stragglers?" Deveaux asked.

"Sir, we followed the trails of those who fled and managed to round up all of them. They have been executed as you ordered."

Deveaux grunted. "And buried?"

"Yes, sir. All except that thing out there. The men don't wish to get too close to it."

Deveaux stopped chewing and shook his head angrily. "Stupid bastards. It's dead, isn't it?"

"With all respect, sir. The men fear it's an omen."

"Set it alight," Deveaux commanded. "Let it burn all night, and in the morning we'll leave behind ashes. That should lay its power to rest."

"But the stench—"

"Not half as bad as the stink of fear," Deveaux growled at the officer. "Let them learn that now."

The officer left, his young face looking paler. Deveaux raised a glass of wine to his lips. Then he cursed as the rim bumped against his protruding front teeth and the wine spilled onto his uniform. He set the glass down and ran a hand through his tangled hair. How easily the things of battle came to him. How graceful he was in killing. He had ridden out and slaughtered the creature that terrified his men. And yet how like an animal he was in the ways of men. None of his officers dined willingly with him. With his beastlike head he ate awkwardly, tearing the food with mismatched teeth, the sound of his chewing echoing in the odd-shaped chambers of his skull. Glasses of wine broke against his teeth if he wasn't careful placing the rim to his lips. And even when he was careful, the wine dribbled down the sides of his mouth.

Irritated, Deveaux stood and stepped out of his tent. He watched his officers set torches to a hastily built pyre around the base of the vulture. The fire whooshed to life, long arms of orange flame reaching into the sky. The fire crackled as it ate into the carcass, turning it red-gold and then blue with the blazing heat. Thick ribbons of smoke were carried aloft and drifted into flat clouds.

The men tending the fire coughed behind their cloth masks and Deveaux was glad that his nose had, as it usually did after eating, become congested. Even the smoke-filled air carried no taste to his tongue.

There were no fires burning in the town, no lights save the quarter moon shining forlornly above the stone walls. Deveaux smiled, his teeth pricking his lower lip. He would rename the village after himself. And he would come back in the spring to see it reborn as a Silean town and himself well rewarded.

Chapter Four

In the chilly afternoon, Market Square was crowded. Even the scant offerings did not dissuade Beldanites from strolling and poking hopefully through the clutter on the carts. The songs of hawkers and barrowboys encouraged buyers to part with their money. Hands slapped palm to palm as deals were concluded, followed by the soft clink of coins being exchanged.

Slipper wandered through the crowd, stopping at various stalls to look before moving on to another. Occasionally he glanced upward, his eyes sweeping the crowd for familiar faces. He rubbed the long planes of his narrow face and tugged at his blue neck scarf. It identified him as a weaver's apprentice, though he had never held a shuttle in his life. The collar of his smock itched and Slipper longed for the comfort of his own shirt. This was Kai's idea, dressing respectably to do the cheat. Readers and Guards didn't look as closely at a Guildsman as they might an ordinary street brat.

And Slipper was getting too old to pass for a street brat. His cheeks showed signs of a new beard and his shoulders had widened over his slim waist. Though he was still slight—the legacy of growing up half starved—his deep-set eyes and the faint furrows that were appearing on his brow denied that he was a child. Slipper rubbed a finger over the new tattoo at the base of his thumb that marked him as a Named adult. A Ghazali woman had done it, using some herbs that had dyed his skin almost the identical blue of the Queen's tattoo mark. Though it might fool a Silean Guard, it wouldn't pass the scrutiny of a Reader's vision. But then, neither would Slipper. He was a water element, and his aura was as blue as Beldan's harbor on a summer's day. For much of his life he had lived with Kai, the leader of a Flock once called the Waterlings. Though a Reader, Kai was born to the street, and she had gathered around her the street children with the old power, hiding them from the Readers. They had lived in the tunnels beneath the streets of Beldan, venturing out only at night.

But all that had changed after the massacre at Firecircle. Slipper went to shove his hand into his vest pocket and then remembered with annoyance that the smock didn't have pockets. After Firecircle he and Kai had taken ownership of a tea shop called the Grinning Bird. They had kept it open as a refuge for the street poor and vaggers. Kai had hoped to use the Bird as a base from which to start an underground army of snitches that would one day assist the New Moon's rebellion. But the Grinning Bird was no more; confiscated by the Sileans when Kai had been arrested. The brightly painted bird that had graced the lintel of the door had been covered with whitewash and the shop was now boarded over.

Slipper shivered in the afternoon sunlight thinking of the underground prisons where he had searched for Kai. The small barred cells were packed with Beldan's people, suffering and dying in the dark. He would have gone alone if need be to find Kai, but the Kirian, Shefek, had been there, casting aside his fear of enclosed spaces to follow Slipper into the tunnels. Neive had been there too. He was an ashboy from Scroggles whose earth element had finally found the path through the tunnels under the city into the older tunnels of the prisons. It was only Kai that Slipper had been thinking of rescuing, but before it was done he had freed a good many prisoners. Neive had guided their escape through the tunnels, bringing them safely to the caverns beneath Market Square.

As before, Slipper lived beneath Beldan's city streets. But where they had once been a motley Flock of pickpockets, they were now a growing rebel army; an army of Oran Guildsmen, journeymen, vaggers coming from Sadar's Keep, Ghazalis bringing and carrying away messages and, as always, the street snitches. There were few who knew the full extent of the tunnels and Kai had argued that it be kept that way. The first time one of their people had been caught and tortured, the Silean guard raided the main tunnel at Market Square. From then on, each time there were arrests, they moved the location of their central headquarters, closing off entrances for a while to confuse the Guards.

Slipper spotted the bright red scarf that Kai wore to hide her short hair. The Sileans had shaved her head in prison and it had grown back into a curly black mop. Kai's old habit of tying her hair into a knot at the nape of her neck was gone. Now she ran stiffened fingers through it, twisting a single lock around her finger until it stayed like a small curled horn at her temple. Kai nodded at him over a pile of brightly colored ribbons. Slipper nodded back and tugged at the scarf that chafed his neck. From the leather pouch at his belt he withdrew two keys linked by a thin chain. He weighed them in his palm and then set off across the square.

He moved smoothly through the crowd, his attention trained on the door of a Silean tavern on the square's border. As he threaded his way through the carts he noted the others stationed throughout the crowd. Soltar, a weaver's son whose parents had been killed by the Guard, lifted his pointed chin. He whistled a shrill tune between his teeth. Almost imperceptibly, Slipper heard the noisy crowd hush as ears caught the tune. Two snitches gambling bones outside the tavern pocketed the loose coins and loitered near the door. An elderly vagger leaning against the side of a stall straightened his stance and his hand slid down to the center of his staff. A knot of cutterlads, freed from their rug looms for the afternoon, slipped their blunt-handled scissors into their hands as they stood around a baker's stall haggling over the price of sweet buns. And despite the jangling of his nerves, Slipper grinned as through the crowds he saw the Petticoat detach herself and angle the wide sweep of her skirts toward the tavern like a sail unfurling before the wind. She gave Slipper one glance, her dark eyes laughing and the white lace of her bodice gleaming like snow on her olive skin. She tossed her woolen cape back over one shoulder and smoothed the front of her dress, her childlike hands fluttering over her breasts. Kai was right, Slipper thought, here was the perfect distraction for the prig they were hoping to catch. Now all they needed was the lighterman to bawl out the hour, and for the man they waited on to emerge.

The loud cries of the lighterman rose above the din of Market Square. And following close behind them, the shrill caw of the Silean whistle marked the end of the firstwatch. Kai pulled the shawl tighter around her shoulders. She watched, worried, as Slipper made his way toward the tavern.

"Whore's shit," she swore privately. Why did it have to be Slipper doing this? If only it could have fallen to someone else. She had had to hide her dismay when Slipper had snagged the short straw. But Slipper had known she was upset anyway. He had become angry with her for doubting his skill at the cheat. It wasn't that, Kai argued. Slipper had always been among the best at light-fingering. He was just too valuable a person to lose should something go wrong.

Slipper was important to the New Moon. His water element often guided them through the night-black tunnels, and he was among the few who never felt frightened by the seemingly endless turns of the underground labyrinth. And Kai knew that it was Slipper who had taken over the organization of the smaller children—snitches, barrowboys, and cutters, even the younger apprentices from the Guildhouses. He had the right touch with them, always a sweet ready in his pocket for the hungry child, a good word and a safe place to rest. He'd a friendly ear for all of them and they in turn strove to please him by bringing him bits of information gleaned from the streets, small nuggets of conversations that had profited the New Moon. Kai thought about the shipment of Oran wheat that two Silean tradesmen had hoped to slip past the customs house and sell on Beldan's newly formed cheaters' market. It was the Petticoat who brought that news, as the two men had chattered on to her about how they would make a fortune from the deal and spend some of it on her, if she'd just spend the night with them.

Kai sucked in her lower lip at the sight of the Petticoat heading for the tavern. "The 'Shift-less' is more like it," she grumbled. And then just as quickly Kai flushed with shame. Stupid jealousy, she nagged herself, will you never outgrow it, Kai? They had a good supply of wheat in store as a result of the Petticoat. Two vaggers had met the riverboat outside the city in the middle of the night and relieved it of its grain. Not a word was said in the city about the theft, no one paid for the crime on the gallows, for the merchants were not in a position to expose themselves. But the Petticoat had demanded a price. Slipper brought her two yards of expensive Silean lace, which Kai could only assume he had nicked. Oh, yes, Kai thought sourly, the girl had her price for everything.

Kai moved away from the stall of ribbons, edging toward the tavern. She sighed, reminding herself that even though the Petticoat was as likely to turn a trick for the promise of money and security elsewhere, for the time being she worked for them. The girl, young as she was, had been a whore a long time. Maybe she had a right to be selfish; at least she was good at what she did.

Kai watched as their prig, Fortuna Re Arras, left the door of the tavern and entered the square. Re Arras was the Secondwatch, in charge of the Silean Guard from afternoon to early evening. He had come from Silea last spring to seek his fortune and had found ambiguous fame as one of the few survivors of the Uprising at Sadar. Kai knew about the battle from the Ghazalis who had come later to Beldan with the news. She knew that to be a Silean survivor of Sadar meant that the man had turned tail and run when Jobber exploded into flames on the battlefield. But all that had been retold by Silean nobles eager to believe themselves superior to the Oran people. Re Arras returned to Beldan a hero, responsible, it seemed, for the death of at least a thousand New Moon rebels where in truth there had only been scattered hundreds in all at the Keep. His reward was his appointment to the position of Secondwatch.

"Frigging bastard," Kai cursed him. In the first month of his appointment there was a leap in the number of arrests. On Baker Street an angry mob of women had protested the rise in the price of bread. In answer to their outraged cries, Re Arras sent the Silean cavalry, and within a short time ten women were dead and the rest had fled, carrying the wounded who could still walk or run.

Re Arras was a big man, and he rubbed a contented hand over his bulging stomach. Shaggy black eyebrows shaded the eyes that were partially hidden in the generous folds of flesh. His nose spread like a pitted mushroom in the middle of his face. A thin mustache failed to hide the thick lips that jutted out over a brace of chins. Kai watched him as he surveyed Market Square with a look of arrogance. He smoothed his receding hair and replaced his black hat, the white feathers dragging down his back. Hooking his hand around the handle of his sword he started toward the High Street. Behind him two uniformed Guards conversed, following at a respectful distance.

"Now!" Kai whispered urgently, suddenly fearful that the Petticoat would miss her mark and then Slipper would be out the cheat. "Get in," she hissed, frustrated by the Petticoat's slow amble into the oncoming path of the Secondwatch. The Petticoat called his name, and the arrogant expression on Re Arras's face changed to interested curiosity. The Petticoat gracefully tilted her head, the dark eyes capturing Re Arras's attention. She said something. He answered, his mouth widening into a leer. The Petticoat laughed and tapped him coyly on the chest with one tiny hand.

It was as Re Arras stepped closer to her, his two hands squeezing the Petticoat's shoulders, that Kai saw Slipper's blue neck scarf. He jostled the Secondwatch's shoulder, but the man was too captivated by the Petticoat to notice. Only an experienced eye like Kai's saw the darting motion of Slipper's hand as it dug into the Secondwatch's pocket.

Kai held her breath, waiting for Slipper to finish. "The keys, switch the frigging keys," she muttered, and her hands curled at her sides.

Two keys were the object of the cheat: two keys that opened the securely locked doors of the Silean armory. Only the Firstwatch Gonmer and the Secondwatch Re Arras had the keys. The Firstwatch was a dangerous swordswoman and much more difficult to distract than Re Arras. Kai knew that an uprising and break-in of the armory would cost too many lives, both in the storming of the armory and in the reprisals that were sure to follow. But with the keys they could plan a quiet little break-in—the few Guards stationed there at night would not be thinking of the New Moon walking through the front doors. And, Kai hoped, a pair of false keys might also buy them time, as she knew that Re Arras was not often given the command to open the armory. Kai had followed how the Firstwatch Gonmer had shortened Re Arras's duties as Secondwatch, almost as if she too had little trust of the man. They could clean the armory of weapons and not be discovered for a good day or more. The whole thing could go very naffy.

But it wasn't going naffy, Kai realized with a sudden chill. Something was wrong. Slipper was still there, his hand still dug into the pocket. Even the Petticoat was beginning to look concerned, her smile strained.

"Frigging get out," Kai said out loud.

"Oy, go the fuck away yourself," a barrowboy snarled back, thinking it was to him she had addressed her words.

Kai pushed past him, the alarms clanging in her head. The other two Guards had seen Slipper and were approaching slowly, their questioning expressions growing darker.

He's going to get caught! Kai's mind reeled.

"Soltar!" she shouted, and watched the boy scramble into the crowd. "Cutters!" she yelled as she ran. The cutters scattered in all directions and Kai lost sight of them as she stared at the large figure of Re Arras turning, his elbow brushing against Slipper. "Zorah's tits!" she exploded. "Get out, Slipper!"

So close. Slipper felt his hand wiggle into the deep pocket. He dropped in the fake set of keys, letting them down slowly.

Then his fingers touched the hard iron of the right keys and he smiled as he started to pull them out. Easy, he breathed, sweet and easy. The smile froze on his face as he felt the keys snag on something else in the pocket.

Slipper's gaze shot up, trying to discern the position of the other two Guards. They were far away enough not to notice his standing so close to the Secondwatch. He tugged gently at the keys. They were still stuck on something. Sweat made his upper lip itch. He twisted the keys slightly, but nothing changed. Then he tried pulling them, lifting out whatever else the keys had caught on.

His fingers brushed against the smooth surface of a packet. It was wrapped with string and he felt the hard, bumpy crust of sealing wax. The chain of the keys had become entangled in the string of the packet. It was no good. He couldn't bring out one without the other. But the packet was large and would not be shifted easily.

Whore's shit, Slipper thought, hearing the Petticoat's nervous laugh, I should get out. But even as he brought his hand out, he felt the packet slip into the channel of the pocket and begin to dislodge itself. That's it, I can do it! and he stayed, easing out ever so gently the keys and the packet together.

"Oy, you there! What are you doing?" One of the Guards had seen him and called out. Re Arras's body jerked, as if only now acknowledging Slipper's intimate touch.

All subtlety aside, Slipper wrenched the packet and keys out with a final fierce tug. Re Arras bellowed angrily and one huge hand shot out, snatching him by the collar of his smock. Slipper gagged as the collar was jerked tight against his throat. With one hand he pulled at the collar, trying to tear it free of Re Arras's grip. Then he heard a solid thump and Re Arras bellowed again, this time with pain. The grip on his collar was suddenly released.

Like a fox sprung from the trap, Slipper bolted, chancing one glance behind him. The elderly vagger was withdrawing his staff, preparing to bring it down again across Re Arras's legs. Re Arras was hunched over, an arm hugging his middle. The Guards were torn as to whether to assist the Secondwatch or capture the fleeing thief.

"Get the little bastard!" Re Arras shouted through clenched teeth, "and get *him!*" He pointed to where the vagger had been standing ready to strike, but he was already gone. Re Arras swiveled around, his eyes searching the crowds, his lower lip quivering with rage. There was no sign of the brown robes, or the tall staff. The Petticoat, too, had disappeared.

Slipper ran, dodging in and out of the crowds. A Guard pursued him, shouting at people to stop him. Slipper knew they wouldn't. If anything, the crowd packed together more tightly, like a closing thicket. Slipper stooped low, running hard, his heart pounding to the rhythm of his feet. He had the keys and the packet. Try as the Guards might, they'd not catch him now. Slipper sniffed the sweet rotting odor of the vegetable stalls located in the western corner of the square. He was looking for one vegetable stall, painted blue and white. The shrill caw of the Guards' alarm urged him to find it quickly.

There it was! Radigan was standing in front of the awning, roasting potatoes. Seeing the dark, hawklike profile against the afternoon sky, Slipper recognized the family resemblance of Radigan to his sister, Faul. Thin and tall, he held a small knife and deftly peeled potatoes, watching the crowd with casual interest.

Slipper darted toward the line of vegetable stalls, getting behind them. He crouched, keeping his head low. When he came to the back of Radigan's stall, he dove under the wagon, the sides and wheels of which had been covered with a huge blue cloth to create a small tent beneath the wagon. There wrapped in a bundle were Slipper's shirt, vest, and jacket. And best of all, the battered black lighterman's hat he always wore. Gulping for air, Slipper stripped off the smock and neck scarf and hid them beneath a box of potatoes. The cold air was bracing on his sweat-covered skin. He drew on the shirt and vest, jamming the keys and packet into the breast pocket. He reached eagerly for his jacket.

"Hie up," warned Radigan in a low voice. "They're coming."

Grabbing his jacket and the lighterman's hat, Slipper rolled from beneath the wagon and slid around behind another stall. His hat clenched between his teeth he shoved his arms through the jacket's sleeves.

He could see the Guards, three stalls down, their swords scraping under every wagon and stabbing into barrels. He placed the hat firmly on his head, drawing the old brim down over his forehead to shade his eyes. Hands in his pockets, he ambled to the front of Radigan's stall.

"Give us one," Slipper said pointing to a potato roasting on the fire. He struggled to slow his breathing and hoped his face wasn't too red from the exertion of running. Slipper handed a two-copper piece to Radigan.

"Can you stand it hot?" Radigan asked with a sly smile.

"Yeah, I think so," Slipper answered as the Guards peered under Radigan's wagon. Slipper tensed, wondering if in his hurry he had managed to completely hide the smock and neck scarf. Whether he had or not, though, didn't seem to matter. The Guards had their minds set on finding a snitch and weren't looking for clothing. They continued down the row of stalls, cursing as they came up empty-handed.

"Here you go," Radigan said handing him the potato wrapped in paper. "Don't get burned."

"Never," Slipper said grinning. Radigan laughed and clapped him on the shoulder. Then he picked up a new potato and returned to peeling the brown skin.

Slipper hurried down the High Street and turned into an alley that led behind the Silean shops. It was quiet after the noise of Market Square. At the end of the alley was a small deserted courtyard that had once held a garden. An old fountain of pink and gray Oran granite graced the middle of the garden, though it was filled now with bits of trash hardened in dirty rainwater. To one side of the old garden there was a stone wall, and embedded in the wall was a huge carved face. It was a comic face, the bulging eyes staring crosswise. The nose was droopy and long, hanging over a wide-open mouth from which a stone tongue lolled out into the scrubby bushes below.

Slipper entered the garden cautiously, making sure there was no one about. At this hour, though, most of the shopkeepers were attending to the demands of their customers. He walked briskly across the garden and leaned down at the open mouth of the huge face.

Just beyond the tongue was a narrow opening, big enough for a child or a small, determined adult. Going feetfirst, Slipper angled his body through the carved mouth and wriggled himself over the tongue. His feet dangled as the opening behind the mouth turned downward. When his head disappeared into the mouth, Slipper clung by his hands to the ledge. Then, taking a breath and closing his eyes, he let go and allowed himself to drop.

He knew it wasn't a long way down, but each time he entered the tunnels through the face he felt as if he were being swallowed alive. He huffed as his feet hit the rock bed of the tunnel. He brushed himself off, making sure the keys and packet were safe in his pocket. Then, setting out in complete darkness, he headed for the main tunnel beneath Market Square.

Traveling in the dark tunnels didn't bother him. There was always the water, whether in a trickle at his feet or dripping down the corrugated sides of the tunnels, to tell him where he was. The water spoke to him, a thin, feathery voice that whispered his location, directing him to the other camps scattered underground.

He saw a pale gold globe of light and knew it was Kai coming to meet him. As she approached he could make out her stern face, the scarf pushed down around her neck. A thick coil of hair curled above her temple and Slipper knew that she was furious.

"Zorah's tits, Slipper, what happened out there?"

"It's all right," he said. "I got what we wanted."

"Yeah, but—"

"I said it's all right," Slipper repeated more firmly. Kai's face softened, relief washing over the rigid features. Her eyes glittered raven black, but her lips parted into a half smile.

"Old habits, Slipper. You know that." She shrugged.

"And you know that I'm a good snitch."

"Yeah, I do," Kai agreed, "but frigging all you had me worried."

Slipper retrieved the keys from his vest pocket along with the packet. "This was the trouble. Keys were wrapped up in this bunch of papers."

"Let's have a look," Kai said curiously. She handed Slipper the torch to hold and took the packet from him. She untangled the keys and handed them back to Slipper, who replaced them in his pocket. Then she broke the seal and slipped the string from the folded wad of paper.

Slipper watched her as she stood in the torchlight reading. Shefek had taught them how to read, but Slipper had made a poor student. Kai, however, had taken to it, studying hard, though her lips still moved soundlessly with the words as she read. Slipper shifted the heavy torch into the other hand, growing impatient in the silence.

"Did Re Arras get the fake keys?" Slipper asked. "Did the switch work?"

"Hmm?" Kai said distracted and then answered quickly, "Yeah, worked naffy. I stuck around long enough to hear the old pig tell the Guard the thief didn't get away with nothing."

Suddenly Kai swore as she rapidly scanned the rest of the pages. "Z'blood, Slipper, the frigging bastards."

"What? What is it, then?" Slipper asked peering at the scrawled writing.

"Do you know what you've snitched here?"

"Dirty love letters?"

"No! Re Arras, the bastard, wrote a letter home to his people asking for money to outfit him in grand scale. Seems the Silean army has arranged a winter campaign against the Oran villages along the Sairas River. A General Deveaux Re Silve is arriving soon with an army to crush the Oran rebellion. The butcherboys in Beldan will join him when he reaches Asturas for another assault on Sadar."

"That ain't good."

"Not by half. We're going to have to get word out to the villages and to Sadar. I only hope we aren't too late."

Kai grabbed the torch from Slipper and hurried down the tunnel, the sheets of paper gripped tightly in her hand. Despite the limp she still carried from the beating in prison, she could move quickly when aroused.

"We must get word to Orian in Doberan."

"Oy, Kai!" Slipper called. "Hold on will you!"

"Can't," Kai yelled. "Can't you see the danger?"

"But the armory, when do we nick the armory?"

"Tonight," she said over her shoulder. "We rob it tonight, and set about cutting down the ranks of the new butcherboys. The fewer that make it to Asturas the better."

Slipper watched the light of her torch fade into the tunnel recesses. He sighed in the dark, pulling the brim of his lighterman's hat down lower. With his hand tucked deep into his pocket, he slowly followed Kai. Faint voices lifted from thin streams of trickling water. Slipper stopped to listen, his arms pressed close to his chilled sides as he heard the whispered message of despair.

Chapter Five

Jobber glared at the broken glass of the high window. A light scattering of snow blew in with every shift of the wind. Her red hair was pulled back, braided into place with thin strands of leather. Snow floated down from the window to land cold and wet on her face.

Why was Faul never bothered by such things? Jobber wondered as she flicked a tentative gaze to the rigid form of her swordmaster. Faul's angular face was motionless, her gray eyes half shut. She sat on her knees, her feet tucked beneath her buttocks and the wooden training sword at her side. In the bare room, Faul had grown so silent in her meditation that she appeared no more than a shadow cast on the stone wall. Jobber was supposed to be meditating on the Fire Sword lying at her knee. She should have been clearing her mind of clutter, making it as reflective as the mirrored surface of the sword itself; she should not have been distracted by the occasional wet flakes of snow. But she was distracted, and she wrinkled her nose to chase away a melted flake.

An instant later, Jobber was dead. Faul had wakened to life

with a deadly motion as Jobber had succumbed to the urge to wipe away the snow tear. Faul rose up on one knee and her wooden sword slashed out, the blade side touching Jobber's neck. Jobber fumbled, but her hand never made it to her sword. Dead, Jobber swore, dead, dead. That made three times today that she had lost against Faul without so much as a chance to use her sword in defense.

"Frigging shit," Jobber groaned.

"Precisely," Faul said coolly. She withdrew her sword, resettling her thighs neatly over her knees.

"Aw look, Faul, it's the snow."

"Yesterday it was the sun in your eyes."

"Yeah, well . . ."

"And before that it was a cramp in your leg."

"Z'blood . . . ," Jobber hissed, irritation prickling her heated scalp.

"Don't curse in here," Faul commanded.

Jobber scowled. "It ain't a sacred place."

"To me it is."

"And what makes it so?" Jobber demanded.

"You," Faul answered with a wry smile. "You and the Fire Sword, together."

Jobber's angry words dissolved like the snow. She plucked at her fraying braid. "I'm awful at this, ain't I?"

"Yes," Faul agreed. Jobber could see by the strained expression on Faul's face that she was worse than awful.

"You could spare my pride," Jobber protested.

"I could. But it would gain you nothing."

"I know, I know," Jobber said, standing up and shaking the blood back into her cramped legs. "The path of the sword begins with death," she intoned, repeating the oft-heard lesson. "But haven't I died enough these last few days? Am I ever gonna get to scaffer you first?"

"Even when you are able to scaffer me—"

"Well, at least you said *when*, not *if*, " Jobber broke in.

"Even then," Faul continued, "I'm not the Fire Queen Zorah. And this wooden sword," she said holding her weapon perpendicular to her face, "is not a Fire Sword."

"Z'blood," Jobber swore and then shrugged apologetically at Faul. She eyed her wooden sword miserably. The sword's way wasn't meant for her. No matter what she did it felt alien in her hand, no more useful than a rock she would have pitched through a glass window.

"What's wrong then?" Jobber asked.

"Heart's not there," Faul answered. She stood and smoothed the front of her black tunic.

"You saying I don't care?"

"No. I know you care." Faul frowned as she searched for the right words to explain. "But you need discipline to master the sword."

"I got discipline!" Jobber argued.

"And patience," Faul said.

Jobber bowed her head, accepting defeat.

"The heart I'm talking about has to do with balance," Faul tried again. "A harmony in yourself that allows you to understand what needs to be done without having to think about it. In a fight there is no room for second-guessing. That's true even in the old style of hand-fighting that you practice. It's a way of being ready, open to everything, without losing sense of your own place in the movement."

Jobber rolled her eyes. "You sound like a vagger, preaching something out the dust."

Faul stowed her wooden sword on brackets set into the wall. Jobber followed her and silently placed her own training sword beneath it.

"There was a time, Jobber, when the vaggers did more than preach, and when swordmasters did more than kill," Faul said wearily. "The Fire Sword was forged in a time of peace when there was no difference between it and the beauty of Ghazali poetry."

"It ain't part of my life, Faul," Jobber answered. "There ain't never been peace."

Faul pinched the bridge of her nose and shut her eyes. Then she dropped her hand to her side again. "Jobber, my life has not been so different from yours. Except for the sword." Bitterness tinged her words. The slate-colored eyes held Jobber's guilty stare. "Look, it's not something understood in words. You learn it in the sweat of training."

"Oy, Faul! Faul!" a girl called out from the bottom of the spiral staircase. Jobber's face brightened and she hurried Faul out of the room, glad to escape any more disapproval.

Jobber peered down the stairs and saw Finch climbing recklessly up the crumbling stone steps. Her yellow hair spread out like the tufted head of a dandelion.

"What is it?" Faul barked.

Finch braced a hand against the wall, panting with the exertion of her climb. She glanced warily up at Faul's severe face.

"Don't mean to break in on you," Finch apologized.

"It's all right," Faul said more gently. "We're finished for the day."

"Good then," the girl said. "There's someone calling for you, Faul. At the main gate. Won't state his reasons, just keeps on about how he's to speak to you and no one else. Gateman don't want to let him in and I can't say as I blame him. He's a queer thumb. Looks like a bonepicker. But he carries a vagger's staff tied across his back." She was staring at Jobber now, spreading the word as any Beldan snitch might while waiting at the corner.

"One of your relatives, Faul?" Jobber asked, digging an elbow into Faul's side.

"Shut up," Faul snapped. Her eyes clouded over as she considered Finch's news. "Tall was he?"

"Short. Round as a tun of Beldan brandy."

Faul lowered her head, still thinking. Then all at once her head jerked up and a look of fury filled her face. "Did he give his name?"

"Oh yeah, forgot," Finch said, her eyes almost hidden by the crown of wild hair. "Shefek."

Faul exploded with a curse and ran down the spiral stairs. Finch pressed against the wall to let her pass. Then she and Jobber exchanged amazed glances, hasty grins lighting their faces. Without another word, they clambered after Faul, wanting to be at the gate when she arrived.

* * *

Faul strode up to the gateman, trying to catch her breath. The run from the training room had given her time to collect her anger and store it behind a veneer of control. She opened a latched peephole and peered out. Shefek waited beyond the gate, humming a tune. Snow collected on his bare head and shoulders. White flakes mingled with the gray of his beard, and above his mustache his nose bloomed red in the cold. His sharp eyes followed the outline of the gate and Faul could almost hear the calculations rattling in his thoughts. She could see the staff, set at an odd angle across his back. After five years of eluding her, what did he want with her now? she thought archly. Bastard, Faul swore, but she couldn't deny the thread of excitement that traveled up her stomach and etched a line down her arms.

She shut the latch over the peephole. "Give me your sword," she ordered the gateman. The gateman withdrew his sword from his belt and handed it to her. She glanced at it sourly. More for looks than fighting. Heavy, badly weighted, probably too dull to cut cheese. "Open the gates," she said, and waited as the old gates creaked apart.

She slipped out between the two doors, not wanting this meeting with Shefek to occur in front of the assembled curious in the courtyard. It was stupid, she knew. They'd all listen anyway from the ramparts overhead. But she didn't want any distractions. That had been her undoing last time.

A playful smile lifted the corners of Shefek's mouth as he saw her approach. Faul kept her expression flat. His eyes gleamed, and from beneath the collected rags and blankets he wore his arms stretched forth to greet her. The arms were still strong, his forearms thickly muscled, his palms smooth except for a ridge of yellow calluses at the base of his fingers.

She waited for him to speak.

He saw she would not take his hands and, showing his disappointment, returned them to the warmth of the rags. A full head shorter than Faul, Shefek's gaze wandered over her body, lingering at her breasts. Then slowly he looked up and quietly studied her face.

"Faul, my owlet," he crooned. "Untouched by time."

"Shefek, you vulture," she retorted. "Untouched by truth."

He laughed, a deep chuckle, and moved closer. Faul raised

the sword as a warning. He gave the sword an incredulous smile. Snow whirled around his shoulders. "With that?"

"With my bare hands if I have to."

"That's certainly more interesting."

"Why are you here, Shefek?" Faul demanded.

"It's cold. I've traveled a long way. Let me in, Faul, and we'll talk."

Standing close to him, Faul noticed the new creases that aged his eyes. His cheeks were weather-beaten and scarred with wind burns.

"Where's my gold chain?" Faul asked bitterly.

He looked wounded by her acid tone. "Surely I gave you something more precious. I've not forgotten that night, Faul. It was a blessing. You remember it, don't you?"

Faul blushed. "Shut up," she said quickly. "You robbed me. Damn the Kirians and their tricks."

"But you never told anyone about me, did you, my owlet?" Shefek answered smugly.

"Don't call me that," Faul snapped.

Shefek's eyes strayed to the snow-covered Keep rising behind Faul. Then he inhaled sharply and his golden eyes blazed at her. "I have some new things to show you," he said softly. "Little trinkets that will interest you."

"What sort of things?" Faul asked, stalling. The golden eyes held her transfixed. Why did she feel like the goose staring stupidly at the fox?

"It's cold out here. Let's talk over a meal," he replied blowing warm air on his chilled fingers.

Faul relented and her mouth formed a wary smile. Shefek took it as an encouraging sign. He reached out to embrace her. She jabbed him in the belly with the hilt of her sword. The hilt hit something hard and she grunted at the unexpected impact.

"What are you wearing under those rags?" she asked suspiciously.

"Only if you let me see what you're wearing under this." Shefek laughed and fingered the laces of her tunic.

"You never change," she said and brushed away his inquisitive fingers.

"Ah, but I have, I have," he replied mournfully.

"Perhaps we both have," Faul said, anguish at the recent past unexpectedly touching her thoughts. "All right," Faul agreed and motioned Shefek to the gate. "But first I'll send someone to show you where you can wash. You stink, Shefek. . . ." She wrinkled her nose at the reek of his clothing.

"Oran's peace!" Shefek roared cheerfully as they passed beneath the ramparts and into the courtyard. "The human joy of being clean. To be rid of the vermin that have bedded in my skin."

"As always, Shefek, none too careful about who you lay down with."

"Does that include you, Faul?" he said loud enough to be heard by the gathering crowd trying to look gainfully occupied while they eavesdropped.

Faul could feel the stares burning holes in her back, but she refused to answer Shefek's accusation. It wasn't anyone's business with whom, or in this case what, she slept with, and even if she did try to deny it no one here would believe her. To say anything more would only succeed in making her look foolish. But she'd get him for that remark. Later, at dinner. She smiled wickedly. He had some new things to show her—well, she'd picked up a few tricks since Beldan too. And if they didn't kill each other with them, it might prove to be an enjoyable evening.

"Oy, Shedwyn!" Jobber burst into the storage cribs, knocking a stack of pots off the counter and just as nimbly catching them before they fell.

"What it is, Jobber?" Shedwyn said, annoyed at being interrupted. She was standing at the entrance to the storeroom counting sacks of grain. Her skirts were pinned up to her waist to keep them clean while she worked. The ragged petticoat beneath did little to hide her broken clogs and bare calves.

"Hear about the strange new vagger?" Jobber's green eyes sparkled. She reached for a dried apple hanging on a string near the counter. Shedwyn smacked her hand away and went on counting.

"They're all strange," she replied, one finger ticking off the sacks. "Five, six, with another four . . ."

"Shedwyn!" Jobber said more loudly and tugged the woman's braids.

"Or was it six? Now look what you've done. I've lost count."

"Oy, farmergirl."

"Don't start that."

"Start what?"

"When you start calling me farmergirl I know I'm about to get a snootful of Beldan brass."

"Well, it's true. Don't you farmers ever think about anything besides the weather and sacks of grain?"

"What else keeps us alive?" Shedwyn retorted. She placed her hands on her wide hips, yellow millet flour streaking her bodice.

"All right, all right," Jobber conceded. "But look here, a vagger came today at the gate, asking for Faul."

Shedwyn's eyebrow lifted. "So what's strange about this vagger, aside from the fact that Faul knows him?" A black cat wound itself around Shedwyn's legs, mewing for a tidbit.

"He's got no face tattoos. He's old, short, and heavyset. But"—Jobber held her fists up in a guard position—"he moves like a fighter." She punched the air. "Carries a vagger staff, only wears it across his back."

"What's he want?"

"A meal."

Shedwyn opened her hands to the air. "Don't we all?"

"Faul sent me down here to ask whether you thought there might be some extra to spare. A bit of meat perhaps . . . ?"

Shedwyn shook her head. "Too tight. Meat's just too scarce. I'd be taking it from the little ones. Besides, if word got out they'd all be in here shouting that I'd let them starve while others ate well. No, he'll have to take his share like the rest."

"Yeah, you're right," Jobber said with disappointment. She stared at the cat weaving a pattern at Shedwyn's ankles. Jobber carried a scar on her ankle from the last time one of the creatures came too close to her. "What about—"

"Don't even think it," Shedwyn said, correctly guessing Jobber's thought. "Without this scrawny cat here the rats and mice would have eaten more than half our stores."

Jobber sighed. "Fair enough. A bowl of Sadar's best, then. There's always that."

"Aye." Shedwyn smiled, brushing strands of brown hair from her weary face. She ladled three bowls of the steaming soup called "Sadar porridge," a broth barely seasoned with the scent of meat and dappled with small pearls of barley. A wizened root floated on the surface. "Go on, then," Shedwyn said to Jobber, who'd taken out a wooden tray and set the three bowls down on it. "Cut some bread if you like."

Jobber grabbed for a wheel of bread and taking up the knife hacked at the bread on the counter.

"Not like that!" Shedwyn said irritably, stopping her. She picked up the bread and took the knife from Jobber. Holding the wheel firmly against her chest, she sawed thick slices, cutting inward toward her heart.

"Why does it matter how you cut the bread?" Jobber asked.

"This is bread, not wood," Shedwyn answered patiently, as if talking to a child. "It's a sign of respect. To cut toward the heart. It's like giving honor to the land for the bread we eat."

"Does the land really care?" Jobber asked harshly. Sadar's Keep was overcrowded with laborers and farmers, all of whom had worked hard on the land, slaving each day and starving every year as the land slowly died from the drought.

"You're asking me?" Shedwyn asked in a somber voice. "I am the land, Jobber," she said. "It's my element, just as you are fire. And I care a good deal about the suffering of my people."

"Yeah, sure," Jobber murmured, embarrassed. She started to take the tray of soup bowls and bread.

"Wait," Shedwyn called. "Will you light the ovens?"

"I ain't a flint," Jobber answered, annoyed.

"But you can save us wood," Shedwyn ventured. "I'll add a bottle of brandy for your meal."

Jobber's pale cheeks pinked. "Fair deal," she said and set the tray down. Shedwyn moved toward the door, but Jobber waited by the counter.

"Well, aren't you coming?" Shedwyn asked.

"Let's see it first," Jobber answered.

"Aw, come on, Jobber," Shedwyn protested.

"Nah. I learned that from you farmers. Hold the goods. That's the better half of the deal."

"Silly raver . . .," Shedwyn muttered and ducked into the darkened storeroom. She reappeared with a bottle of Oran brandy, condensation glistening on its black sides. "Here then," she said, indignantly holding it up.

Jobber reached for it, but Shedwyn pulled it back.

"Fire first," Shedwyn demanded.

Jobber smiled broadly, imagining the sweet burning taste of brandy. Z'blood, how long had it been since she'd really had a decent draught of anything? The wretched millet beer that the Oran farmers brewed bloated her stomach and made her stink like old trousers.

Jobber followed Shedwyn into the kitchens, crowded with women making bread and cooking the day's meal. A baby dangled in a makeshift swing near the archway, his toes kicking up dust on the floor. He wore a little red cap of wool and was sucking on one of the strings, waving his fists delightedly in the air. Across the room, his mother pounded, pinched, and rolled the lumpy dough into loaves, setting them aside with the mountain of other loaves waiting on the counter. Two children sat beneath the long table playing a game of catch and toss. The boy lost and pulled the girl's braids. She gave him a savage kick with her clog that sent him scurrying out from under the table. An old black dog wandered in and started barking, which set the baby to bawling. A woman in a red skirt shooed the dog away and gave the child a bit of bread dough to quiet him.

Jobber liked this room. The air smelled of yeast, wet wool, and the musky scent of women. It struck an odd contrast to the starkness of the training room, with its bare walls and Faul's thin figure barking orders. The kitchens were alive, bubbling as the women argued and gossiped, scolded or praised the children that were always underfoot. In one corner an elderly woman broke out in harsh laughter and Jobber caught sight of old Veda, her two remaining teeth like daggers in her empty mouth. Telling tales on the men again, Jobber guessed. In another corner a woman nursed her new baby, the child's head tiny compared to the swollen bulge of her breast. She was singing, her voice light, but the song was sad.

"Hie up," yelled Calid to the other women clustered in the courtyard near the kitchens. "Jobber's come to light the fires."

Shouts of praise and welcoming claps on her back made Jobber smile shyly.

"All right, all right. Give me a shawl, will you? I hate that frigging snow," she said roughly.

Someone passed her a black shawl and Jobber threw it over her head. The shawl reeked of wood smoke and the grassy scent of henna. She crossed the courtyard, heading for the great beehived ovens. Once lit they would burn for the day, slowly heating the bread and baking the hundred-odd loaves eaten by the Keep's inhabitants.

Jobber peered into the ovens and saw the stacked wood waiting. Around her, standing in the snow, the women gathered in a quiet half circle. Their heads and shoulders were covered with black shawls that draped over skirts of red, blue, and brown wool. Some had no shoes; others wore cracked wooden clogs. They were silent, and on their faces Jobber saw the fearful awe. Many of them had been at the Uprising of Sadar. They had seen Jobber transformed into a destructive column of flame.

Still afraid of me, Jobber thought, sensing the tension in the air. This is why I hate doing this, she thought sullenly.

Then Shedwyn, wrapped in her own shawl, appeared. She moved easily among the women, smiling and chatting as she set them at their ease. They laughed, nervously at first, and then more naturally in Shedwyn's reassuring presence. She's one of them, Jobber thought, knowing that many of them believed it was Shedwyn who had quenched Jobber's uncontrollable fire at the battle of Sadar.

Jobber bent to the task, reaching for the fire element within her. She closed her eyes, sighing as the surface of her skin flushed with heat. She sensed the flickering of flames beneath her brittle skin . . . and heard the steady beat of her pulse, like a forge's bellow fanning the fire in her heart. The rose of fire opened and molten flames flowed outward on the petaled tips. A heart of fire, its center white and blue, its edges bursting like a ripe orange with petals of red flames. When balanced under her control, it was radiant and beneficent. But out of balance, it was destructive. Balance the heart, she thought, remembering Faul's warning. Learn to balance it on the edge of a sword.

Jobber gasped as the fire leaped from her fingers to the wood. White-hot sparks erupted, sucking in the air from the draft holes at the base of the oven. Gray smoke curled up from the chimney and the air was peppered with the sharp scent of burning pine.

A small cheer rose from the women who crowded around, patting the tops of the ovens affectionately and giving thanks to Jobber.

Jobber swayed, closing her eyes to the sudden sense of loss as the fire-rose closed in her heart.

Shedwyn was there with the tray and the bottle. "Dine well."

"At least I'll drink well."

"Come down later and tell me about it. Old Veda has promised her pipe if you'll share the news."

Jobber grimaced at the thought of the old woman's tobacco. It was coarse, and worse, it stank like manured straw. "I'll come, but not for a smoke."

"I'll see if I can find anything more suitable," Shedwyn said knowingly. "Eneas has some put by."

"Sure he won't mind?" Jobber asked, thinking it was bold of Shedwyn to offer Eneas's tobacco to her. Though he had joined the New Moon and shed a good many of his Silean attitudes at the Uprising of Sadar, when it came to tobacco his refined palate remained Silean.

Shedwyn laughed at the skeptical expression on Jobber's face. "He'll not deny me," she said.

"Done, then," Jobber answered, setting the brandy bottle on the food tray.

"Jobber, wait," Shedwyn called as Jobber reached the door.

Jobber turned impatiently. Shedwyn's face looked pale, dark circles beneath her eyes. "Well, what is it?" Jobber asked, suddenly concerned.

Shedwyn hesitated and then abruptly waved Jobber on with one hand. "Nah, go on," she said. "Another time."

"I'll be back later," Jobber called over her shoulder as she opened the door and left the kitchen.

The tray wobbled as Jobber passed a window in the tower staircase, and her eyes strayed to the pale moon rising in the late-afternoon sky. Snow clouds had rolled away and the wedged moon hung like an icicle. She stared at the plain, stretched out below the Keep like a flat sea of gravel. Though it was beautiful in its stark fashion, it couldn't compete with the city of Beldan. If only she could see the smoke rising from Crier's Forge, sending its black plumes skyward to mingle with the blue smoke of the tanneries and the gray-green smoke of the hearth fires. She longed for the smell of the city, salty with the sea and sweet with the breweries. She wanted to hear the street noises: the lightermen crying the hour, the barrowboys shouting, and the teaman ringing his bells as he chugged through the streets with his brass tea urn strapped to his back. Jobber winced with the pain of her homesickness.

"Frigging shit," she swore, "here I am gogging at the moon."

Jobber continued on her way up the stairs. She knocked at Faul's door, the only private chamber in the whole of the Keep. Faul had insisted on privacy, saying that she was willing to forgo other privileges if she could but have this one. Jobber envied her hidey-hole in the otherwise crowded fortress. Whole families gathered in the common rooms and on the ground floors of the Keep. At night even the animals were brought in to keep them safe from the mountain storms.

"Come in," Faul's voice answered.

Balancing the tray with one hand, grumbling, Jobber pushed the door open with the other.

Shefek and Faul sat opposite each other at a small table. Their faces glowed with expectation, their posture poised like a pair of sparring cats. The room crackled with tension. Jobber frowned, confused at finding herself completely ignored.

She set the bowls down and only then did Faul see the third bowl that Jobber had brought for herself.

"I didn't invite you," Faul said.

"Let her stay," Shefek countered.

"Why?"

"It might be interesting."

"Dangerous?" Faul asked raising one eyebrow.

"Perhaps." Shefek shrugged.

"Over there, then," Faul said, pointing to a chair close to the wall. "Keep still and watch," she warned.

Jobber took her bowl and bread in one hand and, since no one seemed to notice it, the bottle of brandy in the other over to the chair Faul indicated. She sat down slowly, staring at them. Faul was more elaborately dressed than usual. She wore a quilted tunic that hid most of her shape and the white sleeves of her shirt were loosely tied at the wrist. Her red wool trousers had been tucked into her boots, the folds carefully arranged around the edge of the boot. But it was Faul's hair that puzzled Jobber. Except in battle, she always wore it loose at chin's length. But now it was held back from her face by an ornate Silean hairpin.

Shefek on the other hand seemed scarcely changed from when Jobber had first seen him. His face was a ruddy color in the firelight, his hawk nose more prominent than ever. He wore his hair back in a single braid that lay draped on the front of his shoulder. The tassel end of the braid was decorated with an ornament in the shape of a silver leaf. He'd combed out his beard, and it framed his face like an owl's ruff. Something in his eyes gave Jobber pause. They glowed, first an eerie green, and then, as he turned to smile at her, the color shifted into gold.

Jobber put the bottle of brandy between her feet and took a spoonful of soup. She stopped midway to her mouth as a dart spun from Faul's hand toward Shefek's head. She had only flexed her fingers as if to pick up her spoon and the shining steel-tipped dart had snapped from her sleeve. Shefek jerked his head to one side, his smile intact, his eyes glowing brighter. He shifted the other way as a second dart whirled through the air. Both passed his ears and clunked against the stone walls.

"Inn darts?" Shefek asked amused.

"Altered, of course."

"Of course." He reached for his spoon and Jobber saw Faul tense. So did Shefek. He picked up his spoon and waved it harmlessly in the air. He lowered it to the bowl, stirring the already cooled soup. Then his other hand snapped open. Jobber cried a strangled warning as a stout-handled knife with a short, curved blade sailed through the air.

Faul knocked it away with a wedge of bread. "An oyster knife?"

"Altered, of course," Shefek smirked.

A glint of amusement shone in Faul's eyes. Z'blood, Jobber breathed, they were enjoying this! She put down her soup bowl and took up the brandy bottle instead. She uncorked it as silently as possible, fearing to draw attention to herself. She took a deep swallow, bringing the bottle down in time to see Faul smooth back her hair and reach for the Silean hairpin. Shefek almost didn't see it, his gaze lowered as he snatched a spoonful of soup. The ornament spun through the air, its tines sharpened. He must have heard it, for he ducked his head and it passed over him. As he came up, the silver leaf from his braid whipped back at Faul. She gave a sharp laugh and twisted to the side. The leaf embedded itself in the headrest of her chair, trapped by two of its jagged points.

"Lovely," she murmured, carefully removing the leaf from the chair.

Shefek reached under his leather vest for something and in her corner, Jobber crouched. He withdrew a full fist and slammed the contents onto the tabletop.

"Oran stars," he said as the handful of small projectiles scattered across the table. They were round steel balls studded with spikes.

"Moons!" shouted Faul as she reached into her own pocket and laid down two silvery crescents, their inner edge sharpened like miniature scythes.

"Throat biters!"

"Gougers!"

"Widow makers!"

"Castraters!"

Jobber gaped as Faul and Shefek reached into hidden pockets and pulled out one throwing weapon after another, all of them small and deadly. The bowls of soup disappeared amid the clutter of steel objects.

Then, satisfied, they leaned back in their chairs as if to take stock. Jobber took another hasty gulp of brandy.

"Enough with the small toys," Faul said in a husky voice.

Shefek's eyes narrowed and his smile stretched. He ran a hand through his beard, as if considering his next move.

Jobber stared so hard at them, paused in the gathering tension, that she nearly missed seeing it. Moving in unison like the wheels of a cart, Shefek and Faul dove from their chairs and reached for their weapons, hidden in the folds of their clothing.

Faul pulled a short sword from her trouser leg where it tucked into her boot. She lunged, slashing Shefek's ample midriff.

Nimbly he jumped back, snatching a short sword from his sleeve. The two swords clashed and then sheered away from each other. The combatants circled each other, the short swords tossed from hand to hand as they played for an opening in each other's defenses. Jobber pressed her back into the wall, the bottle of brandy held snug against her chest. Whore's shit, she swore silently as the pair darted back and forth, the blades flicking dangerously. Shit, shit, shit. She had to get out of here!

Jobber edged along the wall, the rough stones scratching her back through the thin fabric of her shirt.

"Not so fast, Jobber," Faul said as she delivered a thrust. "It's not over."

"Yeah, well, I am done," Jobber insisted.

"But it's just getting interesting," Shefek replied, grunting as he narrowly missed one of Faul's overhand cuts. As her sword arm came down, he stepped in, one arm blocking the sword arm in its downward stroke. He slashed upward toward Faul's exposed head.

Jobber flung herself into the fray, intending to stop him. Instead she was knocked back by Shefek's toppling body as Faul provided her own defense. She had followed the flow of Shefek's block, bending her body low to avoid the attack to her head as she used her other arm to sweep him off his feet. He fell backward, and Jobber behind him just missed getting stabbed by his sword as it was knocked from his grasp.

"I told you to stay out of the way!" Faul shouted at Jobber.

"I'm frigging trying!" Jobber yelled as she scuttled to the side of the room, looking for a safe spot to hide until their madness was over.

On the floor Shefek reached for his staff and held it up as a defense. Faul sneered and grabbed its end, intending to twist it out of his grasp. It broke apart, and half of the wooden staff came away in her hand, revealing a long, straight blade jutting out of the wooden handle.

Faul gave a delighted laugh and leapt backward as Shefek got to his feet again.

"Clever," she said, breathing heavily.

"Yes, isn't it?" Shefek answered proudly, snapping the blade in the air. He lunged for Faul, but she tipped a chair in his path. It detained him long enough for her to snatch her own long sword, lying near her chair, and pull it free from its scabbard.

With the table between them, Faul and Shefek faced off, just as Jobber had seen them when she had first entered the room. But now their intent was clear. They were braced like their unsheathed swords. The fire in the grate hissed at a wild gust of wind. Jobber stared from one to the other, their breathing calmed so as not to betray any hint of motion. Their faces glistened with sweat and Jobber saw on Faul's a look of youthful rapture. Opposite her, Shefek smiled, the edges of his mouth stretched wide, his eyes glowing with their unnatural sheen.

They both sidestepped the table, feet treading carefully, step over step. Faul clutched her sword in a two-handed grasp, the blade's tip facing Shefek's throat as he held his staff-sword upright, the blade's edge turned in.

Jobber held her breath.

Faul's sword slashed in a skyward stroke. Shefek's staff blocked it neatly and twisted downward. A scream caught in Jobber's throat. Faul danced back as Shefek's sword missed cutting her knees. When the staff finished its downward journey, Faul shifted in again, swinging her sword in a wide arc. Shefek blocked it with the wooden end of his staff. The wood cracked smartly as each of Faul's strokes landed on its barrel. As their bodies closed in, their weapons were crossed until they were face to face between the quivering swords.

Jobber swallowed hard, air hissing softly from between her clenched teeth. The closer to death, the more the pair vibrated with life. In this strange duel, each demanded total commitment from the other. There was integrity in every attack. Accepting death together, the swift cuts and deadly strokes became as intimate and meaningful as a lover's embrace.

Jobber watched them struggle, pressing closer together, merging into one terrible four-armed monster. Faul's downturned face showed the strain, but she refused to surrender to Shefek. On Shefek's upturned face the smile froze as all of his energy centered on pressing for an advantage.

And then, exhaling noisily, Shefek and Faul withdrew, conceding by mutual consent. Silent except for their labored breathing, they stowed their weapons. Jobber's cheeks ballooned with a breath of relief and she slumped against the wall. Exhausted, Shefek and Faul draped themselves once more in their chairs.

"Oy, Jobber," Faul said at last. "Give me the brandy."

As she stood, Jobber realized her knees were shaking. She handed the bottle to Faul, being careful not to pass too close to Shefek. Jobber believed Faul to be the best sword fighter she'd ever known. But Zorah's tits, who was Shefek? She stole a wary glance at him. Now that the fight was over, he resembled nothing more than a tired, portly man with gray hair and a red nose that suggested overindulgence. Even his eyes, which had glowed so unnaturally, were dim, their color barely discernible beneath the drooping lids.

"Well?" he asked her and Jobber jumped, spooked.

"Well what?"

"Was it interesting?"

"Oh yeah, if you like getting killed."

"Isn't that what it's about?" Shefek asked, leaning forward in his chair to peer at her. His eyes glowed softly like tarnished brass. "The path of the sword is through death," he said. "What does that mean to you?"

Jobber shrugged. "To be good with the sword you have to be ready to die."

"More than ready. Each time you pick up the sword, it must be as if you have already crossed over. The heart must be still. Only then can you move freely with strength."

"If you think you're already dead, then what's the point of fighting?" Jobber asked tartly. Vagger talk, that's all this was. And the more of it she heard, the less she understood.

Shefek smiled. "To surrender to the moment is to give it life."

Jobber wanted to understand. She could see Faul nodding, agreeing with the words whose meaning remained opaque to

Jobber. But it was no good. It just didn't mean anything to her. She knew what street fighting was; she had the knuckles and calluses to prove it. Growler had taught her the basics long ago and she'd picked up the rest from experience. Hit first, hit hard, and don't quit. It was just that simple. But this . . .

"Bah," scoffed Shefek. "Words are a poor substitute for the real work." Then, looking at Faul he added: "Tomorrow, we'll begin."

"Begin what?" Jobber asked suspiciously.

"You're in luck, Jobber. Shefek and I will train you together," Faul answered.

"Z'blood!" Jobber groaned. It was wretched enough with Faul, but now Shefek and all his incomprehensible words . . .

"A toast," Shefek called, splashing a few drops of the brandy into two cups. He passed one to Jobber and the other to Faul. Shefek lifted the nearly full bottle. "To a new Fire Queen. May she burn pure in heart." Shefek put his lips to the bottle and tipped it back. Jobber's mouth gaped open as Shefek drank without pause, without breath. He continued lifting the bottle higher as the amber liquid drained into his throat. When the last drops were emptied into Shefek's mouth, he set the bottle down again and his eyes glowed like gold coins.

"You can go now, Jobber," Faul said, staring across the table at Shefek.

"But—"

"Go," Faul repeated more sharply.

Jobber left the room, the wooden door shutting noisily behind her. Alone in the corridor Jobber stood, perplexed and confused. What was Shefek? If only Lirrel were here to tell her what was going on behind the mask that Shefek seemed to wear. Why, when she needed her, was Lirrel off chasing a girl who might not even exist? Angrily, Jobber headed down the stairs to the kitchens, frustration igniting in small sparks around her hair.

Chapter Six

A young woman sat on the rocky bluffs staring at the dark green sea. She sighed, wrapping her hands deeper into the folds of her black shawl. She could taste the snow gathering in the scudding clouds. Tayleb looked down the deserted strip of sandy beach, hemmed on either side by the steeply rising bluffs. Hope faded in her stubborn heart. There was no sign of the Namires; she must accept that they were gone for the winter months. She must wait until spring again.

Tayleb missed them terribly, the loneliness of the cold, empty beach overwhelming her. The Namires were her friends. And yet she had told no one about them. Not even her parents. The Namires were not supposed to exist. They had been hunted long ago, when the Silean warships came to the Burning. At least that's what they said in the village, when the old men sat around and swapped tales. Cautionary tales they were, of how the Namire women, with their beautiful long green hair and their gilled necks, seduced mortal fisherfolk to their deaths in the sea; of how the Namires brought every disaster imaginable to the Islanders, from the sudden squalls that washed men overboard to the torn nets that meant the loss of a day's catch.

None of it was true, Tayleb thought angrily. They didn't even have green hair. She stood, her bare feet gripping the slippery rocks for balance. Crabs scuttled past her in search of tide pools. Purple-black kelp clung to the lower rocks, waving back and forth with the incoming tide. The Namires weren't sea demons at all. And no one on the island but Tayleb knew that.

She had been diving for clams when she first met them a year ago. She had thought them seals swimming underwater. . . .

The water was cloudy with swirling sand. They reached out, pulling playfully at her hair and tugging at her loincloth. She broke free and darted to the surface. One head, then another, and then three more popped up, staring at her with round, wide-set eyes. One gave her a dimpled smile and laughed. Not seals, Tayleb realized, and panicked at the sight of their smiling faces. She dove again, hoping to outswim them to the rocks. With hurried strokes, she swam against the ocean current. But they followed close behind, and when she scrambled over the rocks they climbed out after her.

"Stop, don't run away. Please don't be frightened."

How strange the Namires looked out of water, standing awkwardly on the rocks, unused to solid ground. They were completely naked and all of them female. Their shoulders and arms were muscled like a man's, but they had small hard breasts and narrow hips.

"Who are you?" Tayleb had asked. "Why did you grab me in the water?"

"We are Namires and we thought you were one of us."

"The Namires don't exist," she announced.

They laughed, slapping their lean thighs. One pointed to her with an impish grin. "We know what we are, but what strange fish are you? You're scaled like the Namires, but you've no neck gills!"

Tayleb glanced down at her arms. Naked, her skin shimmered like the scales of a mackerel across her chest, shoulders, and down her arms. The skin wasn't rough but supple, the soft colors rippling like a fish's underbelly.

Her mam had told her it was a birthmark. She had dreamed of the sea the night Tayleb was conceived, and every night thereafter until her birth. Her da teased her. "Lucky it weren't a sea bass she dreamed of or you'd be walking about with whiskers hanging off yer chin and a great gaping mouth!"

"Are you really Namires?" she had asked them, more curious than afraid.

"Swim with us and see for yourself," they challenged and dove back into the sea. Tayleb hesitated, and then growing bolder, joined them in the sea. . . .

They had met every day that spring and summer to swim in the ocean. Tayleb had lost her fear of them and instead grew to love them like sisters: Kire, with her long black hair and pale blue eyes was the oldest and shoal leader. She claimed responsibility for the safety of the rest and drew Tayleb under her protection. Tammi was a trickster, her green eyes twinkling with mischief as she played pranks that set them flinging seaweed at her head. Mari was serious, worrying about the Islanders' boats coming too near their swimming grounds, while the adventurous Kana was always threatening to swim closer to the boats to give the Islanders a scare. And last was Ril, the youngest and although shy, Tayleb's closest friend in the shoal. She had close-cropped hair the color of brown kelp and small, delicate features. She made strings of collected shells that she wore around her neck. With Ril, Tayleb had exchanged friendship rings carved out of mother-of-pearl in the shape of two fish meeting.

That summer and this, Tayleb's skin had been crusted with dried salt from her daily swims with the Namires. Tayleb had drifted as far out into the sea as she dared, though they begged her to follow farther yet. There were times when she'd grown frightened, lured out into the deep water by the laughter of the Namires only to see the shore a thin blue line in the distance. But no matter how far Tayleb had strayed, Kire always brought her safely to shore again.

Tayleb picked her way down the steep bluff, stopping every now and then to search the tide pools. Little silver fish darted back and forth as she wriggled her fingers in the ice-cold water. A crab held up a warning claw. She splashed a little water on him and he retreated sideways, bearing himself proudly despite the indignity.

On the sand she walked slowly toward home, not wanting to go there. She scratched a design in the sand with her big toe, and then rubbed it out again. The hardest part was keeping quiet, telling no one about the Namires. She would have liked to have at least confided in her mother. But fear prevented her. Already the villagers gossiped that she was past the age for Naming and when were her parents going to take her to a Reader? She had heard her mam beg off—Tayleb was her only child—heard her father make excuses that she was still too young, not yet ready for Naming and the marriage that would follow. But Tayleb guessed the true reason they waited. Though it was never said, they feared she had the old power. The Readers would see the aura and she would be destroyed as the Namires had once been hunted. Alone on the beach, Tayleb tried to quell her fear.

If she had the old power, it was quiet, like an unseen current beneath the surface of the waves. She tried to find it, to separate it from the rest of her senses. But it wasn't a thing distinct from the other workings of her body. It drifted as she drifted. Tayleb let her shawl slip to her shoulders, freeing her hair to the blustering winds. If she told her parents about the Namires, then what was silent would have to be spoken. What was ignored would have to be faced.

Tayleb looked out at the rolling waves, a white mantle of foam layering the surf. Her hands clutched the billowing ends of her shawl. She was afraid of the Readers. There was nowhere on the island to hide. Tynor's Rock was a small place in the ocean. Soon after Tayleb had met the Namires, she knew that before she'd face the Readers she would flee Tynor's Rock and seek refuge in the smaller uninhabited islands farther out in the ocean. The Namires would find her and, except for the winter, she would not be alone.

Tayleb skipped a flat stone across the water. A life of solitude. Not much of a future. Tayleb retied her shawl over her head, giving the lowering clouds a frown. Even the noisy gulls were hiding from the approaching storm. The rain was imminent. You're as gloomy as the day, she chided herself. Go home and sit by the fire. She started walking, and her heels dug little cones into the wet sand.

"Lirrel, are you sure?" Alwir asked, his face showing the strain of rowing. Salt coated his sparse beard and he squinted his eyes against the spray. His hands gripped the oars tightly as he fought against the rough waves.

"Of course I'm sure," Lirrel answered irritably. The wind flapped the wide sleeves of her black dress so that she resembled a young crow taking flight.

"You said that about the last island."

"And she wasn't too far off, was she?" Dagar said, defending Lirrel. He sat next to Lirrel and wiped his wet face with the corner of a neck scarf.

"We're looking for a girl, not a boy, remember?" Alwir muttered and jerked the oars harder through the rough sea.

"But he had power," Lirrel reminded Alwir. "And you were able to convince him to join the New Moon before the Readers discovered it. Wasn't it worth it after all?" Lirrel held down her blowing hair, trying to see Alwir's face. He was looking more gaunt than usual, his lips turning purple with the cold. Well, she thought worriedly, they were all looking worn. Even Dagar had lost his usual good nature, fatigue and cold making his teeth chatter. They could do with a rest. But not until they found her. Lirrel was certain the girl was here. She had sensed her presence growing stronger with each stroke Alwir took in the driving current.

"But if you are wrong," Alwir was saying between gritted teeth, "we will be stuck on this frigging island. They warned us on Handfast that this storm would be bad. We stand out enough on the Islands as it is. I don't like these people getting too many ideas about what to do with us."

"I know, Alwir," Lirrel said softly. A wave rocked the boat and she clutched its sides. "I know. But I feel as if I can almost reach out . . ."

Rain pattered on the water, lightly at first and then more heavily. Cold water landed on their faces, and the waves rose around them, splashing over the sides of their longboat.

"Z'blood," Alwir yelled at the rain. "Where is the island?"

Lirrel stared through the curtain of sleet, desperately searching for a sight of the shore. The wind gusted, driving the sleet away from her face. And then she saw it, a ragged black line of bluffs rising above a curved beach.

"Land, Alwir," she cried. "Straight ahead."

Alwir swore, bending his back deeper to the demanding oars.

In the rasp of waves Lirrel heard a fragment of music. She leaned forward in the boat, using not her eyes but her senses, the currents of air guiding her. The music grew stronger, the gentle lilt sad and lonely. She could almost see her . . . A woman, the damp sand clinging to her heels. Lirrel blinked through the rain. A vision. No, she realized with excitement.

"There! Dagar, look, it's her! The girl of my vision." She stood up excitedly in the boat. "Oy!" Lirrel called, her arms waving frantically over her head. "Oy! Over here!"

"Lirrel, get down!" Alwir ordered as the boat, already buffeted by the waves, began rocking dangerously. "Z'blood, get down or you'll capsize us," he yelled, trying to balance the boat with his oars.

"It's her I tell you!" Lirrel cried, ignoring his order and continuing to wave her arms high over her head. Please, she prayed, look over here!

The figure on the beach turned and stared in their direction. Driving lines of rain crossed the bow of the little boat, obscuring the sight of the figure. But Lirrel could hear her and the song in her head played an increasingly complicated melody. The lilt dissolved suddenly, crashing like the breakers against the headlands.

The crash of breakers . . . Lirrel stopped waving and twisted around to see a huge swell rising high above the boat, a white crest frothing over the edge.

"Get down!" Alwir shouted, rowing harder to pull the boat away from the tumbling wall of water.

The wave sucked the longboat straight up toward the foaming crest. Lirrel screamed and was pitched backward into Alwir's lap. He swore as he lost his grip on an oar. As he scrabbled to regain his hold on the second oar, the wave smashed across the stern and tipped the boat over.

Lirrel was cast into the icy cold water, gasping from the shock. She floundered helplessly in the waves, her face rising once to the surface amidst a seething boil of white foam. She drew a frantic breath before she was swept under again, her long garments weighing her down.

On the shore Tayleb had been rushing home through the rain. This was the price of dallying too long on the beach. Then she stopped. A voice had called out to her. She glanced hopefully at the water. The Namires! They had come back one more time!

But through the swirling sleet she saw only a longboat and someone standing, waving. Landsiders, she thought seeing the fool standing in the middle of the boat. Did they want to get themselves drowned? But the fool called out to her, waving its arms.

From the beach she saw the huge wave rising behind the longboat and knew before it crashed that the Landsiders were lost. She ripped off her shawl and then her blouse. As she stepped out of her heavy wool skirt she saw the boat, its upside-down hull floating like a forlorn beetle. She waded into the water clad in only her shift.

"Damn the rain!" she shouted. "Can't you stop, you miserable clouds!" Her gaze skirted the water for signs of them. If they were Landsiders, chances were good they couldn't swim. She spotted black garments floating like kelp and she swam toward them. She caught a Landsider under the chin, and with great effort lifted a head out of the water. She was surprised to find it was a woman.

"Can you loosen your skirts?" she said, kicking her legs to keep them both afloat. Under the hand that held the woman's chin above the water, she felt her shake her head no. "To the boat then!" Tayleb answered and kicked out her legs, guiding them through the water to the upturned boat. She drew the Landsider alongside the boat and waited until she had taken ahold of the side.

"Can you hold on?"

The woman nodded, coughing up water and shivering violently.

"You're near enough to the shore. Just hang on and the boat will take you in."

"My friends . . . ," the woman said weakly.

"I'll find them," Tayleb answered. She turned back to the ocean and realized that the rain had abated, giving her a clearer view of the sea. She saw a head pop up, look around, and then dive under the water. Well, at least one of them can swim, she thought, relieved.

She swam out and met him as he came up, shaking the water from his face like a dog. He was startled to see her.

"Over there!" Tayleb pointed. "Get to the boat."

Relief and gratitude flashed over the boy's wet face before he dipped momentarily under a rising swell.

"There's another man," he said as he came up again.

"Go help the woman. I'll find the other," Tayleb answered.

Then Tayleb dove deeply beneath the water, pulling herself in the current with long swift strokes. The water was murky and the light dim. Once she thought she had him, but when she reached out it was only an oar floating on the surface of the water. She came up for air again, bobbing on the water, turning slowly in the rolling waves.

And then she spotted him, not far off. She didn't see all of him, just his arm thrown over the second oar, the rest of his body submerged beneath the surface of the water. She was tired and the cold had crept into her joints. Her arms growing numb, she swam weakly toward the drowning man.

She brought his head out of the water and saw the blood flowing from a gash on his forehead. His face was white as a gull's breast and for a frightened moment she wondered if she clutched a dead man. She grasped him firmly under the chin and kicked her legs out. The rest of his body floated grudgingly to the surface and she towed him toward shore. She glanced at his face once more and saw that his eyes were open and that he was blinking, a dazed expression on his face.

"It stopped raining," he said.

"Kick!" Tayleb gasped, and was relieved when his legs wavered back and forth in a lazy action that brought his body closer to the surface and easier to pull into shore.

Tayleb reached down with one toe and cried out as she felt the rippled sand beneath her foot. Another few feet and she'd be able to stand. She looked up to the shore and saw that the longboat had reached the shallow water. The woman, helped by her companion, swayed from side to side, stumbling in the surf like a drunk from a tavern.

"Almost there," Tayleb said and felt the injured man kick a little harder. She put her foot down again, finding the sandy ocean floor. She dragged the Landsider by the scruff of his neck, taking care to keep his face out of the water. When she had reached the shallows the other two roused themselves from the sand and helped her tow him into shore.

"Thank you. Thank you so much for rescuing us," the woman was murmuring as they lifted her companion's wet and sagging body from the water.

"It's naught . . . ," Tayleb answered and then stopped at the sight of the woman's face. Long black hair framed a pointed face, with skin a polished brown. But it was her eyes that claimed Tayleb's attention, for they were a gleaming white, the pupils small dots of gray. Tayleb averted her gaze to the young man holding up the injured man's long, spindly legs. Wet hair was pushed up over a wide forehead, his face intent on his task. His eyes, at least, were dark.

She glanced down at the man they were dragging over the sand. He was tall and thin, his face like a battered scarecrow's. The gash on his forehead left a dotted trail of blood.

"Here now, leave him," Tayleb said and they laid him down on the sand. He groaned and his head rolled to one side. Tayleb bent over him, placing her hands firmly against his chest, and pushed. "He's swallowed a lot of seawater. It'll have to come out." Water dribbled out the corners of his mouth and she pushed again. His head rolled the other way, another moan escaping with the seawater.

She pushed again and he started choking. Tayleb turned him over just as he began vomiting onto the sand. He retched noisily, his legs drawn up close to his chest. When he was done heaving,

Tayleb ripped the hem of her shift and applied the cloth to his head. He flinched at the touch and then relaxed.

Strange folk indeed, Tayleb thought as she pressed evenly on the cloth, trying to stanch the bleeding. What were they doing here, and at this time of the year? She burned with a dozen questions, knowing that she'd not ask a one of them. She was an Islander and she would hold her tongue and wait.

Tayleb studied the injured man as she pressed on the cloth. Pale and drawn, he looked like a ghost with mottled purple lips. He opened his eyes and they glittered like two blue chips off a crab's shell. He stared back at her openly, his eyes following the lines of her face. He started to speak but was stopped by another wave of retching that coiled him into a knot and set him vomiting again on the sand.

"Come on," Tayleb said, reaching for her clothes. Quickly she slipped on her skirt and blouse over her wet shift. "Help him to stand. We need to get him inside. My home is just over there, beyond that bluff. Do you think you can make it that far?" she asked the others.

"Yes," the woman answered and raised the injured man by the shoulders to a sitting position.

She and her companion hauled him upright between them, where he wobbled like a puppet waiting for someone to pull the strings taut.

"Here, keep him warm with this," Tayleb said, handing the woman her black shawl.

She gently wrapped it around his shoulders. Against the black wool his pallor grew more stark.

"That way, then," Tayleb said, pointing to the bluff.

"Lirrel . . . ?" the injured man said in a hoarse voice.

"Easy, Alwir. Go easy. *Ahal*, I'm sorry I made this happen," the woman apologized, near tears.

"You were right," the man said, and then groaned with pain.

Tayleb glanced back at the trio with concern. She was surprised to see the one called Alwir smiling despite his obvious pain, though on his gaunt, blood-streaked face the smile made for a grim spectacle. Well, she reasoned, returning her attention to the rocky path, he'd reason to be happy. After all, he wasn't dead, though stealing another glance at him supported by his two sea-washed friends, it was hard to believe that he was still alive.

Overhead she heard the warning rumble of thunder and knew that if they didn't hurry they'd be drenched again in the cold rain. *Wait*, she pleaded to it. *Just wait until we are at the door.*

The thunder growled in protest, but no rain fell as they stumbled along the path to the cottage. Tayleb nearly cried with relief at the sight of her home, a warm, lighted glow showing in the window. She fell back to the struggling trio, relieving the exhausted woman by taking her part in supporting the injured man. Together they arrived at the cottage.

As Tayleb turned the latch on the cottage door, the thunder boomed once more. She could hear the driving rain sweeping across the bluffs. Quickly she pushed the woman and her companion through the open door and succeeded in dragging the injured man in with her just as the rain lashed the cottage walls.

Chapter Seven

"**M**am," Tayleb called out as soon as she crossed the threshold of the cottage. "There's Landsiders here needing help."

Her mother turned from her loom at the sound of Tayleb's voice. The hearth fire hissed with the cold rain that blustered into the cottage. The woman rose quickly from the loom bench and let drop a black shawl from her shoulders. Her long brown hair was tightly braided into a figure eight at the base of her neck. Her face was soft and rounded. Faint blue lines etched whorled patterns on her cheeks and across the wide forehead. Intelligent green eyes appraised the bedraggled couple dripping water on the flagstone floor. Then her brow creased at the sight of Alwir's slumped form, balanced awkwardly on Tayleb's shoulder.

"Bring him here," she beckoned, drawing back a little curtain to reveal a snug bed built into the wall. "Get them wet things off him," the woman ordered, opening a cupboard.

The young man struggled with Alwir's trousers, trying to pull the wet garment down and off his legs. Tayleb and Lirrel stood discreetly aside.

"Let me give you a hand," said her mother brusquely. "Weren't the first time I undressed a man. Leastways this one isn't a corpse yet. Tayleb, get the kettle going," she called over her shoulder, "and mind you get something warm for yourself and the other girl there to put on as well."

Tayleb set a black kettle on the hook over the hearth.

"Here, these are mine and should fit you," Tayleb said to the Landsider woman as she pulled a red woolen skirt, a plain shirt, and a shift from the cupboard. "You'll want this too," she added, handing her a black shawl. With murmured thanks the shivering woman went into a small bedroom to change.

Tayleb returned to help her mother and the younger man. They were holding Alwir upright as they undid his vest and then slid his wet shirt over his head. On the man's slender chest the ribs raised like whalebone beneath the porcelain skin. His teeth chattered and he groaned as the wet shirt went over his head. "Well, your da's shirt may be too short, but at least it's dry," Tayleb's mother said.

As Tayleb hastily pulled the shirt over the man's exposed limbs, his companion wrestled his dangling arms into the sleeves. Then Tayleb's mother carefully laid him down on the pillows. She began to wrap a dry cloth dressing around his head as Tayleb drew the covers up over his shivering body.

"That's it," her mother murmured, "get him good and warm. Wound isn't so bad. But he'll need rest." The younger man waited at the foot of the bed, bloodstains on his shoulders, his wet clothes clinging to his body. "There's another needing dry clothes," she said to Tayleb and then, seeing her daughter's wet garments added, "and you, too, wet to the bone you are. Go on now and change. I'll show the boy to your father's clothes." She gave him a little push. "Come on, this way now."

Tayleb stole another worried glance at the injured man. In the dim firelight the shadows darkened his gaunt cheeks. He stirred, his eyes fluttering open to stare at her. Though his body shook with the cold, his penetrating gaze was steady. Tayleb blushed, embarrassed by the scrutiny.

"Are you feeling better then?" she asked.

Alwir was silent, his eyes studying her face. And then he

closed them and sighed. She placed her fingertips against his neck, relieved to feel the faint beat of his pulse. "Poor man," she said.

"Tayleb, I'll look after him now," her mother said softly. "See that you get out of them wet things."

Tayleb went quickly into her own room, where the woman with the strange eyes was almost finished dressing by the light of an oil lamp. Tayleb's shirt was too wide for the woman's slim frame. It gaped at the neck and bunched around the waist. She rolled up the sleeves and smiled at Tayleb.

"*Ahal*, it is good to be dry again. I can't thank you enough."

Tayleb stripped off her wet clothes, trying not to stare at those silver eyes. "It was odd, that. I was on my way home, but I could have sworn someone called out my name, so I stopped. It was chance I was there when you went over the side."

"My name is Lirrel," the woman said, pulling on a pair of black stockings.

"Tayleb," she answered shyly.

Lirrel reached into the pocket of her wet dress and pulled out a flute, the dull gray shaft covered with markings. She dried it carefully on the hem of the borrowed skirt. "I am a Ghazali musician."

"I've only heard stories of the Ghazali. We don't see many Landsiders on the Islands," Tayleb said, pulling a dry shift over her head.

"We're not much for water. My people do better on the hard road. It was my fault that our boat capsized," Lirrel explained.

Tayleb reached for a skirt hanging on a hook beside the door. Like Lirrel's it was woven of thick red wool and hemmed with bands of black ribbon. As she reached for her shirt, she saw Lirrel quietly staring at her. The iridescent scales on Tayleb's wet arms glistened in the lamplight like mother-of-pearl. She jerked her shirt on and buttoned the cuffs. I'm no stranger than you with your eyes, she thought angrily as she slipped her feet into woolen socks and then into a pair of dry wooden clogs.

A sharp whistle from the hearth called to her. "Come now," she said to Lirrel, "there'll be something hot to drink."

They stepped into the main room and Lirrel laughed at the sight of her companion. He wore a shirt several sizes too large, tucked into a pair of trousers he had folded and belted around his waist. Black woolen stockings covered his legs, the toes extending beyond his own into wrinkled points. On his head, Tayleb's mother had placed a red fisherman's cap. He smiled agreeably at her, his hands warming around a mug of steaming tea.

"Go on, laugh. But if you'd a glass, you'd see you cut a new figure yourself," he replied.

Tayleb's mother was kneeling at the hearth, prodding the fire with an iron poker. She looked up from the hearth, smiling, until her eyes met Lirrel's. And then the poker slipped from her hand.

The two women stared silently at each other. Then slowly the older woman stood, one hand clapped over her mouth. She closed her eyes, but tears formed beneath the lids and trickled down the sides of her cheeks.

"Mam," Tayleb called. "Mam," she whispered urgently, standing close to her. She tugged at her shawl. "What ails you?"

Her mother drew an arm over Tayleb's shoulders, pulling her close to her side. She sniffed hard, wiping away the tears with the back of her hand.

"So," she said thickly, facing Lirrel at last. "It is time."

"*Ahal.*" Lirrel nodded in agreement.

"It has passed so quickly. I hadn't realized this moment would be so hard."

"Mam, what are you talking about?" Tayleb asked, growing alarmed. Her mother was never bothered to tears, never upset, even when the boats returned late and Tayleb's father was still on the water. Her mother waited patiently at the shore's edge until she saw the light of his lantern as his boat carried him to the bay. Never would she cry so easily as this. And never before strangers.

"What do you want with her?" Tayleb demanded of Lirrel.

"Shush, now," her mother said. "Go get your da. He's down by the pier helping to tie up the boats. Go and fetch him."

Tayleb hesitated, her gaze shifting between her mother and

Lirrel, searching for an explanation. The tears had dried, and her mother's eyes shone brightly in the firelight. Lirrel bowed her head, as if in apology.

"Go fetch your da," Tayleb's mother repeated, and this time her voice was sharp. Tayleb jumped at the order and, grabbing a shawl, fled out the door and into the rain again.

Outside, the wind was blowing hard, the rain striking her from different directions. Tayleb folded the shawl around her face and followed her feet, the clogs sticking in the soft mud of the path. A flash of lightning and the crack of thunder lifted her head in the dark. She saw the black rectangles of the piers and the humpbacked bodies of the men pulling the longboats higher onto the shore.

Tayleb hurried on, the questions pounding harder than the rain that chilled her face.

She knew her father by his rough gravelly voice as he shouted over the racket of the wind to the other men. Tayleb saw that his own boat, the *Turtle*, was already stowed safely up the beach and weighted down. It was like him to stay and help the others lifting their boats out of the rough sea.

He was the last man of five tugging on a rope, hauling in Gaulder's boat, when Tayleb grabbed him by the jacket. The wool was wet and spongy from the rain.

"Da!" Tayleb shouted into his ear. "Da, Mam wants you home now."

"Eh?" Her father angled his head toward her. He was grunting with the effort of pulling the boat ashore.

"Mam wants you home," Tayleb repeated. "She sent me to fetch you."

He looked at her, frowning. "Why?"

"Some Landsiders have come—"

Her father let go of the line and the man in front of him cursed at the sudden impact of the extra weight in his hands.

"Describe them," he demanded, grabbing her by the shoulders.

"Ghazali girl one of them. With white eyes."

Her father took her by the arm and started up the muddy path toward the cottage. Tayleb grew scared as he gripped her tightly, nearly dragging her in his hurry. She slipped once, and cried out in fright as he wrenched her upright again.

At the door of the cottage, Tayleb wrestled herself free from his grasp.

"What's going on?" she demanded. "Who are these people?"

"Won't know 'til I see them," answered her father.

"Da," Tayleb pleaded, "who are you expecting? It's Mam crying in there, and you tearing up the path in fury. Are we in trouble?"

Her father rubbed his face, brushing the water droplets that clung to the wiry beard. His gnarled hand reached out to touch Tayleb's sodden hair. "It's too wet out here for words, lass. We'll go in."

Her father pushed open the door and entered. Tayleb resisted, not wanting to be a part of what awaited them. But she could not remain where she was and so reluctantly, she followed.

On the cottage threshold, she turned to latch the door. With her back to the room, she heard the dreadful silence. Judging by the reaction of her parents, whatever news these Landsiders had brought, it was nothing to rejoice over. Her heart drummed anxiously as she faced the room and let the shawl slip from her shoulders.

It struck her that everything familiar had changed. The room and all the things in it seemed brittle, as if made of colored glass. Even her parents looked different as they stood together by the hearth, her father taking a mug of tea from her mother. Her mother stood like a soldier, her shoulders thrown back, the round point of her chin lifted. The old tattoos on her face rippled across her cheeks. Her father took a small jug and poured a measure of Oran whiskey into his tea. His smile was gone, and his face sagged with fatigue, his eyes clouded. At the table Lirrel sat next to her companion, steam from the mugs of tea bathing their faces. The curtains fluttered as the wind whistled between the cracked panes. In the rafters above, the dried fish waved, the leather ties creaking as they scraped against the beams.

Tayleb didn't like it, the strangeness and the quiet, as if they were afraid to speak. Afraid to speak to her.

"*Aha!*, then I must begin," Lirrel said softly.

"No," said her mother quickly. "It is my task to speak first." She set down her mug of tea and beckoned Tayleb to the table. "Join me here, daughter."

Tayleb went, the cold seeping into her fingers.

"What's going on?" she asked nervously.

"When I was a young woman," her mother started, "I came from good people. I was born Moire Hest. The Hest family had served the Queens' quarter knot for more generations than I could name, and when the time came and I was old enough, I too served as a member of the Queens' Guard. I served the Earth Queen Huld."

"But Mam," Tayleb argued, "there is no Queen Huld."

Moire looked squarely at Tayleb and again Tayleb felt the shiver of strangeness.

"Two hundred years ago, the Fire Queen Zorah betrayed her people. She believed she could destroy the Queens' quarter knot and gain for herself immortality."

"But she did, didn't she?" Tayleb asked, confused. Every child in the village knew the story of the Burning, of the Fire Queen Zorah preventing Oran from slipping into Chaos as she herself embraced immortality.

Moire shook her head. "No. I went with Huld's armies, I fought at Sadar against the ravages of the Fire Queen and the Silean armies. And when it was clear that we would lose, Huld changed herself, and us, to wait for a better time."

"Changed? What do you mean changed *us?*" Tayleb demanded. With every word her mother spoke, Tayleb's hands grew colder, until the chill had crept up the length of her arms and across her chest. She hugged herself, shivering. Lirrel gave her a mug of tea. Tayleb placed her hands along the warm sides of the cup.

"We were changed to trees," Moire replied. "Avadares pines. They age so slowly that our lives would be preserved until such time as Huld could call us out again. The markings on my face are what is left of the tree I was. These lines trace the years when I was rooted in the earth. Queen Huld remained a tree, so as to slow the stream of Oran magic that flows into the Chaos because of Zorah's act.''

"This doesn't make any sense at all," Tayleb said angrily.

"About twenty seasons ago Huld returned some of us to our human form again. Oh, how the world had changed for us." Her mother sighed. "Even in the simple act of walking the world moved so fast." She clenched her fists. "When I think of how I wept within my tree, how I detested both Queens for imprisoning me . . . But in time I accepted the prison and learned to hear the slow heartbeat of the earth and the wordless language of the sky. And when I was released, I wept again—both for the joy of my freedom and the loss of such serenity."

"Why did Huld release you?" Tayleb asked.

"She gave us the last of her strength, and gifted four of us with the ability to produce a child of the old power. To Growler the gift of fire, to Zein the gift of air, to Althen the gift of earth, and to myself the gift of water."

"Your mam came here the year both my parents died of the fever," Tayleb's father put in. "I still remember it. She were a Landsider and there was few on the island that would trust her. Except the Widow Laile."

"And only that because she had nothing left to lose that was precious to her. And she needed my help," Moire said.

"Oh aye, that she did, and it's comfortable her last years with you were." Tayleb's father sat down beside them. He took his pipe from the pocket of his vest and knocked the ashes into the hearth before refilling it. "I was living alone then. And not doing the best job of it. 'Teck the Lost' they called me in the village. I ate when I thought on it and I slept in my clothes. Every day when I come to the pier, I seen your mam there, basket on her arm and her face cold as cod waiting on the day's catch. Well, the widow died in the winter, but it wasn't until the following spring that I seen your mother for true. Still standing straight backed waiting for the catch, but this time," her father said raising the pipe stem toward Moire in emphasis, "I seen the look on her face and knew it to be like my own. Lonely. A kind of numbing pain I myself had been feeling since my parents died. So I courted her, and much to everyone's surprise, excepting my own, she agreed to marry me."

"Before we married, I told Teck the truth about me," Moire said.

"A rare trust," Lirrel said softly.

"But one I knew to be well placed," Moire answered. "I would have a child of the old power, I told him. And one day Queen Huld would call that child to Sadar and she would be ours no longer."

"What makes you think I've the power?" Tayleb asked. "Maybe Queen Huld was wrong."

"I know you have the old power. Each child has to bear the mark of their element for the others to know her by. The fire element was to have the red hair of the Queen, the earth element a tree of life stained into the skin of her belly, the air element with eyes like the moon."

Tayleb stared at Lirrel's pearl-colored eyes.

"*Aha!*, I am an air element, and my father was Zein."

"Tayleb," Moire said softly, "your arm shines with soft scales. You are the fourth element to join the Queens' quarter knot. Haven't you felt the power in you?"

"I don't know," Tayleb said, not trusting herself to any other reply.

"Whether you have or not, you must leave Tynor and go with these people to Sadar," Moire said firmly.

"And then?" Tayleb asked as the panic rose in her chest.

"You are the last element to form the Queens' quarter knot," Lirrel answered. "We need you to help us fight the Fire Queen Zorah and free Oran from her control."

"Me?" Tayleb whispered. She turned to her parents. "I know nothing outside of this island. And now you would have me leave with strangers, go to the mainland, join with people I don't know, and do something I can't even begin to imagine?"

"It was like that for all of us," Lirrel said, hunching over her tea. "None of us was asked, or even prepared for this."

"There must be someone else," Tayleb said stubbornly, leaning back from the table. "There have been other children born with the old power."

"I have traveled a long way to find you," Lirrel said wearily. "Believe me when I tell you, there is no one else like you, no one else who can take your place."

"And there is no place for you on the island," her father said soberly. "The Readers will come and Mam and I will not be able to protect you. They will hang you as they have done those other children with power."

Tayleb's face blazed with anger. "Then I won't stay here. There are the far Islands where I can hide."

"And abandon Oran so easily?" her mother asked. "Can you live so alone?"

Tayleb thought of the Namires.

"No," Lirrel said, putting her mug of tea down hard on the table. "No, the Namires will not find you. As with the rest of Oran, you will be abandoning them too."

"How can you know about the Namires?" Tayleb demanded furiously.

"I can't help it," Lirrel said, raising her voice. "Your thoughts are loud in my head. I am forced to hear even if I don't want to." Lirrel stared at the ceiling trying to regain her composure. When she spoke again, her voice was sad. "I will tell you again; the Namires will not come to you. Because of Zorah they will not survive. As Zorah drains away the magic, she drains the power that keeps them alive."

Tayleb closed her eyes, the tears stinging beneath her eyelids. She folded her arms on the table and cradled her head on her forearms. Angry sobs filled her throat and she choked them back.

"It has been the same for all of us, Tayleb," Lirrel said gently. "All of us have been torn from people we loved."

"I'm scared," Tayleb said.

"We all are," Lirrel answered. "But we need you."

Tayleb lifted her head from her arms. "How soon must we leave?"

"As soon as we can," Lirrel replied.

"You'll go nowhere for at least three days," Teck stated. "The storm is bound to hold for that long at least."

"And your friend there will be in no shape to travel," Moire added, pointing to Alwir.

"We may have to leave him," Lirrel said, raking her teeth over her lower lip. "It's urgent that we return to Sadar as soon as possible."

Tayleb stood and wrapped the shawl around her shoulders. "I need a little time. To prepare," she said, her voice sounding small to her.

Lirrel stifled a yawn. "I understand."

"In the meantime, you must sleep, all of you," Moire said. "I'll watch your friend through the night. In the morning, if the storm continues, there will be time to talk," she said to Tayleb.

"Aye, tomorrow then," Tayleb said. Her limbs trembled with fatigue as she stumbled toward her bed. She crawled beneath the quilts, leaving room on one side of the bed for Lirrel.

Lirrel climbed in beside her and curled into a ball. Though she was exhausted, sleep refused to come to Tayleb. Each time she drifted to its edge, she imagined Kire or Ril dying and her body would jerk awake. She realized that when she left the island she might never see them again. Or her parents. She turned fitfully in her sleep.

"Maybe having time to think is a curse," Lirrel whispered in the dark.

"This is awful. I feel tossed over the side of a cliff. I'm falling, but so slowly that I can count the rocks below," Tayleb moaned.

Lirrel sighed. "You won't hit them."

"But there is the sea, then."

"It's your element, isn't it?"

"So you say."

"So I know. Trust in yourself, Tayleb. I have to," Lirrel answered.

Tayleb was quiet, listening to the wind beat against the shuttered windows. She thought of her mother spending years as a tree, of her father silent with grief. She gave a small choked laugh, thinking of how little she had known them. Or they her. Tayleb screwed herself farther down into the warm quilts and tried to imagine herself like the sea, shifting and changing beneath the wind from bright blue to gray. She would have to find the courage. For the Namires and for herself.

Tayleb closed her eyes and tried again to sleep. Long into the night she listened to the restless wind churning the ocean. And when sleep came at last, it carried her out beyond the Islands to vast, empty sea.

Pale sunlight. Weak rays touched his closed eyelids. Alwir squinted as he opened his eyes. In the gray light he saw the crossbeams of an Islander's cottage above him, from which dangled dried fish and garlands of onions, garlic, and tomatoes. He moved his head cautiously, relieved not to feel pain. He raised his hand to his face, staring at it as if it belonged to a stranger. He touched his head, discovering the light dressing of bandages around his forehead. Exhausted by this simple movement, he replaced his hand on the coverlet and drew a deep sigh.

How long had he lain here? The cottage was quiet, and except for himself, empty. His eyes searched the room for signs of Dagar and Lirrel. There was a wooden trestle table covered by a frayed linen cloth. Benches had been neatly tucked beneath it. To one side, near a window, a loom waited. Beside it shuttles nested in a basket. In the hearth, banked coals glowed, and hanging from a chain a black kettle steamed. In the other corner a stool was surrounded by a pile of nets, a mending shuttle waiting atop.

Alwir closed his eyes as he gathered strength. Then he sat up, his shoulders hunched, expecting pain. There was none, but the room slanted as blood drained from his cheeks.

"Frigging shit." He exhaled and then laughed weakly, recognizing Jobber's favorite oath. Ah, well, he thought, she was back at the Keep, probably learning how to slice the strings off Faul's vest with the Fire Sword. At least he hoped she was, he thought, suddenly irritated. After all, what good was it to be out here nearly getting drowned if all she was doing was sitting with her arse to the fire and swilling brandy? And why was he so angry?

He stared, dazed, at the strange room, aware that he was frightened. He didn't know where he was, or what had happened to the others. He had to get up and find them. Worry urged his legs over the side of the bed. While he waited for the room to stop rocking, his mind jumped ahead with questions. Where was Lirrel? Was she safe? Had they been discovered? He sucked in a gasp as his feet touched the cold flagstones. His heart was thudding wildly and he reached out to the wall to steady himself. He was naked except for a shirt, too large across the chest and too short in the sleeves. He looked down, shocked at the sight of his chalk-white legs.

Trousers. Boots. Jacket. Where were they? In mounting panic, he imagined Lirrel in danger, Dagar fighting to rescue her, both of them being lost. And himself to blame for lying here senseless.

He saw his trousers, folded on a chair near the hearth. Beneath the stool were his boots. He took a tentative step and then launched himself across the room. As he was halfway there, the door opened and sunlight spilled in. He jerked around expecting to fight.

"What are you doing out of bed?" a young woman demanded. "Don't move." She quickly shut the door behind her and set her wicker basket down. A gust of cold wind belled Alwir's shirt, lifting it higher on his thighs.

He shivered and pushed the edges of the billowing shirt down over his naked legs. His gaze darted toward his trousers and then the bed sheets, trying to guess which would be the easier of the two to reach. He opted for the bed and started to shuffle back. But he moved too quickly and the floor began to sway. He swore as he stumbled on the flagstones.

The woman caught him and, wrapping her arm around his waist, she led him back to bed.

"My friends," Alwir croaked in a voice unused to speaking.

"Doing well," she answered.

"Better than me?" he asked.

"Oh, aye. They've gone out to help Da bring in the catch."

The relief of knowing that Dagar and Lirrel were safe was immediately replaced with acute embarrassment. Alwir looked at the woman and realized she was young and pretty. Her arm was tight around his waist and he could see the white swell of her breasts above the line of her red-and-black bodice. She smelled of salt and fish and cold air. The hand supporting his chest was chapped, but the fingers were small and neat, half-moons rising from the cuticles. She glanced up at him, the crystal blue of her eyes shaded.

"Lean on me, then. It won't do to crack your head again."

Alwir laid an arm across her shoulder, balancing his unsteady weight against her. Her body pressed close against his felt warm. She steered him to the bed and helped him sit down. She bent to lift his feet but he stopped her.

It was her turn to blush, aware now of the revealing shortness of his shirt. She busied herself elsewhere in the room, stowing away baskets while Alwir endeavored to pull his legs up into the bed and cover himself.

He coughed lightly as a way of letting her know he was finished. She smiled at him and Alwir saw the faint glow of pink before it faded from her cheeks.

"Are you hungry?" she asked.

No, he thought, but he wanted her company so he said: "Yes."

"Mam left some soup here for you, in case you'd wake up and want it."

She brought the hot soup in a blue crockery bowl. Around its sides painted red fishes swam in lapping waves.

"It's good," he said, taking small spoonfuls. And then he realized he was hungry, that he couldn't remember when he had last eaten.

"Was it you that fished us out of the sea?"

She smiled. "Aye, I saw your boat go over." She drew up a stool to sit beside the bed.

"My name is Alwir."

"I know that. Lirrel has spoken of you. I am Tayleb."

"Have I been ill long?" Alwir asked.

"Oh, aye. I wasn't sure you'd make it, you looked so bad. But Mam, well, she thought differently." Tayleb fumbled in her pocket and pulled out a ball of black thread and a tatting shuttle. She started working it, pulling the thread round and round the bone shuttle, making a string of little knots.

Alwir watched her, pleased by the way the sun highlighted strands of red and gold in her curly hair. She glanced at him and then quickly down to her work again. She plyed the shuttle faster.

"I don't remember much of what happened," Alwir said trying to break the uncomfortable silence.

"You cut your head open on an oar when your boat capsized," Tayleb answered. Her blue eyes shifted to a light green. "You bled a good deal."

Alwir touched his head, remembering the cold water and the crack in his skull. He had a faint memory of the beach, sand in his hair and Lirrel and Dagar dragging him along. Then he remembered something else.

"Do you want more soup?" Tayleb asked, getting up.

"No, thank you," he said, setting the bowl aside.

As Tayleb crossed the room, Alwir followed her with his eyes. She was short, her waist slender. She pulled back her curly hair and bound it with a black ribbon. She stripped off the linen tablecloth and placed her basket on one end of the trestle table. Then, rolling her white sleeves to above the elbow, she reached in and pulled out a mackerel.

Scales flew from her knife like tiny flecks of mica; little prisms of light sparkled on her hands and arms.

Alwir stared hard at her bare arms. It wasn't the fish scales but her own skin that glimmered. He remembered now seeing the blue aura when he lay on the sand. Lirrel had been right. Tayleb was the fourth girl, the final Queen in the Queens' quarter knot.

How much does she know? Alwir wondered. His head ached with conflicting emotions: relief and excitement at finding the fourth girl, but despair as Tayleb looked at him, a smile on her face. She was pretty, and her face stung him with unexpected gladness. If she had been an ordinary girl he would have charmed her to keep her smiling for him alone. But she wasn't an ordinary girl. The Queens' quarter knot would come first. There would be no place for him in her life once they left the island.

He leaned back into the pillows and closed his eyes, trying to convince himself that it didn't matter, that he could serve her as a loyal soldier and that would be enough.

"Are you well?" Tayleb asked, coming to stand near him.

"I'll be better soon," he replied gruffly, not opening his eyes.

Chapter Eight

Beneath the moon's reflection, the white forms of the Namires floated toward the surface of the water, attracted by the underwater sounds of the anchored Silean ship. Schools of silvery herring dashed past them. They broke through the surface with a quiet splash and then drifted, staring at the black silhouette of a Silean vessel listing on the waves.

"But what's it doing here?" Mari asked Kire. "What can it mean?"

"Trouble," answered Kire. Her hands sculled the water nervously. "It's not a trading ship, but a warship."

"Here, to the Islands? But why? The Naming is over. Surely they can't be bringing Readers now?" Mari argued.

"Tayleb?" asked Ril, fingering the small friendship ring. "Do you think the Queen has come to know of her? Tammi said it would happen one day."

"I hope not, Ril," Kire said. "But we can't take the chance."

"I say we swim alongside and see if there's anything more to be learned." Kana turned onto her back, her arms stroking the rough sea languorously as she contemplated the darkening sky.

"Too dangerous!" Mari blurted out. "That's a warship, Kana! Those ships used to hunt us."

"And now they might be hunting Tayleb," Ril said as she kicked her feet harder to keep pace with her shoal sisters. "For once I agree with Kana. We must go alongside. If they've come for Tayleb then we must warn her. What say you, Kire?"

Kire breasted the waves, her long powerful arms sweeping to her sides as she swam to meet the black ship. "Tayleb is our responsibility. We have kept her safe thus far. But this ship is trouble. I say we go closer."

"I don't like it," Mari repeated.

"So you've said," Kire snapped irritably. "But we have no choice. So swim."

Kire ducked her head underwater, the rising curve of her back and buttocks lifting out of the water. The white soles of her feet flashed before she disappeared under the dark water. Ril followed quickly so as not to fall behind. Tammi and Kana cleaved the waves with their dives, their white bodies rippling beneath the water's surface. Mari hesitated, not wanting to go and not wanting to remain behind. Angrily, she dove into the wake of bubbles and reluctantly followed after her shoal sisters.

The riggings creaked, the halyards slapping the mast as the ship pitched slowly from side to side in the wintry sea. On one side of the horizon, the last streaks of sunlight stretched behind a bank of dark clouds, while on the other side a half-moon rose in a clearing sky. Ener Re Aston, hunched in his black cloak, wondered at the wisdom of leaving the mainland so late in the season. The night mist made the joints of his hands ache. He'd come topside only because he found he could no longer abide the company of the Sileans settled in the warm hold below. Their contempt for Oran and its people filled their talk until Ener found the pretense of laughing at their insulting humor impossible. Perhaps they did it to prick his skin, though more likely it didn't matter to them what he thought.

Glumly, Ener watched the last orange glow fade from the horizon. One more night on this ship and they'd reach the cluster of rugged islands and begin their search. If he was lucky, he would resolve this business quickly. The girl had to be on one of the islands. His informers had learned that she had not yet come to Sadar, that the New Moon still searched for her. A water element would be at home on the Islands, and it was remote enough for her to have avoided the Readers. He had staked his future and the future of the Reader families on it.

The door to the hold banged open and coarse laughter bellowed out. Ener steeled himself as an officer shambled toward him, his boots scraping across the wooden planks of the deck.

"Too good to drink with us, Re Aston?" a belligerent voice accused.

Ener checked his ire and hid his disgust. Turning to the man, he formed a pleasant smile. The officer was Re Torras, one of the younger Guardsmen. He was a big man, with loose-jointed limbs and a shuffling walk. But Ener was not fooled by the slowness of his step, nor the heavy-lidded eyes that seemed on the verge of sleep. The man had a quick temper and a deadly aim with the Silean crossbow. Ener needed care handling this one.

"Not at all, Re Torras. I've had too much to drink already. The air seemed a good idea to cool my heated blood."

"Bah," Re Torras scoffed, partially satisfied with the answer and partially not, Ener thought, since it offered him no opportunity to vent his spleen.

"Stinking Islands," the man grumbled, throwing his weight forward on the railing of the ship. He rested with arms over the side, and with a finger pressed against one nostril blew his nose into the ocean. The snorting exhale was followed by a rough hack. "What do you think then?" Re Torras asked, turning to lean his back against the railing. "All this running around for an Oran bitch. I could be in Beldan, playing knucklebones and drinking decent beer instead of this horse's piss."

Ener reached into the pocket of his cloak for a small flask he carried. Better to make an alliance with a man like this than an enemy, he decided. "Try this," he said, handing the flask to the Guardsman.

"What is it?" Re Torras squinted at the clear liquid.

"Mother's tears."

"I've heard of it," he exclaimed, a smile parting the lazy mouth. He grabbed the bottle and took a desperate swig of the illegal Oran liquor. He freed his mouth from the bottle and gasped, air whistling into his throat. "Not bad," he said hoarsely and took another, more cautious sip. "Not bad at all."

He corked the flask and tucked it into his vest pocket. With quiet disappointment, Ener watched the flask disappear. It was a small price to pay for the man's good humor.

Re Torras reached for his crossbow, which was stowed in a coil of thick rope. He had been practicing shooting fish off the bow earlier in the day, even though it wasted bolts. He took the weapon now and rubbed its stock affectionately. Then he aimed it toward Ener's head.

Ener's expression remained impassive, though his gloved hands clenched behind his back.

"Oy, so what do you really think, then, eh?" Re Torras asked. Re Torras lowered the crossbow with a leer. "Is the bitch out here?"

"Yes," Ener replied.

"Think she's pretty?" Re Torras asked as he reached down and grabbed a bolt. He turned the winch on his crossbow, placing the thick-headed bolt in the shaft. "Wouldn't mind this frigging chase if I could make it worth my while. I'd have her screaming." He laughed unpleasantly, hoisting the loaded crossbow again to his shoulder.

Ener gave him a sidelong glance and his lips curled in annoyance. "Could be she's dangerous."

"If she ever got the chance. She won't know her own name when I'm through with her. They're all the same I tell you."

"Who?" Ener asked, momentarily confused.

"Women. Frigging bitches all of them," he said confidently. "Give them the back of your hand."

Ener looked angrily into the black water below. He was going to make his reply when something in the water stopped him. "Z'blood," he swore as he saw faces staring up at him. Women's faces, stippled with the bright gleam of moonlight as they floated on the surface of the water. "Look, there's something in the water," he shouted to Re Torras. Two of the faces disappeared.

Re Torras flashed his crossbow down and fired. The hard thwack of the bolt was joined by a short scream. Ener stared in horror as a child bobbed to the surface, the bolt embedded in the white chest. Hands floated on either side and a terrified face gazed up at him. Blood streamed over a necklace of shells. A wave rolled the body over and then it was gone, submerged by the weight of the bolt. Beside him Re Torras was cursing as he loaded another bolt.

Re Torras aimed the crossbow over the edge of the railing and peered down. Nothing rose to disturb the water except for the waves that lapped rhythmically against the hull of the ship. After a few moments of waiting, he swore loudly and fired the bolt into the empty sea.

"What the frigging shit was that?" he asked angrily.

"Namires," Ener answered, still awed by the sight of the child's face.

"Docksiders blow," he spat contemptuously.

"No. There were once great schools of them, though they were to have died out long ago. Hunted by your Silean forebears. But I know that's what they were. How else could there have been a child out here, far from any shore!" Ener slammed his palm flat on the railing. It made a crisp smacking sound against the wet wood. "She's here. I know it. The girl is here. Tomorrow will prove me right." Ener smiled triumphantly at the moon-speckled sea, confident of his future for the first time since they had left Beldan.

"Wet work, this," Dagar said over his shoulder, catching Lirrel's eye. He pulled hard at the fishing nets as they dragged in the foaming sea.

"*Ahal,*" she answered breathlessly, the wet rope digging furrows into her palms. Why did the nets seem so heavy? she wondered.

"Backs to it!" shouted Teck.

"We should be leaving, Lirrel," Dagar said.

Lirrel didn't answer. She was winded from hauling in nets

and too irritated to give a reply. It wasn't that she didn't like work, or that she was lazy. It was just that hauling nets, gutting and cleaning slippery fish, was not the way she wanted to work. She was Ghazali. She wanted to be traveling, playing her flute at different villages along the road. Then she sighed, discontented with herself. I'm conceited, she thought, and pulled earnestly on the rope. I want to play music that reflects the joy of labor as long as that labor is done by someone other than myself. And she knew with a twinge of guilt that as it was, Dagar pulled doubly hard so that she, standing in line behind him, would not have to take her share of the weight.

She had grown accustomed to Dagar's always taking on her share of the work. If Teck gave them baskets of fish for cleaning, within a short time Dagar would have done his and would be taking the fish from her basket, cleaning them twice as fast as she could. He had changed much since Cairns. He was short for a man, but now taller than herself. His face was youthful, but on his upper lip a shadow of soft, dark hair was appearing. His chin, once pointed with thinness, had filled out, growing more square. The air was cold, but the hard work had made him warm. He had stripped off the black coat and his sweat-soaked shirt stuck to his back. The muscles bunched over the flat shoulder blades as he reached for the nets.

His hand flashed like a brown thrush as he reached forward for a handhold on the rope. Despite her bad mood, Lirrel smiled, charmed by the sight of Dagar's hand, which looked stronger and more capable than when she had held it at Cairns.

"We leave soon. I've only been waiting until Alwir was well enough," she answered.

"Oy, look to it now," Teck cried in a gravelly voice. "Net's coming in."

As Lirrel pulled on her line, an unease stirred in her mind, like a cloud passing over the sun. She groaned as the unease became fear and pressed against her temples.

"Damn the nets, what is it I've caught?" Teck shouted as the black cords of the net rose out of the muddied water. Only a few fish flapped their bright tails in the foamy surf. The weight belonged to a body trapped in the net. Hair was tangled in the knots and the body glistened with water droplets, white as a bleached shell.

Lirrel stifled a scream and dropped her hold on the nets. She splashed into the shallow water and Dagar followed behind her, reaching the curled figure before she did.

They hauled the body onto the shore and carefully disentangled it from the netting.

Lirrel's hands covered her mouth as she saw the corpse of a young girl, the short black hair washed back from the stark white face. Eyes like dull agates stared up at the gray sky. A Silean bolt rose obscenely from the middle of her chest. Lirrel bent down closer and touched the small hand, seeing the friendship ring on the white finger. It matched the one on Tayleb's hand.

Teck was muttering and when Lirrel glanced up at him she realized he was praying.

"Namire," he said thickly, pointing to the thin gill slits that sluiced water from either side of her neck. "I'd always wanted to see them. But not like this." He covered his face with his hand, the swollen knuckles and thick fingers hiding his eyes.

"Sileans," Dagar said, touching Lirrel's shoulder.

"We must leave. Now," Lirrel said, trying to swallow the nausea that stuck in her throat.

"Tayleb," Dagar said.

"Ahal." Lirrel nodded. "I'll tell her." She stood and brushed the sand from her skirts, chewing the inside of her cheek. "Dagar, would you please see to the body?"

Dagar's face was unreadable. "Of course," he said.

"I'll help you," Teck offered.

Leaving them, Lirrel ran, following the sandy trail through the withered grass that covered the banks. How long before the Sileans arrived? The sea had been calm the last few days. Alwir seemed to be healing rapidly, and so she had agreed that they would remain longer in hopes that he would be well enough to return with them. Now she feared they were too late.

Lirrel folded her shawl around her face as she entered the village. The streets were empty except for a dog barking a warning. She didn't stop, but hurried up the cobbled streets. On a fair-weather day like today, the men would be out in the boats.

The women would be too busy with their chores to pay much attention to her hurrying past. Teck and Moire's cottage was on the outer edge of the village, clinging to the rocky ledge of the bluffs. Her lungs demanding air, Lirrel stopped to rest on the climbing path. And then she turned to the village, only then aware of the unnatural quiet.

From the hill she saw the black-and-gray flags flying from the tall-masted ship. A Silean warship was docked on the far side of the island where a small natural harbor provided deeper water for the larger ships. The village women would have seen the ship's approach. They would be there, trying to do a bit of trade. A Silean alarm cawed out shrilly over the quiet village and gulls scattered into the sky.

Cold with panic, Lirrel continued her uphill run. Panting hard, she reached the cottage door as Alwir swung it open.

"Sileans," Lirrel gasped out. "Here."

"I heard the alarm," he said. His eyes searched the village. "Where's Dagar?"

"At the sand flats."

"We have to get Tayleb out of here."

"I know," Lirrel said. "And there's something else too."

Tayleb was standing by the window, her frightened face drained of color. Moire had already begun gathering supplies.

"Quick now," she hissed at Tayleb, "get the bread and the dried cheese. You can hide until tonight out in the caves on the bluffs and leave after moonrise."

"Mam," Tayleb said weakly, "suppose it isn't me they're after."

"It is," Lirrel replied. She came close to Tayleb and took her by the hands. They were clammy. "Just now at the sand flats, the nets hauled in the body of a Namire. A girl with a ring like yours."

"Ril," Tayleb moaned and tried to pull her hands away from Lirrel's. Lirrel held her fast.

"She had been killed with a Silean crossbow. They know you're here, Tayleb."

Tayleb crumpled as she started to cry. She folded her arms over her chest, but Lirrel grabbed her firmly by the shoulders.

"Not now," Lirrel urged. "Push your grief away. Now we must run."

Moire handed a tied bundle to Alwir. Then she held her daughter tight in her arms to silence the sobs. "Take them to the caves," she whispered fiercely into Tayleb's ear. "Do what must be done now."

Tayleb nodded as she stifled her cries. Moire released her and pushed her gently toward Alwir. "Mam," Tayleb pleaded.

"Go now!" Moire ordered. She gave Alwir a sharp glance. "Watch out for her."

Alwir took Tayleb by the arm and together they left the cottage.

Lirrel touched Moire on the arm in a gesture of farewell. Moire turned to her, a stony expression masking her pain.

"I'll send Dagar out by the beaches to the bluffs. Look for him."

"*Ahal,*" Lirrel said and then slipped through the door. Outside the cottage she heard the shrill caw of the Silean alarm as it carried over the village.

Lirrel started up the rocky path to the bluffs, turning once to see Moire's shawl-covered head disappear down the hillside toward the sand flats. Her heart ached with worry for Dagar, but she couldn't stop to contemplate it. He would have to find his own way to them. Farther up the path Tayleb was moving rapidly along the edge of the bluffs. Her hair was blowing wildly around her face, the shawl trailing in the wind. Alwir marched behind her, his hands grabbing for the rocks to support his unsteady legs. Lirrel followed, hearing the roar of Tayleb's unspoken anguish. Lirrel closed her eyes as images of Ril crashed like the waves against the rocks. She took a deep breath and steadied herself. Then she urged her legs to march uphill and against the pounding wake of Tayleb's grief.

Chapter Nine

Dagar and Teck laid the body of the young Namire in a sailcloth that had been left to dry on the shore. Teck snapped the fletch end of the bolt and threw it away on the sand. Dagar folded the coarse sheet around the body. He stared a moment at the young face and saw again the corpse of his little sister when he buried her at Cairns. Dagar's heart began to beat violently as he covered her face. He pressed a hand against his chest as his heart banged against his ribs. Sweat prickled on his upper lip.

Teck hoisted the body over his shoulder and, head bent, started walking up the grassy banks. The wind rustled through the slender stalks of withered grass and scattered the faded purple blossoms of the sea asters. Dagar trudged behind Teck, searching for a Ghazali song that might offer solace to the wild beating of his heart. He remembered one, a slow measured tune, which he hummed, his throat tightening with emotion.

There was one small graveyard at the edge of the village. Almost all the graves belonged to the women of the village. On the Islands, it was an accomplishment to die on land and be interred in the soil. Few men were buried on Tynor; more often they died at sea, and their bodies were never recovered. Teck entered through an old iron gate and laid the body down on the grass.

He was sweating in the cool air and tears stained his cheeks and beard. Dagar found a shovel that had been stowed in a little shed.

"I'll dig," Dagar said.

"Nay, lad, just give me a rest," Teck protested.

"I'd rather do it," Dagar insisted.

Dagar drove the spade into the ground, surprised at the looseness of the soil. At Cairns, and later at Sadar, the drought had compacted the soil to a hard clay that resisted every effort with the spade. Here the grass tore easily as he dug, spidery roots pulling away with the black sandy soil. Dagar started humming again, and then, finding the words in Ghazali, he sang aloud. His voice grew more confident as the music lent a rhythm to the digging spade.

The shrill caw of a Silean alarm silenced him.

"It's coming from the other side of the village," Teck said, getting to his feet in alarm. "There must be a ship in the harbor."

"I've got to hurry," Dagar said quickly and resumed digging.

Teck grabbed a second spade, his eyes straying worriedly to the village as he dug. The two men worked quickly, and the loose soil piled up beside the open grave.

As they settled the body into the grave, Teck saw Moire coming down the hill, her black shawl flapping around her shoulders and her skirts billowing in the wind.

"Moire!" Teck called. She spotted them and veered off the sandy path to cut her way down the steep grassy banks of the hill.

"There's a Silean ship," she said.

"We heard the alarm," Teck answered. "Where's Tayleb?"

"She's taken Lirrel and Alwir to the caves to wait for night-fall. The tide's out and they'd never get the *Turtle* in the water and away fast enough without being seen." Moire addressed Dagar. "You're to go back to the beach and follow the shore to where you first came. Do you remember it?"

"The crescent beach, with the bluffs all around?"

"Aye, that one. They will be looking out for you. Now go quickly."

"I must finish here first," Dagar said, returning his spade to the loose soil. He tossed a shovelful of dirt over the body of the Namire. The dull thud of the soil as it landed on the shroud brought a lump to his throat. How he hated the emptiness of that sound.

"We'll do it, you go on now," Moire urged, roughly taking the spade from Dagar's hand.

She held his gaze steady, a look of understanding in her eyes. "The dead don't rebuke us for flight when it's necessary. I left many of my own dead on battlefields and only these long years have taught me that they didn't cling to me as hard as I tried to cling to them."

Dagar nodded sadly. *"Ahal,"* he murmured softly.

"Go, Dagar," Moire said. "Lirrel waits for you."

"Z'blood," Teck swore as over the brow of the hill a troop of Silean Guards appeared, led by villagers. They were pointing up the path toward Teck and Moire's cottage.

"Go by the sand flats," Moire ordered Dagar.

"Too late," Dagar answered as he saw a second band of Silean Guards spreading out over the sand flats beach, checking beneath the overturned boats on the shore.

A Guard on the hill hailed them, demanding that they approach. Three Guards lifted their crossbows in warning and the thickheaded bolts glinted dangerously.

"What do we do?" Teck asked Moire.

"We stall."

"But your face," Teck said. His hand touched his wife's cheek. "They will question the marks on your face."

"Aye," Moire replied taking Teck's hand in hers as she walked slowly toward the entrance of the graveyard. "But they will get no answers they can use."

Dagar followed the couple, trampling the old grass with his heavy tread. His heart began to pound again and this time it was not with rage or grief, but fear.

* * *

A full moon had risen above the rim of the sea, casting a rippled path along the waves. Tayleb ventured cautiously out of the cave and peered at the beach below the bluffs. Throughout the day they had hidden in the deep recesses of a cave hearing the shouts of the Silean Guard as they searched for them. Now the shore was empty and, except for the murmuring of the waves with the rising tide, it was quiet.

"Tide's in. We must leave soon," Tayleb said anxiously.

"I want to wait a little longer for Dagar," Lirrel said as she and Alwir appeared at Tayleb's side.

Alwir laid a hand on Lirrel's shoulder but she stepped away from it. It was meant to comfort, but she didn't want comfort because that would mean accepting the possibility that Dagar would not come.

"How much longer can we wait?" Alwir asked Tayleb.

Tayleb appraised the waves breaking along the eroded base of the bluffs. The beach had narrowed to a sliver of white sand. "We can't wait. Tide's at high-water mark."

Alwir scratched windblown sand from his beard and then spoke to Lirrel. "All right, then. Lirrel, you go with Tayleb to the *Turtle*. I'll go to the village to see if I can find Dagar."

"Thank you," Lirrel said softly, the twin moons of her eyes glowing in the dark.

"And my parents too, Alwir," Tayleb added. "I scarcely bid my Mam farewell, and my Da not at all."

"I'll try. But don't wait any longer than you have to. If Dagar and your parents have bartered time for us, we would be wasting a precious gift."

"Fair enough," Tayleb said and, shouldering a netted bag of food, she led the way down the rocky face of the bluffs.

They walked carefully, following a sandy trail hidden between the clefts of the rocks. The fresh scent of the sea rose to meet them and the wind blew fine sand in their faces. As they neared the water Tayleb took off her clogs to clamber barefoot over the slippery kelp-covered rocks. Lirrel followed her example, gasping as her feet found purchase in tide pools of cold seawater. Alwir's boots crunched noisily as he crushed dense clusters of mussels beneath his heels.

The huge pocked boulders of the bluff broke apart into smaller and smaller rocks that tumbled down to the shore and the rising waves. Lirrel sighed with relief when she felt the sand again under her aching bare feet.

On the beach Tayleb stopped and stared out at the lapping waves.

"What is it?" Lirrel asked, hearing wariness in Tayleb's thoughts.

"Something in the water," Tayleb answered.

"Look, there!" Lirrel said and pointed to a shadow that darkened the path of the moonlight. Four figures rose out of the waves, the white foam clinging to their shoulders and flanks.

Tayleb gave a cry and ran into the waves to greet them. She threw her arms around the tallest one and the others circled round her.

"The Namires," Lirrel said to Alwir's unspoken question.

Wonder filled Alwir's gaunt face. "I never thought they were real," he said.

"So much of our history is lost. The Namires are remembered only in stories. But they were part of the Oran people once, living more in the sea than out of it. Where we had villages, they had great schools that farmed the coastal waters."

"What happened?"

"Sileans. Their clerics proclaimed the Namires abominations. They were hunted."

"And Zorah permitted it," Alwir said bitterly.

"*Ahal,* for she feared any remaining source of Oran magic. The Namires fought back, but too many were lost."

Lirrel was quiet then as Tayleb and the Namires approached them. The four young women crowded around Tayleb, waiting nervously. Their round heads were slick with wet hair and their bodies glistened. Strapped across their backs they carried small bags woven of kelp strands. One of them stepped forward, her expression challenging.

"This is Kire, shoal leader," Tayleb said introducing her. "And this is Mari, Kana, and Tammi," she added, indicating each one. "And this is Lirrel and Alwir, my friends," she told the Namires.

"Na ahlan," Kire said solemnly to Lirrel and held out her hands.

Lirrel's eyes sparkled with pleasure at the Ghazali greeting. *"Beran,"* she replied and stepped forward to take the girl's hands. Kire's hands were cold and wet; translucent webbing connected the fingers.

Kire kissed Lirrel formally on both cheeks and Lirrel closed her eyes as her own lips brushed against the salty skin.

"It's all the Ghazali I can remember," Kire said apologetically. "Our grandmother spoke it fluently. She used to meet with the Ghazali on the shores of Soring Marsh in the summer for the poetry contests." Kire gave a half smile. "She told us the Ghazali didn't like water but were curious about what lay beneath the surface."

Lirrel nodded in agreement. *"Ahal,* it is the same even now among the Ghazali."

"Though we are all that's left of the Namires," Kire finished, "and I'm not much of a poet."

"All that's left?" Tayleb asked, shocked.

Kire nodded. "There were no males born in the last hatching. And those that were our relations have died over these last seasons, their bodies gray-scaled with disease."

"Zorah," Alwir said flatly. "The Namires must be suffering too from the drain of Oran magic."

"There's no more time for talk," Tammi blurted rudely. "We've come to take Tayleb off the island. The Sileans must not find her here."

"There are Guards posted all along the sand flats," Kana said to Tayleb. "You won't be able to reach the *Turtle*."

"Then how are we to leave? The only other boats are the longboats used by the Sileans. And those are docked at the harbor pier," Tayleb said.

"I had not thought there would be three of you," Kire said with a frown.

"Four," Lirrel corrected. "Another is in the village."

"Prisoner?" Kire asked.

"We don't know," Alwir answered. "I am going there to see if I can find out."

"All right then," Kire said, "here's a plan." She held her hands up and the moonlight shone through the webbing of her outstretched fingers. "Tayleb comes with us—"

"How?" Alwir asked.

Impatiently, Kire flipped the wet hair back from her shoulder. "How else but through the sea? You and Lirrel go to the village. If you can find your friend, bring him to the harbor pier."

"There will be Guards—" Alwir protested.

"Aye, but not nearly as many as those camped along the flats. They don't expect you to walk into the village." She turned to Lirrel. "With a shawl over your head, you'll pass for an Islander."

"It's too risky," Alwir argued. "Is there any way you can take Lirrel with you now? I'd rather chance the village on my own."

"No. Not unless Lirrel can survive swimming in the open sea," Kire said flatly.

"Kire, even I can't survive swimming in the open sea now. The water's too cold. I won't make it," Tayleb insisted.

"You will," Kire said. "Because of who you are."

"I told you we should have taught her sooner," Tammi grumbled.

"No," Kire snapped. "She needed to trust us first."

"I don't understand," said Tayleb, shaking her head.

Kire stared at a beached wave spreading thick foam over the sand. The water retreated with a rasping whisper. "It will be easy for you. The Namires swim in warm currents. Deep under the waves."

"But I'll drown."

"No you won't," Mari said. "You're a water element. The water won't harm you. We'll take you down with us and you'll breathe water."

"Breathe water?" Tayleb repeated softly.

"There's no time to waste," Kire said to Alwir. "When you get to the pier, take one of the longboats and row out into the harbor. We'll meet you there and help you cross the open sea. One thing more," Kire said. "Tayleb, give Lirrel your clothes. They'll be of no use to you in the water."

"Aye," Tayleb said, and with stilted movements began undressing. She undid the waist buttons of her skirt and let it fall. Then pulling off her blouse, she stood shivering in her shift. Lirrel gathered up her cast-off garments.

"Tayleb, you swim with the Namires," Kire said gently. "Give Lirrel your shift."

Alwir edged away, his head downcast to avoid looking at her. Tayleb stripped off her shift and handed it to Lirrel. She pressed her hands against her bare thighs, her shoulders hunched against the night wind.

"Right," Kire said to Lirrel. "Beyond the harbor."

"Wait." Lirrel stopped Kire, one hand on the woman's shoulder. "I am sorry about Ril."

Kire hesitated, as if wanting to speak. She squeezed her eyes shut and then opened them slowly, blinking away tears. "Thank you," she said in a low voice. Then she turned back to the sea and, taking Tayleb by the hand, led her into the shallow waves.

Lirrel ran to join Alwir, who waited farther down the shore.

"Is she gone?" Alwir asked as Lirrel reached him.

Lirrel looked back and saw Tayleb wading into the sea. A wave broke against her, splashing water high up on her breasts and shoulders. Lirrel heard the startled cry in Tayleb's thoughts at the slap of cold water. Then at once the shrillness of her thoughts was muted as Tayleb plunged beneath the waves and disappeared.

"*Ahal*, she is gone," Lirrel said.

The muscles in Tayleb's legs cramped in the icy cold water. Ahead of her the Namires continued to glide over the surface, fragmenting the silvery moonlight.

"I can't," Tayleb gasped, swallowing water. "Too cold."

Tayleb's numbed arms and legs became motionless. Only her face floated on the surface as the cold weight of the water seemed to collapse around her chest.

"Tayleb, listen to me," Kire said, tucking a hand beneath Tayleb's chin to keep her afloat.

Tayleb saw the outline of Kire's face, the moon rising behind her shoulder. Tammi and Kana joined her, their hands under

Tayleb's armpits, lifting her to float on the water. The iridescent scales of Tayleb's arms sparkled brilliantly.

"We'll take you below, Tayleb, to where the currents are warm. You are safe with us," Kana was saying in her ear.

"I'm afraid," Tayleb answered, her feet stirring with panic.

"Don't be. You are the water, let it flow through you," Tammi said.

"Tayleb, look at me," Kire said brusquely. "If there had been more time, we would have done this slowly so that you would not fear. We would have celebrated your arrival below the surface. But there is no time. Ril is dead and you are being hunted. You must trust us."

"Aye," Tayleb answered weakly, though her courage was drained away by the cold, dark water.

"We'll take you down. Don't cling to the air. It will only make it harder for you."

Tayleb wanted to say yes, but before she could speak the Namires dove into the water, Kire on one side of her, Kana on the other. Together they held her hands and pulled her below the surface. For a terrifying instant, Tayleb saw the full moon, shattering into rings of white light as the water closed over her head.

She held her breath, even though Kire warned her not to. The hoarded air buoyed her chest, resisting the downward tug of the Namires' hands. Her neck stretched upward, her eyes straining to see the moon. Bubbles escaped at the corners of her mouth and joined the stream of other bubbles fleeing to the surface.

The water grew colder still, stabbing her with a dagger of ice. Her hands weakly struggled against the firm grasp of the Namires. The moon shrank to a pinpoint of light and then disappeared as the water became black.

Tayleb opened her mouth and the last of her air escaped. Her back arched and her body convulsed as she sucked in a breath of water.

She had no choice but to surrender herself to the water. Without air, without even a glimpse of the surface far above her, Tayleb closed her eyes. Her terror ebbed as the cold filled her veins and the wracking pain of her lungs subsided. She heard a distant roar in her ears, her blood still clamoring for a breath of air. But her reserves were gone. She allowed the water to invade her and drown her fear with a strange calm. She had no sense of direction, and only the tug of Kire's hand and the current of water spiraling around her body gave her a sense of movement.

Seawater filled the hollow corridor of her throat and entered her lungs. It was all one, she thought vaguely as she felt the water infuse her veins. An exhaled stream of water warmed her face, its taste momentarily sweet.

And then Tayleb shuddered awake, confused by the unexpected sensation of warmth. Her eyes opened, and in the murky water she saw a glimmer of light. A faint light formed around her from the luminous shine of jellyfish, their phosphorescent glow like artificial stars. They circled her in the warm water, lighting on her shoulders and arms. She flinched, expecting a sting, but felt instead only the velvety stroke of their tentacles.

Tayleb cried out in amazement and a curtain of bubbles cascaded around her.

A hand touched her and Tayleb drifted around and saw the Namires, each haloed by the light of the jellyfish.

They touched her reassuringly, stroking her cheek and arms.

Tayleb tried to speak but there was only the murmur of bubbles.

Then Kire kicked out her legs, urging Tayleb to follow her. The warm currents carried Tayleb along the floor of the ocean. Sand rose in little puffs of clouds, displaced by the powerful strokes of the swimmers. Tayleb's eyes grew accustomed to the wavering light of the deep sea, her senses constantly startled by the sudden appearance of mackerel, sea bream, and gar, their eyes shining bright green. Schools of herring swam alongside like an escort, their silvery tails flashing in the eerie phosphorous glow of the jellyfish.

In the womb of the ocean, Tayleb's skin thinned into a porous boundary. She swam without effort or resistance. Turning, she saw the Namires struggling to keep pace behind her. She stretched her hands forward in the water and they appeared transparent, the bones of her fingers like bleached coral.

Tayleb felt the long-denied power waken in her at last. She delighted in her new-found element and discovered that she could sense the ocean currents as they swerved along the rugged coast of Oran. She felt the water as it rose from hidden springs, joined the snow of Avadares, and plunged over the cliffs to fill streams and lakes throughout Oran. And at the mouths of the rivers, at Remmerton, Doberan, and Beldan, tongues of fresh water lapped far out into the salty ocean.

Even in the dark water, Tayleb knew exactly where she was. Ships resting on the surface itched her skin as if the wooden hulls were cockleburrs scraping against her back. She thrust her body upward toward the surface again. The white dot of the moon appeared and then swelled as she neared the surface. The luminous jellyfish trailed beneath her like a comet's tail.

The water churned and a white spray exploded into mist as her head and shoulders broke through the waves. Water clung to her lashes and she blinked, astonished by the cool, arid touch of the wind on her cheeks. She choked in the wind and floated on her back as she struggled to breathe air again. Water sluiced from her nostrils; gradually the swallowed gulps of air replaced the sea. A faint ocean mist was laden with the spice of land and the scents of human beings.

The swirling water murmured to her the approach of the Namires. Tayleb straightened in the water to face them as first Kire, then Tammi and Kana together, and finally Mari broke through the waves, spouting water.

"Is it well with you?" Kire asked.

Tayleb nodded. "Aye," she answered simply, surprised at the lightness of her voice. "Very well."

"Good," Kire answered with a sigh. "Twice before we failed. But our patience has been rewarded."

Tayleb's happiness suddenly chilled. "What happened to the others?"

"They drowned," Tammi said sadly. "But you are the one we have been searching for. You, Tayleb, are the Water Queen promised us."

"But you didn't know that when you pulled me down."

"Not for certain," Kire answered reluctantly.

"You told me to trust you," Tayleb said. "But you could have been wrong. You could have pulled me to my death."

"That's why we waited, that's why we swam so much with you last season and this, hoping to learn the truth first," Kana explained. "We didn't want to make a mistake again."

Mari swam toward Tayleb, her face distressed. "Please don't be angry."

Tayleb swam away from the Namires, her eyes scanning the lights of the village sprinkled across the brow of the hill. "My friends are waiting," she answered coldly. "I must go."

As Tayleb swam for the harbor, she heard the creaking boards of the Silean ship and the gentle rasp of the waves on the shore. But louder still was the confusion of her heart; the joy of merging with the water warred with her anger at the Namires for drowning others before her. The triumph of her accomplishment seemed tarnished by those innocent deaths. She was still an Islander, and she felt her trust in the Namires betrayed by those drownings.

Tayleb forced away those unhappy thoughts as she spotted the longboats tied to the piers. She drifted on the tide, searching for a sight of Alwir or Lirrel. She prayed that Dagar would be with them and that there would be news of her parents.

"Where do you think they are?" Alwir asked Lirrel as they hid behind the rocks, staring down at Tayleb's small cottage. There was no fire and the windows of the cottage were dark.

"Perhaps they've taken them to the headman's cottage. It's the largest house in the village and close to the harbor," Lirrel answered.

Alwir touched the bandage on his head wound and cursed silently. "I don't like not knowing where I am," he explained. "This damn wound left me ignorant of all but Tayleb's cottage."

"I'll lead us," Lirrel said, brushing the sand from her skirt hem. She clutched the bundle of Tayleb's clothing and wondered where Tayleb was now. She had heard the moment of terror before Tayleb surrendered to the water, and then the flood of joy that filled Tayleb's thoughts as she became aware of her element. But her thoughts were silent now.

"Behind the cottages, this way," Lirrel said, beckoning Alwir down a narrow, sandy path.

The village was quiet, doors latched and windows shuttered as if expecting a storm. Even the dogs had been brought in. The only sound that carried through the streets was the occasional raised voices of the Silean Guard camped along the sand flats.

As they approached the harbor, Lirrel halted in the shadows.

"Oh, no," she breathed.

"What is it?" Alwir asked sharply.

"Over there, that's the headman's house." Lirrel pointed to a large house, its base built of stone. Battered wooden shutters were pulled tightly over the windows. No light shone from between the cracks and from the chimney no smoke columned into the air. "They're not there."

"Are you sure?" Alwir asked again.

"There are no Guards," Lirrel said. "If a Reader was there, wouldn't there be a Guard?"

"So where are they?" Alwir questioned the night. He stared angrily at the anchored Silean warship and then swore to himself again.

Lirrel groaned, catching the shape of Alwir's thought. "They're on the ship. Of course. They brought them back to the ship."

"Lirrel," Alwir said soberly, "do you know if Dagar is still alive?"

Lirrel's stomach tightened. That worry had gripped her since they had left the caves. "Yes. But something is very wrong."

"Then we must free him."

"I owe you thanks again, Alwir," Lirrel said.

"For what?" he whispered, taking her by the arm and leading her down the street.

"For taking this chance. For not doing the wise thing and leaving Dagar to his fate."

Alwir shrugged. "Dagar is my friend too, Lirrel. I couldn't abandon him to the Sileans."

They traveled slowly, hugging the shadows of the narrow street. At the end of a row of cottages, the road opened into a broad path that led down a grassy hill to the pier jutting out from the beach. Two huge camp fires of driftwood burned brightly on either side of the pier, and settled around the fires, the Silean

Guards were relaxing on duty. One Guard was standing, his gaze sweeping back and forth over the grassy embankment, a crossbow poised in his arms. Quickly he lifted the crossbow and shot a bolt into the long grass. The squeal of a rabbit followed the hard twang of the bolt. The other Guards cheered as the crossbowman scrambled up the embankment and retrieved the freshly killed rabbit. He jerked the heavy bolt free and then proudly held up the carcass.

"Right," Alwir said softly. "The longboat is at the end of the pier. Somehow we have to walk down there, through the Guards, and out to the pier without being noticed." He turned to Lirrel, his expression skeptical. "Any ideas?"

"Ahal," Lirrel answered, thinking of the rabbit. "A distraction, to keep them occupied. Like the rabbit. Larger, maybe, but still vulnerable."

"A woman," Alwir said quickly.

Lirrel grimaced and Alwir turned his palms skyward.

"They're Sileans, Lirrel."

"I know, I know," Lirrel answered sounding annoyed. "It just makes me feel unclean."

"Can you give them an illusion like at Sadar?" Alwir asked.

"Yes. But I need to pick someone real from the village to create the illusion. Like Moire."

"But young," Alwir said. "When she first arrived at Tynor's Rock."

"Ahal," Lirrel agreed and closed her eyes. She concentrated on Moire's face, imagining it at twenty-odd years. The face grew thinner, her eyes larger as the flesh tightened with youth. She stood arrow straight, her arms held loosely in front of her. The grass stirred as the image of Moire was lifted from the remembering earth. Lirrel saw the suppleness of Moire's limbs, her hair still scented with the tart fragrance of pitch.

Lirrel heard the sharp intake of Alwir's breath as a vision of Moire appeared on the hill above the Sileans. The light of the bonfire flickered over her skirts.

"Oy, you there," a Guard called. "Come here."

Moire's figure didn't move.

"I told you to come here!"

Lirrel reached deeper into the past and at once the figure of Moire changed. Her face clean of tattoos, she aimed a longbow, ready to fire. It was the time of the Burning. Lirrel's eyes teared with the sting of remembered smoke and ash.

The Guard shouted a warning and the others scattered before the figure of Moire, quickly knocking an arrow in her longbow. The Guards flattened themselves into the sandy banks, but no arrow was released. They looked up cautiously, seeing Moire retreat. Several Guards rose and began to give chase.

Moire's figure wavered in the firelight and then disappeared in the shadows.

Lirrel inhaled a shaky breath and touched her fingers to her sweating brow. "Come on," she whispered hoarsely to Alwir. "I can't do this very long."

As Alwir and Lirrel started down the road, the Guards gave another shout. Moire appeared higher up the embankment, the longbow raised arrogantly above her head. The remaining Guards along the pier sounded the alarm, all of them spreading out along the grassy hill to find Moire.

"Now," Alwir ordered the moment he saw the pier was emptied of Guards.

Alwir held Lirrel's arm tightly as they walked so she would not fall while she concentrated on the image of Moire. Lirrel gave a low-throated growl and at once Moire's voice rose above the Guards' shouting an ancient battle cry. They reached the pier unnoticed by the Guards. Then they ran down its length, the loose boards drumming beneath their heels.

Alwir reached the end of the pier first and, grabbing the line, pulled in a longboat.

"Get in!" he said to Lirrel. She tumbled limply into the gently rocking longboat. Still crouched, Alwir tied off the line and rolled into the longboat after her. The freed boat began to bounce on the waves, the current pushing it toward the shore. Alwir raised his head enough to peer over the side and saw the Guards fanned out over the embankment searching in vain for Moire. Then he sat up and reached for the oars. Tugging them quickly and cleanly through the water, he rowed the longboat out beyond the pier and into the harbor.

"Lirrel?" Alwir called, worried as she huddled in silence at the bottom of the longboat.

"Ahal," came the weak reply. Lirrel sat up slowly and wrapped the shawl around her shoulders. She wiped her face with a trembling hand. "It's hard to call up the past. I am possessed by the thoughts of those that came before as well as their image. Moire was a strong woman then, filled with anger and passion. She denied her nature in order to make a life on Tynor's Rock. I felt I was strangling on her desperation." Lirrel rubbed a hand over her throat. "It's not the same for her now, but then life here was barely better than her imprisonment in Huld's forest."

There was a splash and the longboat pitched to one side. Two white hands appeared on the rim of the boat. Tayleb's head and shoulders rose out of the water as she pulled herself up on the side of the boat.

"Tayleb!" Lirrel called and reached a hand to help her into the boat.

Tayleb shook her head. "No, I am fine where I am," she replied. Then she smiled as Alwir gave a surprised cry at the luminous trail of jellyfish. Lirrel could just make out the rest of Tayleb's body in the eerie glow, her legs scissoring lazily in the water. The other Namires drifted a short distance away and Lirrel frowned, troubled by a feeling of division. They wanted to come closer, but they held back, their eyes watching Tayleb.

"Where's Dagar? And my parents?" Tayleb asked eagerly.

"They're not in the village," Alwir answered. "We think the Sileans have them on their ship."

Tayleb drew a quick breath. "All right. Give me the line. We'll tow the longboat through the water. If you row, the noise might alert someone on the ship."

Tayleb kicked and the glowing jellyfish scattered in the water. On the dark water, the moon sketched a broken pattern of light. Tayleb took the rope from Alwir and then glanced over her shoulder to the Namires. They scurried to join her. Stroking the water they towed the longboat silently across the harbor toward the Silean ship.

"Tayleb," Lirrel whispered, leaning over the side to be closer to Tayleb's head. "Tayleb, what's wrong?"

Tayleb swallowed a mouthful of water and then spouted it back into the waves. "I'll tell you later."

Lirrel leaned back as a growing anxiety settled around her shoulders. She could sense Alwir's fatigue and the faint rhythm of his throbbing wound. She heard anguish in the Namires' thoughts and angry confusion in Tayleb's. And as she looked out at the black riggings of the Silean warship, her dread increased.

"Dagar," she cried softly, afraid for him. Her fears drifted on the currents of air that snapped the shrouds and halyards of the ship and fluttered the flags on the mast. She needed reassurance, the feel of Dagar's presence. A breeze circled the ship and returned carrying the metallic taste of blood.

The Namires towed the longboat to the stern of the ship, stowing it in the shadow of the rudder. High above them the broad hull was checkered with squares of golden light spilling from the windows of the captain's quarters. A window opened with a snap of its hinges and a half-eaten apple was tossed into the sea. Alwir and Lirrel withdrew into the rudder's shadow as their boat floated peacefully beneath the window.

"Damn these Oran bastards!" a voice cursed. "Frigging kill the whole lot of them and be done with it."

"Well, you've almost succeeded," came a curt reply.

In the gold light Lirrel saw Alwir's face harden. His lips formed a soundless curse.

"That's my father, Re Aston," he said to Lirrel, the words forced from between clenched teeth.

"I told you, Islanders are not ordinary peasants. They don't tattle with a little bruising!" Re Aston was saying.

"There's no other way to make them sing. Just wait," reasoned the second voice calmly. "I'm telling you, Re Aston, have patience. When they come around again—"

"—if they come around again. Z'blood, you're a hard man, Re Torres," Re Aston complained.

"Even the strong ones break. And before they die, they sing for me. It's just a matter of time."

"One's already dead without telling you anything."

"No more," Alwir said thickly and without another word of explanation slid quietly over the side of the longboat. The boat rocked with his passing.

"Alwir," Lirrel called softly.

His head resurfaced, his mouth gasping at the shock of the cold water. "Wait here," he said brokenly, "but be prepared to pull away quickly." Then he ducked his head underwater again and began swimming alongside the ship.

"I'll go with him," Tayleb said. "He may need my help." She turned to Kire. "Give me your knife," she demanded. Unhappily, Kire handed over a netted bag that carried a short-handled knife. Tayleb slipped the bag over her neck and rested it against her back. With a small splash and a flick of her white soles she dove into the water after Alwir.

Alwir shivered as he swam to the middle of the ship, looking for the ladder built into its planks. Though his teeth chattered he was grateful that the cold momentarily dulled the throbbing of his head wound. He saw the ladder nestled between the channels where the shrouds were secured. He reached for it gratefully and hauled himself out of the water.

His hands numbed, he could scarcely feel the rough wooden rungs. He stopped to rest, his head leaning against the tarred wood, as he tried to catch his breath. Briefly he praised Faul, remembering when he had served on the *Marigold*. There wasn't a member of her crew who had not spent time either mastheaded atop the ship or lowered down to the waterline of the hull to scrape barnacles. His hands reached out and his feet followed, planting themselves firmly on the slippery ladder.

He was halfway up the side when he felt the wood vibrate with another body. He glanced down and saw Tayleb climbing up behind him. Though he wished she had not come, it was too late to stop her.

He continued climbing though his arms ached and his knees scraped against the hull. The ship seemed unusually quiet to him as he peered over the gangway. A galley door opened, and a long rectangle of light spilled over the deck.

Alwir swore as he spotted the three bound figures huddled

next to the mainmast. They were slumped, their heads bowed like weary sleepers'. The door to the galley slammed shut and the deck was returned to the shadows.

Alwir cautiously swung his leg over the gangway, alert for the Guards. He crouched behind a hatch, waiting for Tayleb. She slipped easily over the gangway, her naked skin gleaming like that of a newly caught fish.

"Where are they?" she whispered in his ear.

"Over there, by the mainmast. Z'blood, I've no knife to free them."

"Here," she said and tugged at the little bag around her back. She pulled out a short, curved knife. The handle was whalebone, the grip indented with ridges for the fingers.

"Where did you get this?" he asked, surprised at the unusual blade.

"The Namires."

Alwir's fingers fit neatly into the ridged handle. He felt better, now that he was armed. "Stay close," he warned.

Alwir crept across the smooth planks of the deck, taking care not to trip over the coils of rope. By the mast, he knelt down to the bound trio.

The first was Teck. One touch of his shoulder and Alwir knew he was dead. He grabbed Tayleb behind him, afraid that she might cry out. He spoke quietly. "Teck is dead."

She moaned, her shoulders going limp. Then she reached out a hand and cradled Teck's downturned face. Her palm came away sticky with blood.

Moire's head stirred as Alwir's knife cut into her bonds.

"No," she said, her voice slurred. "Forget me. Free Dagar."

"We'll free you both," Alwir insisted, sawing the short-bladed knife deeper into the ropes.

"No," Moire's voice hissed. Alwir looked more closely and saw her battered face. Her jaw was broken, her swollen eyes hollowed with pain. "I've other wounds. I'm dying."

Alwir's hand curled into a fist. He wanted to shout with rage. But he forced himself to remain steady and obey Moire's request. Tayleb leaned beside her mother, her strangled cries almost more than Alwir could stand.

"Dagar," Alwir said, nudging the slumped body gently. He was relieved when Dagar's head lifted drowsily.

"What are you doing here?" Dagar asked dreamily as Alwir sawed with rapid strokes through the ropes.

"Rescuing you," Alwir said tersely. Like Moire, Dagar's face was battered, his lips swollen and bleeding. "Can you stand?" Alwir asked as the last rope fell away and Dagar's body tumbled forward.

"I think so," he answered, sounding more alert. "Just help me."

Dagar unfolded stiffly and, with a moan, raised himself on trembling arms.

"Z'blood, Dagar. What have the bastards done to you?" Alwir asked. Dagar clung like a drowning man to Alwir's arms as he struggled to his feet.

Alwir wrapped an arm around Dagar's waist and half dragged the staggering boy toward the railing. Tayleb still knelt beside Moire, holding the limp hand and weeping. Alwir saw in Moire's eyes the wide-open stare of the dead. "Come on, Tayleb," he urged. "We must get off the ship."

Tayleb wiped the tears off her face and shuddered with a final sob. Then, seeing Dagar wobbling at Alwir's side, she joined them, lending a second arm to support Dagar.

Dagar stumbled over the coiled rope and groaned, his body suddenly going slack. His chin drooped and Alwir's knees buckled as Dagar's weight lurched forward.

"Dagar, stay with us," Alwir encouraged.

"By all means," cracked a voice from behind them. "Stay with us. Unless you wish a bolt through the woman's throat."

Alwir froze, one hand gripped around Dagar's waist. The other hand, holding the knife, was hidden from the speaker by Dagar's body.

"Turn around," the voice ordered. "Slowly."

Alwir glanced at Tayleb. "Jump," he mouthed to her. She stared at him, rigid and unmoving.

"I said turn around," the voice commanded again, "or the girl dies."

Alwir's eyes lowered to the knife. "When I turn, jump," he

whispered again. This time Tayleb nodded, understanding. She let go of Dagar. Dagar roused himself and, though weak, Alwir felt his body brace.

Alwir rotated slowly, one hand still supporting Dagar. He had to judge where the voice was coming from. He guessed that the voice belonged to Re Torres, the man his father had been talking to in the captain's quarters. The man who had tortured Moire and Teck. Alwir's thoughts fired rapidly as he chanced everything on one move.

Three-quarters of the way around, he shouted, "NOW!" to Tayleb and spun to face the man, flinging the Namire blade hard in the direction of the voice.

The world fractured as Alwir's mind grappled to follow the blade. Behind him, he heard Tayleb grunt softly as she flung herself over the side. A splash followed. The blade left his hand, flying toward a Silean, who at the same time lifted a crossbow. But another man darted in the blade's path, shoving the Silean to one side with a loud warning.

The warning quickly changed into a garbled cry as the knife buried itself in the man's chest.

"Father!" Alwir cried out stunned, seeing Re Aston fall against Re Torres, his hands grasping the Silean's shoulders for support. Re Aston coughed and blood spattered the Silean's uniform.

"Get off, you frigging whore's shit!" Re Torres shouted as Re Aston's falling body knocked him off balance. The crossbow slipped from his hands, the bolt discharging harmlessly into the coiled ropes. Re Torres swore furiously, shoving the dying man away from him.

The galley doors opened, the light blocked by more Guards summoned by the sound of Re Torres' rantings.

Alwir helped Dagar up over the side of the ship's railing. He watched as Dagar fell into the waiting sea and then, heaving himself over the side, jumped in after him.

The fall into the water was brief. And in that fall, Alwir saw again his father, dying from the knife that his own hand had cast. The waves splashed against the hull, reaching up with whitened arms of foam to receive him. When his body collided with the sea Alwir screamed in rage. He had hated his father; feared him as a child and then despised him when he'd tried to force him into the life of a Reader. At Firefaire, Alwir had felt betrayed when his father abandoned him to the gallows.

He should not feel as he did at this moment, the sea slashing him with its sharp, cold fingers. He should not feel shame. And yet he did. His body sunk below the waves, seeking a deeper coldness that would end the cascade of emotions. He had killed his father; his hate should have been satisfied. But he grieved for the man, grieved for an imperfect love mingled in the hate.

A hand reached for him down in the water and, refusing to let go, dragged him to the surface. Around him the water seethed with the brilliant shine of the phosphorous jellyfish. Looking up, Alwir saw it was Tayleb dragging him to the surface. As his head broke the water, Tayleb shouted in his ear.

"Get to the boat. They're shooting at us."

"Get rid of the light!" Alwir choked as a Silean bolt jetted into the waves near them.

"We had to find you and Dagar in the dark water," Tayleb snapped.

A second twang was followed by a shrill scream. Mari thrashed wildly in the water, and the white foam was stained red. Another bolt pounded into the water and Kana's body disappeared beneath the rippling waves.

Tayleb stirred the water fiercely, scattering the dim light of the jellyfish. "Away," she trilled to Kire on the other side of the longboat. "Pull the boat away!"

Dagar and Lirrel lay flat in the bottom of the longboat, Lirrel's black shawl covering them both. Alwir clung to the sides of the boat, his legs kicking wildly. At the prow of the longboat, Kire and Tammi hauled the line, frantically driving the longboat through the waves. One more bolt exploded toward the water and with terrifying accuracy slammed into Tammi's back. She floundered and then slipped into the dark sea. With a cry of anguish, Kire released her hold on the line and dove beneath the water to her dying sister.

The longboat seemed to drift despite Alwir's weakening efforts to push it out of range of the crossbow. Suddenly Tayleb was beside him, her hands clinging to him, shaking him as if to tear him from the sides of the boat.

"Dead! They're all dead!" she cried.

"Tayleb," Lirrel called weakly from the longboat. "Call the water from above and I will stir the air to shroud us."

"I don't know how!"

"Think of mist."

The wind stirred, a sudden breeze scudding over the water. White foam spumed forth, breaking into a fine shower of water droplets. The wind continued to rise, twisting the drops of water higher. As Alwir looked up he saw a column of spinning water stretching up over the longboat. Streamers of water dripped from the funnel. Tayleb's hand gripped his shoulder, her face tilted toward the rising column of water. She exhaled and the water burst from the confines of the funnel, dissolving into a thick-misted spray.

The wind circled around, distributing the freed drops into the formless mass of a cloud. The moonlight paled as the longboat drifted into a thick pearl-gray mist. Water clung to his face like a wet cloth and when Alwir inhaled he felt as if he was drowning. He heard the shouted curses of the Sileans, but soon even that was muffled and then silenced as the longboat was shrouded in the dense mist.

"Go," Tayleb said to Alwir. "Get in the boat. I'll pull the line." Her head slipped under the water, her hair fanning out on the surface just before it streamed behind her as she swam away. Exhausted and numbed with cold, Alwir hauled himself into the longboat. He lay down beside Lirrel, whose arms wrapped protectively around Dagar. Dagar slept fitfully and Alwir could hear the whistle of his labored breathing. Alwir found Tayleb's black shawl, still reasonably dry. He covered his head and shivering body with it.

"Dagar?" he asked.

"Alive," came Lirrel's tired reply. "But only just."

"And you?"

"I hardly know myself," she said.

The water lapped against the sides of the boat as Tayleb, somewhere ahead of them in the water, guided it through the mist. Alwir's eyes closed, and then snapped open again, seeing the knife strike his father. Had Re Aston known it was Alwir? Had he shoved himself against Re Torres to prevent the man from shooting his son or was he protecting the Silean from Alwir's attack? Despite the cold of his body, Alwir's thoughts burned feverishly. He could not shield himself from the memory of his father's death. It pried his eyes open to view and then review that one terrible moment.

A sob shook him loose from the grip of his thoughts. It was Lirrel weeping loudly as she lay at the bottom of the longboat. He had never heard her cry before, not even when they had buried her father, Zein. And now sobs wracked her back and shoulders.

Alwir tried to offer comfort, but nothing he said seemed to penetrate the relentless chorus of her sobs.

It was exhaustion that finally quieted her, the sobs dissipating into whimpers. A few ragged sighs escaped before she settled into a deep sleep. Then Alwir, too, closed his eyes, which were rimmed with salt and swollen with fatigue. The waves rocked the longboat like a cradle as it glided beyond the harbor and into the open sea.

Chapter Ten

"*I hear he's a monster.*" *Elena Re Manos smoothed a stray* lock of hair from her carefully done coif. She smiled at Antoni, her lips stained red with wine.

"Merely a good soldier," replied Antoni, brushing the tips of his mustache.

"It's the same thing," Elena insisted. "Women know that what makes a good soldier is a man's bestial nature."

"And honor and duty?"

"Second only to savagery and cunning." She laughed lightly and took another delicate sip from her glass.

She thinks she's clever, Antoni thought with irritation. He bent his head, his mouth close to her ear. "And isn't it true," Antoni murmured, "that women admire the beast far more than the man?"

She laughed again and tapped him on the shoulder. "You aren't suggesting that you fight battles to please women?" Her breath as she exhaled was moist with wine.

"Does it please you?" he asked.

Elena Re Manos took a small step back, away from the shadow

of Antoni's face. She smiled coyly. "I admit only to being curious about General Deveaux Re Silve. Is he as ugly as they
say?"

"Incomparably ugly."

"And his body?"

"Like a soldier's, hardened by training. Skilled with a
sword." Antoni watched a pink flush color Elena's cheeks. Her
eyes sparkled with private imaginings. Antoni went on in a harsh
whisper. "The dispatches also say that at Doberan he ordered
every man, woman, and child put to the sword. The corpses
were tossed into a common grave. He did the same at the village
of Gallen and he means to do the same at every Oran village
between the coast and Asturas." It was with a certain satisfaction that Antoni watched the color drain from Elena's face.

"So," she said coolly. "A true beast."

"And an intelligent soldier. He plans to end this rebellion
before it begins. Even if it means the murder of women and
children."

A thin ridge of disapproval creased her neat forehead and she
regarded Antoni with distaste. He had breached court protocol
by speaking something other than pleasant and inane conversation. Antoni bowed curtly as she rustled her skirts in preparation
to leave. He watched her go and grunted softly to himself. He
hadn't told her half of what the dispatches wrote about Deveaux's
bloody campaign.

He took another sip of wine and his eyes swept the room with
impatience. He had come to despise these court affairs. Once
they had been a political game to him, a matter of intrigue,
playing one Silean noble off another, securing his position as
Advisor against all other newcomers. At other times it had provided a game of seduction, the sport of undoing the reputation
of a loyal wife, or spoiling the virgin offering of a Silean family.
And when he had become the Upright Man, there was yet another secret pleasure in hearing their angry tales of being
robbed—while he carried their stolen treasures in his pocket.

Antoni's eyes came to rest on the Fire Queen Zorah. She stood
alone amid a circle of disinterested nobles. She, too, was
changed. She no longer wore the keen profile of youth that had

once made it painful to look at her. Then her coppery hair had flamed like the rising sun around the flawless cream-colored skin. Her green eyes had shone with arrogance, brightened by flickering yellow flames. Her body had been slim, her breasts small and hard over a narrow waist and a long, nearly hipless torso.

But Zorah's youth had vanished with the Uprising of Sadar. Her face was softer, her cheekbones more prominent, her chin and jaw rounded. The fiery hair was rusted and a few pale strands denied any color. The skin puffed slightly around the green eyes that were now hard as malachite stones. Her body had matured, her shoulders wider and her breasts sloped. Her hips swelled beneath the narrow waist. Antoni saw that the arrogance was tempered by an aloof dignity. She seemed to no longer care for the court, nor the pettiness of Silean affairs.

Antoni guessed that in the Fire Queen's mind other battles were being fought and it was difficult to say who was winning. Re Aston had been right, he reflected, when he said that the Queen was weakening. Antoni had felt the gradual drain of power in the past months. Compared to her, he'd only a small measure of magic, and still he sensed it slipping away from his grasp, as a man loses a hat to a brisk wind. He had fought to gain what little power he had; he didn't want to lose it to Zorah's failing obsession with youth.

Antoni motioned to a servant for more wine and as he did he was jolted out of his musings by the sight of the Petticoat, standing at Re Fortuna's elbow. His mind issued a warning to turn away, but he hesitated, curious at seeing her at the court. The Petticoat looked across the room and met his gaze. Her brown eyes widened with recognition. An enigmatic smile appeared on her face as she lowered her gaze again.

"Frigging whore!" Antoni swore, "she's marked me." Antoni crossed the room with one thought rapping in his mind. *Dead.* He wanted her dead. There was no way he could risk the whore fingering him.

Stupid bastard, Antoni thought of Re Fortuna as he neared the mismatched pair. He wondered how the man intended to explain his whore at the court. And noting the way the other noblewomen avoided them, it was obvious to everyone but Re

Felice that the Petticoat did not belong here. Antoni smoothed his beard and assembled a smile on his face.

"Re Felice, it seems you are well favored this evening," Antoni greeted him.

"Indeed," Re Felice answered. "The wine is excellent." He was a portly man, his complexion ruddy, a sheen of sweat on his forehead and balding pate.

Antoni waited for the nobleman to present the Petticoat. Re Felice averted his gaze, seeming to ignore the young woman standing at his side. But Antoni was not so easily put off, knowing that etiquette would demand that Re Felice acknowledge the woman. The moment passed uneasily until Re Felice gave a small shrug of defeat.

"May I present my . . . niece." He stumbled over the word. "My niece, Sara Re Felice," he said, sounding more confident.

The Petticoat arched an amused eyebrow at Re Felice but gave a graceful curtsy to Antoni. She had been well dressed for the occasion, the white petticoats of her trade hidden beneath a dress of blue silk. Her black hair had been coiled with a small string of pearls. Expensive pearls, Antoni thought, disturbed by the easy way this young woman had insinuated herself among Silean nobility. But neither the pearls nor the dress of Silean make could disguise her Oran face, with its high cheekbones and olive skin. Her dark eyes glittered like those of a child pleased with a prank.

"And how do you find the court, Sara?" Antoni asked, concealing his agitation.

"Very interesting, sir. There is much to see. And much to learn." Accusation sparkled in the Petticoat's dark eyes.

Antoni wanted to get her alone, away from the protective shelter of Re Felice. He wanted to strangle her swan's neck before she exposed him. Re Felice laid a heavy hand on the Petticoat's shoulder, silently declaring his ownership of the girl.

"Let me present your niece to the Fire Queen, Re Felice," Antoni offered, knowing full well the man could neither duplicate nor refuse the honor.

Re Felice's eyes narrowed as he sensed he was outmaneuvered. Reluctantly he removed his hand from the girl's shoulder.

Antoni gave her his arm, which she took with an eager curiosity. He steered her through the crowd, feeling in her arm her pulse racing excitedly. All caution was erased from her face, her lips parted in expectation, as she stared in wonder at the Fire Queen. Antoni was distracted by the alarms that clanged furiously in his head. This street brat had marked him and had managed by her own cunning to be here at the court. As he glanced sideways at the delicate profile he briefly thought it a shame and a waste of talent that she had to die.

The Fire Queen Zorah inhaled slowly, aware of the subtle reek of copper mingled with the scents of Silean perfume. Her pulse throbbed in her temples as her heart drummed anxiously of its own accord. The crowded room flickered in her vision. Her dry felt stretched over the bones of her face. She exhaled with caution. The former certainty of her world was now assaulted by panicked moments where it seemed that too quick a breath, too sharp a turn of her head, and her solid existence might shatter. Zorah commanded herself to remain calm, her hands carefully folded together over her thighs. The Silean nobles eddied near her, drifting close and then away from her cold quiet.

Zorah swallowed thickly, her throat parched.

"Would you care for some wine, madam?" The Firstwatch Gonmer was standing attentively nearby and Zorah realized the woman had been watching her closely.

Zorah allowed a brief smile. "Yes." The Firstwatch snapped her fingers at her page, Lais. Lais fetched a gold-rimmed glass of wine and presented it to the Queen.

Zorah took a small sip and was grateful when the warm wine slid easily enough over her dry tongue. She took another sip and then sighed. The attack of fear ebbed, her pulse slowing to normal and her vision becoming steady once more.

"Look how they enjoy themselves at my expense," Zorah said, glaring at the nobles assembled in the stateroom.

The Firstwatch Gonmer silently nodded her assent.

"Like carrion crows. Cawing over the scraps no matter how stinking."

Across the room the Regent Re Ilario burst out into loud laughter at something confided in his ear by a young Silean woman. He took her by the hand and pranced back a few steps, indicating to the musicians that he wished to dance. They picked up their instruments and began playing a Silean dance tune, the music filling the stateroom with a gay noise. From around the room, couples joined in, creating sets of dancers as they patterned themselves on the tiled floor.

"Would Madam care to dance?" a young noble asked the Queen.

Zorah stared derisively at him. Her eyes filled with yellow flame. She didn't recognize his face and could only guess that he had recently arrived from Silea. That would explain his misplaced boldness, if nothing else.

"No," Zorah answered curtly. As he left to ask another woman, Zorah felt the sharp pang of regret. There was a time when she would not have refused a dance. When she would have had men stirred into duels for the simple privilege of partnering her in the dance. But no more. No one knew the demanding concentration it took to keep Oran intact. The whirlpool of power that insulated her from the flow of time had grown more constricting as Oran magic bled faster and faster into its narrowing stream. She felt encased, her arms pinned to her sides as the eroding magic hemmed her ever tighter. She could hardly hear the dance music for the deafening winds of Chaos, howling from beyond the fragile boundaries of Oran's cradle.

Zorah took another sip of wine and frowned. A new sound vibrated against her eardrum, like the angry buzzing of a wasp caught beneath a glass. It grew louder, disrupting her concentration. She searched the dancers trying to find its source. The silk dresses of the women merged into a swirling pattern of shifting color, jeweled combs and brooches casting spangles of light. Zorah squinted, her vision flickering again as the noise sawed against her molars. She unfocused her eyes, letting the colors of the silk skirts wash over her sight.

And then she gasped, her hand snapping the stem of her wineglass. Seized by fear, she was oblivious to the bloody gash in her palm. Amid the bleeding colors of the Silean dresses she saw the unmistakable halo of light. An aura of magic circled one man, silently proclaiming his Oran power. She drew back, terrified to see that no one color identified it as a single element. Instead it was streaked with spirals of white, blue, and green light, a mixture of elements. All that was missing was the brilliant red of her own fire element.

Zorah focused her gaze and saw the man approaching her, a young Oran woman draped on his arm.

"Traitor!" Zorah hissed. "Frigging bastard!" Zorah flung the broken wineglass to the ground. The bowl and stand splintered into fragments on the tiled floor. Her hair burst forth with a shower of sparks, and the stench of burning copper sizzled in the air. The musicians stopped playing, a few notes dwindling away in confusion. The dancers on the floor looked around in alarm.

Antoni Re Desturo gathered himself beneath Zorah's flame-filled eyes. His face paled and the pupils of his black eyes gleamed red. A feral grin mocked her as he waited for her to speak.

"Madam," Re Ilario said angrily, shoving his way between the stilled dancers. He glanced quickly at Antoni and the Petticoat and continued to approach the Queen. "Surely you can't be offended that the Advisor seeks his pleasure—"

Wordlessly, Zorah snatched Gonmer's sword from her belt. She raised the blade's tip to the Regent's astonished face.

Re Ilario took a hasty step back. "Madam, I insist—" he tried again.

Zorah paid him no attention, her rage centered on the shining aura that circled Antoni's head. How had he managed it? she thought wildly. How had she failed to see it before now? The coppery sheen of her hair rippled with a hot wind and a static charge crackled in the air.

"Get out of my way," she snarled as Re Ilario positioned himself between her and Antoni.

Re Ilario gestured to the Guards standing attentively around the sides of the room. Instantly they drew their weapons and pushed their way through the unsettled crowd to join the Regent and Antoni. "You overstep your authority, madam. This man is a Silean, and my Advisor."

The Firstwatch Gonmer grabbed her page's sword and came to stand beside the Queen.

Zorah lowered her sword a fraction. "Get a Reader," she demanded. She saw Antoni's smile vanish. So, she thought, he had hoped his silence might buy his way out of here.

"For whom?" Re Ilario protested.

"Your Advisor."

"Ridiculous. Antoni Re Desturo is Silean. Not some Oran trash from the country."

Zorah raised the blade inches away from Re Ilario's throat.

"Call one."

"I will not. It is a breach of the treaty. You have no right—"

Re Ilario's words were silenced as without warning Zorah slashed the sword across his throat. Blood sprayed out over Zorah's hand, hissing as it steamed with the heat of her fury. Re Ilario crumpled to the ground amid screams and cries of outrage. The young woman at Antoni's side dragged him back just as the Silean Guard drove forward to attack.

Gonmer stepped before the rigid body of the Queen to meet their advance. With clean precision her sword raked across the first Guard before slashing the next.

Zorah's eyes followed Antoni's flight from the stateroom. She was trembling, her heart pounding wildly. The room flickered as if caught in a net of flames. And in the clashing of swords and the angry shouts of the Guards, Zorah felt the thin veneer of her control crack.

She dropped the sword and crouched, terrified as the howling winds of Chaos blustered through the fissures and snatched away her breath. The room shook, the vibrations subtle at first and then growing more violent. The dance floor buckled and marble tiles were popped from their grout and pitched crashing into walls. The plaster mortar crumbled, falling like hard snow on the clamoring dancers fleeing the stateroom. The exposed tower stones began to grind, chips of rock spitting into the air. And once dislodged from their mortar, the stones were lifted by the howling winds into the night sky, where they burst into a streak of white dust.

"My Queen," Gonmer shouted at Zorah. She grabbed Zorah by the shoulders, forcing her upright on her knees. Zorah's body was stiff, her arms clutching her sides. She couldn't breathe, the drag of power twisting a noose around her neck. Gonmer held her face and yelled, "Stop it! Z'blood, stop this, or we will all be destroyed!"

Zorah wrenched herself free of Gonmer's grasp and crawled to the torn gap in the wall of the tower. The cold wind snatched at strands of her hair and chilled her heated face. More stones were freed and cast into the sky. Clinging to the skeletal remains of the wooden frame, Zorah saw the city of Beldan spread out below her. Gold and blue lights shone from the windows and in the distance Zorah saw the dull orange glow of Scroggles, its fires never quenched. The moon cast white and green spangles across the harbor and it seemed to Zorah that everywhere she looked she saw the auras of Orans as yet uncrushed. Their magic glimmer taunted her as the world disintegrated around her.

She shouted with terrified rage into the wind, and there came an answer from the deadly rumble in the city streets.

Zorah couldn't see the earthquake, but she could feel it in her cracking bones. Stricken with pain she saw the side of a building spin past her, its plastered walls white in the moonlight, the lathing jagged ribs of torn wood.

Zorah curled her body over her knees and began to weep. She clenched her teeth and struggled to contain her panic. She had to hold fast to what was left of her world. She stared up through the blasted ceiling and searched the cold stillness of the stars, clapping her hands over her ears to shut out the keening winds of Chaos. With the practiced discipline of the Fire Sword, she banished her emotions and reached in her mind for a place of utter stillness. She imagined the Fire Sword, straight and pure, like an infinite ribbon of steel with no beginning and no end. She placed herself on its blade like a small gleam of light in an endless road of light. Fear and rage dissolved in the shining light of the sword and a measure of control returned to her. The fierce rapping of her heart slowed, the strangling rope of fleeing magic loosening its grip on her throat. Zorah inhaled deeply. As she exhaled, she withdrew her hands from her ears, and heard silence. The scraping tower stones settled into a tentative peace.

Zorah sagged with exhaustion.

"Madam?" Gonmer ventured.

"It's finished," Zorah said. She gazed down at her filthy dress, her hair lying in tangled knots on her chest. The gash on her palm crusted over with a scab as the magic of Oran slowly healed her once more. She turned to the room, dismayed by the destruction. Re Ilario's body lay sprawled, blood pooling in the dust. Slain Guards joined the ruins of broken tables and chairs. The only light came from the moon, shining through the huge gap in the tower wall.

Gonmer emerged from the shadows like a ghost. She walked carefully, stepping over the remains and kicking aside the debris in her path. "Are you well, madam?" she asked.

"Well enough," Zorah replied. The joints of her knees cracked as she stood and turned slowly to take in the full measure of destruction. "Well enough for now," she murmured and limped from the stateroom.

On the street, the Petticoat and Antoni hid near the gates of the Queen's Keep. The ground had finally stopped bucking and heaving beneath them. They could hear the sounds of people wailing and shouting in the streets. The air was thick with smoke and dust where the old buildings had been blasted into rubbled heaps. They had seen the wall of an inn ripped off and sent hurtling into the sky and watched as cobblestones skipped along the swaying streets like river-washed stones. Now, in the uneasy aftermath, The Petticoat tugged at Antoni's arm as he lingered by the Keep.

"Come on. Butcherboys will be out."

Without warning, Antoni turned and slapped her hard across the face. She staggered beneath the blow, her hand raised to the bruised cheek.

"If it weren't for you, you frigging whore, I'd not be on the run. I'd scaffer you and be done with it." Antoni grabbed a dagger from his boot and lunged toward the cringing girl.

"I said nothing! I didn't give you away," she cried, dodging the slashing dagger.

The blade ripped through the silk of her skirts. She stumbled back into the wall of an inn. Antoni pinned her against the bricks, his dagger drawn up alongside her neck. She closed her eyes, her chest heaving with fright.

"Please sir, don't cut me," she pleaded. Her eyes snapped open again. "I'll hide you."

Antoni paused as the makings of a plan formed out of her desperate offer. He pushed the point of his dagger close to her earlobe to hold the Petticoat still while he thought it over. Perhaps it was time to change his course. The Queen was losing control—after tonight that much was obvious. He would get what he wanted faster as the Upright Man than as Antoni Re Desturo. The Queens' quarter knot would come to Beldan, and like the New Moon, he, too, had his spies.

Antoni stared coldly at the Petticoat's terrified face. She was smart and, with the right coin, loyal. It made sense. He would use her for now, get her to find out what he needed to know. He could always kill her later if she became a problem.

Antoni resheathed his dagger in the cuff of his boot, his hard gaze never leaving the Petticoat.

"I'll give you one chance, my pretty-pretty."

The Petticoat stifled a relieved sigh. Then she smiled thinly. "This way, sir," she said, pointing down a smoke-filled alley. "You can stay at my place. It's just over the Maidenhead. That is," she said looking worriedly at the surrounding ruins, "if the Maidenhead is still standing."

"Pray that it is, girl," Antoni growled in reply. He reached for his silk scarf in the pocket of his cloak and tied it around the lower part of his face. Then he gave the Petticoat a shove to let her know he was ready to leave.

Slipper and Kai stood outside on the High Street, watching a fire burn out of control. An inn had crumbled into ruins, its hearth fire spreading to the closely packed buildings of the street. A woman in the upper window was screaming. Her hair had caught on fire and her white shift blazed golden in the firelight.

Kai muttered a curse as flames shot up along the woman's arms. Still screaming, the woman flung herself from the window to the street below. The crowd scattered in terror, and then gathered again around the woman lying in the street. Someone covered her with a shawl, smoke drifting through the weave of the fabric.

"That's it," Kai growled to Slipper. "We can't stay in the tunnels no more." Furiously she twisted the black hair at her temples. "If it weren't for Neive we'd all be buried in Market Square tunnel."

It was Neive who had felt the tremors first. His earth element had warned him and he cried out to the others to flee the tunnels. Scurrying like rats, the New Moon bolted out of hiding just as the earth began its rumbling and shifting.

"Where do we go then?" asked Slipper. He was watching the crowd too, marking the children that appeared between the shoulders of the adults. Occasionally one would turn, looking for him. Slipper was counting heads, making sure that all of his Flock had gotten out.

"Don't know yet. But one thing is certain," Kai said sourly. "The Queen can't hold on much more. It's time to fight in the open. Start cutting down the butcherboys ourselves."

"What about Jobber and the rest?" Slipper asked, drawing Kai away from the crowd. A squad of Guards had arrived and were pushing the crowd back from the burning building with their swords, preventing anyone from helping those still trapped inside.

"Z'blood," Kai said shaking her head. "They'd better come soon. Between that Deveaux scaffering us in the countryside and the Queen doing us here in Beldan we don't have too long to sit and wait on it. Get a message out to Sadar. The time to move is now."

Slipper and Kai turned up Finnia's Alley, dimly lit by spluttering torches.

"Oy, mistress," called out a hoarse voice and Kai halted beneath the shadows. A lighterman shuffled toward her, his longhandled torch settled on his shoulder. His black coat flapped in the breeze.

He entered a circle of cast light and Kai saw that it was Master Farian, a Guildmaster she had met in prison. His disguise as a lighterman was effective; she would not have known him had he not called to her. He chuckled at her surprised expression.

"I had not thought to fool you," he said.

"How did your people fare in the tunnels?" Slipper asked.

"Most got out." Farian shuddered. "Some were lost, but until day, I won't know for certain how many."

"No more," said Kai. "We meet above ground now."

"I've always hated it below. Look," Farian said edging closer to them. "I say we meet at Crier's Forge. It's abandoned now, and the Guards aren't seen up there anymore."

"Yeah, all right," Kai said. "We meet firstwatch. We've the weapons from the armory. It's time to use them."

"We're outnumbered," Farian reminded her.

"Not for long. If you were Silean and the whole frigging city was going up in smoke would you think it worth your life to stay?"

Farian gave a wry grin. "Maybe not."

"Mark my words," Kai said sharply, "they'll be lining the harbors, paying any sum for safe passage back to Silea."

"We'll do it the way the New Moon did at Sadar," Slipper said, smiling proudly at Farian.

"Get in, get out," Farian nodded in agreement.

"Tomorrow, then," Kai said briskly. "Firstwatch, Crier's Forge. We'll settle it then. Don't be late."

Farian feigned a look of astonishment. "Uh'm a ligh'erman, ain't I?" he said in the thick accent of Beldan's poor. "It ain't firstwatch 'til I say it." And then his expression sobered. "Butcherboys are out big tonight."

"The Queen does it," Kai answered glumly. "Kicks over a stone and turns out the maggots."

"Just don't step on any," Farian warned. He pulled the brim of his hat down in farewell and continued his way down the street. At the corner, they heard his hoarse, rasping voice bawling out the hour. And then he turned and was gone, the slim shaft of the lighterman's pole disappearing last.

* * *

Wet snow pelted Sadar's Keep, forming huge white drifts on the peaks at its back and a smooth blanket in the Plains below. In the common room and the kitchens people gathered in subdued conversations or nodded over smoking pipes, waiting. They waited for the storms to end and for news of their villages. A small detachment led by Eneas had left Sadar almost a month ago for the southern villages, hoping to recruit Orans and sympathetic Sileans. In the aftermath of their departure, the storms descended on the Keep, making it difficult for messengers to send word. Isolated in the mountains, the people of Sadar's Keep waited and watched hopefully for riders.

Shedwyn sat at a long wooden table in the kitchen and spun yarn. Fat rolls of carded wool transformed into slender thread as she twirled the spindle by her knee. She tried not to think of Eneas. She tried not to worry about him. But the dull ache in her hips, the tenderness in her breasts, reminded her of her pregnancy and brought her thoughts back to Eneas's promise to return.

Stupid girl, she scolded herself. How could you let this happen now? And then she smiled sadly at the thread slipping between her fingers. How could she not?

She picked up the spindle, wound on the new thread, and dropped the spindle again, giving it a hard twist. Wool spun between her fingers into thread.

You wanted a child, she told herself. You wanted Eneas's child to be a bridge between Sileans and Orans, to prove that a future together as one country, one people, was possible. Shedwyn sighed tiredly. A child born in a time of war to be a promise of peace.

Perhaps she hoped for too much.

She looked up from her spinning at the faces of the women gathered in the kitchen. Many of them had husbands or brothers in the army that had left with Eneas. And she saw her own worry reflected in their quiet, concerned faces. One woman sat between her two children, her arms draped protectively around the shoulders of her young sons. Shedwyn put a hand to her belly, knowing for the first time the burden of a mother's love. Shedwyn knew it was not for her husband nor herself that the woman feared, but for the uncertain future of her children. The boys drowsed sleepily in the warmth of her embrace, ignorant of their mother's fear, aware only of the love that passed between them.

Shedwyn lowered her eyes to her spinning again and watched anxiously as the thread twisted between her fingers, measuring out a smooth and perfect length of yarn. How long would it take? How long must they wait?

"Get your sword up!" Shefek shouted at Jobber. His face was mottled white and red with fury, his hands jerking up an imaginary sword with a frustrated gesture.

On the training floor, Faul thrashed Jobber soundly, her sword crashing into Jobber's ineffective defense.

"Up! Or she'll cut off your head!"

Jobber raised her sword, her weary arms shaking. Faul's wooden sword slammed against Jobber's blade. Jobber's grasp slipped, the sword drooping beneath the impact of Faul's strike and revealing an opening in her defense.

Faul swung the wooden sword overhanded and rapped it hard against Jobber's exposed collarbone.

"Frigging shit!" Jobber swore. Two hot smears of pain bloomed on her pale cheeks. Her hair glowed bright red, the metallic reek of copper mingled with the pungent scent of sweat. "I'm done in," she shouted at Shefek. "I won't fight with a sword."

"You will!" yelled Faul as she readied for another attack. "You have to," she insisted. The gray hair at her temples was nearly black from sweat, and though the room was cold, damp rings appeared on her shirt beneath her arms.

"No, Faul. I don't!" Jobber answered. She started to cast the sword away when Shefek caught her wrist. He closed his hand around her fingers, forcing her to keep hold of the sword's handle.

"Don't even imagine doing that," he whispered angrily. He squeezed hard and the blood drained from Jobber's hand.

"Damn you, Shefek," Jobber snapped wearily. "Let go." She glared into his gold glowing eyes. "Let go, or I'll burn your frigging fingers to the bone," she threatened.

Shefek released his hold, his eerie gaze never leaving her face. Jobber swallowed dryly, hating the coppery stink of her hair and the vague carrion odor of Shefek's rage. Her shoulders sagged but her hand clung unwillingly to the sword.

Faul grabbed Jobber by the shoulders and shook her angrily. "Stubborn arrogant bitch!" she shouted.

"No worse than yourself, Faul," Jobber retorted. Holding the sword between two hands she jerked her arms upward, breaking Faul's grasp on her shoulders. As Faul stumbled, Jobber started forward, her fist cocked for a punch.

Shefek jerked Jobber back by the collar of her shirt. He wedged his body between Faul and Jobber and shoved Jobber away. "Control yourself!" he said. "And you too!" he barked at Faul.

The trio stood apart, their harsh breathing punctuating the tense silence. Jobber felt strangled by her frustration. She looked at the sword in her hand as if it were an enemy.

Then she shook her head and her hair, made brittle with heat, rustled.

"I told you, Shefek and you, Faul. The sword ain't my way."

"Because you refuse to learn," Faul said in a clipped voice. Her jaw was tight, a tick rippling her cheek as she fought to keep her temper. "You are the only one. No one else can use the Fire Sword."

Jobber stared at the beams in the ceiling. "Faul, it don't matter what kind of sword it is, don't you see? It's still a frigging sword. We'd be better off letting you go on, with your blade. At least you know how to use it."

"The Fire Queen Zorah must be taken by another Fire Sword," Faul said.

"No," Jobber said hotly. "The Fire Queen Zorah must be taken by another Fire Queen. It ain't the sword."

Faul was shocked into an angry silence. Even Shefek tilted his head to stare quizzically at Jobber.

"How do you know that?" he demanded.

Jobber groaned, uncertain of why she had said it in the first place. At that moment it had sounded right to her. All the sweating and agonizing with the Fire Sword seemed so pointless. At the battle of Sadar, Zorah had almost succeeded because she had manipulated Jobber into wanting the power of the Fire Sword. It was Zorah who poured her soul, her life into the Fire Sword. But not Jobber.

"I'm going now," Jobber said to Faul and Shefek. "I've had enough."

Suddenly Jobber needed to be alone to think. She needed to be away from Faul's constant disapproval, from Shefek's overbearing superiority. They had boxed her into a corner, forced her into accepting their arguments, and in allowing it, Jobber knew she had lost something of herself. Her mouth tasted as if dry sand coated her tongue.

She replaced the training sword on the wall, aware of Faul and Shefek's thoughtful stares. They let her go without comment and, once outside in the corridor, Jobber gave a thirsty sigh. She wanted beer. Lots of beer. She'd even drink the wretched home brew they made at Sadar. Anything to wash away the taste of failure.

She walked down the steps, listening to the scrunching of the stones beneath her worn boots. It seemed the first time since Shefek's arrival that she had heard a sound other than Faul yelling at her or Shefek giving a long lecture on marital theory. "Moving without moving, action without action . . ." It seemed endless.

Jobber grinned in the darkened stairs. "The way of the sword is death," she intoned in imitation of Shefek. Frigging all, she rolled her eyes. Who cared? *Everything* led to death sooner or later. She struck a pose. "The way of the plow is death," she said sarcastically. Seeing how Sadar was filled to the rafters with half-starved peasants and laborers, it was at least as much of a truth for them as it was for the sword fighter.

Jobber lifted a heavy handful of hair off her neck. The stink of copper was gone. She knew that what made everything worse was that she loved Faul. Wanted Faul's admiration and respect. Wanted very much to be like Faul. Alone and set apart from others. Good with the sword, and coolheaded. Then Jobber laughed out loud at her own stupidity. Good with the sword Faul was, but coolheaded? Jobber shook her head thinking of the tick that rolled across Faul's cheek when she became furious. And maybe she wasn't as alone as Jobber once believed.

Jobber's smile faded as she thought of Shefek. She had entered Faul's chamber two nights ago without knocking. Shefek had been there, in Faul's bed. Jobber retreated hastily from the room and later was stung by jealousy. Though she had avoided sex, Jobber knew what it was. She had seen the whores on Blessing Street plying their trade often enough. But it had not occurred to her that it could have love or friendship attached to it. It wasn't so much that Jobber wanted to be where Shefek was, resting in Faul's bed. It was more the disappointment of knowing that Faul had reason to find sex worthy of her attention. It had seemed to Jobber that in following Faul's example, she might be able to avoid the complications of sex forever. Now, along with everything else, sex took its place next to the other unanswerable questions.

Jobber stopped at the door of the kitchens, catching the stench of burning copper. She frowned at her cool hair. It wasn't her. She put her hand on her chest and felt her heart hammering. She glanced around her, frightened by the growing sound of a low, rattling hum.

The old wooden door burst open and Shedwyn collided into her.

"Out!" she was shouting, giving Jobber a quick shove. "Get everyone out of the Keep. The earth moves!" Behind her in the kitchens, Jobber could see women snatching at shawls and children as they hurried out the doors into the courtyard. A baby wailed, sensing the mounting terror.

"What are you saying?" Jobber shouted, the humming in her ears becoming a loud roar.

"Sadar, something is happening to the earth." Shedwyn yelled her answer as she fled toward the common room. "We've got to get everyone out."

The Keep came alive with shouted warnings. People grabbed blankets and the few small possessions they had and went scurrying through the corridors. Animals penned-in for the night were freed, and they bleated and bawled as their hooves clattered over the stones. Some thought to take torches as they escaped into the snowy night.

Jobber glanced quickly up the stairs to where she had come. Faul and Shefek were still in the tower. She had to warn them. She leapt up the stairs two at a time. There was a loud rumble like thunder and a huge fissure split the tower open. Snow gusted into Jobber's face. The stairs above her exploded and she ducked, shielding her face from the flying debris. Jobber looked ahead and saw the stairs were gone, sheared away as a wedge of the tower was scraped free. The stones groaned and were carried aloft into the swirling snow.

Jobber stared openmouthed as chunks of stone from Sadar's Keep filled the night sky.

She scrambled down the remaining stairs, hearing them grind as they were torn loose behind her.

Jobber ran through the gutted kitchens. One wall was gone and the driving snow hissed in the dying hearth fire. Through the din of crashing stone Jobber heard someone crying. She looked around and in the cloud of dust and snow spotted a red knitted cap. A child was wearing it, sobbing loudly under a table.

"Come on!" Jobber shouted, bending down to stretch out a hand to the terrified child. Near the child Jobber saw his mother, lying dead. All Jobber could see of her was a hand streaked with dust and blood poking out of a pile of stones. The sobbing child clung desperately to the hand.

"Come on, let go and come now to me," Jobber coaxed.

The child cried louder and clung tighter.

"Come now, she's dead! She can't help you! You've got to come with me."

Another groan rumbled, and the old Keep heaved on its foundations.

"The whole frigging place is going to go!" Jobber shouted angrily at the terrified child.

She lunged under the table and dragged the child out by his ankle, trying to avoid getting kicked in the head by the flailing legs. Once freed she picked him up. He surprised her by throwing his hands around her neck and wrapping his legs tightly around her waist.

She hugged him close. "Come on. Let's get out of here."

She ran from the kitchens, her body hunched over the child. As she sprinted past the rounded backs of the ovens, she cursed, seeing them torn from the ground and lifted high into the air. They were carried aloft and then crushed. Shards of brick mingled with snow and drifted back to the earth.

Jobber kept running, seeing the gusting lights of torches moving across the open Plains of Sadar. She fled across the courtyard. Stopping short, the gates thundered angrily, protesting their destruction. The cornerstones bulged as if squatting deeper into the ground. And then with a sucking noise they were wrenched from their earthly sockets and thrown toward the sky.

"The whole frigging place is going into the Chaos!" Jobber cried out.

She continued running, wondering if Faul and Shefek had made it out of the tower in time.

As her legs lunged down the rocky slope toward the Plains, Jobber heard screeching overhead. She looked up and saw the black shape of a gigantic bird drifting down over the Plains. The wide, flapping wings stirred the snow. The wingtips curved upward as the creature banked against the wind. Two round golden eyes stared down at Jobber as it gave out another shriek. Jobber stopped in her tracks. The bird's body dipped downward as it turned and Jobber saw Faul, riding on the back, clinging to the ruffled feathers of its neck.

The giant bird stretched out taloned feet and prepared to land on the Plains. The wings flapped wildly and it settled clumsily on the ground, unable to stand without tilting from one side to the other. The long, curved neck lifted up from between the valley of its wings and it shrieked in frustration. Faul rolled off its back, just before the huge bird toppled sideways.

Even in the heavily falling snow, Jobber could see as the creature began to change its shape. She edged forward cautiously, watching the gigantic bird transform. As it became smaller and darker she saw less, but heard Shefek's familiar bellow. And when she was close enough, she saw Shefek standing beside Faul.

Faul covered him with a blanket as he continued to swear loudly.

Jobber stepped up to him, adjusting her hold on the child in her arms. She hesitated at the sight of Shefek's glowing yellow eyes.

"Z'blood, Shefek. What are you?"

"A Kirian, though not for much longer," he growled.

"One of them vultures with the swords," Jobber said, understanding Shefek at last.

"Look," Shefek said with a groan of despair, pointing behind Jobber.

Jobber turned back to the mountains and the Keep. Through the falling snow Jobber saw a deep black cavity, an emptiness where there had once been the Keep. On either side of the cavity, the tops of the peaks had also disappeared as if bitten off.

Shedwyn appeared out of the snow and stood beside Jobber. She gave Jobber a blanket and went to take the child from her arms. But the boy clung to Jobber, refusing to let go.

"It's all right," Jobber said, so Shedwyn wrapped the blanket around the both of them. "What's happening?" Jobber asked Shedwyn, looking back at the emptiness of the mountains.

"Zorah can't hold on to Oran's cradle anymore. It's all going back into the Chaos," Shedwyn answered.

"But why here?"

"The farthest place from Beldan, her own source of power, perhaps." Shedwyn's voice sounded flat and weary.

"And Huld?" Jobber asked.

"Still she holds. But she too is weak."

"Shedwyn," Jobber said, snow pelting her face with cold wet drops, "we can't stay here."

"I know. I've sent the others down to the woods. They may find a shelter there for the night."

"No," Jobber said, shaking her head. "I mean we can't wait for Lirrel to return to Sadar."

"To Beldan, then? Closer to Zorah?" Shedwyn asked.

"Yeah. Back to Beldan."

"Then you'd better take this," Faul said, handing Jobber the black scabbard of the Fire Sword.

Jobber eyed the sword and hoisted the child higher in her arms. "You carry it. My hands are full."

Then, with Shedwyn at her side, Jobber trudged through the snow, her head lowered against the wind and driving snow.

Chapter Eleven

Deveaux *shrugged deeper into his cloak, staring sullenly at the* lines of passing soliders. In the fading afternoon they looked tired, their faces gray, their eyes listless. Their footsteps shambled over the frost-hardened road. It was evident to Deveaux that their numbers were smaller, a fact that was not lost on his men. The village of Gallen had proved more challenging than he had thought possible. The Oran peasants had held out for three days. Though there had been no surprises, no giant birds such as at Doberan, the Orans had displayed surprisingly good military sense. The villagers had been battle trained; they had fought for their families and their land with discipline and with courage. Bravery had not been enough to help Gallen survive, Deveaux thought coldly, but it had been enough to inflict serious damage on his own troops, and their morale. His horse shifted restively underneath him, sensing Deveaux's agitation.

He had ordered the inhabitants buried, except for the twenty he had hanged from trees along the road to Gallen. There had been women among those hanged. Though it struck him as distasteful, he had said nothing when he saw the female corpses, stripped and mutilated. They would serve to restore the fighting spirit of his men.

The sun broke through low-lying clouds, its rays slanting over the tops of the trees. The gold light pierced the gloomy day and Deveaux's pulse quickened with nervous energy. He planned to take the village of Lauriel next. Scouts had gone ahead to size up the place. It was smaller than Doberan, and surrounded by fields. There were no fortifications, not even a village wall or gates. It was an easy target, ready for the sword.

Deveaux kicked his horse into a loping canter as he rode to the front of the advancing line. He signaled his generals and they called the march to a halt. The foot soldiers in the front lines stopped and sat on the ground, their weapons resting over their shoulders. Deveaux watched, fascinated as always at the sight of his army settling like a rolling wave as the orders traveled to the end of the line. Above their heads, the upright shafts of their weapons resembled a field of ripe grain.

His horse pranced back and forth as he shouted to them in the breaking sunlight. "We will attack the village of Lauriel. It is a village of shit-eating peasants!"

"They can eat my shit any day!" bawled a hoarse voice.

Deveaux paused, letting the coarse laughter ease the mood of his soldiers. Again he watched amazed as the words rippled to the men farther back in line not able to hear the exchange firsthand.

"And so they will," he shouted encouragingly. "But not today. Today we rest. There will be extra rations given and a measure of brandy for every soldier—"

A cheer went up in the front lines, his men shaking their weapons in the air to show their approval.

Deveaux forced a closed-lip smile, knowing that his picket teeth made him look like a grinning bear. His captains were tight-lipped. They didn't like his plan.

"Sir, do you think it wise?" asked Captain Re Vegas. "We are running low on rations. We can't rely on the local Silean estates to sustain a winter campaign."

"Getting more supplies is your concern, Captain. Mine is

seeing that I have men ready and able to fight. The battles have been harder than they expected—''

''With all respect, sir, there is nothing to deter them at Lauriel. It will be an easy conquest.''

Deveaux shook his head, annoyed, and a lock of matted hair fell over one eye. ''If the men are well rested and fed, the victory will be that much quicker, with less loss of life. It will boost morale now and make it easier to demand more of them later. And,'' Deveaux added, brushing the hair out of his eyes, ''this country has too many surprises. It's dangerous to underestimate any of these battles.''

Deveaux rode his horse at a slow trot through the swarm of soldiers. Makeshift camps had been established, small circles of men starting cook fires or settling back to shake out stones from their boots and polish weapons. Thin curls of smoke lifted from the new fires and the hum of conversation was broken by the bark of orders. His soldiers praised him as he passed, arms raised in salutes. One handed him a lit pipe, the strong, pungent smell of Silean tobacco issuing from its bowl. The stem of the pipe rested badly in the corner of Deveaux's mouth. He bit down awkwardly, trying to hold it in place with his huge teeth. A narrow line of saliva collected around the base and Deveaux knew he would drool. He knocked out the ashes and pocketed the pipe for later. Deveaux continued reviewing his army, noting here and there the renewed expressions of determination on the faces of his soldiers.

I may look like a beast, Deveaux thought, but I know the needs of men. He spotted the brightly colored flags of his tent, recently erected in a clearing of trees. He rode toward it gratefully. Despite the excitement of a coming battle, he was tired from the strain of the march. He, too, needed a rest and some privacy before his captains thought to besiege him with their endless concerns.

Eneas sat on a small stool by the camp fire and stared absently into its flames. His face was haggard and his eyes dazed by the flickering orange light. For the last month he had traveled with his small band into the southern villages of the west country, gathering a tentative army.

Tentative, he reminded himself, tasting the fire's soot on his tongue. The plan had been his idea, and his responsibility to carry out. He would come at night with his rebel band to the smaller estates of Silean nobles. Eneas knew many of them by name, knew that their status as Sileans was fragile. Neither wealthy nor influential at the court, they only just survived as gentlemen farmers. They worked side by side in the fields with their Oran laborers, the only difference between them and the few Oran peasants who still owned land being a preferential treatment in the collection of taxes. Eneas relied on the knowledge that most of them, given a chance, were decent people. They feared the New Moon and the loss of their privileged status. But few wanted their sons to serve in the Silean militias, and they regarded the slaughter of Oran villages as shameful.

Eneas forced his way into their manors, rousted them from their beds, driving them into the kitchens. As the men stood angrily by their frightened families, he gave them a choice. Eneas rubbed his gritty eyes while the light of the flames danced behind his closed lids. The choice was simple: join the men and women of the New Moon army and fight to free Oran from the oppression of a foreign Silean parliament.

"And if we don't?" they had asked with drawn faces as they clung to their children.

"We will stay here until morning," Eneas had answered. "And in the light of day, we will leave, supplied with your horses and your grain."

"And what about us?"

"You and your families will be left unharmed," Eneas had told them. "However, let me warn you—it won't look good to the Silean militia."

Relief quickly changed into anger again as they realized what Eneas's gambit would do to them. Either join the New Moon and flee at night, or be accused by the Silean militia of collaborating with the New Moon. If they had at least been beaten or bound, they might argue that the New Moon had robbed them.

But the militia, already looking for an excuse to confiscate land, would never listen to their explanation.

"But they will murder us! You would condemn our wives and children," Re Ferale had shouted.

"This is civil war. You must choose a side," Eneas had replied grimly.

"And the Queen. What about the Queen?" another man had argued. "You can't kill her! Will we be her slaves when this is over?"

"There is to be a new Queens' quarter knot that will lead the New Moon. Even as we fight, they are preparing for their battle with her. Together we will make a new country, one that provides for the Oran people and those Sileans who join us now."

It had not taken much convincing. Their fear of the Silean militia was greater than their reluctance to join the New Moon. They sent their women and children by carriage to Beldan, where they would be housed in inns secretly held by the New Moon. To a man, they had followed Eneas and his army into the night. They brought their sons old enough to carry weapons, fresh horses and food. Oran men and women, the laborers and servants, joined as well, rapidly swelling the rebel ranks as they moved through the plains and marshes of the southwest.

Eneas inhaled deeply, letting the smoke of the camp fire fill his lungs before he exhaled. He missed his pipe, which he had left behind at Sadar. He had gambled, and so far he had won. Most of the Sileans who had come along under duress had changed over the last month. As Orans and Sileans talked and argued around camp fires at night, they had begun to find a common ground in their mutual fears. Clothing was exchanged as supplies from the Silean manors dressed and fed the mostly Oran New Moon. Except for the subtle differences in their faces it was becoming difficult to tell Sileans and Orans apart.

Eneas gently kicked at a log, watching the shower of sparks rise into the night. He had an army. Now what to do with them? They would not be able to return to Sadar until the winter storms subsided. Southeast then, he thought, to the coast. They would be closer to Beldan for the spring offensive. He could billet the army along the beaches of the marsh flats. Last he had heard,

Orian was in Doberan. She would be able to help him train his rebels.

"Sir!" an urgent voice called to Eneas. He glanced up and saw the boy Anard Brestin approaching him. His pale face was washed with the gold light of the fire. Eneas had not wanted the boy to come. He was an earth element and all the children of power were to remain safe at the Keep. But Anard had insisted, wanting to see his family again in the Soring Marsh. Shedwyn had spoken on the boy's behalf, reminding Eneas of their promise to his parents to send word of the child. Eneas had relented, knowing that with her usual stubbornness Shedwyn wasn't going to stop arguing until she got her way.

The lanky boy had proven to be a resourceful assistant. He managed to be everywhere at once and he listened well, bringing Eneas much-needed impressions of his newly formed army.

"What is it?" Eneas asked. His knees cracked as he stood.

"A messenger has arrived with news for you, sir."

"From Sadar?" he asked.

"No. Beldan."

"How did he get here?" Eneas asked, alarmed.

"It's Geffen who found him, rambling in the forest on some old nag. He sent me on ahead to ask what to do with him."

"Bring him here, and while you're at it, fetch Re Ferale, Aberon, and Re Morea. I want them to hear this as well."

Anard nodded and slipped back into the dark shadows of the forest. Eneas paced to warm his cold body, and blew on his hands. Why should a messenger from Beldan be on the road now? The campaign wasn't due to start until spring. Unless something had happened to change the plans . . .

"Oy, get yer hand off me!" snapped a loud voice.

Eneas allowed a smile, recognizing the brassy tone of a Beldan street accent. The man sounded like Jobber.

Geffen came into the clearing, his arm clasped firmly around that of a man wearing a smock beneath his cloak and a blue weaver's scarf around his neck. His face was long and craggy, two deep ruts on either side of his cheeks. Geffen was holding him tightly and his bearded face was scowling.

"Let go of him," Eneas called. "He's to be well treated."

"Frigging right. Z'blood, I ain't a squeal," the man said sharply.

"Nor a weaver," replied Geffen. "You've not the hands for it!"

"This disguise weren't meant for the likes of you, now was it? It was good enough to get me past the butcherboys. Place is thick with them in case you don't know."

"What do you mean?" Geffen demanded, grabbing the man once again by the shoulder.

The man bristled and shook off Geffen's hand, turning to confront him. Geffen's hands curled into fists.

"Hold!" Eneas shouted at the pair. "This is useless. We are on the same side. Let us try to remember that." The two men stepped back stiffly, relinquishing space but not mistrust. Watching them, Eneas felt overwhelmed with fatigue. It seemed impossible, this juggling act with the different factions of his country, trying to make them unite. How was he to combat the hostility between those of the city and those of the country, between the Guildmasters and common laborers, and not the least, between Sileans and Orans, all supposedly fighting on the same side?

"Are you hungry?" Eneas asked.

The man shrugged. "Yeah, I must be. Ain't had much to eat the last four days. Just grabbed what I could find before pushing on."

Anard returned, followed closely by Re Ferale, Re Morea, and Aberon. Word of the messenger's arrival had spread through the camp, and from all over the forest men and women were coming to stand near Eneas's fire to hear the news. The messenger looked nervous at the sight of so many eyes staring at him from beyond the rim of the firelight.

Eneas turned to Anard once again. "Get some food and drink for the messenger—"

"Tyne. They call me Tyne of Harrow Street," the man said.

Eneas nodded. "You can eat first and then talk."

Tyne shook his head. "I'll eat on the run. And I wager so will you. It's rare I got here at all without being scaffered."

Tyne moved closer to the fire, reaching his hands out to warm them.

"What's happened?" Eneas asked.

"A while back," Tyne said, "our people nicked the pocket of the Secondwatch. He prigged the jingles—keys that is—to the armory so as to make a sweet catch without too many getting scaffered in a brangle. But along with the jingles, our man prigged some letters. It was the letters that done the deed."

Eneas frowned, trying to follow the language of the man's story. "What did the letters say?"

"They told about a butcherboy, Re Silve, who was coming over to wipe up the Orans living along the Sairas River. They wanted to tear up a path to the trading villages, since the New Moon has battened most of the trade along the Hamader River."

"A winter campaign?" Geffen asked.

"Yeah. Surprise-like. Plan was to hole up until spring. Then the butcherboys in Beldan would join them for one big final brangle. I got sent out to warn the villages along the coast and if I could, skipper up to Sadar to let them know."

Tyne fell silent. He wiped his face, as if cleaning away cobwebs.

"What happened?" Eneas asked.

"I was too late," Tyne answered. "I went to Doberan first, looking for a vagger named Orian who was to help me." Tyne glanced up at Eneas, his eyes haunted. "There weren't no one when I got there. It was eerie, walking through the village and not seeing anyone. There was plenty of blood. Things looked torn apart. I went out of the village, and in the fields I saw mounds of newly dug dirt."

Anard handed Tyne a small jug. He took a deep swallow, shuddering. "I dug a bit with a stick. Curious-like. Not too far down I found the first body. And next to it another, and then another." He looked up at the watching eyes around the camp fire. "Dead. They was all dead. Every last one of them. Brats as well. And another thing," he added, squinting as he remembered. "There was some kind of corpse they'd tried burning. Only it weren't nothing I recognized from the bones. Huge, like a frigging great bird."

"Are you sure it's Re Silve that killed them?" Re Ferale asked. He was a short man with precise features that gave him a delicate appearance. He ran a finger nervously over his trimmed mustache.

"Oh, it's him all right. I ain't told you all of it, yet. After Doberan I found this old horse out by herself. So I took her and rode up north to Gallen." Tyne's expression hardened. "They didn't bury all of them at Gallen. They hanged some and what they done to the bodies"—Tyne shook his head and took another deep swallow from the jug. "But like Doberan, all of them was dead. I thought to go north still, but last night I nearly run into them. Frigging great army, spread out all over the road like they owned the place. At the head I seen the man Re Silve."

"How could you be sure it was him?" Eneas said.

"His face. Ain't no man ever looked like that. Not even in the back streets of Beldan."

"What's the next village?" Eneas asked Geffen.

"Lauriel. But there's nothing there to interest the Sileans."

"Any from the New Moon there?"

Geffen shook his head. "It's too small a place. Treys and the rest never figured it would be of use. Didn't want to make it a target."

"Well, all I can tell you now," Tyne said grimly, "is that Deveaux Re Silve and his Silean army are about a half day's march from that village and by tomorrow I'd guess that all that will be left of them will be hanging from the trees as well."

"How far are we from Lauriel?" Eneas asked.

"A day's ride," Re Ferale answered quickly. "Do you mean to fight the Sileans? They're sure to have us outnumbered."·

"There would be the element of surprise," Aberon interrupted. He kicked mud from his black boots. He had once been a vagger and the remains of his tattoos still etched his brown cheeks. "If we didn't win against them, we could at least inflict damage."

"Slow them up, and give Tyne the chance to go ahead and sound the warning to the other villages farther north," Eneas agreed, thinking. He looked at the faces that ringed the camp fire. On the faces of the Silean men he saw hesitation. Could he trust them in battle against their kind? On the faces of the Oran men and women he saw fury and the desire for revenge. They were more than ready to fight.

He lowered his eyes and tested the conviction of his own heart. At the Battle of Sadar there had been no such choice. The Sileans had attacked, and he had discovered under siege that one fought purely to stay alive. Then he had been but a soldier. Now he was the leader of soldiers; this newly formed group was his army and they looked to him to make the decision whether to make a stand against the Silean army. Many of them would surely die, he reasoned. But all those living in Lauriel would die without them, and countless others living farther north if Deveaux's army was not slowed down.

Shedwyn. The image of her face, the curve of her breasts, came unbidden to his mind. Shedwyn and their baby. . . .

"What's it to be then?" Geffen demanded, drawing Eneas from his thoughts.

Eneas squared his shoulders and faced the others. "Those of you from the estates, meet among yourselves and choose captains. Choose carefully," he warned. "Choose captains you will listen to, whose orders you will follow without question, who will lead you into battle. Do it quickly. We'll break camp before dawn."

"Are we fighting?" someone called from the shadows.

Eneas paused before answering. He wrestled with his thoughts. This was not part of the plan carefully laid by the council of leaders at Sadar. Was he throwing away the future of the New Moon by agreeing to a foolish act of bravery? If too many died in this battle, would he compromise a later success? "Surprise is possible only if you don't allow for it" Veira Rune, one of Huld's ancient soldiers had once told him. The New Moon had not allowed for Re Silve and he had cut into their flank without their knowing it.

Eneas's resolve hardened. "As I said, I want a meeting of the captains as soon as possible. We'll fight Re Silve's army before they reach Lauriel."

Shouts of approval greeted his words, and he saw the promise of battle illuminate the faces of the rebels more brightly than any flame. Their voices were loud as they called in the dark to one another, gathering into groups, arguing as they decided whom among their numbers to select as captains. Eneas walked through camp, speaking a few words to the Orans he knew from Sadar as they sharpened their weapons and straightened the ruffled fletches of their arrows. They clapped him warmly on the shoulder. He had made the right decision they told him. They were confident and ready. Eneas walked slowly back to his own fire to wait for the captains to join him. But he knew, even before they arrived, that when they faced the Sileans, the New Moon army would be united behind him.

"Cock's shit!" Geffen growled, seeing the Silean army spread along the dirt road to Lauriel. "So many of the bastards!"

Eneas's stomach gripped and he heard the echo of Geffen's dismay in the thudding of his heart. He licked his parched lips and turned to Geffen and the other captains lying against the sheltering brow of a small hill. The road filled with marching Sileans lay beneath them in a small narrow valley. This was the most advantageous place from which to attack, for farther down, the road opened into a huge, flat plain that would offer them no defense.

"Do you understand the plan of attack?" he demanded sharply, wanting to shake off the paralysis of fear. "Sileans fight face on, straight rows. We attack in small groups, hitting the flanks." Eneas spoke with more confidence than he felt, hoping the certainty of his voice would give them courage. "Drive your men like a wedge through the line. We must break them in as many pieces as possible, create as much confusion between the front lines and the back."

"Get in, get out," Geffen repeated.

"If we can pin them down long enough, Tyne will be able to warn the villagers at Lauriel, and those farther north," Eneas continued. "And in any case, we shall see to it that the number of Silean soldiers will be that much smaller. Hit hard while you can and then get out. Take your people out of the battle and head north to the other villages."

Eneas looked his captains over once more, memorizing their faces: Geffen, Aberon, and Finnia, who had come from Sadar;

Re Ferale, Re Morea, and Re Stures from the estates. Despite the clamoring of his heart, Eneas felt the clean stab of pride. Oran and Silean faces stared back at him, and he knew that those who survived today would be the cornerstones of a new society.

"Let's go," Eneas said brusquely, heading toward the horses that waited restlessly among the trees. Anard held the stirrup for Eneas as he mounted his horse. Eneas glanced down, suddenly seeing him. "You're not to stay here!" he ordered the boy. "Do you understand? Take the old gray and head up to the North. Now!"

"Aye, sir," Anard said. "And sir, Huld's luck to you," he added, his chin lifted bravely.

Eneas nodded, his constricted throat preventing reply. He rode to the brow of the hill, his rebels following behind him. He glanced to the side, seeing along the edge of the hill the other bands clustered around their captains. Next to him, Finnia took out an arrow, her thighs clamped tightly against the sides of her horse. Her brown hair fluttered softly in the breeze.

She grinned at him. "It's fairly done, Eneas," she said boldly and nocked her arrow.

Eneas raised his arm, waving a blue flag. Then he dropped his arm and from along the spine of the hill, the New Moon exploded with shouts and battle cries as they descended on the Silean army below.

As in a nightmare, Eneas heard the clubbing roar of battle, his own bellowed shouts, the answering cries of the Sileans, and the shrill neighing of horses. Silean soldiers scattered before him, surprised by the invasion of mounted horsemen. Finnia's arrows snapped, twanging like buzzing wasps, fatally stinging men as they reached for their weapons or turned in utter confusion to their attackers.

Eneas had freed his sword and singlemindedly hacked from side to side at the arms and angry faces that swelled around his horse. A severed arm clung to the horn of his saddle, the hand refusing to relinquish its grip. The arc of a raised sword caught Eneas's attention and he slashed back with his weapon, seeing it cleave through a snarling, bearded face. The bloody face fell against the flank of his horse and Eneas turned away. Through the thickness of heaving bodies he drove his horse, its shrill neighs joined by the screams of men dying beneath its hooves. Sweat stung his face, blinded his eyes, but he never stopped the raking harvest of his sword.

And then his horse broke free, the dense crush of men falling away as Eneas realized he had breached the other side of the line of Sileans. He wheeled his horse around, pulling hard at the bit in the horse's foaming mouth. The surprise had given them a moment's advantage. The Silean army was scattered, fleeing men trampling the dead or wounded that lay like broken crockery.

Eneas saw the narrow path he had cut close as men swarmed into the gap. He kicked his horse and raised his sword for another assault. Others from his band had made it through, and glancing quickly to one side he saw Finnia nocking her last arrow. Blood streamed along the sides of her face, deepening the brown of her hair. Her eyes glared wildly at the gathering wall of Silean soldiers prepared for their attack. She held herself steady, refusing to be daunted by the sight of their approach. She released her last arrow and with a tight smile of gratification watched it pierce the eye socket of an advancing Silean. She threw down her bow and reached for her sword. She raised it high in the air, awaiting Eneas's command.

Eneas shouted, and ducking his head drove his terrified horse forward into the Silean lines again. His sword bit deep into the rising tide of men. It clanged and screeched as steel crashed against steel. A sharp pain snagged his attention and he saw blood oozing from a gash in his thigh. He jerked his eyes away from it as he sensed rather than saw the attack rounding on his other side. He heard the roaring of an animal like a single voice plucked from a chorus of dying men.

He looked up and saw the face of a beast, a mane of gold hair spattered with blood, howls of rage issuing from a mouth that was twisted and tusked. Eyes glittered then rolled back, the whites gleaming with blind madness. The bright flash of a sword arced over Eneas and he lunged to one side. The blade hissed in the misted air and slashed through his horse's withers. The horse bucked with pain, the muscles severed. Its knees buckled and it rolled forward, pulled down to the earth by the weight of its heavy head.

Eneas cried out as he tumbled into the dense swarm of soldiers, swords and axes stabbing the path of his fall. He slammed into the hard frozen earth, made slick with blood. His horse shuddered violently and rolled, trapping Eneas's leg beneath its dying body. Eneas tried desperately to pull himself free, cringing against the bodies that stumbled and fell over him, clinging to him briefly with their lifeless embrace before he pushed them away. He heard a woman scream above him and saw Finnia, her face livid with rage.

She missed her attack, and as her sword returned for another strike, an ax settled deeply in her shoulder, hewing away her arm. She wailed as she crumpled over the back of her horse and slipped to the ground. She landed next to Eneas, her eyes white with pain and shock. He grabbed her and pulled her to his side. She buried her face in his neck. His body was bludgeoned with pain, but it dulled compared to the horror he felt clutching the dying Finnia.

A woman's body. Different from Shedwyn's, but with the familiar softness, breasts and hips laid against him in the intimacy of approaching death. He clung to her, shielding her from the tangled legs of battling soldiers and prancing horses. He could hear the gentle rattle of her breath on his neck, drowning out the battle cries and the sickening grunts of dying men split like staves of kindling. Hot tears burned in Eneas's eyes as Finnia squeezed his shoulder with her remaining hand. Then the hand opened and Eneas heard, amid the clamor of battle, the silence of her death. Exhausted, he laid his head on the earth and Finnia's blood puddled around his cheek. The dark and distant shadows of those above him raged on. He closed his eyes to the flickering light when death parted two dark combatants, and one fell, revealing for an instant the gray sky above.

Chapter Twelve

Lirrel woke to the sound of her own harsh breathing. Her hands were balled into fists, clutching at sand that slipped between her fingers. The sky was a pale gray, the mist thinning as it rose into the new day. A shriek broke the morning stillness and she cringed in terror, her knees drawn up to her chest. She was panting, the sand grating against her lips. She forced her bent legs to straighten and opened her hands. She stared upward and saw a gull wheeling in the sky, his white bullet head cleaving the fading morning mist.

Lirrel relaxed slowly and closed her eyes. The gull's hungry cries were not to be feared. Nor was the rasping sound of the waves scratching against the shore. The terror that had gripped her came from elsewhere. Lirrel touched Dagar, lying close beside her. He stirred and burrowed more deeply into his woolen cloak. Lirrel opened her mind and listened to his thoughts. Despite his beating, he slept without anger. Lirrel heard only the peaceful swishing of mountain grass, the bleat of goats. Farther in his thoughts Lirrel sensed his hidden sorrow, but even in sleep

Dagar avoided it. She retreated, reassured by the quiet of his thoughts.

Lirrel looked for Alwir and saw him lying near the upturned hull of the longboat. His head lay cradled in his arms, his cheeks and beard crusted with dried salt. A breeze from the ocean ruffled his hair and small bits of black kelp scattered across the sand, catching in the folds of his cloak. Lirrel let the thoughts of the sleeping man reach into her mind. Sadness and resentment filled her ears with discordant notes. Alwir shifted in his sleep, shaking free of the jangling melody, but the somber notes returned as he settled again.

Lirrel withdrew from his private anguish. Neither of them was the source of her disturbing nightmare. She sat up and surveyed the beach, suddenly missing Tayleb.

Late in the night Tayleb had brought them to this island that was no more than a beach and an outcrop of rocks and tufted grass. Gratefully they had hauled the longboat onto the shore. Lirrel remembered the way Tayleb had emerged from the foaming surf, her body spangled by moonlit drops of water, kelp twined in her hair and a small crab scuttling off her shoulder and dropping to the sand. She had breathed with difficulty, choking on the misted air, words sounding garbled. With the longboat stowed on the beach, she had dressed, wrapped herself in a cloak, and laid down to sleep. Tayleb had looked strange dressed again in her Islander skirts. Wearing clothing no longer suited her, and Lirrel had sensed her discomfort as her skirts entangled her legs like a net.

Lirrel looked anxiously down the beach, trying to shake the unexplained dread that clung like sand to her skin. It didn't come from the sleepers, and Lirrel was certain it didn't come from Tayleb. She sniffed the wind and caught the odor of newly dug earth. Her mouth flooded with the salty taste of warm blood. Her eyes teared, feeling the burning sting of smoke. The crying of gulls gave way to the harsh cawing of crows. And then the gentle rasping of waves was broken by the insistent snap of bowstrings.

Another vision. It had clawed the edges of her sleep, waiting for her to awaken.

No, Lirrel said as the air thickened and churned around her. No, not again, she pleaded, her bones shrinking into the core of her flesh. She dug her hand into her pocket, clutching the stem of her flute. Was she to have no rest from the visions? She reached for Dagar, wanting to wake him. But she was stopped by the sight of his battered, sleeping face. Lirrel closed her eyes and wished for deafness or blindness, anything that would stop her from witnessing the terror of the visions. But the vision followed her retreat and compelled her to open her eyes and watch. She stepped away from the sleepers and, alone on the beach, allowed the vision to consume her.

The vision seethed around Lirrel's thighs like waves breaking against the rocks. A cry was torn from her lips. Faces, open-mouthed and weeping, appeared in the folds of her skirt. She brushed feverishly at her hair and her chest, trying to scrape away the cold tendrils of the vision. She started walking down the tiny beach, and then broke into a run, but the vision trailed her, clinging to her body, and the clamor of battle filled her ears.

Lirrel felt her courage crumble, and as her resolve snapped, a new voice cried out defiantly within her. She spun on her heel to face the vision and shouted angrily, "No more! Z'blood, no more!" She felt the gentleness of her spirit blister with the heat of a scalding rage. A movement caught her eye and she looked down, seeing the slain corpses of men, women, and children in the black stitched hem of her skirts.

"Away! Away!" Lirrel screamed and violently shook her skirts to scatter the fearful images. From the ground a hideous face maned with yellow hair laughed at her. The huge face neared hers, cold eyes entrapping Lirrel's frightened ones. It was like a man's face, but the breath stank as he opened wide his jaws. On the jagged teeth Lirrel saw the fragments of bodies. She whimpered as black wings covered her with a sheet of darkness and drew her into the snapping jaws.

But the newfound rage in her would not permit surrender. Lirrel's body clenched like a fist and her mouth burst forth with obscenities. She vomited a torrent of curses and threats. Deep within her Lirrel ached with sorrow, not knowing that she had harbored such words of hate. The words rattled like spears and shot from her lips like arrows.

The vision hovered and then shredded, dissolved by Lirrel's rage.

But once begun, Lirrel couldn't stop. Wind gathered around her, drawing up columns of stinging sand. Her voice grew hoarse but the words continued to pour out.

"Lirrel!" someone called. The wind keened loudly in her ears, carrying the bludgeoning sounds of her curses. "Lirrel!" the voice insisted and arms wrapped tightly around her. She struggled against them, not wanting to relinquish the freed torrent of hate. Not yet. She wasn't ready. The arms that held her would demand that she face the visions, would demand that she be a peacekeeper. Lirrel had known what that meant once. Had believed in being Ghazali. But that part of her had been suffocated by the darkness of the visions. One needed light, one needed love to know that peace was possible.

A wet cloth stroked her hot cheeks, and salty water stung the cracks of her dry lips. Her lungs ached and Lirrel became aware that she needed to stop the flow of hateful words and breathe. She gasped and the air gusted through her body, her chest filling like a sail. In the silence of her breath, Lirrel remembered what she was. Slowly, and with effort, she stilled the stream of obscenities. The wind died down as Lirrel's body grew limp. She sank to her knees on the beach, her head bent low, little tunnels of sand echoing with the frantic sound of her labored breathing.

And then silent tears followed.

Tayleb lifted her up and wiped her face with a wet cloth.

"Lirrel, what is it?" she asked.

Lirrel shuddered and pulled the cloak around her chilled body. Their worried faces stared back at her; Tayleb pale and wide-eyed, Alwir's fear masked by concern. And last was Dagar. There was no fear on his face. In his dark eyes she saw only sadness. His hand still rested on her back, and she knew it was he who had held her while she raged.

"I have lost the way," she whispered.

Dagar took her in his arms. "No," he replied. "No, you are still Ghazali."

"I can't be what they want."

"Who?" he asked, smoothing strands of black hair from her temple.

"The New Moon," Lirrel answered. "I am not strong enough."

"You just need rest, Lirrel," Dagar said. "Your strength will return."

Lirrel brushed the sand from her face. She sat up slowly and gazed around her at the tiny beach and the vast stretch of ocean. The world seemed so clam and peaceful again.

But something had changed. Not just in her, but in Oran as well. She studied the clouds gathered over the horizon, their fleecy backs lifting into the sky. She squinted out over the water trying to see the land beyond the rim of the horizon. Across her silvery eyes, a thin band of gray clouds scudded before the wind.

"What is it?" Alwir asked.

Lirrel tensed as she studied the currents of air spiraling over the water. Then she nodded, understanding at last.

"Oran is beginning to unravel. Neither Queen Huld nor Zorah can keep us much longer from the Chaos." Lirrel took the cloth from Tayleb and wiped her face again.

"What are you saying, Lirrel?" Alwir demanded.

"I *am* strong," Lirrel said with conviction. "But power is being torn from me. In its absence there is only doubt. Doubt and fear. *Ahal,* even now as I look to the sky I can't find the patterns that were once clearly there. There's a veil that shields my sight. I can't 'see' as I once did."

"But the visions?" Dagar asked, frowning. "You still have the visions."

"They are visions of a recent past, driving me toward an unknown future. And that's the cause of my doubt."

"How long before we reach the mainland?" Alwir asked Tayleb.

Tayleb glanced at the steady roll of the sea. "We've the current to our stern. We'll be there before midday."

"Do you know where on the mainland?"

"We're fairly south now," Tayleb answered. "I'd say we aren't far from the mouth of the Sairas River. I can sense the fresh water even this far into the ocean.''

"Do you know what village is there, Lirrel?" Alwir asked sharply.

"The Ghazalis used to camp along the marsh flats of the Sairas. There was an Oran village called Doberan.''

"Good. We'll get horses there and head for Sadar." He stood brusquely and went to the task of righting the boat.

Lirrel sensed in Alwir's burst of activity his desperate need to stave off anxiety. It rapped through his pulsing veins like a Ghazali drum. Tayleb joined him and helped turn over the longboat. Her worried gaze shifted back and forth from Alwir to Lirrel.

Dagar waited beside Lirrel. She closed her eyes, swaying with exhaustion. She didn't want to tell them yet that Sadar was gone, that when she thought of it she heard only the howling winds of Chaos.

Lirrel searched her thoughts more deeply, relieved by the faint taste of red soil and a coppery scent in the air. Shedwyn and Jobber were still safe. Then she pursed her lips, sensing something else, its identity elusive. It came to her like a tiny single bloom of lavender, its scent at once dusky and sweet. Without knowing why, a healing balm of gladness spread over Lirrel's troubled heart. It touched her face and her mouth parted with a smile of genuine happiness.

"What is it?" Dagar asked, eyeing her curiously.

Lirrel shrugged. "It's like one of your riddles. I don't have an answer for it." She smiled more widely. "Except that it gives me hope.''

Dagar returned her smile. "Good, we shall need it. Come on, Alwir and Tayleb are waiting for us.''

Alwir was holding the longboat in the water as the waves splashed against the hull. Lirrel shivered as they waded into the cold water toward it. In the boat, Tayleb grabbed a shawl and tied it over her head to hold down the blowing locks of tangled hair. She clutched the oars firmly in her hands as Alwir shoved the longboat farther into the surf. The boat rocked as the tide caught it and the backwash of a wave dragged it out to the sea. Alwir heaved himself in, water splashing up over the sides. Tayleb plied the oars, her lips pressed tight with the strain as the boat broke through the waves and cut a path through the white foam into the open sea.

Shedwyn bent over the small cheerless camp fire, carefully feeding it damp wood. Too much wet wood too soon and she would drown the fire. So she was careful to add one log at a time in hopes that it would dry gradually and then burn. She peered through the dense smoke, one eye closed against its sting, and saw Jobber standing on the other side. The smoke filtered through her hair, stroked her face, but there were no tears in Jobber's eyes. They were bright green, and Shedwyn knew from the small flickering flames they were angry.

"Am I doing it wrong, then?" she asked with a tired smile.

"Eh?" Jobber said distantly.

"The fire." Shedwyn pointed to the spluttering flame at the end of a damp log.

"Yeah, well the wood's wet. Ain't much you can do," Jobber said and lapsed into silence again.

Shedwyn moved away from the curtain of smoke. Through the leafless forest other fires shrouded the woods with a dismal gray mist. At least it had stopped snowing, she thought. The sun was rising and rosy spears of light slanted over the tops of the black trees. Shedwyn stared back at the Plains of Sadar, seeing the morning sunlight spill across the empty chasm that had been the Keep. Only one small peak remained and Shedwyn knew that it was Huld's roots, dug deep into Oran, that had held it in place. The Plains, once flat, were split and canyoned with deep gulleys.

Shedwyn returned her gaze to the scattered camps, seeing the somber hues of the forest brightened by the colored skirts of the women. A baby cried, joined by the mournful howl of a dog. The log in her camp fire crackled unexpectedly as the water hissed and steamed out of it. A corner had dried sufficiently and was catching fire. Shedwyn stretched forth her hands to take its warmth.

As she bent, Shedwyn felt her thickened waist. She smiled, realizing that she had no waist; from her breastbone to her hips she had become as solid as a tree trunk. If she smoothed her skirts tightly beneath her belly she could see the rounded bulge of the baby. Another month and there would be no hiding it. At least she no longer felt nauseated.

"Jobber," Shedwyn said.

"Yeah," Jobber answered, still distracted by her thoughts.

"I'm pregnant." Shedwyn marveled at how easy it had been to say the words.

"What?" Jobber asked, slowly pulling out of her fire-gazing.

"I'm pregnant," Shedwyn repeated and watched Jobber's face change. Her cheeks pinked, the flash of yellow flames brightened in her eyes. She opened her mouth to speak. Shedwyn tensed. The last thing she wanted was a lecture from Jobber.

But Jobber surprised her. She closed her mouth, the red blush fading from her cheeks. She knelt down by the fire and poked it with a twig. The fiery hair glimmered in the morning sun with the soft sheen of polished cooper. She looked up and gave Shedwyn a crooked grin.

"Good news for a change," Jobber said. "Ain't exactly the best time." She laughed and then reached out and grabbed Shedwyn by the wrist. "Are you sure?" she demanded.

Shedwyn took Jobber's hand from her wrist and put it on the hard rise of her belly.

Jobber withdrew her hand and slapped her forehead. "Frigging all, Shedwyn. The world's blowing up, there's civil war, and we still got Zorah to brangle with. I ought to be raving at you. But you know, I just can't." She stared earnestly at Shedwyn. "Seems like the first right thing anyone's done lately."

"Thank you for that," Shedwyn said, settling down beside the fire.

"Told anyone?"

"Only Eneas. And you."

"Guess I'm honored then," Jobber said, smiling. "I figured after Eneas you would have told one of the women."

"You're a woman, Jobber," Shedwyn said wryly.

Jobber rolled her eyes upward. "Well, I'm a dell, that's true.

But I can't say I always know what that means. Fact is, you've caught me thinking about that just now."

"With everything that's going on?" teased Shedwyn.

"Yeah, well, when else? I might not get another chance. Tell me," Jobber asked, "what's it like?"

"Being pregnant? So far it's like being sick!" Shedwyn replied.

"Nah," Jobber said, moving closer to Shedwyn's side. "I mean the old in-and-out. What's it like?"

"You mean being with a man?"

Jobber looked disgusted. "Z'blood, with anyone, or anything for that matter. I mean look at Faul. Who knows what Shefek is when they go at it."

Shedwyn chuckled. "Hard to imagine Faul and Shefek."

"Yeah, that's what I thought 'til I come on them, Shefek all cozy-like in her bed. Caught me by surprise it did." Jobber's expression became serious. "See, I figured nothing much would change for me. First 'cause I figured I'd never live that long. Butcherboys and Readers should have me scaffered long ago. Then when I came here well, there was Faul. Straight-fingered dell, all fighter. Now that suited me. I still didn't think about being anything besides what I always had been."

"Which was?" Shedwyn asked.

Jobber shrugged. "Something in between. Never giving much thought to being a dell, and acting often enough like a man. The in-and-out was something that happened to other people. And mostly it seemed silly."

"And now?"

"Well, when I found out that Faul goes after it too, it sort of shook me up. Her choice in men is naffy, but it was learning that she even thought about it, much less took in someone like Shefek, that was hard. And now, Z'blood, it's all I can think about." Jobber fell into an embarrassed silence.

Shedwyn brushed back her long braid and sighed. "It just happens, Jobber."

"Not to me. Maybe for you, Shedwyn." Jobber grinned at Shedwyn's puzzled expression. "I seen how men stare at you. They stop talking when you pass and sort of gurgle in their beards, their eyes eating the sight of you. And then there's Lirrel. Everything she does is like she was dancing.''

"Ah!" Shedwyn agreed sharply, "I know about that one! Haven't I watched her myself, longing for the same sort of grace? But Lirrel's Ghazali, it's born into her. Truth is, Jobber, I've envied you."

"Get out," Jobber scoffed.

"I used to watch you when we trained in the mountains. When you fight in the old style everything about you gleams like a sword. There's a real beauty in that."

"It scares people. It scares men."

Shedwyn chuckled. "Not all."

"Who, then?" Jobber challenged.

"Have you never noticed Wyer? I've seen him look hard at you."

"Wyer and me are friends," Jobber disagreed. "We go back to Beldan. When he knew me as a boy!" she added pointedly.

"Suit yourself, but I don't think it's the 'boy' in you he watches."

"Oy," Jobber said sternly. "Here comes Finch. Treys must have called a meeting."

"Please—" Shedwyn started to say.

"I won't say nothing about the baby," Jobber finished. She gave Shedwyn a rueful smile. "Maybe I ain't never grown into something else because there ain't never been the time. Always been running." She strolled off toward a group newly gathered around a camp fire.

"I'm coming," Shedwyn told Finch and wrapped her shawl around her shoulders. "Always running," she mumbled as she got slowly up from the ground.

The afternoon sun was cold and gray behind a thick bank of clouds. There would be more snow that night, Jobber thought, looking up with annoyance.

She critically studied the wide clearing between the trees where she had stamped down the snow. The drifts were flattened, packed into a hard, smooth surface. Steam billowed from

Jobber's mouth and her warmed skin was chafed by the wool of her cloak.

In the distance she could hear the muffled sounds of the camps. They were packing, preparing to move farther down the mountains before nightfall. Children complained loudly, their brittle voices carrying over the somber noise of men and women breaking camp. Jobber didn't blame them. Too many had died last night, lost in the terrifying destruction of the Keep. They had to move, but no one could be fooled into thinking it was to a safer place. If it wasn't Oran falling into the sky, it was the Silean militias that might be waiting like wolves farther down the mountains.

Jobber stood in the middle of the cleared space. She balanced her weight over her feet and felt the snow give in to the shape of her foot. She stepped forward, knee bent, blocking an imaginary opponent. She stopped with a frown. Her winter clothing made her feel bulky and awkward. Standing up again, she stripped off the cloak and the heavy leather tunic. She didn't need them for this. Clad in a thin, frayed shirt and trousers, she shivered lightly at first and then breathed deeply. In her mind's eye she saw the fire-rose bloom in her core, felt the petals open as a warming heat surged evenly through her veins. She sucked in the cold and steam wreathed her head as she exhaled hot air.

Warmed by her element, Jobber began to practice the old style that Growler had taught her years ago in Beldan.

The sharp exhales signaled the crisp execution of a technique. She sniffed, a sudden blast of cold air in her nostrils as she pivoted, seeking another imaginary opponent. She moved quickly but without haste, allowing the rhythm of her battle to dictate her speed. Sweat gathered on her forehead. Her muscles stretched and flexed gracefully into the movements. She concentrated on the subtle twist of her wrist, the position of her fingertips as she squeezed her hand into a squared fist. She knew the correct angle of her knee, bent over her carefully planted foot, her turns centered between the ball of her foot and the heel. Jobber's hips rocked into the punches, the weight of her body gathered at her knuckles. Her stance became more solid and balanced as her center of gravity lowered.

The thoughts that had jangled her emotions disappeared in the smooth, fluid motions. She had been trying too hard, butting her head against someone else's intentions. And now, in the constant motion of practice, Jobber realized for the first time her own direction. With each attack, each strike and well-placed kick, Jobber saw the opponents of her private struggle vanquished, replaced by a growing confidence.

Long before she saw her, Jobber heard Faul approach the clearing. She heard Faul's catlike step as it broke the crusted surface of the dried snow. She didn't stop moving, though. She twisted her hips, swiveling to block an imaginary sword. For a brief instant, Jobber remembered Growler, his mouth set in a frown as he studied her. Jobber pressed her fingers tightly together into a dagger of flesh. Growler had yelled at her for being lazy when her fingers splayed apart. "Get them broken that way," he'd mutter, and squeeze her hand shut.

Growler. The memory of him flooded Jobber's mind, the drab brown of his cloak and the whorled vagger tattoos on the planes of his face. Like all vaggers he passed unnoticed in the streets, his clothing common, his intelligent face downturned. There was nothing to attract the attention of the butcherboys. Except his eyes, which Jobber remembered as two bright black stones. But the dark center of his eyes held a yolk of gentleness when he spoke to her, cajoled her out of a temper or encouraged her in her training. Jobber breathed deeply as she moved, feeling her body tire at last. He had given her a simple life and taught her to rely upon herself.

Jobber drew herself erect, her hands folded together in a final salute.

"Well done," said Faul when she had finished.

Jobber turned to see Faul leaning against a tree. She had a hesitant, almost embarrassed expression on her face.

"Reminds me of the old days in Beldan," Jobber said lightly. "Feels good to move."

"Looks good too." Faul's boots scrunched on the snow as she walked toward Jobber. "When you fight in the old style there is precision, balance, concentration''—Faul shook her head—''all the things you lack as soon as someone puts a sword in your hand!''

"Look, Faul, I've been thinking about that," Jobber started to say. But Faul stopped her with a held-up hand.

"I know. You don't want the sword. Shefek said as much to me."

"It ain't because I'm afraid," Jobber answered carefully. "I used to wonder all those times you and Shefek was beating me with a sword why didn't Growler teach me to use one in the first place?"

"Maybe he had planned on it when you were older," Faul suggested.

"Nah," Jobber answered. "He didn't teach me how to use the sword 'cause he wanted me to rely on myself. The Fire Sword is a *thing* of magic, Faul." Jobber tapped her chest. "Me, now, I am magic. I'm Beldan's fire. Every hearth, every forge, every lighterman owes its flame to me. I don't need the sword. In all, I think Growler knew the Fire Sword was a dangerous temptation. Zorah used it to steal power from her sisters and from Oran. She used it to get to me at Sadar. The Fire Sword is all that matters to her now because everything she is bleeds into it. Growler didn't want me to be like that."

"So you said in the training rooms," Faul replied. "The Fire Queen will be destroyed by another Fire Queen."

"Yeah, not a Fire Sword. I have to go to her as myself," Jobber explained.

"But how?" Faul asked, her eyes red-rimmed from the smoke of the campfires. "How will you stand against her?"

Jobber gave a small, tight smile. "Not sure yet. When Zorah and I first faced off, at Firecircle, I was too scared. But I knew even when she was trying to burn me that I was stronger than she was. That there was more to my power than hers. I just didn't know what to do. But I've changed since then."

Faul leaned back her head and burst out laughing. The unexpected sound boomed in the quiet hush of the forest, startling birds from the branches. The afternoon sun lit her face and the black fabric of her cloak faded to charcoal.

Jobber joined her, knowing that it was the memory of their first meeting that had Faul laughing. "I was green enough, then, wasn't I?" Jobber said.

"Not so green," Faul answered, wiping a small tear from one corner of her eye. "I may have drunk you under the table that night, but it cost me a lot of brass to do so!"

"You know, Faul, after Growler I wanted more than anything to be like you," Jobber confessed.

"I want you to be like me too!" Faul retorted. Then she shook her head. "No. I think I wanted to be you. The Fire Sword is a perfect weapon. It drives me mad that I can wield it, at least as an ordinary sword, and you can't."

"Won't," Jobber corrected her. "I won't use it, because it ain't my way, Faul." Jobber scratched her head and tiny blue sparks crinkled in the ends of her hair.

"The way of the sword is death," Faul said. "Isn't that what you need to teach Zorah?"

"All ways lead to death, Faul. But it's what happens between the first breath and the last that matters, ain't it?"

"To the person breathing, anyway," Faul answered dryly.

"Fair enough. I don't ask anyone to make me immortal; I don't even care if they forget me the day after I've cocked up my toes. But while I am breathing, I want my life to frigging matter."

"To whom?" Faul asked.

Jobber thought for a moment before answering. "I'd be stupid if I didn't say it should matter first to me. But I'd be equally stupid if I didn't say it ought to matter to others."

"And how do you do that? Make your life matter to someone else?"

Jobber grinned. "Go on, Faul, you ought to know. It's service to others. Your life mattered most to you when you served the Fire Queen."

"It still matters to me," Faul said archly.

"Yeah, because I mean something to you," Jobber said softly. "It's being with others, serving them as well as yourself that makes death less fearful and life, despite its nasty surprises, worth all the effort. I'm right, ain't I?"

Faul brushed back her gray hair, her jaw angled down to her chest. Her hand slid to the back of her head to rest on her neck. She raised her chin and the cool gray eyes studied Jobber's face. "Jobber, you're a snitch, you'd sooner steal the grub off a plowman's plate. You're all brass and mouth and knuckles. And here you are giving me a lecture about duty. Z'blood, there was more than Sadar lost last night to the sky."

Impulsively Jobber lunged forward and hugged Faul. "I hope I do a better job of convincing Zorah," she cracked in Faul's ear.

Feigning irritation, Faul pulled away from Jobber's embrace. "Convince her of what?" she asked crossly, straightening her cloak.

"Convince her to die for us. But in any case, the Fire Sword is yours, Faul. I've no need for it."

Faul's hand fumbled with the strings of her tunic. Amazement lit her tired face. "I accept the gift," she said softly.

They stood facing each other, waiting silently. But there was nothing more to say.

"Best we return," Faul said thickly.

"Yeah," Jobber answered and reached for her tunic and cloak. "Oy, Faul, I got a question here," Jobber said with a mischievous grin.

"What?" Faul asked warily.

They knew each other too well, Jobber thought, and hurried out with her question. "So what about Shefek?"

"I'm sure I don't know what you mean."

"Come on, Faul. He's short, he's old, and he ain't even human. What's it like, then?"

Faul's mouth twitched with the hint of a smile, but her eyes remained a cold gray.

"Let me correct your muddled thinking, Jobber. Height is irrelevant when laying down; I'm old too; and as for Shefek's casual humanity—well, there's plenty of it to do what's needed."

Jobber's mouth gaped open. "Go on, tell me more."

Faul rolled her eyes to the leafless trees. "No." She started back to camp, her arms swinging aggressively as she plunged through the snow. In the silence of the winter forest Jobber could hear Faul's voice as she spoke to the trees—no doubt, Jobber thought, complaining about her.

Jobber took a last look at the barren clearing and smiled to herself. She had no reason to feel calm, and yet she did. As Jobber started the walk back to the camp, she felt for the first time since she had fled Beldan that she was at last on the right road home.

Anard Brestin slid from the swayed back of his gray horse. The old horse grunted, the scrubby head shaking back and forth. Anard whispered soothing words to the twitching ears. He pulled on the halter, guiding the horse up the brow of the hill. The sun was beginning to set behind him, laying down his shadow among the gold light. He drew a deep breath, fearful of the silence.

He had disobeyed Eneas's order. He had ridden the gray horse deeper into the woods where he had seen an abandoned farm cottage. Standing alone amid the trees it had caught his attention in the morning as they journeyed to meet the Sileans. It had reminded him of home.

The thatch of the roof was rotted and small animals scurried away when he first opened the battered door. There was an old bed, and two chairs remained by the cold hearth. The cottage smelled of damp mold and animals. He sat in one of the chairs and stared at the hearth for most of the day, arguing with himself. He hated leaving the battle. He was old enough to fight. He had fought at Sadar, hadn't he? He hated leaving Eneas. Anard admired the man, even though he was Silean. He was clever and he had courage. And as Anard's gaze settled on the cold hearth and the broken shards of a brown bowl on the stones, he knew that most of all he hated being alone in this cottage that reeked of home.

He waited until his impatience became intolerable. Then, abruptly, he made up his mind. Leading the old gray back the way he had come, Anard headed for the hill. He kept a sharp eye out for men who might be fleeing into the woods. His ears pricked at every noise, straining to hear sounds of battle. But

the forest had remained quiet except for the insistent cawing of
crows.

As he walked up the hill a breeze blew over his face and
Anard gasped at the pungent odor it carried. The gray horse
reared his head in terror and Anard fought to hold him steady.
At the top of the hill, Anard stopped and stared at the carnage
spewed over the road. He had seen the dead at Sadar, but there
it had been different. They had had the illusion of a victory.
Here, there were only signs of defeat. As he surveyed the carnage, it didn't matter to Anard that the sacrifice of these fighters
might have saved Lauriel or any other Oran village. There was
no way he could know that. All he could be certain of, standing
on the hill gazing down, was that they had lost.

He forced himself to continue walking down the hill, nearing
the slain bodies of those he had known as friends. Anguish and
nausea gripped his stomach. He wiped his face on the corner of
his cloak. He spit, trying to rid his mouth of the sour taste of
bile.

The horse whickered nervously and Anard stroked its grizzled
nose. He slid his hand down to feel the velvety lips, and let the
breath of the old gray warm his chilled hand.

It came to him that he had only one reason for being here.
He wanted to find Eneas. If Eneas wasn't among the dead, then
he could leave this place with some hope that the New Moon
had succeeded despite the cost. And if Eneas was dead, then
this, too, he needed to know. It would be up to him to return to
Sadar and tell Shedwyn.

Anard held the old gray's halter tight and urged him down the
hill. He stumbled past the battle-scarred corpses, noting that
there were no Sileans among them. They must have taken their
own for burial, Anard thought, and left the New Moon to the
crows. The dead seemed so numerous, spread out, sometimes
in pieces, along the road. He stared at their faces only long
enough to see that they weren't Eneas.

The setting sun cast long shadows over the broken weapons,
the slain rebel fighters, and the bloating carcasses of the horses.
Anard slipped on blood that had frozen into a thin layer of
ice. The frozen faces of the dead mocked his horror. Then he

saw Eneas's horse, its proud head curled unnaturally into its chest. The severed muscles of its neck had separated, opening the flesh to the spine. A crow perched on the shoulder, its daggerlike beak tugging at sinews.

"Get away! Frigging get away!" Anard shouted at the crow, and it flapped angrily to one side, refusing to give up its perch. Anard shouted more loudly, seeing Eneas lying on the ground, his leg trapped beneath the horse. In the dying sunlight his blond hair was like stubbled wheat. In his arms Eneas held Finnia, her face turned toward the sky, her eyes open.

Anard led the gray horse through a narrow path between the corpses until he reached Eneas. His hands shook as he pulled Finnia's body away. Her stiffened corpse resisted and Anard settled back on his heels, suddenly exhausted and afraid. Dead! his mind reeled. They're all dead!

Then Eneas groaned, his eyes fluttering open and then closing again wearily. He whispered something.

"Eneas!" Anard cried and a renewed urgency flowed into his hands. He tugged at Finnia's corpse, sickened as he realized she was missing an arm. He dragged her away and laid her down on the ground, shutting her eyes with a quick gesture.

"Eneas," he called to the moaning man. "Eneas, it's me, Anard."

Eneas frowned, then his eyes blinked open. The pupils were huge and dark. "Stubborn," he croaked. "Like Shedwyn."

"I've come to bring you out of here, Eneas."

Eneas licked his dried mouth. "Stuck," he said, and one bloodied hand tapped the body of his horse.

Anard leaned back on his heels again and thought frantically. He'd found Eneas, still alive. He wasn't going to leave without him. He forced himself to be calm and to think. He wasn't strong enough alone to raise the bulk of the horse, nor was the old gray. But he could use his element to shift the ground beneath Eneas's leg. Depress the soil and, with the help of the gray, drag Eneas free.

Anard scrambled to his feet. Searching quickly among the fallen horses, he found a length of rope still tied to a saddle. He took it, knotting it rapidly as he returned to Eneas.

"Eneas, are you wounded elsewhere besides your leg?" Anard asked.

"I don't think so," he answered weakly. "Z'blood, I am cold."

Anard slipped the circle of rope around Eneas's shoulders and chest, securing it under his armpits. He tied the other end to the gray's halter. "Stay boy," he urged the old horse, hoping it wouldn't spook.

Anard returned to Eneas and bent down beside him. He concentrated his thoughts on the earth beneath the fallen horse. He could feel the hard soil, rigid with the cold. He let his mind settle deeper and sensed the small trails of blood that wetted the soil with traces of iron. Deeper still he probed with his senses. Here, the earth was warm and yielding. Anard imagined tamping down the softer soil beneath Eneas's leg. He felt the earth compact into a channel. The harder soil above cracked at the edges and molded into the newly formed channel. Beneath Eneas's body a rounded depression formed.

Anard was sweating, his black hair sticking to his temples. He stood quickly, ignoring the sudden dizziness to chuck the old gray under the chin and nudge him backward slowly. The rope went taut around Eneas's body. Eneas groaned as his leg was dragged out through the hollowed channel.

Anard wanted to cry out, seeing the long gash appear on Eneas's thigh. A crust of dried blood split and the wound began to bleed afresh. Eneas thrashed with pain, his back arched, his head straining to rise from the ground. Anard urged the gray to keep moving back, despite Eneas's cries. A final tug freed Eneas's booted leg and Anard was alarmed at the way it twisted oddly at the ankle to one side.

Eneas was moaning, his fists clenching and unclenching with the pain. Anard untied the rope at the gray's halter and rushed to his side.

"Eneas, you're free. Can you stand at all?" Anard asked, undoing the rope and then lifting Eneas by the shoulders. "The gray can carry you."

"I'm cold, I'm cold," Eneas hissed between chattering teeth.

"Come on," Anard pleaded.

Eneas pulled on Anard's waiting shoulder and made an effort to stand. Anard buckled under the extra weight and only his terrified determination succeeded in bringing Eneas at last to a standing position. Eneas leaned on Anard, his good leg barely able to support him. The broken leg dangled uselessly. "I can't," Eneas said. "I can't feel my feet."

Anard wrapped his arm around Eneas's waist, and though the injured man was heavy and his body swayed, Anard managed to keep him upright. Anard whistled for the gray. The horse approached nervously, his ears flickering wildly, the whites of his eyes showing in the twilight.

"Come on, old boy, help us," Anard said softly. The horse came close enough for Anard to grip its mane and steady the frightened beast.

"Eneas," Anard snapped. "Eneas," he called again, trying to rouse Eneas from his stupor of pain. "You've got to help me get you up on the gray."

Eneas stared vacantly at him. Blood was caked down one side of his face.

"You have to help me, Eneas!" Anard demanded, his voice sounding shrill.

Eneas reached out a stiff hand and grabbed the horse's mane. He leaned against the gray's side, his good leg wobbling dangerously. Anard knelt and wedged his body between Eneas's legs. Eneas's buttocks rested firmly on the crest of his shoulder. Slowly Anard pushed himself up from his crouch. Eneas pulled on the gray's mane, lurching his body over the swayed back of the horse.

Eneas sprawled across the horse's withers, his head laid against the gray's neck. Carefully, Anard slid the unbroken leg over the horse's back.

"Hold on," Anard said as much to himself as to Eneas. "It's not far."

Eneas's fingers twined around the coarse hair of the old gray's mane. Anard took the halter and led them away from the battleground.

At the brow of the hill he stopped once to check on Eneas

and to give a final glance to the dead, scattered in the narrow valley below. From where he stood, they had become indistinguishable from shadows. A groan from Eneas reminded Anard to keep moving. With tears burning behind his eyelids, Anard led the horse and its burden out of the last slanting rays of sunlight and into the dark forest.

Chapter Thirteen

Eagerly, Dagar watched the mainland rising out of the thin purple line of the horizon. It formed a long narrow ribbon of gray and brown, carved with slivers of beaches. As they neared the coast, the waves became smaller and more numerous, hurrying the longboat toward the mainland. Dried stalks of marsh grass lined the silty banks where the Sairas River flowed into the sea. Though the sun was hidden behind a bank of clouds, the gulls screeched overhead and blackbirds trilled their songs among the marsh grass. The wind shifted, bringing Dagar the smell of mud and dried kelp.

Alwir was handling the oars. His face was gaunt, the skin scrubbed raw on the cheeks above the sparse beard. His blue eyes were as cloudy as the day, gazing out at the expanse of ocean over which they had traveled. From time to time, he turned his head to glimpse the approaching shoreline. Then, turning back to the oars, his shoulders hunched to the task of rowing the longboat. Dagar's own shoulders throbbed with pain, his hands blistered from his turn at the oars. At Alwir's side, facing the shore, Tayleb called the directions and encouraged Alwir.

She leaned into the wind, her eyes trained to the waving marsh grass that drew them to shore. She seemed changed to Dagar. Her complexion was no longer ruddy from the island winds; instead her skin was always damp and milk pale, her cheeks like the smooth inside of a shell. Her eyes shifted from blue to green even as the water around them changed from salt to fresh.

Dagar touched his swollen lips with a tentative finger. The salt had dried in the cuts and stung his mouth. His lips felt solid and unmovable. He closed his eyes remembering. He could still see the glaring eyes and cold smirk of the Silean Guard. He shivered in the chilly air. Was it truly possible to be a Ghazali in these times, to walk the path of a peacekeeper? Perhaps Zein had been right, Dagar thought sadly, remembering Lirrel's father, the longbow and quiver of arrows over his shoulder. Zein had argued with Lirrel that to preserve the Ghazali way of peace, some had to be willing to fight for it, to be corrupted by the violence they abhorred. Lirrel had not agreed; she would rather remain pure.

He glanced at Lirrel, afraid that she might hear the doubt in his thoughts. She slept in the bottom of the boat, her black cloak pulled tightly around her. Her black hair fluttered in the breeze, revealing the drawn face. An ache stabbed his conscience as he watched her sleep.

Absently he patted the set of reed flutes in his pockets. How he wished he could play them now, find some comfort in the tunes of healing. But his lips were badly bruised and he knew that they would split and bleed anew. He decided to hear the tunes in his head, to lilt them in his mind, that they might settle his uneasiness.

As he concentrated on the tune, tapping his fingers with a quiet beat on his thigh, the nearing shore of a sandy beach beckoned a welcome.

"Aye, pull left," Tayleb said to Alwir, guiding him through the rising humps of sandbars, rocks, and marsh grass to the beach. "Not much more."

Lirrel roused herself, her moonlit eyes opening slowly, a puzzled smile on her mouth. "Is it you singing?" she asked Dagar in a husky voice.

Dagar nodded sheepishly. He touched his lips. "Hurts to play."

Lirrel sat up and looked out at the smooth curve of the beach. The smile on her lips faltered. She looked up at the sky, following the circling patterns of the gulls, and a worried crease lined her brow.

"Hold off," Tayleb said to Alwir and peered over the sides of the boat into the water. She frowned at the silty black mud and the broken stalks of marsh grass.

"What is it?" Alwir asked, his shoulders sagging. The longboat rocked, carried forward by the motion of the waves.

"It looks as though there have been a good many to land here before us," Tayleb said. "See how the marsh is trampled. I can't tell whether they have come from sea to land or gone the other way."

"Can it be fishing boats?" Dagar asked.

"No," Tayleb answered and, taking off her cloak and skirt, eased herself out of the longboat. She was standing waist deep in the water, black silt swirling around her shift as she waded through the marsh grass. A blackbird startled from the grass rose into the sky with a frantic beat of wings. Tayleb twisted around in the water, her hand spooning away the muddy silt. Then she darted forward, her arm sinking below the surface to retrieve something. She pulled up a leather glove. Sand emptied out from its finger holes and she washed it clean in the water. Tayleb brought it over to Alwir.

"Silean," she said softly. "And not long in the water."

Alwir looked up at the shore, his eyes squinting as he scanned the long beach. "Where are the ships?"

"Gone to Beldan, to wait," Lirrel answered.

"Do you know that for certain?" Alwir demanded.

Lirrel nodded, her face stricken.

"But what would they want with a place like Doberan?" Alwir asked. Lirrel remained silent. "Tell me, Lirrel," he insisted, "so we don't walk into danger."

Lirrel opened her mouth, but no words came. Instead tears welled in her eyes. Alwir tugged angrily at his beard and stared impatiently at the shore. "Z'blood, talk to me," he snapped.

"Give o're," Dagar said gruffly, putting his arm around the weeping Lirrel.

Tayleb leaned over the side of the longboat to touch Lirrel's arm. "Is it the vision?" she asked gently, taking Lirrel by the hand.

"Ahal," Lirrel replied weakly. And gradually, in the shelter of his arm Dagar felt her shoulders straighten and her back become erect.

"There is no one here, Alwir. This close to the land I know now what the vision showed me. The village of Doberan was laid to waste," she said.

"By Sileans?" Alwir asked, unbelieving.

"Recently come from Silea. There is a leader among them. He hardly seemed human." Lirrel paused before continuing. "There are no voices or thoughts, not even music in the air. I tell you, Alwir, there is no one alive in the village."

Dagar's heart was chilled by Lirrel's words. Vivid images of Cairns flashed without warning; he heard again the utter silence as he entered the village to find everyone had been slaughtered, his own family lying dead at the doorstep of his house.

"Come on." Alwir spoke harshly. "Let's get this longboat to the shore. We need land beneath our feet, we need a fire, and we need fresh water." He eased his body stiffly into the water beside Tayleb and together they pulled the boat toward shore.

Dagar helped Lirrel as she staggered in the muddy water up to the clean white sand of the shore. She laid down on her back and closed her eyes, her hands flattened to the sand, her fingers splayed. Sand drifted on the wind and settled over her eyelids. Gnawed with worry, Dagar watched over her.

At last Lirrel brushed her face clean of sand and opened her eyes. "Forgive me," she said, turning to meet Dagar's gaze.

"For what?" he asked.

"For being a poor teacher. And a worthless companion."

"Lirrel," Dagar groaned, upset that perhaps she had heard his unspoken doubts. "You *are* a good teacher. I only wish I was more of a Ghazali that I might help you."

Lirrel sat up and stared blankly at the water. It pained Dagar to see the expression of self-loathing on her face.

"I was arrogant enough to think there was only one path to being Ghazali. That as long as you remained true to the way, you were pure and strong. Either you embraced the life of a peacekeeper or you didn't. But now . . ." She lifted her arms to the air. "The visions steal my confidence. Rob me of certainty. Even when I argued with Zein at Sadar, I was without doubt. Now I am filled with it. I have strayed from the lighted path and into the shadows."

Dagar took Lirrel's hands between his two palms. Her hands were small and delicate. "Lirrel, listen to me. You are favored by Oran. You are an air element, born with great power, to do great things."

She looked away, but he tugged at her hands until she returned her gaze to him.

Dagar continued. "All your life you have seen Oran's future rise before you like the clouds. You walked the path of the Ghazali with the confidence that comes from knowledge. And yet, even when you knew the way would be dangerous, you didn't retreat."

"But now I have lost the way," Lirrel said flatly.

"No," Dagar insisted. "The world has changed. Oran has changed. The Chaos steals power not only from Zorah but also from you. Robbed of the light of knowledge, you feel lost on a shadowed road." Dagar gazed steadily into the opal-colored eyes. "Look at me, Lirrel. I walk the path with faith only. I know nothing of the future, expect what my heart may hope for. But I have faith that the path of the peacekeeper is the right one to follow."

Lirrel nodded sadly. "You are right. I mistook knowledge for faith." She turned her head so that he couldn't see her expression. "Come on," she said, standing. "We must help them gather wood for the fire. I shouldn't add laziness to my other shortcomings."

"Lirrel—" Dagar protested.

"I am sorry. I didn't really mean that," she said, smiling and waving away her comment with a hand. But her smile seemed strained to Dagar. She shook the sand from her skirts with an angry jerk before heading to the shore where Tayleb and Alwir had gathered a pile of driftwood. He hadn't eased her mind at all, Dagar thought with disappointment as he watched Lirrel go, her heels driving into the damp sand. Perhaps with rest and food her better humor would return again. Dagar rose wearily from the sand and began to search among the trees for wood to add to the newly smoking fire.

Tayleb squatted by the fire, her skirt tucked beneath her thighs. Over the sparks of the fire she saw the last glow of sunlight, streaking the sky with a rose-colored farewell. Mist formed over the sea, obscuring the edge of the horizon. The shorebirds had grown quiet as the day slipped into twilight and even the pounding of the waves had gentled to a soft rasp.

They had rigged a small shelter beneath the trees of the shoreline. The wind rustled the dried leaves overhead but hardly disturbed the flames of the fire. Alwir had argued that they should go to the village for shelter, but Lirrel refused, and so they had remained on the beach.

Tayleb looked up at the haggard faces of her companions and wondered what was next. They had arrived, but each was so battered, withdrawn into his own shell as they hunkered around the fire. On Lirrel's face was misery. Dagar sat beside her and Tayleb marked the way his eyes worried over her silence. He took out his flutes and though he winced as the reed pressed against his bruised lips, he played a few breathy notes. Lirrel's head bowed between her hands and Dagar stopped playing, as if fearing that his music made it worse for her.

Alwir was sitting cross-legged, his long arms laid over his thighs. Tayleb liked the sight of his hands, the tapered fingers elegant despite the weather-roughened skin and torn nails. His lowered chin was close to his chest, and from beneath the dirty bandage Tayleb saw his eyes staring moodily into the fire.

No words from any of them.

Tayleb's throat thickened in the silence. She thought unwillingly of her own losses: Teck and Moire and the Namires. The grief was unbearable and as she stared at the unfamiliar shore her life seemed unreal. She wanted to cry but instead became angry. From a bag she withdrew the last handful of dried fruit she had brought from Tynor's Rock. Some of the fruit was moist and sticky with saltwater. She laid them down on a strip of bleached wood and took out the last of the dried meat. The long strips were white along the edges where the seawater had soaked them. She laid it out for all of them to share.

No one moved toward the food.

Tayleb snatched a strip of the meat and chewed it. Her tongue instantly swelled with the salt taste.

"Water," she murmured and reached for the water skin. She had filled it from the mouth of the Sairas, and though it was mostly fresh, it still had the faint tang of the sea.

Alwir stood abruptly. "I'm going to the village," he announced. "Even though the Sileans have probably taken everything, perhaps I can find us blankets, food—"

"Weapons?" Lirrel said bitterly.

"Yes," Alwir replied angrily. "There may have been some hidden away. I can't just sit here and wait for Oran's fate to be decided by others. I'm not afraid of the dead if that's all there is at Doberan."

Lirrel hugged her knees. "I'll wait here," she said sullenly.

"I'll go with you, Alwir," Dagar volunteered.

"You don't have to, Dagar," Alwir answered more softly.

"Aye, but I do," Dagar said. "The dead need to be remembered." He patted the flutes in his pocket.

"It might be like Cairns," Alwir warned.

"I must still go."

"I'll stay here with Lirrel," Tayleb said to Alwir. "We'll keep the fire going. Only, don't be long," she added, trying not to sound scared.

Alwir bent down and touched her cheek. His fingertips were cold, dry points on her skin, and she clasped her hands around his to warm it.

"We won't be long," he promised.

Then Alwir and Dagar left, following an old and well-worn trail into the forest. Tayleb watched until she could no longer see them among the trees. The light was going fast and in the looming darkness Tayleb shivered.

Lirrel rubbed her hands over her face. "This is terrible," she moaned. "I have never felt so strange, even to myself."

"Have you always known that you were an air element?" Tayleb asked.

"Always," Lirrel answered. "Among my people it was regarded as a gift, not a curse. To restore peace to the troubled heart is something the Ghazali value highly. As an air element I always knew the right words to speak. Now . . ." Lirrel shrugged, her eyes glistening with tears.

Tayleb leaned forward to the unhappy woman. "Maybe, Lirrel, you should try your skill on your own troubled heart."

Lirrel's expression became thoughtful. And then from the pocket of her skirt she withdrew her bone flute. Her hands settled on its shaft like brown sparrows lighting on a branch as she lifted it to her lips. Tayleb leaned back to listen.

The notes that issued from the flute ambled without a discernible shape. Tayleb tried to hear in them a melody. And when she found she couldn't, she tried to imagine instead the music of her element; the rasping of waves, staccato bursts of spray, and the currents drifting like a long, sustained note. She imagined the rain pattering on the thatched roof of the cottage and water gurgling as it drained from the skin into the kettle. There was the soft whisper of steam and the muted hush of mist on the ocean.

Tayleb closed her eyes. She felt her element like a frozen limb at last given the power of motion. It was another sense, newly wakened to reveal a denser and more complex truth of the world. And as she delved into the core of her power, she heard the blood and water squeezed through Oran's veins, pumped by a glowing heart of fire. It warmed her, and her senses spiraled like steam through pulsing veins. Through the earth-solid flesh of Oran's body she seeped, into every crevice and seam, flowing over the broad places and pooling in the hollows of Oran's throat, collarbone, and belly. On her tongue she tasted salt, rust, and spring water sharpened by the resin of pine. Oran's flesh expanded, drawing breath, and Tayleb inhaled the sour mist of Chaos. The mist was exhaled into a sigh, blown through the hollow core of a flute. A flute that played the sorrow and joy of Oran.

Tayleb opened her eyes in wonder. "Lirrel," she whispered.

Lirrel put her flute down, her face serene again. "We will be one, joined into this flesh," she breathed. She glanced up at Tayleb and gave a startled cry.

Tayleb turned, alarmed, and saw a figure limping up the beach toward them. "Kire," she called, recognizing the Namire. A flood of happiness rushed her footsteps.

Kire waited for Tayleb to reach her. Tayleb's joy quickly changed to distress. Kire's skin was splotched with bruises and her black hair was streaked with gray in the twilight. Her flanks had thinned, her ribs visible on her torso. She breathed with difficulty and the gill flaps on her neck looked dry, their wrinkled edges like the petals of a wilted flower.

Tayleb pulled off her cloak and spread it over Kire's shoulders. "You're ill. Come by the fire," Tayleb said, guiding Kire up the beach. But the Namire stopped her with a hand.

"No," she rasped. "I can't stay long out of the water. Too hard to breathe."

"But what has happened?" Tayleb asked.

"It's the wasting disease. I am the last to die. It might have been better if the Sileans had killed me, except for this."

Tears welled in Tayleb's eyes and Kire's face swam before her vision, her form rippling as it did in the sea. "What are you saying?"

"I came to ask your forgiveness, Tayleb. I don't want to die knowing that you were angry with us. With me."

Tayleb clasped Kire gently. Tears lined her face. "There is nothing to forgive, Kire. You are my sister."

"We had no choice. There was so little time left. Zorah's curse drains us. We mourned those who in our desperation we drowned. But now that you are found, I can join my shoal sisters in death."

"Kire, I promise the Namires will live again. That your name will be remembered."

Kire shook her head. "Those times are over. The Namires

belong to Oran's past.'' Air rattled in Kire's throat. "I must go.''

Reluctantly, Tayleb released her. Kire slid the cloak from her shoulders and slipped it back around Tayleb. She kissed Tayleb on both cheeks. Then she turned and limped down the sandy beach to the water. The waves spread out over the sand and Tayleb heard Kire cry out as her feet touched the water. She waded into the waves, turning once to raise her hand in a final salute before she dove beneath the surface.

Tayleb stood watching the blue-white foam that capped the waves. The warm tears cooled on her cheeks and chafed the skin. Shivering in the cold winds, Tayleb was forced to leave the beach. She walked slowly up the shore to the trees, where Lirrel waited for her by the crackling fire.

Behind Alwir, Dagar listened to the quiet sound of their footfall on the sandy trail that led to the village. He glanced up at the sky between the leafless branches. A fading rose color lined the bottom of the low-lying clouds and then was absorbed by the darkness. The silence of the approaching night seemed strange and Dagar realized he was missing the constant splash of the waves.

"Will Lirrel be all right?" Alwir asked softly and Dagar jumped at the unexpected sound of his voice.

"Aye. Just give her a little time.''

"We don't have much time," Alwir answered sharply.

"She's wounded," Dagar said. "But she's also strong.''

Dagar could feel the unspoken heat of Alwir's anger, see it in the stiff set of his shoulders.

Dagar stopped him with a hand on his arm. As Alwir tensed, expecting danger, Dagar spoke quickly. "I meant to thank you for saving me. It cost you much to get me off the ship.''

Dagar heard the ragged intake of Alwir's breath and then he exhaled with a low moan. His body weaved slightly.

"Did I do the right thing, Dagar?"

"I don't know," Dagar answered, understanding Alwir's question. He knew what had eaten into Alwir's heart since Tynor's Rock.

"Did my father move to protect me from the Silean's arrow, or did he move to protect the Silean from my knife?"

Dagar shook his head. "There is no answer to that."

"I hated my father. I hated what he stood for, what he tried to make me do as a Reader. And for all that," Alwir whispered angrily, "and for all that, at the last moment he may have moved to protect me. The only time my father might have acted as my father and I murder him for it."

Dagar's arms opened with helplessness. "Nothing we've done in this war is right. But we do as we have to, in the moment we are given."

"You wouldn't have done that," Alwir challenged. "You're too much of a Ghazali even now."

"I wouldn't have done as you, Alwir, but then if it had been up to me, none of us would be here now arguing the point. We'd be dead. You did as the moment commanded and out of pure intention—"

"Not so pure. I *intended* to murder someone."

Dagar lowered his eyes to his feet. They were hard to see in the dark. A shadowy path, indeed. "There's no way to understand the Chaos," he said. "We can only survive it and hope for a future in spite of it." Dagar raised his head, his chin thrust forward. "Come on, Alwir," Dagar urged. "Dream a hero's dream, not the nightmare of Chaos, but of the world to come. And with a hero's will, make it happen."

It was hard to make out Alwir's features, but Dagar saw him nod, reluctantly at first and then with more conviction.

"A hero's dream, huh?" Alwir gave a dry laugh. "Sounds like the name of a tune. A tune that's too complicated for anyone to play."

Relieved by the sound of Alwir's laugh, Dagar laughed as well. "I'll work on it."

"So will I then," Alwir agreed. "It'll be a duet. But in the meantime, there is still Chaos calling the dance."

He started walking up the path again and Dagar followed, touching the reeds of his flute for comfort.

* * *

Lirrel rested her chin on her kneecaps. Something was nagging at her. It wasn't the dreadful expectation of another vision, but something like a long-forgotten song resurrecting note by note. Lirrel cocked her head to listen.

"What is it?" Tayleb asked.

At the sound of Tayleb's voice a flurry of new notes chased into her head. "Something important," Lirrel said, hushed. A crack from the fire caught Lirrel's attention and it, too, joined its crisp voice with the song being shaped in her mind.

Lirrel realized it wasn't just one song demanding to be remembered. Every note of the tune was changed as it mingled with the other sounds of the night. The hoarse waves carried a brushing rhythm and the creak of the trees thickened the base of the music. Lirrel began to tap with a little stick on the sand. She could almost see the music, shaping a pattern in the drifting smoke. She looked up at Tayleb, a smile opening her face.

"Sing," she demanded of Tayleb.

"Sing what?"

"Anything. Just sing."

Still bewildered by Lirrel's request, Tayleb folded her hands in her lap and began to sing an Islander's song. Her voice wavered at first, throaty as she reached for the higher notes. Then it grew stronger and clearer as Tayleb relaxed and enjoyed the singing. Grace notes tumbled between phrases as the song traveled like a stream.

Tayleb's voice rose above the gathering fragments of Lirrel's song. Lirrel placed her flute to her lips and, blowing softly, joined the melody with Tayleb's voice. On the bones of Tayleb's song Lirrel built a delicate structure of music, each fragment of sound shaping muscle and sinew; the subtle planes of a face, the contours of a body, at once graceful and strong. She drew together the heat and crackle of fire, the slow pulse of the earth, the flow of water and the breath of air that blew the tune into Oran's universe.

The music lifted Lirrel's spirits and gave her courage. She could not see the future anymore perhaps, but she could still hear Oran and she knew what was needed. And needed now.

At the snap of a branch Tayleb stopped singing. The music scattered like a handful of tossed pebbles.

"Alwir?" Tayleb called out to the dark trees.

Lirrel was jarred out of the music. With resignation, she carefully wiped her flute dry before she returned it to her pocket. Already she could hear the anguish in Alwir and Dagar's minds as they approached. But she felt calm, certain once more of herself and the need to act.

Alwir broke through the darkness and into the circle of firelight. There was a hard gleam in his eyes. He carried a bow slung over one shoulder and clutched a handful of arrows, the fletches torn. A short sword was shoved through his belt. In the other hand he carried two blankets, a water skin, and a small jug of Mother's Tears.

Dagar approached the fire after Alwir. His face was ashen but his features were quiet, his mouth soft. He set down an armload of cloaks and a basket of dried cheese.

"There's nothing left of them." Alwir spit the words furiously. He tossed down the two blankets and the water skin. Sitting near the fire he undid the cork of the jug and took a draught of the Mother's Tears.

"But the people?" Tayleb asked.

Alwir shook his head. "There's a huge grave outside the village walls. Animals have been scratching at it and you can find the remains of the villagers all over the Plains. Just bones."

"There is something else, Lirrel," Dagar said softly, retrieving a headscarf from his pocket. His hand trembled slightly as he handed the scarf to Lirrel. It smelled of henna and salt. She tied it around her head, grateful for its warmth.

"What is it?" she asked, edging closer to Dagar. His lip was bleeding and she knew he must have been playing his reed flutes. A song to ease the despair of war.

"There is a carcass of a giant creature. Shaped like a bird, only the size of four men laid together. The wings are picked clean of flesh but there are still feathers clinging to it."

"A Kirian," Lirrel replied. "Most were killed in the first Burning, destroyed when Zorah severed the knot. But a few may have survived until now."

"Like the Namires?" Tayleb added.

"*Ahal,* and like them it must have been among the last of its kind."

"Frigging shit," Alwir shouted. "We have to make some decisions. We can't stay here. Look, I have no desire to lead us right into the Silean army. From the looks of the road out of Doberan, they went north. And with no horses, and probably every village between here and that army sacked, it could take us a long time to reach Sadar."

"We will not return to Sadar," Lirrel interrupted him.

"But Jobber and Shedwyn . . . How will you form the knot?" asked Dagar.

"We don't need to be together for that to happen. I think I can use the music of my flute to bring us together. We have these bodies," Lirrel started to explain, "but we are also elements in Oran's body."

Lirrel searched the armload of cloaks until she found one with its hem unraveling. She pulled a long strand of wool from it, retied it into a circle of thread, and placed it between her hands. Then she wove her fingers through it and created a pattern like stars in the middle of the circle.

Looking up at the others, she smiled and undid the yarn again. She started over with the loop around her hands. "Oran's cradle is the same as the Queens' quarter knot. Watch how the four threads are tied into the knot," Lirrel continued. "We are those threads. Shedwyn, Jobber, Tayleb, and I."

She bent her fingers around the string again, and as each thread twined into its place, Lirrel felt the solid ground beneath her thin. The little stones in the sand eroded and became the glassy surface of water. Then the water steamed and became hot and silky as bright flame. And last it changed again, the flames drawn into smoke. Gray wisps of smoke were carried aloft into the night.

A night of wind and distant stars.

Chapter Fourteen

Jobber leaned forward to shift the wood burning in the fire. She shoved a reluctant log deeper into the bed of glowing embers. Around her voices rose in heated argument.

"The New Moon should stay in the North until spring," Grouter insisted. He was a miner, recently joined to the New Moon, a huge man with stooped shoulders and skin dyed a faint blue from the black dust of the mines.

"Too dangerous," countered Treys. "How much of the North will be left come spring? You saw what happened at Sadar. We can't rely on Queen Huld to protect us any longer."

Jobber looked up at Treys, his face weary with argument, the whorled tree marks on his face etched deeper into his skin. His beard had become salted with gray over the winter. In his broad, callused hands he smoothed the sides of a longstaff.

"What are you saying then?" Grouter demanded.

"We go to Asturas," Treys answered calmly, "and we take the city. No more hiding in the woods."

"And the militias?" Faul asked skeptically.

"We've no choice but to move against them and hope we can

raise the other Orans in the city to join us. We have people there. And there are more bands of New Moon to the west of the city.''

"Too soon," spoke Shefek, shaking his head. "I came through Asturas on my way to Sadar. The Orans there were half starved or overworked. You won't make a fighting army of them to challenge the militias.''

"So far we've fought the trade roads," Faul said. "The New Moon has only had to plunder the odd cart coming through with grain; now you talk of taking possession of the town." Faul shook her head. "They're not the same thing. We'd be digging in and not following our own strategy: get in, get out.''

"And the children?" demanded Hanne, a young woman from the western Plains. Hanne's face was long and thin, the high cheekbones of her Oran face carving two sharp arches beneath her dark eyes. "Do you expect them to fight?" She gestured toward the straggly camps of children bedded down through the trees.

Treys growled at the ground. Then he looked up and his eyes held a challenge. "What else then?"

There was silence around the fire as each contemplated a reply.

"I think Treys is right," Shedwyn said, breaking the silence.

Jobber looked over, curious that Shedwyn should bring her voice into this argument. They had tried to keep themselves free of the arguing and planning, knowing that whatever the New Moon army did, their own role was already decided elsewhere. The New Moon might plan its strategy against the Sileans, but it was up to Shedwyn, Jobber, and Lirrel, if she found the fourth girl, to form the knot that would challenge the Oran Queen.

"Look," Shedwyn was saying, her palms held up as if to catch the light of the fire, "there is no more time left. I can feel it. The earth is slipping away. Come spring there will be naught left of Oran to defend. The Sileans won't matter, we won't matter.''

As Shedwyn spoke, Jobber was distracted by another sound murmuring through the forest. She glanced up at the trees, trying to locate the source. It grew louder, shaking the tops of the trees and brushing the branches together in a noisy rustle. Then it changed, and the rustle became a shrill whine. Shedwyn's voice faded, drowned beneath the keening wind.

Jobber lowered her eyes to the others, still arguing, deaf to the sound. Jobber started to speak and saw their faces suddenly merge into a single streak of colored light. As she felt herself stretched into a thread of fiery light she saw Shedwyn's astonished face, shining bright as an emerald, her mouth rounded with surprise.

Then there was nothing but a night of wind and distant stars.

"Frigging shit!" Jobber breathed in the stream of light and it dissolved, leaving her drifting in a dark sky. Close by her, Jobber saw Shedwyn, her mouth still open with shock. She hovered, glowing like a star, the green light of her element twinkling around her body. She floated, her arms held aloft by a wind, her braid curling in the air. Jobber stared down at her arms and saw the lick of bright orange flames.

"Shedwyn?" Jobber called and the sound of her voice whispered across the empty expanse of sky. Other stars trembled as if disturbed by the sound.

"Jobber, where are we?" Shedwyn asked. The sound of their voices pulled them together.

"Look down there." Jobber pointed as below them in the night sky an island of earth drifted. It shimmered with green and gold, broken here and there with ribbons of blue. A thin vein of white snaked around it, bundling it with the gossamer of spider silk. Frail threads lifted into the night, some of them frayed and torn, others disappearing into the blackness.

"Oran," Shedwyn said. She untangled a vine of green light from her arm, plucking it off her shoulders, down the length of her body, and unwinding it from her thighs and calves. She held the green vine out to show Jobber where the end of it trailed downward as a fine thread of light attached somewhere below to Oran's earthly flesh.

Jobber looked at the flames on her own arm and saw now the pale red-gold strand, the thickness of one of her copper-colored hairs, spinning from the tips of her fingers out into the night. If she squinted she could see its light reach down to Oran below.

"How did we get here?" Jobber asked alarmed. "Is it like Sadar? Have we just . . . disappeared into the sky?"

"Look there!" Shedwyn answered, pointing to a flash of white light.

Jobber squinted in the brilliant streak of light. It blazed white like sunlight glancing off the surface of water. A sharp line of blue twisted around it. The light arched toward them and as it neared, Jobber heard the sweet hollow voice of a flute.

"Lirrel! Lirrel!" Jobber called. She could see now the black outlines of her form eclipsing the core of the light. Her raised hands rested on the shaft of the flute. The music stopped and Lirrel looked up. In the dark shadow of her form, two moonlit eyes stared back.

"*Aha!* Jobber, it is me!"

She drifted forward, the light rising out of the dark sky to illuminate them all.

Another woman drifted beside Lirrel and Jobber grinned, seeing the blue waves of light draped like a cloak over the fourth girl.

She had a small, heart-shaped face surrounded by a mass of wavy curls. In Lirrel's white light her skin gleamed like mother-of-pearl, except for the shifting blue-green of her eyes staring shyly back at Jobber.

Shedwyn moved forward to greet them, her hands outstretched in welcome. Jobber followed her, startled by the sensation of motion in such a strange place.

Lirrel smiled in greeting and placed her flute in her pocket.

"It is good to see you both again. I wasn't sure I could do this."

Shedwyn reached out and touched Lirrel. Sparks of white and green snapped like tiny stars in the air. Shedwyn laughed at the sight. "Well, whatever you did, it worked. And I can tell you this is much more lovely than where we just were."

"And are we still there?" Jobber asked.

Lirrel nodded. "Do you remember the day I saw the vision of the massacre of Cairns?"

"Yeah." Jobber nodded and the flames on her arm flared with the painful memory.

"It was to this place I fled."

"But it was all dark then," Shedwyn said. "And we couldn't see the stars, nor Oran below us."

"I didn't know Oran the way I do now," Lirrel replied. "And we weren't all together then. I've learned much since I saw you last."

"So have we," added Jobber grimly.

"You are the fourth then, the water element," Shedwyn said facing Tayleb. "I am Shedwyn."

Tayleb came forward with a nervous smile. "Lirrel has told me about you. I am Tayleb."

"An Islander?" Jobber asked.

"Aye. And you're Jobber, Beldan bred, are you not?" she asked.

"Oy, Lirrel," Jobber said tartly. "What have you told her about me?"

"Nothing you aren't proud of saying about yourself."

Jobber laughed softly. Then she put her arms around Lirrel. "I've missed you," she whispered fiercely.

"And I you," Lirrel whispered back. "I thought I would find a bit of peace away from you. But instead I missed your temper."

Jobber rolled her eyes. "Well, you're the only one."

Then she released Lirrel and stepped back. As they hovered in the glow of light they studied each other in glad silence.

"Well," Jobber said, "there's a reason for your bringing us together like this."

Lirrel's expression slipped, and for an instant Jobber saw the fear Lirrel struggled to contain.

"The reason is this: we need to form the knot now. We can't wait until spring when we are together in body."

"Last night Sadar's Keep was destroyed," Shedwyn said.

"By whom?" Lirrel asked, though it seemed to Jobber that she was not surprised by the news.

"Zorah most likely. The stones just lifted into the sky, torn right out of the earth. Even Huld can't prevent it anymore and she can't hold on to the land.''

Lirrel nodded. ''I have lost some of my sight and my ability to see the future,'' she confessed. Jobber heard the pain in her voice. ''There is another reason, though, which you must know,'' Lirrel went on. ''We are now on Oran's coast, near Doberan.''

''Orian's there,'' Jobber interrupted.

''No,'' Tayleb spoke up. ''The village was laid to waste. There was no one left alive. Lirrel saw it happen in a vision. There is a Silean army, moving north along the Sairas River.''

''They must be coming to Asturas,'' Shedwyn guessed.

''Yes,'' Lirrel agreed. ''You must leave for Beldan at once. We'll meet you there, and the sooner the better.''

''Do you know the Ribbons?'' Jobber asked Lirrel.

''The bits of marshland at the throat of Beldan's harbor?''

''Yeah, that's it. Kai and Slipper used to have shacks there. At any rate it was Waterling territory. It ought still to be safe. Go there and wait for us.''

Lirrel turned to Tayleb. ''Can we take the boat up the coast to the harbor?''

''Too far to row,'' Tayleb said. ''But there's sure to be a skiff from the village. I'll send Alwir to look for it.''

''Are Alwir and Dagar well?'' Shedwyn asked and Tayleb hesitated before answering.

''Aye, well enough,'' she said at last.

''It's been a hard journey,'' Lirrel said. ''Too many deaths. Tell Treys that Moire, Tayleb's mother, is dead.''

''The Namires, too, are gone,'' Tayleb added softly. ''And on the field outside of Doberan there is the carcass of a slain Kirian.''

Jobber groaned and closed her eyes. She would have to tell Shefek. He would know who it was.

''We must hurry now,'' Lirrel said quickly. ''I don't know how long I can hold us here.''

''Why is it so calm here?'' Shedwyn asked, puzzled. ''I would have thought this close to Chaos all we'd hear is the wind.''

''Look above,'' Lirrel said softly.

Jobber and Shedwyn raised their heads warily. Jobber swore,

seeing the churning mass of black and gray clouds. The air above them seethed, twisting in a drawn funnel of roiling clouds. And in the center of the circling tide of clouds hovered a long flaming sword.

"Zorah's Fire Sword," Jobber spat. "The cause of all this misery."

"I joined Tayleb's power to mine," Lirrel explained. "We are suspended in a bubble, air held by the thinnest sheath of water. But it's fragile and I can't hold us here for long."

"Lirrel, do you know how to form the Queens' quarter knot?" Shedwyn asked.

Lirrel shook her head and her black hair floated away from her shoulders. "I doubt there is anyone left who can tell us that. Moire, Zein, Growler, and your father, too, Shedwyn, are all dead. We must do this on our own. But I am not without ideas," she added and smiled at them.

Lirrel withdrew from her pocket the long circle of string. "Do you remember, Jobber, when I showed you the game of Oran's cradle?"

"Yeah," Jobber said, her eyes fixed like a child's on the string stretched between Lirrel's palms.

"Perhaps that is all the knot has ever been. Oran's cradle. And our elements, are the threads in the game." Lirrel put the string away and lifted the coiled thread of light from her arm. It stretched away on either side of her, with no start and no ending. As she held it up it gleamed white and smooth. "Here, each of you, hand me some of your thread."

Shedwyn unwound the vine of green light from her arm and held out a section to Lirrel. Jobber shook out from the tips of her fingers a hair-fine coil of red light. As it touched the other two threads it flushed brightly and sprouted blooms of flames along its length. Lastly, Tayleb handed a soft thread of glittering blue light.

They floated close together, shoulders touching, and the light of their elemental threads illuminated their expectant faces. Jobber could see the fatigue and worry in Lirrel's eyes, the purple shadows that smudged her eyelids. She saw Tayleb's pale face, the dusting of freckles over her nose and the salty powder that dried on her eyelashes. She glanced at Shedwyn and saw in the planes of her brown oval face a calmness. Her eyelids drooped as her eyes turned inward to view another world. She moved her lips in a quietly worded message.

"Wait," Jobber said and Lirrel looked up startled. "Shedwyn is pregnant. Will this harm the baby?"

Lirrel's face lost its tension, her lips relaxing into a smile. She kissed Shedwyn on both cheeks. And then laughed. "I have felt the spark of your child. It gave me hope. No, the baby won't suffer ill. I think we will gain by its promise."

"Her promise," Shedwyn corrected. "The child is a girl."

"So the next knot is already waiting to be born," Lirrel said. "We'd better form this one then, to give her the chance."

Lirrel returned her attention to the strands of light in her hand. She wound them together loosely, giving them the semblance of unity in a single strand. White over red, over green, over blue, and then white again.

"This is us," she said, and placed the circle of colored light between her palms. "In the beginning, Oran's world was a toy, formed out of the Chaos and blown by the howling winds." Lirrel began to weave the threads of light, following the words of the old Oran story. "To protect His creations from the destruction of Chaos, Oran's mother Amatersoran gave to Him the strength of four elements, each to be a strand in a cradle that would shield Oran's world. But the world became too heavy for the cradle, filled with the humans Oran created. Amatersoran gave Oran death to lighten the load of His cradle. But even that was not enough. And so much did Oran love His people that He eased Himself into the cradle and gave it the strength of His flesh. The strands of elements became His heart of warming fire, the water His blood and tears, His flesh transformed into earth, and His breath the air and wind."

In Lirrel's hands the knot drew ever tighter and more complicated. Each strand doubled back and twisted around its partners until it was impossible to tell where it began and where it ended.

Lirrel finished her story and resting between her palms was a knot of light, suspended between the separate lines of colored light. "Oran's cradle is our knot. We are the flesh, the blood, the heart, and the breath of Oran." Lirrel slipped a colored strand off her fingers and gave one back to Jobber, another to Shedwyn and Tayleb, and kept the last for herself.

The fiery red strand of light settled again like a coral snake around Jobber's wrist.

The knot still hovered, suspended between them. They each moved back cautiously. The strands lengthened, but the core of the knot remained.

"Oy, you feel any different?" Jobber asked Shedwyn, filled with awe.

"No," Shedwyn answered, sounding a little disappointed. "What about you, Lirrel?"

Lirrel laughed, her white teeth gleaming in the night. "I do! I feel even more clearly your presence and can hear the noise of your thoughts."

"Wait, so do I," said Tayleb, her head cocked to one side. "But it's strange. I smell smoke and heated iron. The taste of pine and earth." She placed her finger to her tongue. "Salty water, but clean, not like the ocean."

"The womb, then," answered Shedwyn, the green light of her thread shimmering a bright spring green. "I feel it now too. It's in the senses." She grinned at Tayleb. "Lime, tasting sweet in the acid soil."

"From shells!" Tayleb answered.

Shedwyn bent her head. "Spring water, hidden below the Plains of Sadar. Cold—"

"And wet!" wailed Jobber. "Z'blood how I hate the feel of wet."

"Steam," shouted Lirrel. "Heat, dry and crackling."

"Do you know, Lirrel," Jobber said wiping away at the sudden sensation of rain on her cheeks, "I can hear the notes of a tune. Z'blood, I'll bet I can sing."

She opened her mouth and then promptly shut it again. "Nah. That would be too much magic."

Lirrel's smile tightened and her brow creased over her moonlit eyes. "I can't hold back the Chaos much longer. Even with the knot, I don't have that kind of strength." She drew a ragged breath and Jobber sensed in the knot Lirrel's bone-deep exhaustion. "When I release the bubble we will be at the mercy of Chaos. Keep the knot in your mind and hold tight to your threads. They will guide you back to your bodies below."

"We'll see you at the Ribbons," Jobber said.

"At the Ribbons," Lirrel echoed, the sound of her voice already fading.

The winds of Chaos shredded the fragile boundaries of Lirrel's bubble. Jobber's breath was snatched away by a powerful gust of wind. The shrieking wind spun her around, tumbling her like a dried autumn leaf. Jobber panicked, helpless as the wind stole every breath she tried to gain. Her hair lashed across her face like heated wire.

Jobber grabbed ahold of her thread and pulled hard on the fiery strand. At once she stopped tumbling, though her legs trailed out like ribbons fluttering on the crown of a woman's hat. Jobber clung to the thread of light as it bounced in the wind. Hand over hand, she pulled herself downward along its taut length. The strand of light vibrated, thrummed by the wind, but held steady by Jobber's rage. Through the roiling clouds, Jobber could make out the distant glimmer of Oran.

"Frigging long way down," she muttered and the winds carried away her words.

And yet it took very little time. She reached down, growing stronger as the winds of Chaos scudded furiously above her. And then, as if abruptly released, the taut strand of light relaxed and coiled in the air. Jobber gasped as she plummeted downward with eyes wide open, the thread of light scattering around her like sparks from a fire.

"Z'blood!" Jobber screeched and bolted upright from the ground. Her stomach lurched as gravity weighed on her shoulders. Her head drooped forward with dizziness and her eyes ached.

"What is it?" a voice demanded.

Jobber swallowed thickly and peered up into Faul's worried face.

"Z'blood, Faul, I thought I was going to wind up splattered."

A groan brought Jobber's head up farther and she saw Shedwyn lying beside her, her body curled into a protective knot. She was breathing hard and one hand reached out with splayed fingers.

Jobber grabbed her hand and gently pulled her upright. Shedwyn's eyes fluttered open, fearful and shocked. She stared dazed at Jobber, the color drained from her cheeks.

"You're all right," Jobber said.

"I'm going to throw up," Shedwyn said weakly and Jobber quickly released her hand. Shedwyn lumbered to her hands and knees and stayed there, swaying.

Jobber waited, looking up at the tops of the trees, imagining her own stomach hovering somewhere above. She was surprised to see that the sky was a pale gray. Dawn already.

A few moments passed in silence. And then Shedwyn settled back on her heels. "Maybe I'm not." She sighed.

"Naffy way down, ain't it?" Jobber replied.

"What's happened?" Faul barked, her voice sharp. "We've been watching you all night and you've both lain like the dead. If it weren't for Shefek saying otherwise, we'd have buried you."

Shefek leaned down close to Jobber and brushed her hair away from her face. "So, my young chick, you've seen Chaos," he said, his strange eyes glinting gold as they caught the first rays of sunlight.

"Yeah. Not a place I'd recommend," Jobber answered.

Shefek gave a grin and patted her heavily on the shoulder.

Shedwyn tried to speak, her voice cracking dryly. Faul motioned Hanne to bring some water.

"Lirrel has found the fourth girl," Shedwyn announced to the growing circle of people. Murmured words scattered through the crowd as the message was sent back.

"She found a way to bring us together, somewhere between Oran and Chaos," Jobber explained.

"But the winds . . ." Shefek frowned.

"She used Tayleb, that's the fourth girl. With water and air together, she made a bubble and protected us."

"And the knot?" asked Treys, his face tense with anticipation.

"Aye," Shedwyn replied. "We formed the knot. Lirrel drew our threads together into the likeness of Oran's cradle."

Tears brimmed in Treys' eyes. "A Queens' quarter knot," he breathed. "How long I have waited to hear such news."

"But the rest of the news ain't at all good," Jobber said grimly. "Lirrel and Tayleb are with Alwir and Dagar along the coast near Doberan. They say a Silean army is cutting a path up Asturas. The butcherboys slaughtered everyone in Doberan." Jobber inhaled deeply and then continued. "She also said they found the remains of a Kirian. It must have fought with the villagers at Doberan."

"Orian," Shefek hissed. His face sagged, his cheeks a waxy color. Faul reached out a hand to steady his shoulder.

"I'm sorry, Shefek," Jobber said, shaken at hearing Orian's name. "I didn't know she was a Kirian."

"Orian was my daughter," Shefek said quietly. "She and I are the last of the Kirians." The gold gleam of his eyes was tarnished. "So, I am to come to Chaos alone."

"Jobber and I must leave here at once," Shedwyn said softly. "We are to meet Lirrel and Tayleb in Beldan. At a place called the Ribbons."

Shefek roused himself, his movements brusque. "I will fly ahead to Beldan to tell Kai and Slipper. They will be there, waiting for you when you come."

Faul stood, brushing back her graying hair from her face. In the early morning light her pale skin looked drawn. "We'll need horses. I'm going with you to Beldan. You're going to need some protection along the way."

"Me too!" shouted a voice from the onlookers. Jobber saw Finch's head of bright yellow hair emerge from between two thick-set laborers. "Oy, Jobbernowl, you ain't going back to Beldan without me!"

"This isn't a faire day!" Faul said angrily. "We have to make the trip with speed. And it's dangerous."

"I'm coming," Wyer spoke up. He smiled at Jobber and reached down a hand to help pull her up from the cold ground.

"Frigging Beldanites!" Faul swore. "You're all just home-sick."

"That's right," Finch said proudly. "I've been away too long. If the whole world's gonna go up, I want to be in my city."

"Oy, look," Jobber said with her hand held up for silence. Faul pressed her lips tightly together with annoyance. "You, Finch, and Wyer," she said. "That ain't too many."

"Why Finch?" Faul asked. "They'll need her here."

"Cause she's Beldan bred, like me. And we both want to see home. As much as you do, Faul. Go on, admit it."

Faul's expression softened and her eyes shone a soft blue gray. "A decent glass of brandy," she moaned.

"In a decent tavern," Finch added, straightening the blue ribbons of her bodice.

"The Anvil—" said Wyer.

"The Maidenhead!" countered Jobber.

"Huld's peace," Shedwyn said tartly, "have you forgotten the reason for going to Beldan?"

"No," Jobber replied, more soberly. "But it was nice for a moment to think of something else."

"It's best we were gone," Shedwyn said flatly. She broke away abruptly from the group. Jobber watched her storm through the trees, not stopping to reply to the women who called after her. Faul and Shefek left too, bent on their own separate tasks. Finch went to gather up blankets and food. Only Wyer remained beside Jobber.

"She's worried about Eneas," Jobber explained to Wyer, sensing Shedwyn's anger through the new intimacy of the knot.

Jobber turned back to Wyer and saw he watched her closely. She reddened under the friendly stare, but for once didn't turn away from it. She found herself reappraising Wyer's familiar features. His face was rugged, not so much handsome, she thought as appealing in its plainness. His brown hair fell in thick locks over a forehead lined with a crease dyed with the soot of the forge. His green eyes were blended with iron-colored flecks.

"How does it feel?" he asked and Jobber frowned, not understanding the question. "The knot," he prompted. "Does it change you?"

Jobber grinned. "Yeah," she said softly, "it does. I know

more, not so much in the head, but here," she pointed to her chest, "in the heart. It's like there's a world inside of me."

"Oran?" Wyer asked, his voice reverent. Standing so close to him Jobber caught the faint peppery scent of his skin, and the drift of smoke that permeated his hair.

"Yeah, even the Chaos. If I listen, I can hear the winds. I can also hear the scratching of Lirrel's thoughts. And the beating of Shedwyn's heart, and I can taste the sea, from Tayleb, the fourth girl."

"My father must have known all along how special you were, Jobber. He was a good smith and he must have seen the fire in you."

"And you?" Jobber asked boldly. "What did you see in me?"

Wyer grinned and scuffed his boot in the snow. "You made me uncomfortable. I knew you as a bellows lad, but my thoughts were stirred whenever you came to the forge. You can't know the happiness and then the misery it caused me when I first saw your hair, freed from the cap, and knew you were a dell—and a fire element at that."

"And now?"

"Now," Wyer said, shoving his hands into his pockets and rocking back on his heels. "There is still pleasure in the sight of you," he said simply.

Jobber backed away, suddenly mistrusting her quickened pulse. "Wyer, I ain't good with this stuff."

"Z'blood, Jobber, you asked."

"Yeah, but maybe I ain't ready for the answer."

"Then know that I'm a patient man and I'll wait 'til you are ready."

"You mean that?" Jobber cocked her head to one side. "I can't promise I'll ever be ready."

Wyer shrugged. "I'll still be here. No smith in his right mind leaves a good forge unattended." Then he looked out, beyond her shoulder. "Oy, Faul's waving us on," he said.

"Right, best go then," Jobber answered awkwardly and wondered to herself how she had ever managed such a conversation and at such a time. She was a long way from the luxury of simple things like courtship. Jobber stopped in her tracks. But if not now, when? There might never be another time. Impulsively she slipped her hand into Wyer's and squeezed it.

He smiled, surprised, but squeezed her hand back.

Then she released him and, shoving her hands into the pockets of her trousers, set her feet toward Faul. It wasn't much, she thought, but the feel of his hand lingered in her palm, as did the warm blush on her face.

Jobber and Wyer joined Faul, who was deep in discussion with Treys and Shefek. They were scratching out plans on the hard snow at their feet. The New Moon would gather at Asturas and begin a march south to meet the Silean army. They would pull out everything they had battling the advancing army. Shefek would fly to Beldan to arrange with Kai and Slipper to meet them at the Ribbons. He would stay there and help organize an uprising in Beldan to attack the Silean army stationed there. They would wait no longer. And if they had the luck with them, come spring the Sileans would be trapped between Beldan and Asturas, and the Fire Queen destroyed.

"Not much of a plan," Treys said sadly.

"Not much of a choice," Faul answered.

"We'll lose so many."

"We'll lose it all any other way."

"Aye," Treys admitted, brushing out the snowy patterns.

The camp came loudly to life as people scurried to pack blankets, food, and weapons. Crying babies were hoisted to their mothers' backs, while the older children scampered underfoot, peeling the bark from sticks as pretend weapons. Jobber went through the ragtag camps in search of Shedwyn.

She found her standing beside a pine tree, one arm wrapped around the trunk, her head leaning against it. By the heaving of her shoulders, Jobber knew she was crying.

"Shedwyn," she called.

The shoulders straightened and a hand wiped across her face before she turned around. Shedwyn's face was mottled, her eyes red from weeping.

"I'm being foolish," Shedwyn said, her voice thick.

"Eneas is a good man. He's clever and won't get himself caught," Jobber said trying to cheer her up.

"Aye," Shedwyn agreed thinly. "I just wish I could see him. Talk to him." Then she grimaced, as if disgusted with her weakness. A hand strayed to the rounded bulge of her baby. "Come on," she said to Jobber. "We should be going."

"You know, Beldan ain't that bad," Jobber teased.

"Did you never get used to the country, Jobber?" Shedwyn asked.

"Never. There ain't nothing to do out here. Nothing to see."

Shedwyn laughed and teased Jobber back. "Beldan born, Beldan bred—"

"Long in the arm and thick in the head," Jobber finished. "Z'blood, wonder if I can still nick a purse?"

Shedwyn placed her balled fists on her hips. "Jobber, there's more important things to worry about!"

"I know," Jobber snipped. "But it ain't half bad just to be a snitch for a little while longer. Zorah may have slowed time, but it's coming soon enough for us and the days of stumbling 'round the woods are over. I'm ready, but I also know that whatever happens, I'll never walk Beldan streets again like I once did. I'd nothing in my pocket then, but the whole city was still mine. Weren't a thing I couldn't snitch if I needed it bad enough."

"Except a future," Shedwyn retorted.

"And that's the sweetest snitch of all. Right from Zorah's pocket, I'll nick out Time again. A future for us and that little baby of yours." Jobber threw her arm over Shedwyn's shoulder with a burst of renewed enthusiasm. "Come on, farmergirl, ain't no sense waiting here."

They walked through the trees and Jobber, hearing the crunch of snow beneath her feet, could think only of the hard, cobbled streets of home.

Beldan, beautiful Beldan, she sighed to herself. And somewhere in her memory, she heard the ringing clang of a smith's hammer beating the shaft of a new blade.

Chapter Fifteen

Lais stared glumly into her tankard of stale beer. The inn was nearly empty at the late hour except for an old man chewing bread crusts by the dying remains of a hearth fire. The torchlight was feeble, casting dismal shadows on the smoky walls. The wooden table was sticky with handprints, and a small beetle climbed out from a tiny round hole in the wooden plank and ambled across the tabletop. Frigging dreary place, Lais thought and took another sip of the ale. It tasted flat and watery. A rumbling noise brought her head up sharply, her eyes straining to see the door. The innkeeper clutched the edges of the bar and his white-faced wife grabbed the crockery pitchers in her arms. The old man at the hearth swallowed quickly, as though the mouthful were his last. Even the roving beetle stopped and waited.

"Shitting cart," Gonmer said sourly and glowered at Lais. "It's a frigging cart. Don't start jumping out of your skins!" She slammed her tankard down and dragged her hand over her drawn face. The bloodshot eyes rested on the stilled beetle.

Lais bowed her head, embarrassed, as out in the street a cart rumbled harmlessly past, the clopping of the horse's hooves rapping the cobblestones. The innkeeper's wife sighed and set the crockery pitchers down on the bar again. Lais looked at the beetle and saw it ambling once more near the edge of the table. With an angry swipe she brushed it to the floor and made to step on it with the toe of her muddied boot.

"Don't," Gonmer said. She raised her tankard to signal the innkeeper.

"Why not?" Lais snapped, but moved her toe aside.

Gonmer gave a humorless smile and leaned forward, the hard points of her elbows resting on the table. "Let's say I feel a kinship with it."

"Z'blood," Lais grumbled softly. From bad to worse. The Queen was wretched enough to be with, but now Gonmer had gone strange as well. Lais clenched her fists on her lap. The space between her shoulder blades ached with tension. Fatigue scratched her eyes like dry sand, and when she closed them she saw again the Queen slitting the Regent's throat faster than a heartbeat. And then she remembered the awful sound, and the terror as the room crumbled away into the sky.

"Pondering the end, are you?" Gonmer asked and Lais was startled to find the Firstwatch studying her.

"The end of what?" Lais replied sullenly.

Gonmer chuckled and cast an arm out to the empty room. "The world's turned upside down, ain't it? The sky falls in our laps, and we frigging fall into the sky." Gonmer shook her head with the same cheerless smile.

The innkeeper put another tankard down in front of the Firstwatch. The woman closed a long hand around it.

"Gonmer," Lais said, reaching out to stop the woman from drinking. "Gonmer, what's going to happen to us? Don't you worry on it?"

Gonmer paused, her brow knitted in thought. Then, picking up the tankard, she pursed her lips and sighed. "No. I don't worry. I'm like that beetle there. I crawl out of one hole, and if I'm lucky I make it to another hole. But maybe I won't be lucky, and a heel will finish it."

"But the Fire Queen," Lais insisted. "Don't you care about

your duty to the Queen?'' The accusation in her voice masked the rising fear in her heart.

"Duty!" Gonmer spat the word out as if it were a mouthful of mud. "You dare to ask me about duty?" She pulled her shoulders upright, her eyes narrowed to angry slits. "Don't frigging accuse me of shirking my duty, you skinny-backed dell. I know my duty. It's my life, ain't it?" She took a deep breath and hiccupped. "My duty is to the Queen's honor." She pointed a finger at Lais. "Her honor, mind you, not her person, for who can defend a woman who's immortal? She needs me to clean the shit from the streets so it don't touch her skirts. Knackerman," she hissed and slapped the top of the table. "I'm the stinking Knackerman." Gonmer looked gloomily into her glass and then abruptly picked up her head. "Do you know what the Queen called me?" she asked sourly.

Lais shook her head, her hands trembling as they reached for the security of her tankard. The wooden sides were wet and sticky.

"Serena. She called me Serena."

Lais frowned, not understanding.

"She was the Firstwatch maybe thirty years ago." Gonmer lunged forward across the table with renewed fury. "The Queen doesn't even frigging know me! We're all the same, us Knackermen, one face, one sword, one duty."

Gonmer lurched to her feet and stood there, swaying unsteadily. She reached into the pocket of her tunic and drew out a handful of coins, which she tossed over the table. They landed with a clatter and rolled over the sides onto the floor.

"Duty demands I return," she said thickly. She started for the door, her thigh banging into a chair as she staggered.

"Damn," Lais swore. She was going to have to see that Gonmer stayed on her feet and made it back to the Keep. And then she was going to have to report to the Queen on her own. Lais followed angrily behind the stumbling figure of the Firstwatch, cursing the Queen, the Sileans, and even the Chaos that seemed to hang like a sword over the neck of the city.

Since Zorah had murdered the Regent Ilario, the Silean Guards had refused to take orders from Gonmer, and Lais knew that only the delicate diplomacy of the past accounted for their present survival. And she doubted that it would last much longer. The Silean noblemen of Beldan and the Guards had turned to Re Fortuna, the Secondwatch, and elected him the new Firstwatch. Gonmer had been certain that it was Re Fortuna's stupidity that had caused the bold theft of weapons from the Keep's armory, but she had been unable to prove it. Now until the General Deveaux Re Silve could be called from the field of battle, Re Fortuna would hold the post of Regent and Firstwatch. The Queen had made no protest. She had withdrawn from everyone, locked herself in her chambers and refused to take an audience with the new Regent. For now, the Sileans permitted it. And while the Queen turned her face to the few walls that remained, Lais thought bitterly, the Sileans destroyed what little peace could be found in the city.

No one was safe anymore. If it wasn't the Silean butcherboys, it was the New Moon, now electing to do their fighting in the open. Barricades were conjured like quick summer storms, and the thick smoke of set fires and the hard twang of arrows suddenly filled the narrow streets. The rebels would slay as many guards as they could before dispersing, leaving behind the smoldering remains of their makeshift trenches.

And if it wasn't the New Moon, Lais thought stopping beneath the eaves of the inn and casting a worried glance upward into the cold sky, it was Oran Himself, the cradle heaving and casting them into the Chaos. What was she to do, when even the earth beneath her feet seemed to have abandoned her?

"Oy, you there! Stop where you are," commanded a harsh voice. Standing unseen in the shadows Lais instinctively crouched in the protective darkness. Gonmer was in the narrow street, a wall torch spreading a long oval of light before her. She turned slowly toward two Guards approaching from one end of the street. Gonmer's face tightened, her lips curled back in a sneer. She rested her hand deliberately on the hilt of her sword.

"Who in whore's shit are you to command me?" she bellowed back.

Lais dug deeper into the shadows, the dulling effects of the ale chased from her head by fear. The scabbard of her sword pressed a warning into her thigh.

"Well, well," said a Guard, "a bitch in trousers." He was a short, barrel-chested man, his legs bowed to carry the weight of his belly. His ornate Silean blade hung from his waist, nearly dragging on the ground. Lais appraised him quickly and saw no danger. Gonmer would kill him long before he'd be able to free that ridiculously long blade. The price of his vanity, she thought, would be his life if he were foolish enough to go against her.

"Mind now, Re Coranos," warned the second Guard. "She's a bitch with claws."

Lais swore softly at the sight of the second Guard, a man named Re Amedios. She had seen him fight before and knew he was good with a blade. A decent enough match for Gonmer, even when she was sober. He was tall, with a lean torso that was well balanced over his hips. His face was handsome, a thin-lipped smile forming at the edges of his mouth. His eyes were dark, one brow arched to give him a pleasant expression that belied the hand clasped firmly around the hilt of his sword. His legs parted as he settled his stance.

"Fuck you both," shouted Gonmer thickly. "I'm the Fire Queen's Firstwatch and I go as I please. I take no orders from shit-eating butcherboys." She stood proudly, her black braid coiled around her neck like a snake. The torchlight blazed in her eyes.

"Hah," laughed Re Coranos. "As to being Firstwatch, you've lost that duty, you drunken bitch. And as to your Fire Queen," he leered, "she'll be buggered like any whore by the Silean Guard before we're done with this frigging country."

Gonmer's face became rigid, but her shoulders relaxed. She opened her free hand and stretched her fingers lightly. Her chest rose as she inhaled and exhaled, slowly and without haste. Her thumb pushed gently against the latch of the scabbard and Lais heard the soft snick of the freed blade. Gonmer's half-lowered eyelids hid the burning rage reflected in the pupils.

"Your words stain the Fire Queen's honor," she said.

Lais held her breath, counted the beats of her heart as Re Coranos, leering more widely, swaggered forward. How could he be such a fool? Lais thought. Anyone with sense could see it coming. From the corner of her eye, she glimpsed Re Amedios. He, too, was watching Gonmer, waiting for her to make a move.

Lais slipped her hand from her tunic and clutched her sword. As quietly as possible she straightened herself, her eyes flickering back and forth between Gonmer and Re Amedios.

Re Coranos was close to Gonmer and as the toe of his scuffed black boot set itself down inside the circle of light, she struck. With a whispered hiss, her sword swung free of the scabbard in a swiftly curving arc. The light glinted on the squared tip of the blade before it slashed across Re Coranos' chest, slicing through the leather tunic and the thin linen shirt. Blood trailed the fine line across his chest and he roared in shocked rage. His hands windmilled, confused, and then he tried to grab his sword. But the hilt slipped from his feeble grasp. Gonmer's sword had reached the apex of its upward journey and she snapped it, turning it sharply in the air before cleaving it down across Re Coranos' shoulder. She stepped back, one bent leg balanced beneath her, as the man stumbled forward and sprawled onto the street. The point of her sword rested briefly in a black pool of blood.

Re Amedios sprang up, the stabbing thrust of his sword lunging toward Gonmer. She moved back, away from the corpse of Re Coranos, and lifted her weapon in defense. The two swords met and screeched as they sheared against each other. He thrust the blade at her face and she parried it, twisting to one side. She countered and he was quick enough to strike at the oncoming attack. Again their weapons clashed, sparks snapping on the points.

For the first time in months, Lais saw the shadow of a genuine smile cross Gonmer's face. Sweat gleamed on her forehead and her breath came in short, heavy pants. Re Amedios pressed his attacks and Lais saw now that Gonmer's replies were reckless and chaotic. Re Amedios frowned, unnerved by Gonmer's unexpected sword fight. A cold river of sweat trickled against the ache in Lais's shoulder blades. She knew what Gonmer was doing: she was intending to die.

Gonmer opened wide her own defense to clip Re Amedios on the shoulder and he pranced back, shocked by her boldness. The expression hardened on Re Amedios's face as he recognized the abandonment in Gonmer's attacks. Her moves were careless, and yet deadly in their unexpectedness. His lips pressed tightly together, Re Amedios redoubled his attack, his sword slashing furiously back and forth, leaving a trail of silvery light. Gonmer blocked one, then the next. But before she could counter the third stroke, the force of Re Amedios's blade penetrated her guard and scored a bloody line across her midriff. Lais gasped, seeing Gonmer's dark eyes rimmed white, her mouth gaping open. Her sword arm dangled limply at her side, the sword point dragging on the ground. Her other hand pressed against the deep wound and she groaned as blood seeped through her fingers. Her knees buckled and she dropped to the ground, the black coil of her braid dragging her head toward the cobblestones. Re Amedios raised his sword over the white rectangle of her neck.

Lais burst from the shadows and ran, her sword clutched in a two-handed grip at her side.

"Re Amedios," she shouted to his back and saw his shoulders jerk with surprise. He spun on his heel to face her, his sword still poised for a strike. But it was too late. She was already in close and her sword's point jabbed into his exposed chest. She drove the sword upward, feeling the blade skitter against the ribs. She laid her weight against the hilt as he shuddered, suspended on her weapon. He groaned and tried to beat her away with the hilt of his own weapon.

She let go of the sword and fell back from his blows. He twisted and turned, his hand grasping the protruding hilt of her sword as he tried in vain to pull it from his body. When he turned, Lais saw the dark point of her sword emerging from his back. Abruptly he stopped his frantic movements. His back arched like a strung bow and his jaw thrust upward. With his hands still clinging to the hilt, he fell, sprawling backward into the street. Lais heard the point of her sword scrape against the cobblestones.

She waited, hearing in the silence of the street the rattle of her heartbeat and the pounding of blood in her ears. She moved woodenly, her body cold and numb.

"Gonmer," she whispered, bending down and gently turning over the woman's prone body.

Gonmer's face in the light was slack, her cheeks sunken. The eyes stared mutely back like two black stones. Lais closed Gonmer's eyes, her spirit frayed.

"Frigging shit," she whispered. "What about your duty to *me*, Gonmer?" she said to the empty face. "What am I supposed to do now?" She shook Gonmer by the shoulders, feeling tears of frustration burning her eyes.

An approaching cart rumbled, its wheels battering the cobblestones of the street. Lais glanced up, seeing the horse's head bobbing as it neared her. Terrified, she let go of Gonmer and reached for Gonmer's sword. Then she rose to her feet and sprinted for the dark alleyways. As she ran she could hear behind her the wheels of the cart screeching to a halt and the cries of a trader calling for the Guard. But she ducked her head, the sword heavy in her fist, as she escaped unseen down the dark street.

Zorah walked through the ancient corridors of the Keep, stopping now and again to lift her candle and stare at the remains of frescoes, their once-vivid scenes a faded chalk color. It had been a long time since she had walked these halls. After the Burning she had moved her chambers to the new towers of the Keep. Servants had bedded in the rooms that once housed Oran's Queens. She had grown accustomed to the cold whiteness of Silean marble and she had preferred the glassed windows that opened out to a view of Beldan's harbor. But walking here in the shadow of her past, the floors a pale pink and gray granite from Avadares, Zorah felt pricked by unfamiliar nostalgia. She touched a headless figure on the wall, the plaster crumbling beneath her touch. The arms were raised in a graceful dance. Long ago she had known the names of all the figures represented on the frescoes, for they were portraits of Oran's long lineage of Queens.

Zorah let her hand drop and continued walking. She had come here for another reason. To learn of a thief. Antoni Re Desturo, a Silean nobleman, had stolen Oran magic and Zorah wanted to know how he had done it. She had questioned his servants and discovered that in the old quarters of the Keep he had a private study to which no one was allowed admission. Zorah cursed herself for not having kept a closer watch on the man. She had known he was dangerous, but she had severely underestimated him. A wooden door loomed at the end of the corridor, its iron bands dull in the faint candlelight. She paused at the threshold, suddenly wary. Then, gritting her teeth, she put her candle down at her feet and shoved the door open.

As Zorah stepped inside, her foot knocked the candle holder over. The light dimmed as melted wax spilled out over the wick. In the sudden darkness Zorah panicked, a hand flailing against the wall for support. Then she bent to straighten the candle before the wick was drowned by wax. The candle spluttered weakly, its tiny blue flame clinging to the blackened edges of the wick.

"Burn now for me," the Queen demanded and an orange flame flowered brightly.

With one hand cupped protectively around the candle's flame, Zorah entered Antonio's study. She saw two more candles resting in their holders on the table and quickly lit them. Setting her own down alongside, she looked curiously around as the room gradually brightened.

The room was crowded with crates of musty-smelling books. More books lined the walls, and wedged between them on the shelves were oddities from Oran's past, curios collected by Antoni: a Namire blade, the short hilt of mother-of-pearl broken in two places, a Ghazali bone flute, a lump of iron ore. Zorah scowled as she picked up a green shard, thinking it a curved slice of marble, and then smiled astonished as she recognized the fragment of a Kirian's egg. How had he found this? she wondered, setting it down again.

She shivered at the sight of a skull, resting atop a sheaf of papers. Batting it to one side, she bent to read what he had written. There, in his small precise script, Zorah discovered that Antoni had chronicled his story, little dreaming that a time would come when he would be forced to flee the Keep and leave this vain and damning document behind. She held up the papers to the light and felt the hot flush of anger sear her cheeks as she learned about the Upright Man.

"He's been buggering us both," she spat out loud to the quiet room. "Sileans and Orans alike."

She glanced through the papers, frowning at the mention of his Oran heritage. It was strange, Zorah thought, feeling suddenly as if she had not journeyed the last two hundred years alone. Antoni's maternal ancestor had been Oran, alive when Zorah had brought the Sileans and the Burning to Oran. The blood had stayed, thinning over the generations, but flowing nonetheless until Antoni had taken up his heritage and come here to claim it. A woman's voice called to her out of the shameful past. That woman had sent forward in time a child to rebuke Zorah and to be her undoing.

Zorah put down the papers and crossed to the walls of books. She read the titles, tilting her head to the side. Oran books, written in the Oran language and not seen in Beldan for nearly two hundred years. The words leapt out at her, the old script beckoning. She pulled out a small leather bound volume, its cover molding, its spine dusted with a powdery white mildew. *The Council of Knowledge,* she read, her fingertips smoothing over the faint embossed words on its cover. Turning the stiff pages, she found the marked passages that Antoni had used to learn his deadly skill. Zorah closed the book carefully. She would keep this and read it herself. There was something here for her, something she had forgotten over so many years.

She turned to leave, her curiosity satisfied. But at the doorway she stopped, a cold smile on her face. Antoni's notes gave her an idea. She crossed back to the table and quickly found the wooden box he had described in his papers resting on a shelf behind the table. She opened the top and laughed with delight. Inside were stolen signet rings of prominent Silean noblemen, prigged by the Flocks and fenced to the Upright Man. These were the proofs he kept for himself to remind him of Silean stupidity and his own superior position. Zorah reached in and took a handful of the rings, rolling them over in her palm. The jeweled rings glittered brightly in the candlelight as she quickly identified most of them.

She shoved them into her pocket along with the book and left the study, carefully closing and locking the door behind her.

When she returned to the privacy of her own chambers, Zorah called a servant to bring her food and wine.

"Madam?" the young woman asked, her eyes blinking in surprise.

"I said, food and drink. And I want it now."

"Are you well, then? You've not wanted a thing but water for three days."

Zorah's fiery hair crackled with her impatience. "I'm ready now. Tell Re Fortuna that I want him here." The room filled with the metallic stink of heated copper. Alarmed, the serving girl quickly backed away from the Queen and bolted from the room.

Zorah stared down at her clothes, realizing she had worn them for three days, ever since the disaster at the ball. The front of the dress was torn and dirty, stained dark brown with dried blood, while the skirts were a deep red from spilled wine. She sniffed and grimaced at the unwashed smell of her skin. The dust of the old Keep clung to her and she carried forth from Antoni's study the musty odor of decay.

She threw off the filthy dress and, grabbing a linen cloth, dabbed clean, cold water to cleanse her skin. The water in the bowl settled and she caught the reflection of her face. It still shocked her to see the years that had appeared so rapidly. But it didn't matter at the moment. She felt a sense of strength returning, a calming peace that enabled her to tackle the problems at hand.

She pulled on a linen shirt and a comfortable pair of trousers, the wool pleasantly scratchy on her skin. She whistled an old tune between her teeth as she drew on her hose and then laced up a pair of boots.

She laid the little book on the bed beside her, her eyes straying to it as she dressed. There was something she had forgotten, something she would remember in the old Oran language, in the descriptions of magic, in the memory of the past.

Zorah stood and took a brush to her wiry copper hair. It crackled warmly beneath her hands, drying away the fresh chill of the washing water. Zorah stared out the wide window, amused at the light flurry of snow that drifted down on Beldan from thick, gray clouds.

When was the last time it had snowed in Beldan? she asked herself. Only twice before that she could recall.

Zorah twisted the window latch and pushed open the glass.

She inhaled sharply, letting the cold air sting her nostrils. Then she smiled, assessing herself.

Something had changed. She felt strong. The constricting pain of the last months had abated. She could breathe, move freely without the threat of panic unraveling her. Even the winds of Chaos had dimmed, their sound no longer keening in her ears. The nightmares remained, but she shrugged at that. They were as much her companions as her tormenters.

She watched the swirling patterns of the snowflakes as they wove in and out between the currents of air. If she squinted she could see the same pattern making its way over the rough waves of the harbor. She bowed her head and with a fingertip traced a line in a frail drift of snow.

Then, trembling with excitement, Zorah slammed the window shut and reached for the bag of knucklebones that lay on the gaming table. She shook them in their pouch and cast them out across the table. They fell in a pattern resembling the waves of the harbor and the driving snow. Her gaze lifted to the flames of the candles and for the first time she saw, etched in blue and green, the same pattern in the tendrils of the flame.

Every knot laid its mark on the world of Oran like the whorling print of a thumb. And as Zorah stared tracing the delicate lines of this new pattern, she knew what had changed.

"They have formed a Queens' quarter knot," she breathed, and the flame leapt in reply.

Zorah sat down, pensively setting the book of Oran knowledge on her lap. The new knot acted as a restraint against the current of destruction. Instead of feeling weakened, she was buoyed by their presence, the weight of Oran's draining magic on their shoulders and for once not hers. She smiled to herself, feeling the warm flush of heat settle on her face, her shoulders.

Zorah opened the book and began to read slowly, the Oran words pouring off her tongue like thick, sweet brandy. She had missed the sound of them, missed the depth of their subtlety. The words expressed Oran's mystery, gave it shape and form, lifted it from the scratching of ink on the page into the fullness of her heart. The answer she sought was here, in this text. She no longer feared the new Queens, or the power of their knot.

She would have it for herself before long. The Firegirl would come here to the Keep, to find Zorah. She was Beldan's fire, the bright, burning gleam of the future. And Zorah would pluck her like a flaming rose and graft power to the root of the old knot. Zorah would survive. And Oran would survive. And the other Queens would be hers to command.

"Madam." The servant returned, breathless and frightened.

Zorah frowned at the interruption. After the beauty of the Oran text the Silean language sounded ugly to her ear. "What?" she demanded angrily.

The servant ducked her head, her hands wringing at her skirts. "Re Fortuna says he will not be sent for. If you wish an audience, then you must come to him."

"Bastard," Zorah shouted, yellow flames rising in her green eyes. She rose from the chair and pushed past the cringing servant. Smoke eddied in gray wisps about her head and she let the sudden rise of her fury color her cheeks bright red.

Her heels clicked smartly against the cold marble, and when she pushed open the door of the stateroom the wood scorched beneath her fingers, driving a pungent smell into the room.

Re Fortuna was leaning over a table crowded with papers, two generals arguing at his side. When he saw Zorah, he backed up, his face paling. The two generals closed in front of him, to protect him from Zorah's rage.

"Don't think you can do your will without me, you disgusting little prig," Zorah shouted and scattered the papers from the table. "You and your frigging whore. Do you know who she worked for, do you know her pimp?" Zorah demanded.

"I've no idea what you're talking about, madam. And I suggest you cease this rage before you destroy even more of the Keep," Re Fortuna answered, pushing the words through his thick lips.

"Antoni Re Desturo, your own Advisor, has been using his whores and his Flocks for years to thieve on you. Look what I found in his study." Zorah pulled out the handful of rings and tossed them on the table. Re Fortuna's eyes bulged and he threw himself on the rings, searching every one.

"Looking for your own, no doubt," Zorah said smugly and stepped away from the glare of the two generals. "When Antoni's found, I suggest you waste no time in hanging him like a common thief. He means your destruction as much as mine and he has no loyalty to either of us."

Re Fortuna pounced on a large gold signet ring with a grunt of satisfaction. He picked up his ring and slipped it back on his finger. Then he clasped his hands behind his back and began to strut.

"I bow to you, madam. Though I must tell you that Silea is no longer willing to accommodate its interest to yours. The situation in Oran has changed," he began. "We are at war."

"With whom?"

"The New Moon. They have risen like rats from a flooded tunnel and they swarm the streets. My Guard have been hard at putting them down."

"Who's winning?" asked Zorah sarcastically.

Re Fortuna's back stiffened. "There is no question who is the superior army here. I have sent for Deveaux Re Silve, asking him to replace Ilario as Regent of Oran." Re Fortuna sneered at Zorah. "He is an excellent general, though I fear, madam, he will not be to your liking."

"Something he will share with his predecessors," Zorah retorted. "I want only one thing."

Re Fortuna's eyes narrowed. "And what is that?"

"Among the New Moon there is a girl with red hair." Zorah smiled enigmatically.

"And what does she have for you?" Re Fortuna asked suspiciously.

Zorah brushed back her fiery red hair. "Time," she answered simply. "Find her and Oran is yours to do with as Silea wishes."

Zorah turned on her heel and left the room, not wishing to see the greed that covered Re Fortuna's features. The Oran book lying on her chair called her to a higher purpose. And she didn't want to waste another moment talking to fools.

Chapter Sixteen

Slipper pulled the lighterman's hat down over his eyes to keep the snowflakes from landing on his eyelashes. He hunched his shoulders against the wind and watched the cold steam that issued from his open mouth. All he wanted at that moment was a warm hearth and a tankard of ale. He looked up around him, checking the street and trying to decide if there was time enough to slip into one of the inns and grab a quick one. Kai wouldn't know. He expected the meeting would be crowded, she wouldn't see him arrive late.

He stopped in front of an old inn. Carved in wood over the lintel of the door was the figure of a smiling woman, breasts rounded out from an unlaced bodice. He smiled back, recognizing the doorway to the Maidenhead. His mind was made up, he set his foot to the threshold and then hesitated, seeing a cloaked figure limping up the street.

It was the smallness of her frame that caught his eye, and her head, bared to the cold snow. Dark, wet hair lay matted to her scalp and the snow stained the cloak with black tears. The hem of her white dress was mud-spattered and torn. In her arms she clutched a penny loaf of bread.

"Petticoat?" Slipper said, concern edging out surprise.

Her head lurched up and fear-haunted eyes stared back. A purple bruise capped one cheek, making it bulge unnaturally. Her lip was split near the middle, blood caked on the wound.

Slipper reached out a hand to help her. "Z'blood, what happened to you?" he asked as she ducked her head and averted her eyes.

"Nothing," she muttered.

"Don't say that!" Slipper cried, outraged at the battered face. "Who done it to you? I'll scaffer the bastard."

The Petticoat shook her head violently. "No! No, I said leave it be. It ain't your business."

"Frigging all, no man has a right to use you so. It *is* my business, I say."

"I can handle it, do you hear!" she snapped. "Now go on, Slipper, and leave off. You'd only make it worse for me if he sees you here." She pushed rudely past. He heard her stifle a moan as her arm brushed against him.

Slipper stepped away, the desire for a drink drying on his tongue. "Shitting bastard," he muttered as he watched her scurry through the door. He crossed the street and stared up to the small window near the gabled roof where her room looked out on the street. A lace curtain was briefly pulled aside and a man looked out.

Slipper hid in the curve of a doorway and tried to see the man in the window. The dirty glass made it difficult to see clearly. What man, he asked himself, could get pleasure from beating a woman? The face in the window was dark and seemed shadowed with a beard. It stirred a vague memory in Slipper's mind. Familiar and frightening. He watched the face until the curtain was replaced and it disappeared behind the lace. Slipper turned over the image of the face in his mind. The Petticoat was known for her independence, and perhaps someone had decided it was time to clip her wages. Slipper knew most of Beldan's pimps, but this man was unknown to him.

He looked up again and frowned, the face refusing to leave his mind.

"Naffy, ain't it?"

Slipper jumped at the sound of Stickit's smug voice so close to his elbow.

"What are you on about?" he clipped. He didn't like the woman and had never understood why Kai had joined her to the Waterlings in the first place. She could handle the boats and she knew the Ribbons well enough, but she was also deceitful, selfish and, Slipper thought, easily made jealous.

"Well, the brass whore's getting a coming down, ain't she?" Stickit exclaimed. "Looks right brangled now."

"Who's the fancy man?" Slipper asked hotly.

"Ah no, I don't give secrets like that," Stickit replied, wagging a chubby finger at him.

"Yeah, well." Slipper shrugged his shoulders. "Don't care much anyway on it." He shoved his hands in his pockets as if uninterested. "You coming to the meeting?" he asked, changing the subject.

Stickit's mouth formed a pout in the doughy face. " 'Sides, if I did tell, I'd be looking a sight worse than that dell."

"Yeah, right," Slipper said, sounding bored. The other thing he knew about Stickit was her mouth ran over if she thought it might add to her prestige. If he was quiet, he guessed, she'd keep squealing information on her own.

"He's well up, you know. Titled and all. Wouldn't do good to let anyone know he's down here with the Flocks."

A warning sounded in Slipper's mind as Stickit continued to drop hints. His thoughts scattered around, trying to tell him something, trying to reassemble the foggy image of a man's face.

Then Stickit fell silent, as if realizing she may have said too much already.

"Come on," Slipper said angrily. "Throw yer leg into it or we'll be late."

"I'm going as fast as I care to," Stickit whined. "It's this snow, makes me slip."

Slipper cursed beneath his breath and hurried his feet. He

wanted to get away from Stickit, away from her whining voice and puzzle out his worry over the Petticoat. Her bruised face made him queasy and he was furious that he could not stay to help her. His legs stretched and behind him he heard Stickit's voice growing more distant as she failed to match his stride.

Though Shefek hated the way the snow weighed on his tired wings, he was grateful for the cloud cover. His arrival in Beldan might just go unnoticed if he flew within the dense gray body of the clouds.

As he approached the Plains beyond the city gates, Shefek could see the vague outlines of the city, veiled in mist. It seemed smaller; the towers that had once risen above the arched gates lay in heaps of tumbled stone and brick.

Sadar's Keep was not the only place to suffer Zorah's loosening grip, he guessed.

He could feel Zorah's weakness in the ache of his wings, the stiffness of his legs, and the slowness of his talons to curl. The winds of Chaos whistled in the ruff of feathers around his neck, and his eyes, which had once pierced the rim of the sky to gaze upon the elemental strands of Oran's cradle, now saw only the clouded vision of a decaying city. Shefek banked in the clouds, feeling in the shift of currents the shape of the buildings and the narrow city streets below.

He would make this flight to Beldan to tell Kai of the knot's arrival at the Ribbons. But he would not stay. It was already over for him and he had decided last night as he left Sadar that he would choose his final battle site.

The old world of Oran was ending, and in its decline he could no longer be a Kirian, proud and distant from the mortal weaknesses of human beings. Though he could still fly as a Kirian, he had acquired the weight of love and revenge. He felt himself falling with the burden of those emotions from the lofty heights of Oran's cradle, where as a fledgling he had basked in the winds of Chaos.

He thought of Faul, envisioned the thin angles of her body, her chin, the rise of her collarbones, the twin points of her hips. Even the faint swell of her breasts was punctuated by her nipples, which rose like new buds. For a woman who was so hard and mean at times, he mused, the inside of her thigh was the softest span of human skin he had known.

And Jobber. He loved her as the teacher who learns wisdom blurted from the mouth of a rebellious student. The bright coppery sheen of her hair, the flames of her eyes, reminded him of Oran's heart, in whose flames he had singed his wings.

And Orian. Shefek lifted his wings with fury, rearing back his head to screech at the clouds. Love and hate twined together, choking him in wordless rage. His daughter, his one precious weakness. He had known they would die in this final change of Queens. Even if Jobber was successful, they would not survive Zorah's death. They were tied to her, their power so entwined with hers that they must share the same fate. The old order would be washed clean of its magnificence as well as its corruption.

But he had believed that he and Orian would be together at the end. That he would guide her into the winds of Chaos, take her to the black night beyond the boundaries of Oran's flesh in a final flight. That he would not go alone.

Alone, he thought savagely. That is my final degradation. I fear to be alone. As a Kirian I was never alone. On this world and in the night sky there was always the drifting flocks that called, always the rumbling of Oran's voice that connected us, even when we could not see one another. But the Kirians are gone and I fall from the sky like a man.

Shefek beat his wings to stave off his anger. He braced himself on the current, seeing the face of a monster, yellow-haired and tusked. He had taken the image from the air, seen it sent on the winds that blew from Doberan, Gallen, and Lauriel. This general was not unlike himself, Shefek thought, another beast in the borrowed shape of a man. Who better to accompany him? He screeched triumphantly to the sky, vowing that on his final flight to Chaos he would indeed not go alone.

Shefek swooped low over the Guild district, surprised by the scene of a battle in a twisting street. Smoldering barricades were strewn between the shells of buildings and behind them were crouched Oran archers and pikemen, just waiting. In front, on horseback, the Silean cavalry prepared for a charge. In the windows above, children fluttered blue flags and flung cobblestones and bricks out the windows at the Sileans. The horses pranced, rearing back from the hail of rocks. The squad captain sounded the alarm, and the Silean Guard charged the barricade.

As the cavalry approached, the New Moon rose up, archers letting fly a volley of arrows. Three Guards went down, falling heavily off their horses into the street. A child, wearing a cutter's smock, darted into the street from a small door and gathered up the spent arrows before quickly disappearing again. For those Guards who breached the barricade, pikemen, still wearing the colored neck scarves of their Guilds, raised the long-handled pikes and returned the attack.

A second squad of Silean horsemen rounded the narrow street from the other side, filling the lanes and trapping the New Moon. From above Shefek cursed and wheeled around. He stretched forth his neck, aiming the beak of polished iron as he swooped on the advancing Guards. The steady thump of Shefek's wings caused one to look up, and Shefek saw the Guard's startled face before his prone talons struck the man in the chest, knocking him, bloodied and torn, from the back of his horse. Shefek's wings flapped furiously as he maintained his upright position over the Guards. The horses reared in terror, throwing off their riders in an attempt to flee the sharp talons of the creature above them. Shefek lifted into the air and circled, watching the Sileans scatter in confusion. The squad captain was sounding the harsh caw of the alarm, trying in vain to rally his men. Shefek folded his wings and dove for the man. The Guard's horse rocked back on its haunches, the front forelegs scraping the air at Shefek's approach. The Guard clung to the neck of his terrified beast, his horn clattering to the street. From the periphery of his vision, Shefek saw another Guard setting a bolt into his crossbow and taking aim. He screeched, and the shrill sound of it echoed loudly through the narrow street. A boy flung a rock and it hit the Guard squarely in the back of the head. The man fell forward over the neck of his horse, his crossbow firing its bolt harmlessly into the street. Shefek reached the captain and, raising the high arch of his wings for balance, snatched the Guard from the back of his horse. Like sharpened scythes, the talons closed around the chest of the screaming man. Shefek dragged his struggling burden into the thickheaded clouds, the hoarse screams of the man muffled by the mist. And then, as the weight of the body wrenched his tired limbs, Shefek released the Guard. His wingtips caught an updraft as he was suddenly freed of the weight. The wind lifted him effortlessly and he turned his head slowly, the golden eyes watching how the man dropped through the sky, arms and legs splayed to the rushing wind.

Then, banking once more in the clouds, Shefek returned to the barricaded street. He slowed his flight and lowered his legs to land on the highest point of the barricade.

Shefek cursed as his talons struggled to find a solid purchase amid the uneven rubble of the barricade. One wing draped to the side and he floundered, off balance, as he tried to right himself.

The Kirians were never meant for human cities, he grumbled, furious with the untidiness of his landing. In the air he was swift and agile, but on land he resembled a fledgling, tilting from side to side as it hobbled on unsteady legs. His beak clapped noisily out of frustration as he tried to regain his balance and his dignity.

Except for those lying dead, the Guards were gone, dispersed by the unexpected arrival of the Kirian.

Well, Shefek, if you wanted to pass unnoticed you haven't done a good job of it, he told himself. By the next watch every Silean would be armed with a crossbow—and a fearful glance to the sky.

Two weavers were stripping the boots and clothing off a dead Guard as Shefek struggled with his landing. They stopped and backed away uncertainly. But a boy in a large black coat burst from the doorway and ran fearlessly toward the huge bird.

"Oy, Shefek!" he called, waving his arm and smiling broadly.

Shefek concentrated on changing his form, sensing the moment the scrape of his talons became flat feet, the black tarsi lost their scales and smoothed into the legs of a man. His feathered wings were stretched out to the edges of the street, the pinions brushing against the black, hollowed windows. He felt them shrink, the space between the ribs of feathers becoming more solid as they wove into cloth. Then there was the moment when the hidden privacy of his sex was visible in transformation between Kirian and man. It had never bothered him as a young Kirian, for he paid as little attention to human modesty as he did other human emotions. But now it did bother him, he thought ruefully. It was one more way in which the habit of being human had changed him. He was glad when the feathers covered him with the faded white robes of a vagger. With a hand he touched his nose, reassuring himself that he had not made it too large, and then smoothed the ruff of a beard.

He blinked, hearing his name called. The weavers were waiting by the partially naked body of the Silean Guard, open-mouthed and awed.

"Oy, Shefek," the boy called again and stopped, breathless. " 'Member me?" he asked hopefully.

"Neive, the ashboy who led us through the tunnels," Shefek answered, reaching out a hand to clap the boy across the shoulder. Dust and soot flaked off his coat into a little cloud. The boy beamed back at him and Shefek marked the cocksure expression. Much different from the last time they had met. "So my young rat, is this how it goes?" he asked, gesturing to the barricades with his hand.

"Oh yeah," Neive answered, grinning proudly. Exhaustion washed over Shefek and, without intending to, he leaned hard against the boy as he tried to regain his equilibrium. "And you, Shefek?" asked Neive, bearing up under the weight of the Kirian. "How is it with you? You look . . ." The boy hesitated as his eyes traveled up the length of Shefek's body and then rested on his face, his expression less sure.

"Older," Shefek ventured.

"Feathers are whiter."

"At least I don't stink," Shefek chuckled. "Not like last time."

Neive laughed and pinched his nose between two fingers. "Z'blood, it was awful, Shefek. First time you collared me I was about sick from the stench of yer wound."

"Just so. I hide my wounds now, and though they do not smell, they give me more pain," Shefek said in a low voice. Neive's young face became pensive. Well, thought Shefek, we have both seen enough grief. Shefek clicked his tongue and gave the boy a little shove. "Come, take me to Kai and Slipper. I've news for them." Shefek felt better seeing Neive's expression brighten again.

They walked past the weavers, who had continued stripping the Guard, their eyes never leaving Shefek as they worked. Neive scrambled over the remains of the barricade, but Shefek moved slowly and more cautiously. When they were free of it, Shefek brushed his palms together, dusting off the dirt.

"And how is Mistress Kai?" he asked as they walked.

"Naffy enough. Has her hand in everything the New Moon does."

"And Slipper?"

"Oh, he's well too. Flock leader, but not just of snitches. Cutter lads, Guild 'prentices, frameboys, strawgirls, even the stockingeers from the Pirate cloth houses come to Slipper. Got 'em all organized, he does."

"To do what?"

Neive shrugged. "Whatever we can, Shefek. We're everywhere, getting bits of this and that. Sometimes it pays off. Those weavers back there weren't too sure of you. But I knew who you were straight off."

"Your arm that threw the rock?" Shefek asked, staring down at the boy.

"Yeah," Neive said proudly. "Kissed it and told it where to go."

Shefek chuckled. "And as an earth element, it had to obey you."

Neive grinned, thrusting his hands in his pockets and swaggering. "Oy, those of us got the stuff use it now. No point in hiding it anymore. The noddy-noose is for anyone against the Sileans, not just those with the old power."

"I suppose there is comfort in being equally persecuted," Shefek replied dryly.

They turned down a back alley, the stench of the tanneries congealing in the damp air. A boy in a leather apron came out of a blackened doorway and fell into step beside them.

"Oy, Rilker," Neive said.

"You weren't at the meeting," Rilker accused. His leather apron was streaked with dye stains and old blood.

"I was caught up in a brangle on Forge Street. Kai still there?"

He shook his head. "Last I saw, she and Slipper headed for the tunnels."

Shefek groaned and gave a slight shudder. "Anywhere but there."

Neive grinned. "Come on, Shefek. I'll take you down. Won't be nothing to worry on."

"Hear Slipper's latest game?" Rilker said quickly.

"What's that?" Neive asked.

"Flocks is stealing street signs. Ain't none of the new butcherboys knows where the piss they are." He laughed, showing a mouthful of missing back teeth.

"Yeah, most of them now is only interested in where the docks are." Neive grinned at Shefek. "Looking for a ship out of here. Ever since the last rattler shook up the city they haven't felt too naffy 'bout staying long."

"I'm in a hurry," Shefek answered gruffly.

Neive nodded a quick farewell to Rilker and led Shefek through the maze of back streets. The cutters had already been hard at their work and Shefek saw the clean, empty rectangles where signs had once named the street. Neive stopped in front of an old tunnel entrance. He pushed back the boards and motioned Shefek in.

At the dark mouth of the tunnel Shefek balked, sweat beading his forehead. He hated the tunnels, the closed-in spaces. To a Kirian it was the same as being buried alive.

Neive grabbed ahold of his arm. "Come on, 'member how you pushed me in the first time. I promise Shefek, we'll get in and get out quick as rats."

Shefek smiled thinly at the familiar strategy. "Get in, get out," he repeated through gritted teeth and surrendered himself to Neive's guidance.

Kai sat at an old wooden table staring bleakly at the figures scratched on paper. The candle flame flickered with the capricious wind that gusted through the tunnels. She sighed and raised her hands to her skull, digging her fingers through her hair.

"Go easy," Slipper said softly. He poured her a small neat drink of Mother's Tears into a chipped glass. "Oy, when was the last time you slept?" he asked.

Kai thought about it as she accepted the drink. She tossed it down her throat, grateful for the scorching taste that seemed to rouse her momentarily from her exhaustion. "Don't know. I don't sleep anymore. I close my eyes and there's a battle. Butcherboys march across one eye and the New Moon marches across the other."

"Who wins?" Slipper asked.

Kai smiled weakly. "That's when I open my eyes and find out I ain't been sleeping but watching a brangle or getting a report, like this one," she added gesturing to the paper. "Z'blood, it's all like a dream. Waking or sleeping. I need some good news, Slipper," Kai said, suddenly urgent. "I need to know there's a frigging good reason for going on like this day after day. Look at the list of the dead here," she said sharply, holding up the paper from the table. "I know a good half of them." She pointed a finger to one name. "Faulter, an ironmonger. Got scaffered three days ago. Left behind a wife and a baby." She held up another list. "And now here's his wife, Mauyra. She got scaffered last night at the brangle in the High Street." Kai sucked in her lower lip, her finger tracing down the list of names, slowing over the familiar ones. "Dennen, the teaman, Genie and her sister Fiona, whores from Blessing Street, Soltar, the weaver's son—"

"One of mine," said Slipper thickly, remembering the boy. Soltar had seen his mother murdered by the Guards and later his father sentenced to hang on the gallows at Firefaire. He had been important to the New Moon, bringing them the children of the Guilds, the apprentices and odd jobbers who roamed the city streets.

"The list goes on . . ." Kai's voice trailed off.

"It's a price," Slipper said, "but it's worth it."

"Is it?" Kai asked, her fingers twisting locks of hair at her temples. Her large eyes grew black in the shadowy light of the tunnels. A tiny flame flickered in each pupil. "Once I was certain. But now I feel like all I do is line up people and send them out to get scaffered.''

''Now ain't the time to lose heart, Kai. The New Moon is making a difference. The butcherboys don't know which end is up. We've got them screwed around. And more of them are cocking up their toes than us.''

Kai fell silent, hearing the dry buzzing in her ears. Z'blood! she was tired of the war. She was tired of pretending to be without fear. Worry and grief were like tightly laced boots that would never come off. The scuffle of footsteps brought her head up in alarm.

''Friend,'' said Slipper quickly, his ear cocked to the silent voice of water trickles in the tunnels.

''Oy, Kai,'' Neive called out from the darkness and his voice echoed in the chambers.

Kai inhaled deeply and then swallowed the sour taste of worry. ''This way,'' she answered and shuffled the papers into a neat pile. Her mouth settled in a grim line. ''There was a brangle up at Forge Street today. Neive must be bringing in his report. More for the list,'' she added darkly.

Neive's shadow appeared on the wall before he did and was followed by a second shadow. As he rounded the entrance to the cavern Kai gave a joyful cry.

''Shefek!'' she shouted. Both she and Slipper jumped up from the table to greet the old man. He waited for her, a tired smile on his face, as she rushed toward him. She clasped him firmly about the neck, feeling his arms circle her waist in reply. She closed her eyes, her chin digging into his shoulder. Tears blistered her eyes, washing out the grit of the tunnels.

''Well met, my raven,'' Shefek said softly.

Kai pulled away from him, quickly wiping away her tears. ''It's good to see you, Shefek.''

Shefek glanced up at Slipper and clapped him hard on the shoulder. ''So, you too have changed,'' he said, staring intently into Slipper's face. ''A hawk now, not a fledgling.''

Slipper tucked his hands in his pockets. ''Out of the egg at last, Shefek.'' He smiled back.

Shefek chuckled and his round golden eyes spotted the jug of

Mother's Tears. "Praise Chaos," he murmured. "Something to wash away the desperate closeness of this place."

Kai grinned, a balled fist resting on one hip. "It ain't brandy, Shefek, it's Mother's Tears—"

"Better still," groaned Shefek, heading for the jug.

"So go easy. We'll all be needing it."

Shefek nodded absently, his eyes concentrating on the clear liquid he poured from the jug into the chipped glass. He tossed it down and, while swallowing, poured another round. He drank that one too and then turned back to them, exhaling slowly. Kai could smell the sharp anise fragrance of the liquor on his breath.

She joined him at the table and, taking two other glasses, poured one for herself and one for Slipper. Neive gave a hopeful smile, but she ignored him.

"To your return, Shefek," she said raising her glass. She drank quickly, holding her breath as the liquor coursed down her throat. It burned like a small fire between her breasts.

Slipper pulled up two more ancient chairs and they sat around the table.

"So, the news, then," Kai said seriously. Shefek's face seemed to swim before her eyes. The Mother's Tears had loosened the bundled tension in her body and she felt strangely at ease for the first time in days. Her fingers rested quietly on the table instead of twisting her hair.

Shefek nodded, a gnarled hand smoothing the wide ruff of his white beard. His nose was bright red in the candlelight. "Sadar has fallen," he started.

Kai shivered as the moment of peace evaporated. Shefek's words touched her like a cold hand. "How did it fall? Have Deveaux's armies made it so far north?"

Shefek's eyes widened. "So you know about the beast general?"

"I found out about it through some letters Slipper nicked. We sent Tyne of Harrow out to warn the villages."

"He was too late. The village of Doberan was sacked. Gallen too."

Slipper swore and clutched angrily at his glass. He poured another round for the three of them.

"And the others?" Kai asked, her fingers curling into her palms.

"I don't know for sure."

"Then what happened at Sadar?" Slipper asked tensely, raising his glass to his lips.

"Zorah can no longer hold the old knot together. Oran's cradle is tearing apart, slipping piece by piece into the Chaos. Sadar's Keep was wrenched out of the mountains and sent spinning into the sky. Most of the New Moon got out in time. Most, not all."

Kai leaned back in her chair, her face sagging. "Z'blood. It's happening here, too. Whole streets going up into the sky."

"But there is good news, and that is why I am here," Shefek continued. "Lirrel has found the fourth girl. And the four of them have tied the new Queens' quarter knot."

Kai's lips parted with surprise, her large eyes sparkling with sudden hope. "Can they do it? Can Jobber do it? Fight Zorah before it's too late?"

Shefek dropped his gaze to his hands, studying them before he answered. When he lifted his head Kai saw a mixture of emotions on his face: pride, confidence, and the jagged lines of grief. "Yes. I think she can."

"What do you want us to do?" Slipper asked, leaning forward on his elbows. Neive crowded next to him waiting to hear.

"Jobber and Shedwyn will be coming through the western Plains. Lirrel and Tayleb, the fourth girl, are coming up the coast. They plan on meeting at the Ribbons."

"When?" Kai asked.

Shefek shook his head. "I can't answer that for certain. But you must send someone out to watch for them. Someone you can trust."

"I'll go," Slipper said.

"No, I need you here," Kai said. "Pick someone else."

"Fair enough," Slipper agreed reluctantly. Then he gave a half smile. "It'll be good to see Jobber again. Is she the same?" he asked Shefek.

Shefek shrugged, smiling good-naturedly. "Like you, she's out of the egg."

"And the Fire Sword?" Kai asked, one finger curling around a black lock. "Can she use it well enough to fight the Queen?"

"Jobber has discovered her own weapon," Shefek answered.

His eyes glowed brighter. "One that will stand her in better stead when it comes to facing the Queen."

"Has to be that temper of hers," Slipper ventured. "Figured it had to be good for something other than smarting off to butcherboys and getting herself in a brangle."

Kai leaned forward and laid a hand on Shefek's arm. "Just tell me true, Shefek, can she do it? Is all this fighting and dying going to mean something?"

Shefek laid his hand over Kai's. "Among other human weaknesses I have acquired I include hope. Yes, I have faith in Jobber. Shedwyn and Lirrel are also strong forces, and I have no doubt that the fourth girl is able to match the strength of her sisters. It was precious seed that Queen Huld flung into the future, but I pray you shall live to see it bear fruit."

Kai leaned back in her chair, her narrow shoulders slumping with fatigue.

"Thank you for that, Shefek."

Shefek stood, shuddering lightly as he glanced up at the vaulted ceiling of the cavern. "I must go," he said.

Kai frowned, forcing herself to stand. Her limbs ached with weariness, her legs trembling. "Will you not stay here?"

"We could use the help," Slipper added.

Shefek shook his head. "No. The end for me lies elsewhere."

Kai's eyes softened and she blinked slowly, her lids heavy. "That's it then, ain't it, Shefek? We won't see you any more after this."

Shefek smoothed his beard, his eyes glinting a bright gold. "No. I belong to the past," he said softly. Shefek turned to Slipper and the young man straightened his shoulders, his chin thrust out. Then Shefek gazed back at Kai's tired face. He smiled at the pair. "Courage," he whispered. Then he grabbed Neive. "And now I must get out of here!" he roared.

Neive scurried before Shefek, leading the way out of the cavern, back through the tunnels. As they entered the mouth of the tunnel, Kai was certain she saw another shadow hovering at the entrance. For a brief instant she saw the flash of yellow hair and the rounded front and skirts of a woman. She squinted into the dark, but the shadow was gone. A Waterling, or one of Slipper's

Flock, she thought wearily, otherwise Slipper would have been forewarned. She must have been scared off when she realized others were present. She'd come back later.

"The news is good," Slipper said, taking ahold of Kai's hand. He peered into her face.

She smiled thinly at him. "Yeah, it's good, ain't it? A Queens' quarter knot. It makes the war worth it, don't it?" Her question held a note of pleading.

Slipper pulled her up out of the chair and, circling an arm tightly around her waist, walked her toward the tunnel. "It makes it worth a night's sleep, Kai."

"Can't," she protested.

"Can. And I'm the one to see to it. You take to the bed. I'll keep watch and wake you if there's news that needs you."

"But Slipper," Kai started to say and found herself unable to argue.

"The New Moon will fight without you for a few hours."

"And you'll get someone to go to the Ribbons?"

"Yeah, I'll get someone to go to the Ribbons. Just as soon as I get you to a bed."

Kai sighed and relinquished herself to Slipper's arm. She'd be better after sleep, she told herself. In the tunnels she stumbled as exhaustion claimed her, and only Slipper's strong arm kept her from pitching forward in the dark.

In the Petticoat's tiny room, the Upright Man paced in angry frustration. He stopped his pacing and snatched at a white lace skirt, hung on a hook. He cursed loudly as he tore it into shreds, the sound of rent fabric scraping the air. The Petticoat huddled in a corner, her hands clamped over her mouth to quiet her sobs.

The Upright Man heard her and wheeled around, glowering over her.

"You stupid bitch of a whore!" he shouted, a fist raised over her prone body. "Who were you talking to?" he demanded. "I saw you from the window. You can't keep your frigging mouth closed."

"I didn't squeal!" the Petticoat protested. "I swear, I didn't say nothing!"

The Upright Man leveled a hard kick at the cowering figure.

His boot impacted against the soft flesh of her thigh. She folded into a smaller bundle, her legs drawn up protectively. With her cloak drawn across her face, she muffled her cries of pain.

Antoni Re Desturo stepped back from her, rage boiling in his veins. Red points of light glared in his eyes. "You've ruined my plans, you frigging bitch! Now I am trapped in this"—he turned in the room, his arms lifted to the walls—"this stinking cage. My Flocks dispersed, the New Moon taking the streets, and myself hunted by the very bastards that once served me! I'll make you pay for this," he finished savagely.

He lunged down, grabbing the Petticoat up by the collar of her cloak.

"No more," she pleaded, "Z'blood, no more." She cried out, her face livid with bruises. She struggled violently in his grasp, trying to avoid the open hand that swung in the air and slapped her hard across the face. The open hand changed to a closed fist.

"Oy, open up!" came a call from the door.

Antoni stayed his hand, his head turned sharply to the door. The girl in his grasp shook with silent terror.

"Oy, I said open up! It's me, Stickit!"

Antoni's expression shifted, the hard line of his mouth parting with expectation. He glared again at the Petticoat, disgusted by the battered face.

"Open the door," he commanded in a harsh whisper. He released the girl with a shove and went to stand behind the door. He withdrew a knife from his boot and nodded at the Petticoat to answer Stickit's insistent knock.

The Petticoat hobbled over to the door, eyes dazed, her expression empty. She opened it a crack and peered out.

"Let me in," Stickit whispered. "I got new for *him*."

Antoni reached for the door, opening it wider, knife still in hand. He roughly hauled Stickit in by the sleeve of her dress. "Anyone see you?" he demanded.

"Nah," she answered, brushing her sleeve down again. "I came alone, didn't I? I ain't stupid—" Stickit glanced up at the Petticoat, who lowered her eyes with shame. "Not like some," she added.

"Get out," Antoni said to the Petticoat.

"Where?" she asked weakly.

"Just get out, and keep out of sight," he said. "Or I'll finish you off, I will."

The Petticoat gave a strangled sob and bolted through the door. As she left, Stickit closed it behind her.

Antoni darted toward the woman, watching with pleasure as the color drained from her cheeks. He still held the knife, which he placed along a crease on her thick throat. "Don't be cocky with me, girl, or I'll serve you as I served the whore that just left. Now give me the news."

"I can't talk like this," she whined, her eyes rolling back in her head.

Antoni eased away from her, but his nerves snapped with eagerness. He couldn't wait anymore. Since he had fled the Keep with the Petticoat what little power he had drained from Oran's lost children was slipping rapidly back into the Chaos. Holding on to it was like holding water in a sieve. His senses were dulled, and as the one spark of his future began to die out he grew enraged with frustration.

"Go on," he growled at Stickit, furious that his fate should rest with the tattled tales of this whiny whore.

Stickit began eagerly, rubbing her neck where the cold blade had lain against it. "Well, I heard tell today in the tunnels that they've done it. Made a new knot. Seems like they found the fourth girl all right." Stickit stopped.

"What else?" Antoni asked, trying to calm the rattle of his heart. Ambition flared in his mind at the thought of a Queens' quarter knot, whole and undamaged.

Stickit looked around the room as if thinking.

Conniving bitch, Antoni thought as he watched the girl frame a demand, a payment for the news.

"Name your price," he ordered.

Stickit smiled and sucked in her lower lip, exposing her yellow teeth. "This here room. I want it. I don't want to sleep in the doorways no more, or bed down in the tunnels."

"And the Petticoat?" he asked, not surprised by her demand.

Stickit shrugged. "The way you use her, she won't need it much longer. And what I got to tell is worth it."

"I'll hear it first," Antoni said, his voice dangerously cold.

Stickit came close to the Upright Man, the words stuttered with eagerness.

"I heard a vagger tell Kai that the knot is meeting at the Ribbons. Jobber and another are coming overland, but the other, along with the water girl, is coming by the coast."

"The water girl?" Antoni asked, his eyes narrowing.

"Yeah. And I can be there to meet them. I know the Ribbons better than anybody."

Antoni reeled back from the woman, air forcing its way out of his lungs as he exhaled hard. His hands closed into fists and his eyes squeezed shut. Then they snapped open and he looked out on the bleak remains of the street below. The water girl would come, Stickit would bring her here to him. No one would question her, for she was known as a member of the New Moon and the Waterlings. Then he would take the fourth girl, drain her of her power as he had all the others before. And when he was finished, he would be the water element in Oran's knot. The other three would be forced into dealing with him, forced into giving him the power he wanted.

He turned slowly to Stickit. "The room is yours. But not until I've taken the water girl. Bring her here. Just her. She's all I need."

Stickit grinned and she looked around the room, her eyes already taking possession. "An easy prig. Easier than a fancy man's pocket."

She left then, the door closing quietly behind her. Antoni Re Desturo stood by the window, his hand resting on the sill. He caught a glimpse of his cream-colored nails, jagged and torn. With a scowl, he took a small paring knife from the top of a dresser and sat down to smooth the edges of his nails. They must be perfect, he thought with a smile as he trimmed the torn edges. And very sharp.

Chapter Seventeen

Thick smoke, layered like cotton batting, hung in the air as Deveaux rode his horse away from the jagged front line. Around him trees crackled with flames, the wind whipping ash and sparking embers into the sky. Deveaux swallowed, gagging at the acrid taste of charred wood. The dense smoke was impenetrable in the low-lying gulleys. But Deveaux didn't need his eyes to tell him that his army had taken another costly strike at its flank. On the narrow plain between the forests, his men lay on the ground, some badly wounded, a fair number already dead. A horse neighed shrilly until the twang of a crossbow bolt silenced it. A slight breeze parted the clouds of smoke and Deveaux saw his remaining soldiers, battle weary and sullen as they marched in ghostly silence, hands clutched tightly around their weapons.

Deveaux swore and his teeth scraped the lower edge of his parched lip. His hair was matted with blood. Black soot clung greasily to his face and hands and beneath the leather jerkin he could smell the rank odor of his own sweat. His horse's neck drooped with fatigue, its hooves stepping cautiously amid the abandoned corpses. Under his thighs he felt the animal tremble. Steam snorted from the flared nostrils as foam collected at the bit.

He had misjudged the New Moon. He had not thought them capable of any more surprises. He had not thought them capable of a deadly assault. And yet, both had happened. In the last few days as they had traveled north to Asturas his army had been attacked with increasing regularity along its slow-moving flank. The New Moon was mobile, quick to engage and then disengage when his own army rounded on it. They scattered rapidly, disappearing into the woods, into the air it seemed, only to reappear later farther down the road. The villages had been forewarned. When the Silean army arrived the cottages were empty, the gates standing open.

"Damn the bastards!" Deveaux cursed loudly and his horse startled at the crack of the general's voice. The New Moon now chose the battle sites, not the Sileans, and each site disadvantageous to the advancing Silean army.

Deveaux reached the bank of the Sairas River and, sliding off his horse's back, he went to the river's edge. The water moved swiftly and quietly, strands of grass waving in the current. He reached a hand in and retrieved a palmful of water to drink. Its coldness sliced his tongue, but its purity washed down the sour taste of a failed battle.

There were other things that disturbed him. They had captured a number of Oran families fleeing from the North. It had intrigued him at first. Why should they flee the North, the stronghold of the New Moon? What was chasing them out and into the advancing lines of an enemy army? Most of them had been poor peasants, women with small children, old people, and they were filled with fantastic tales of the earth lifting and disappearing into the sky. The New Moon stronghold of Sadar's Keep was no more. Deveaux had not believed them until one of his sergeants brought him a vagger they had found hiding in the woods. They had tortured the man, slowly and carefully, so that his spirit would break but his body would hold out until they could learn what they wanted to know. For two days the man remained silent. But on the third day, he talked. Deveaux had been alone with the man, and had bent his head close to hear the whispered words.

Deveaux lowered his hand into the water again and took another sip. The whole island was disintegrating, the vagger had confided with the calm of a dying man who has ceased to have interest in mortal questions. There was no way the Sileans could win. If the New Moon was not successful in stopping Zorah, the land would continue its violent spasms until it was torn apart and returned to the Chaos out of which it had come. If the New Moon did win, the Silean armies could not hope to succeed against the Oran people and the power of the new Queens' quarter knot. It was all one fate for the Sileans.

Deveaux had told no one. But he knew now the reason the New Moon army had increased in strength and boldness. They were holding nothing back. There would be no spring campaign. This was it: their last chance, and they fought with all the combined strength of a desperate people.

And you, Deveaux, he asked himself, what are you here for? There was nothing to win, nothing to gain here. The parliament had done well to send him to this frigging useless war. Deveaux snarled and plunged his head into the water. He shook his tangled mane of yellow hair, wanting to wash away the drying blood of battle. He came up for air and, grabbing another breath, returned his head to the water. The cold scorched his cheeks, dug needles of pain into his scalp. But it was free of the stink of oiled weapons, burning leather, and the harsh, metallic taste of blood. Then he surfaced and shook his head like a dog, spraying water over the bank.

"Sir?" a voice called tentatively.

Deveaux squinted through the water droplets that clung to his eyelashes and saw two soldiers waiting for him. One of them wore the uniform of his army, but the other Guard was dressed in the older style of uniform not seen in Silea for many years. The shocked look on the Guard's face betrayed his ignorance of Deveaux. A messenger, surmised Deveaux, as he rose to his feet. From that prick Ilario. Probably wanting to know how things are going while he's back in Beldan sitting his arse on a cushion. Deveaux dried his face on the rough wool of his sleeve. The messenger gawked as Deveaux neared him.

"From Beldan, aren't you?" Deveaux demanded.

"Yes, sir," the man shot back, trying to regain his composure. "I've come to escort you to Beldan, sir."

Deveaux stared at the man in silence. "To Beldan," he said at last. "And why Beldan?"

"Sir, the Regent Re Ilario has been murdered. It was decided that you would be the best replacement at this time. The First-watch Re Fortuna, in accordance with the wishes of the Silean nobility, has requested that you come at once."

Deveaux's gaze narrowed. "Who murdered him?"

The messenger shifted his feet uncomfortably. "The Queen, sir," he answered.

Deveaux snapped his tongue against the roof of his mouth and sneered in disgust. "He gets himself killed in some frigging lovers' spat and I'm to leave my army?"

"It wasn't like that, sir," the messenger said quickly. "He was defending the honor of the Silean Advisor when the Queen grabbed a sword and cut open his throat."

"Where's the Advisor now?"

"He's disappeared, sir," the messenger said miserably.

"Disappeared," Deveaux repeated incredulously. "What manner of honor is being defended here, when a Regent gets himself sliced by a woman and the man in question turns tail and disappears?" Deveaux shifted his glance from the Guard to meet his soldier's gaze. A communal rage passed between them. What were they doing here after all? Deveaux dismissed the soldier but asked the messenger to remain.

The messenger waited uneasily as Deveaux came close enough to catch the scent of fear on the man's skin.

"What's really happening in Beldan?" he asked.

"Sir?"

"How long do you think it will be before the whole island breaks apart like a clod of mud?"

The messenger paused, as if considering the correct answer. Deveaux saw his expression shift, the diplomatic mask crumbling as a frightened man appeared from behind it. The messenger shook his head. "Not much longer, I'll wager. Best choice, sir, is to get yourself boarded on a ship home. The sooner the better."

"Is that what you've planned?"

The messenger shrugged. "If I could, sir. But demand is high and ships few. Only those with gold in their pockets is getting out now."

Deveaux thought it over. It would be worth it to see the look on the parliament leader's face if he should arrive home, unscathed by this worthless adventure. Still, it would be a desertion of duty if he left Oran before the end, and for that there could be penalties. Then Deveaux smiled, letting his teeth escape over the confines of his lips. There were ways around that. It was just a matter of timing. He would think about it on his way to Beldan. Glancing up at the thick veil of smoke through the trees, he reasoned almost anything was better than this pointless battle.

"Tell my page to make the horse ready. And let him know that I wish to have a meeting with the captains. We leave before nightfall," Deveaux said brusquely.

The messenger left, relieved, Deveaux imagined, to be spared the unpleasant sight of his face. Deveaux returned to the riverbank and, despite the wind, stripped off his clothing. He waited, poised on the bank, his mane of yellow hair brushing his naked shoulders. He looked down at himself, the old scars seamed across his muscles. A chip of bone protruded beneath the tent of skin across his hips. His skin was white beneath his clothes, only his hands dark brown and callused. He waded into the water, the current lapping at his thighs. He shuddered, his breath coming in gasps as the cold water circled around his legs. As he lowered himself slowly into the river, the water washed away the layers of dirt and sweat. He would not go to Beldan stinking of battle. Despite his face, he was a man, not a bloody-muzzled wolf newly come from the kill. Deveaux scrubbed his arms in the cold water as he contemplated his future. He would stay in Beldan just long enough to find passage away from Oran. The coffers were half filled with his soldiers' pay and there were not so many left alive to collect it. The money would be enough to set him free somewhere else if he chose not to return to Silea.

Contented with this plan, Deveaux climbed out of the water, cold but refreshed. He felt confident that he would once more survive the treachery of the Silean parliament. He reached for his trousers and slipped suddenly on the muddy bank. Falling against the stones, he gave his thigh a bloody scrape.

Shefek soared high in the air, rising above a bank of smoke-thickened clouds. He caught the prickling odor of battle, lingering in the mist that beaded in droplets on the smooth surface of his beak. He blinked his eyes with extreme slowness and lowered the curled arch of his neck. The wings parted the clouds, opening a path through the mist. He broke through the lower surface and saw the flames that licked the tops of the high trees and the long black scars across the dry, wintry plains. Corpses lay in bloody heaps as soldiers, their faces covered by cloth masks, committed them into the flames of the burning forest. Shefek angled his body over the ground and watched as two soldiers, catching sight of him, dropped a corpse in terror and fled toward a collection of muddy tents.

A crossbowman knocked a bolt and aimed it toward Shefek. He pumped his wings, driving his heavy body higher and out of range. He heard the wind whistle as the bolt sped in the sky and fell short of its target. Then Shefek screeched shrilly, seeing a man with a tangled mane of blond hair and the distorted face of the beast emerge from a tent. Shefek circled again, marking the man, knowing him, catching the peculiar scent of his skin. Shefek screeched again in defiance and beat his wings furiously in the air. A wind spiraled around him, lifting the trampled grass of the field. He flew over the tents, and the cloth walls flapped in the driving wind, straining at the ropes. The man below him was unmoved, looking upward to take the full measure of Shefek's flight. His eyes followed Shefek's movements like a cat before the bird, his lips parted to reveal the fangs.

Shefek cackled, the closest to laughter he could manage. Then he banked in the clouds and flew away, seeing a second crossbowman set a bolt into his crossbow. This was not how he wanted it to be. Shefek wanted Deveaux firmly locked within the cage of his talons. He planned to carry the beast all the way to the edge of Oran's cradle and then into the howling winds of Chaos.

Shefek settled his enormous body down on a flat plain a short ways west of Deveaux's camp. His wings battered the ground as he fought to gain his balance, cursing at the shock of landing. It was the last time, he promised himself, that he would transform into the likeness of a man. The whitened garments of a vagger cloaked his body and after a habitual touch to his nose he headed across the plain for the Silean camp.

The sun was a pale white circle as it hovered over the tops of the trees. Its bleached light gave off no warmth and as it dipped between the blackened spurs of the trees it shone like a counterfeit moon. Shefek walked without haste, his hands tucked into the folds of his vagger robes for warmth. He was impatient and irritated with his human form. He had grown tired of its limitations, of the flat, callused feet, the worthless arms that gave nothing to the glory of flight. He was a Kirian and he longed for the freedom of the air, not the confines of skin.

He stopped on the road, seeing two horsemen cantering toward him. He smiled at the tangled mane of yellow hair on one of the riders. He could not have chosen a better road and he murmured a silent thanks to Oran. Shefek planted himself in the middle of the track and watched with satisfaction as Deveaux pulled in the reins of his horse cautiously at the sight of the vagger. Just waiting.

Deveaux's eyes narrowed and he scanned the edges of the trees, looking for others who might be waiting in ambush. He held his hand up as a warning to the other rider.

"No one but me," Shefek said softly under his breath. "Come on, you mangy cat, let your curiosity bring you closer yet."

Deveaux drew his sword, holding it out in readiness. His horse trotted uneasily toward Shefek, its eyes rolling white. At least the horse knows me, Shefek thought, and so, it seems, does the cat on its back. The Silean Guard beside Deveaux looked perplexed by Deveaux's caution.

"State your business!" Deveaux shouted.

Shefek remained silent. There was no sunlight to catch the

golden glint in his eyes. Instead they reflected the cloud-covered sky, dull as pewter mirrors.

Deveaux's horse grew more restive.

"I intend to kill you if you do not speak," Deveaux snarled again, raising his sword.

Without a word, Shefek started walking quickly toward Deveaux. The horse pranced backward, seeing the long-legged stride of the white-cloaked vagger approaching him. Deveaux swore at the beast and dug his frustrated heels into its flanks. Enraged, he slapped the reins down hard across the neck of his horse and it bolted, terrified, toward Shefek.

Shefek's walk became faster, almost a run as Deveaux's horse unwillingly cantered toward him. With a fierce joy he abandoned his human form, the Kirian's spirit bursting the confines of the man's flesh. He could feel the rapid transformation occurring as he ran. He had no reason to do it carefully or patiently. He didn't need this man's body anymore. The thin sheath of skin tore violently, shredding into ribbons as the fingers ripped open to reveal pinion feathers. The remains of his human mask was split in two by the emerging point of a Kirian's beak.

The horse reared back, neighing in terror as the Kirian's huge wings engulfed it and the vulture's head shrieked above it. The horse stumbled, falling forward to it knees, its head colliding with the hard winter ground. Deveaux clung to its neck as it toppled over and then he fell from its back and rolled to the side. He sat dazed by his fall, the sword lying on the ground beside him. Shefek's talons dug bloody gashes as they latched onto the horse's neck as a perch. His beating wings thundered in the air.

Deveaux scrambled to reclaim his sword. At the moment his hand clasped around the hilt, Shefek's taloned claw reached out and snapped shut around Deveaux's body. The huge wings tilted as he was off balanced by the extra weight. He gave a few awkward steps as he prepared to fly, aware that Deveaux, trapped in his grip, was dragged along the ground. He could hear Deveaux bellowing and feel within the smooth hardness of his talons Deveaux's desperate squirming. Shefek flexed his legs, and then sprang into the air with a victorious screech.

His wings ached as he beat them furiously, lifting his body

and his struggling prey from the ground. The point of his arrowed beak cleaved a path between the clouds and the winds gusted coldly, fluttering the white bands of breast feathers. The man trapped in his talons continued to shout, though his voice grew faint in the rushing air. As Shefek flew higher and higher, the veneer of a borrowed humanity fell away and he remembered only his Kirian self—at one with the wind's currents, lifted and carried away from the weight of the earth. He could hear again Oran's thoughts, hear the mournful cries of the winds of Chaos calling him back. The self that had once walked the dusty roads, that had embraced the shape of a man and chained itself to the weakness of emotions, dissolved in the thinning air. He was a Kirian, and the last of his once-proud race.

Shefek felt his strength return. He felt freed of sorrow, of love, even of the need for revenge by the emptiness of the darkening sky, the wide black distances between the glimmering stars. How long had it been since he had flown so high? Since he had taken the Kirian's route home?

A sharp pain caused him to look down in surprise. A sword protruded from the feathers of his underbelly. He saw a creature trapped in the grip of his talons. Shefek regarded the limp body curiously. He knew that at one time this man creature had been important to him. He had clung to it for reasons he could no longer understand. Here among the stars, in the vast black night of Oran's cradle, those things had ceased to have any meaning for him.

He opened his talons and released his catch. The man tumbled in the winds, skipped like a stone over the surface of a quiet pond. Long, long he fell, back toward the hardness of the earth. Shefek watched for a moment and then turned away with no other interest in that past.

But pain dug at him, drawn from his belly, where the man's sword had opened a wound. He was growing weary, his wings slowing, his heart hammering in his breast as he reached for the last of his strength. He could see ahead of him the welcoming threads of colored light: the wrapped cocoon of Oran's cradle hanging delicately in the air. He heard the keening of wind and saw the boiling sky drawing all things into its seething heart. Chaos loomed above him, threatening and exhilarating.

With a final burst of energy, he reached with his talons and wrapped them smartly around a thread of fading light. It hummed, shining more brightly as it recognized the long-departed feel of a Kirian's talons. With his wings folded against his back, Shefek arched his long neck, his head tilted so that one gold eye stared into Chaos. Circling in the roiling mass of clouds Shefek saw Oran's past, its creation side by side with its future as the winds of Chaos stirred Time together in a raging whirlpool. The golden eye gleamed brighter as he leaned closer still, fascinated by the howling Chaos.

The wind ruffled his feathers, snatched the pinions with fierce gusts as it tried to suck him into its driving current. He flapped his wings in a final gesture of self-preservation. But he could not sustain his hold on the thread of dying light. With a Kirian's shrill cry, he opened wide his wings. The winds bore him aloft easily, whirling him madly in their current. And then he was caught in the stilled core of the whirlpool, confronted with Zorah's Fire Sword.

Shefek hung suspended for an instant above the world of Oran; then the winds shifted again, sucking him back into the boiling clouds. He scraped against the Fire Sword and it halved the Kirian's body. The winds of Chaos tore the halves apart into fragments until the Kirian was no more than particles of dust joined to the dense mass of seething clouds. Only a few white feathers remained, drifting in the calm air between the strands of Oran's cradle.

Chapter Eighteen

Faul squatted by the small camp fire, glancing uneasily at the shadows their figures cast against the trees. She didn't like having this fire. It was too dangerous. But it had snowed again during the early part of the day, and except for Jobber they were all wet and cold down to the bone. Faul's jaw ached where she had clenched it to keep her teeth from chattering. The horses remained near, huddled close together. Steam rose from their flanks and their soft muzzles. Faul tucked another small branch of wood into the glowing coals and sat back.

"Oy, Faul," Jobber said, "take another piece." She had divided the dried meat and handed Faul a black strip.

"Z'blood," Faul answered shaking her head. "It's no better than a tanner's apron."

"A bit cleaner," Finch put in, chewing her piece noisily with her back teeth.

"You Waterlings never were very fussy," Jobber snorted.

Finch shot back with a grin. "Oy, I seen you pinch the mold off a crust or two!"

"Ain't no shame in that."

"And it was you eyeing the cat with a long tooth," Shedwyn added, pointing an accusing finger at Jobber.

"Yeah, well, Shefek must have beat me to it 'cause I never saw the beastie again after he came."

Faul grunted, a half smile at the corners of her mouth. Jobber waited, her eyebrows raised in anticipation of protest. There was none, and even Finch blanched at Faul's silent agreement.

"Well, then," Jobber said finally, "each to his own dish, I guess."

Faul gazed up at the night sky. It was clear, and between the spires of the trees the stars twinkled coldly. She thought of Shefek and wondered where he was. She knew she would never see him again. And yet, she chided herself, that's what she had thought the first time he had left her, after seducing her and then disappearing with her good gold chain. They had argued about it at Sadar. "You gave it as a token," he had insisted innocently. Well, it hardly mattered anymore, she thought sadly. The smile faded on her face and a chilly breeze touched her cheeks. The truth lay like a hard stone in the pit of her stomach: this time he is gone for good.

What was it that had so captured her about Shefek? she wondered, leaning her chin forward to rest on her knees. Jobber burst into laughter at something Wyer had said and Faul glanced in their direction. Jobber's face glowed, lit from within by a secret fire. Her eyes sparkled green and gold as she spoke to Wyer. Her long, sturdy hands wiped self-consciously at her cheek, as if she imagined a smudge of dirt lay there. Wyer too had altered from his usual taciturn manner. He smiled when he spoke, his teeth white against his soot-stained skin. They sat close together, shoulders almost touching. Faul returned her gaze skyward. Just so, she thought, remembering the way the heat flared in her cheeks at Shefek's touch. To every dell, a digger; to every woman, the right man. Faul smiled at the stars. Well, in my case, she thought wryly, the right man wasn't a man at all.

And that was it, she decided. Shefek came to her with the power of Oran's past. Like the Queen and like Jobber, it was the crackle of magic that had attracted Faul. In the dark dullness that she believed her own life to be they were shimmering blades of light, unpredictable and challenging. There was in Shefek's embrace not just the pleasure of a capable lover, but the distant music of Chaos, the glimmer of stars in his golden eyes and on his skin the feathery softness of plumage. Faul sighed, then looked quickly at the others, embarrassed for having forgotten herself in their company.

But she needn't have worried. They were hunkered close to the fire, their faces tired but caught up in the merriment of their own conversation. A blush on Finch's face made Faul realize they were sharing vulgar gossip. Shedwyn leaned back to rest on her elbows. The firelight cast a bright orange glow on the fabric of her skirt, pulled tight over her swelling belly. With a start, Faul recognized the curve of Shedwyn's pregnancy. She frowned, annoyed that she had not seen the obvious sooner. No wonder the young woman had looked so worn of late. Shedwyn laughed at something Jobber said, a hand reaching to stroke the oval of her belly.

"Oy!" Finch cried, cutting short the laughter. She bolted to her feet, glancing around in panic. Her blond hair fluttered around the small, terrified face.

"What is it?" Faul growled, immediately kicking dirt on the fire to douse the light.

"Metal! Steel. And it's close by," Finch said holding her fingers out.

Faul listened and heard the quiet chink of a chain.

Shedwyn lumbered to her feet and clicked softly with her tongue. The horses lifted their curious heads in reply. They shifted nervously in their stance, sensing the tension. Heads bobbing, they came quietly to nuzzle Shedwyn's shoulder and head.

"Mount up," Faul ordered. She waited on the ground until Shedwyn and Jobber were up on the backs of their horses. Her hand rested on the hilt of the Fire Sword as she let her eyes adjust to the sudden darkness. The coals from the camp fire were dying slowly beneath the covering of dirt.

"Which direction?" she asked Finch. Finch reached up for the mane of her horse and turned her head slightly. "Z'blood," she whispered fearfully, "I can't tell."

"Shedwyn?"

"There." She pointed to a stand of trees just beyond the circle of the camp.

"Wyer," Faul said, "take them east."

"And you?"

"A diversion to give you time."

"No," said Jobber. "They won't find us in the dark."

"They've already marked us," Faul answered quietly. Her head jerked around to the sound of a twig crackling, and then the rustle of bushes. "On my word," she warned. She leaned down and took a branch still twigged with dry needles and stuck it into the dying embers. It flared to life, flames licking the dried needles. She lobbed it toward the trees, and out of the shadows appeared the startled face of a Silean soldier. He roared, and from the darkened forest came the buzz of arrows. "Go!" Faul commanded and slapped Jobber's horse on the rump.

The horse sprang forward at Faul's strike. Jobber swore loudly but ducked her head as the low-lying branches threatened to tear her from the horse's back. Shedwyn followed and then Wyer. As Finch's horse entered the woods another arrow whistled in the air. Faul heard the girl scream, and the harsh snapping of branches as she was pitched to the ground.

"Finch!" Faul called out even as she backed into the darker shadows to hide herself. There was no answer from the girl. The loud drumming of hooves and breaking branches commanded Faul's attention.

A rider and horse broke through the trees and entered the camp. Faul loosened the Fire Sword from its scabbard and held it ready. As the horse's hooves scattered the coals of the old camp fire, Faul stepped forth from the shadows and slashed the blade upward through the horse's chest. Light from the scattered coals flared and the Fire Sword gleamed like a stream of red blood. It sliced through flesh and bone easily and without resistance. The horse buckled and stumbled forward. Its rider, cursing as he fell, hacked the air with his own sword. Faul shifted her stance, twisted her hold on the hilt, and drove the sword down across the tumbling soldier. The sword cut him cleanly at the waist.

Soldiers were spilling out of the trees into the camp, flinging themselves at Faul as she wove in and out of the shadows. Her hands grew slick as she moved from one adversary to another, dodging their blows and cutting them open as quickly as possible in reply. A few coals from the gutted fire smoldered, catching the dry ends of fallen branches. A spark crackled, and then another. Faul saw the circle grow lighter as fire smoked and then flickered into life. A second horseman rounded on her and she had but an instant to turn and meet him.

Too late! she thought with a detached sense of calm. She stumbled uncertainly in her turn as the Silean blade angled down toward her with terrifying speed. Reflexively she raised the Fire Sword and heard the scrape of the blades as they met. The Silean sword hovered and then gained the advantage, slashing deep across her collarbone. She staggered back, surprised by the red welt of skin exposed through the torn fabric. She hardly felt the wound, its pain echoing elsewhere in her senses, but not here, at the point of battle. She raised the Fire Sword for another attack, furious that her legs had begun to wobble. Again she was slow and she watched, disgusted, as the Silean sword stabbed at her waist and tore up. With a clumsy thrust, she drove her sword into the rider's thigh. The Fire Sword pierced the leg through to the horse's side. The man bellowed, pinned to the back of the terrified horse, which bucked wildly, trying to throw off the man and the sword.

"Z'blood," Faul swore and collapsed to the ground. She lay curled, pine needles digging into her cheeks. The pain was intense and she could taste the warm salt of blood in her mouth. Nothing in her moved, nothing answered her angry command to rise. Her hands opened and shut of their own accord but would not lift the sword that lay just out of reach.

And then gradually a numbness stole over her, made her float away from the pain, from the disappointment of having failed. She opened her eyes and saw the black hooves of the Silean's horse prancing in the firelight, the longs legs breaking the light into slender rectangles of orange and black. She stared wide-eyed at a tiny flame, sparking to life amid the pine needles near her face.

Fire. She imagined herself reaching out to its warmth. Beldan's Fire, she smiled, seeing in the flame the red torch of Jobber's hair. She exhaled slowly and watched with satisfaction as the small flame burned more brightly with her breath.

Well, Faul, she congratulated herself dryly, not such a bad death after all. The flames continued to dance, spreading out around the camp fire as Faul's eyes saw the blackened shapes of the men she had killed. Not bad at all, she thought as darkness covered her eyes, shutting out the bright flames. She felt herself grow hollow, emptied as her blood seeped into the forest floor. And in her final exhale, she heard the keening winds as she surrendered to the Chaos.

"Stop," Shedwyn pleaded, tugging on the reins of her horse. "Huld's peace, we must stop. I can go no farther."

Jobber following behind her pulled her horse up short, the bit digging into its mouth. Its sides heaved with the effort of the run and its head drooped as it panted. Jobber slid from the back of the horse, her hips flaring with pain from the jarring ride. She crossed to Shedwyn, who rested her head on her horse's mane, tears pouring down her cheeks. Jobber touched Shedwyn's hand, worried at the coldness of her skin.

"I can't," Shedwyn said between choked sobs. "I can't ride like this. Not now."

Wyer drew alongside them, straightening his legs in the saddle to stare back at the way they had come. Then he eased himself down, his shoulders sagging with fatigue.

"I don't hear them," he murmured. "Perhaps its safe to walk a ways."

"How long before light?" Jobber asked, staring up at the night sky. The stars had faded, and over the east edge of the trees the black sheen of the night had softened.

"Not long," he answered and swung down off his horse to join Jobber.

He picked up the reins to Shedwyn's horse and urged it forward at a slow, gentle walk.

Shedwyn moaned softly as the horse moved but held on.

Jobber's heels dug angrily into the ground. The wintry smell of pine needles and decayed leaves was joined by the sudden odor of burning copper.

"What is it?" Wyer asked.

"Faul," Jobber answered miserably. "And Finch. They're dead, ain't they?"

Wyer sighed and nodded his head. "I saw Finch downed. Faul would have been here by now if she had survived."

"But what if she's still alive? What if she's only injured, holed up under a bush somewhere. What if she dies only 'cause I'm here running away—"

"Jobber." Wyer cut her off sharply. "You're not running away. You and Shedwyn, it's not the same as it is for the rest of us. We would give our lives for you."

"And what do we give you, eh, Wyer? I ain't done so much for anyone. A Beldan snitch—"

"A Fire Queen!" Wyer retorted.

"But what does that mean? Zorah, as poisoned as she is, still managed to rule a country. I don't know how to do that. What's more, I don't think I even *want* to do that."

Wyer spat in disgust. "My father told me once that every forge in Beldan was but a fragment of Oran's heart. The forge was a sacred place to him. But Jobber, you have His heart within you. You bring the strength and power of Oran's heart to us. To Beldan."

"Of what use is it, if everyone I ever cared about dies?" Jobber asked bitterly.

"It's best you find that out, Jobber, and soon," Wyer answered softly.

"I want to go back. To find Faul," Jobber said stubbornly.

"Impossible," Wyer said, growing angry.

Jobber seethed with silent rage and frustration. The metallic stink of her hair thickened in the night air. Strands of coppery hair billowed around her head. The horses shied away from her in fright, jerking at the reins. Wyer glanced over at her, tight-lipped in his irritation.

Jobber sighed with weary resignation. "I'm sorry," she apologized weakly. "I'm sorry for being a raver." She smoothed her hands over her scalp, running her fingers through her hair.

Yellow sparks crackled between her fingers, flying into the air, where they faded in little puffs of smoke. Her horse whinnied softly, still anxious until she calmed it, gently stroking its sweating neck.

The smell of copper dissipated, but the aroma of smoke still lingered in the air.

Shedwyn picked up her head and pointed through the trees. "Look, a cottage. Please, I need to rest."

Wyer frowned. "Someone's there already. They've a fire going."

"I'll chance it," Shedwyn insisted.

Wyer looked at Jobber, who hesitated, her expression full of misgivings.

Wyer caught Shedwyn around the waist as she eased herself down from the back of her horse. He lowered her to the ground and she stumbled with a small cry of pain. A horrified expression twisted her face.

"No," she moaned and dug her hand beneath her skirts to feel between her thighs. "No!" she cried out as she withdrew her hand and saw her fingers were wet with blood. Her face folded with grief and she sagged to the ground.

"Wyer," Jobber ordered, all traces of doubt vanished. "Quick, carry her to the hut. We'll take our chances."

Wyer lifted Shedwyn up into his arms, staggering beneath her weight. Shedwyn wrapped her arms around his neck and laid her head on his shoulder, shaking with silent sobs. Jobber marched before them, looking back now and again to stare anxiously at the pair.

The sky was growing light, the faint gray dawn bleaching everything of color except for the wet black trunks of the trees. The forester's hut was dreary, the roof leaning dangerously to one side. Moss bunched along the rim of the eaves between the tattered remains of bird's nests. The door was warped, and from a gap at the bottom Jobber could see the yellow flicker of firelight.

Jobber stopped before the door, her hands in ready fists. She could hear Wyer grunting softly with the burden of carrying Shedwyn. "Oy there, is anyone about?" Jobber called out.

An old gray horse leaned around from the side of the cottage, staring at them with curious eyes. But the door remained closed.

Jobber gritted her teeth, deciding it was better to charge the door than give whoever was within a second chance to find a weapon. She stepped up in preparation to force the door open when it was opened abruptly from inside.

A boy stood there, his mouth rounded in surprise as Jobber pulled back a cocked fist.

"Jobber! It's me, Anard!" he cried raising his hands.

"Anard?" Jobber answered, astonished. She dropped her fist and clasped the boy gratefully by the shoulders, laughing with surprise. He was thin and pale, his dark eyes huge above the hollow cheeks. Then her face sobered and she turned to Wyer, stepping out of the way of the door. "Come, bring Shedwyn in quickly to the fire."

Wyer pushed past them, squeezing through the narrow doorway with Shedwyn.

Jobber started to ask Anard what he was doing there when Shedwyn gave a loud, anguished cry. Jobber rushed through the door. Anard was buzzing with words behind her but she couldn't make them out.

Inside the hut, Wyer had laid Shedwyn down on a straw pallet beside a second figure. She was stroking his haggard face, tears staining her cheeks. Jobber groaned, recognizing Eneas by the long strands of dirty blond hair. His waxy skin was stretched thin as parchment over his bones. The lids fluttered open and he stared at Shedwyn feverishly, his eyes black with widened pupils.

The small room stank of infection and smoke. Jobber came close to Eneas and took one of his hands in hers. It was dry and hot, though his forehead was shining with beads of sweat. His lips were cracked, the skin flaking at the corners of his mouth.

"I tried, Shedwyn," Anard was saying. "I tried to find those few roots that might help bring down the fever, but nothing seems to be working."

Shedwyn sat up, and in the light of the hearth fire her skin was the color of driftwood. She smiled at Eneas, her lips tense against her teeth. "I'm here now," she said quietly to Eneas.

Then she raised her sharp glance at Jobber. "I need you to help me."

"Anything," Jobber replied.

"Anard, you and Wyer must bring me digger's root. You'll find it growing beside the gacklebushes. Two handfuls, at least. Go now." She waited until they had left and then turned to Jobber. "Pull back the covers, I need to see how bad the wound is."

Though she had prepared herself, Jobber gasped at the sight of Eneas's leg. The wound had swollen, pus gathering at the center of a red gash. Purple streaks extended beyond the wound, reaching up to his groin and hip.

Shedwyn wiped a shaking hand across her forehead. "It must be cleaned properly," she said. "Take a wet cloth until it steams in your hands, but not hot enough to burn flesh." She motioned to a bowl of water and a few rags that Anard had used to wipe Eneas's forehead.

Jobber grabbed one, dipping it in the cold water and then clasping it between her hands. She closed her eyes and felt her senses travel inward to the rose of fire in her heart. It bloomed, the heat spreading out to her fingertips, and hot steam hissed in the cloth between her clenched hands.

"Good," Shedwyn was saying, "now apply it to the wound."

Jobber opened her eyes and laid the steaming cloth on Eneas's leg. The silent man jerked awake, a hoarse scream coming from his lips. His shoulders lifted off the pallet and Shedwyn laid herself over him to keep him from thrashing.

Again and again Jobber rinsed and heated the cloths between her hands and applied them to the wound. It drained more freely, and the cleaned edges of the wound began to glisten. Eneas drifted in and out of knowing, sometimes crying out an unfinished order, other times murmuring words that Jobber couldn't hear, but that Shedwyn answered in whispers of her own.

"Fairly done," Shedwyn said at last, examining the cleansed wound.

Wyer and Anard returned with a full sack. Anard set some of the cleaned root in an old kettle over the fire to boil. Shedwyn had Wyer grind another portion into a paste and then applied it directly to the wound. When the boiling root had tinged the water an amber color, she pulled it off the fire and poured it into a cup. Wyer lifted Eneas's head and, after she had cooled it with her breath, Shedwyn spooned some of the liquid into Eneas's mouth. He coughed at the taste, but swallowed it at Shedwyn's encouragement.

Satisfied at last, Shedwyn lay back exhausted on the straw pallet. "I must sleep now. But please see that he drinks some of this before the day is half over. And change the dressing once more. The digger's root will cause the infection to drain."

Shedwyn curled herself into her cloak and, reaching one hand protectively over Eneas's chest, settled herself to sleep. Anard fed the fire, keeping the chilly room warm.

Wyer got up stiffly from his stool and started out the door. Concerned, Jobber followed him.

He walked to the old gray, his face lost in thought. As he ran his hand along the scrubby mane, Jobber saw his jaw set as he came to a decision. He brought the gray out and, grabbing its mane, swung a leg over its back.

"I'm going back to find Faul," he said to Jobber. "Seeing Eneas . . ." He paused. "Well, he's not out of it yet, but I'd wager with a woman like Shedwyn he's got a better chance than most."

"Let me go with you," Jobber asked.

"No. It's foolish enough for me to go. You must stay here with Shedwyn. She's going to need help. And I doubt she'll be willing to leave until she is certain Eneas is well enough to remain without her." Wyer bit down on his lower lip, a question lingering. "Shedwyn's bleeding, does it mean she's with child?" he asked finally.

Jobber nodded slowly. "Yeah. At least I think she still is."

"I'll be back as soon as I can," Wyer said, kicking the coarse flanks of the old horse.

"Wyer," Jobber called anxiously. He craned his head to hear her, the horse still plodding on its way. "Have a care," Jobber said, the words catching in her throat.

Wyer waved his hand and then, leaning his body forward, urged the old horse to a canter through the trees.

* * *

For three days Jobber and Anard sweated Eneas's wound and spooned the warm liquid into his throat. Anard went out daily to hunt for digger's root, even though it snowed on the second day. He brought back a small rabbit he had caught in a snare. Cursing her clumsiness, Jobber managed to cook it without burning it too badly and got Shedwyn to eat. Shedwyn had stopped bleeding, but she still looked worn, her skin ashen and her brow knitted in worry over Eneas. Jobber had her own fears and though she tried to offer encouragement, her time was split between anxiously watching the trees for signs of Wyer and caring for Shedwyn.

On the third day, Jobber was relieved to discover Shedwyn sitting on the pallet beside Eneas, combing her hair with her fingers. Her face looked more relaxed, the color returning to her cheeks.

"The fever's going down," Shedwyn said to Jobber. "See, his forehead is dry. It's cooler, too, and he's sleeping easier."

"Wound ain't so red," Jobber said, rubbing the grit from her eyes. She stirred the coals of the old fire, the dreary room brightening a bit.

"He'll mend," Shedwyn said softly.

"And you?" Jobber asked, appraising Shedwyn's face. "Are you all right?"

She sighed heavily, her fingers threading through the thick hair. "It was too much, too soon. The end of Sadar, and that ride through the woods. The bleeding has stopped for now, but I don't know yet if harm was done."

Anard came bursting through the door, dropping his sack of digger's root. A few of the brown roots rolled onto the floor. "Wyer's back!" he cried.

Jobber sprang to the door, her heart thudding with expectation. She caught a glimpse of him, draped with the morning mist as he rode slowly through the trees. His head hung down as if he slept in the saddle, the horse plodding wearily to the hut.

Wyer was alone. Jobber's throat tightened.

The gray stopped and Wyer lifted his head to Jobber. A new beard grizzled his cheeks and his eyes were dull. He swung down from the horse with slow, stiff movements. He retrieved the feathery carcass of a woodcock tied to his saddle. The bird dangled forlornly as he held up the body by the legs. In his other hand he held the Fire Sword in its long black scabbard.

Jobber moaned as Wyer placed the Fire Sword in her unwilling hands.

"She was dead when I got there," Wyer began in a low voice. "She died fighting and she took a fair number of the butcherboys with her. I put her and Finch together and covered them with stones. Only this was left and I didn't know whether or not you'd want it back again."

Jobber nodded silently, despising the sword she held in her hands. It was ugly, a worthless thing, for it had not saved Faul. She would have thrown it away, tossed it from her hand like a hideous snake but for the memory of Shefek's command.

"Should have buried it with Faul," Jobber said sharply and then looked quickly, her face pained. "I'm sorry," she apologized to Wyer, seeing anger cloud his eyes. "I don't want to be harsh. It means a lot to me that you went. That I know about Faul. It's just this . . . thing," she hissed, holding the sword out, away from her body. "It has more glory than it deserves."

"How are Shedwyn and Eneas?" Wyer asked.

"Mending, it seems."

"Good, good." Wyer nodded. Then he held up the woodcock. "I brought this down for us."

"How'd you catch it?" Jobber asked, puzzled.

Wyer pulled out a slingshot. "It was Eneas's. Remember how we made fun of it?"

Jobber gave a brittle laugh. A small ray of morning sun slanted over the trees, changing the black bark to a shining gold color. "Come in, come in and see Shedwyn," she said, and pulled him by the cloak to the hut.

Inside Shedwyn was sitting up, a bowl of tea between her hands. Anard was sitting by the fire, stirring digger's root into a kettle of boiling water. Shedwyn gave Wyer a warm smile and Jobber noted that the worried crease in her forehead had been smoothed away.

"Wyer, come in by the fire," Shedwyn said. "There is still a bit of rabbit left. You must eat."

"Always nursing everyone, Shedwyn," he teased lightly. And then he knelt by Eneas, a hand reaching out to touch the sleeping man on his shoulder. "And how goes it?"

"Better. Much better," she whispered. "With both of us."

Eneas's eyes opened at Wyer's voice. He was still pale, but a more natural hue had replaced the waxy color. His eyes were blue and clear.

"I live, so she tells me," Eneas croaked with a faint smile.

"You're mending. Living comes later," she retorted.

"It's good to see you again, Eneas," Wyer said.

"Aye, though I wish it were for different reasons. Shedwyn has been telling me of Sadar. I want to do something but—"

"You already have, Eneas," Shedwyn soothed. "Your part now is to rest."

"She's right, Eneas. Just sleep and heal quickly. There'll be time enough later for work." Wyer stood and went to warm his hands by the fire. Jobber saw him sway, his eyes half lidded with exhaustion.

"Oy, same for you Wyer," she said. "Get some sleep."

He nodded, and settling down in the corner near the fire he wrapped himself in his cloak, his head pillowed in the bent crook of his arm.

Jobber took the kettle of boiling water and plunged the woodcock into it to scald the feathers. She started plucking it, feathers drifting around the drafty room. Long before she had finished her task she heard Wyer's deep-throated snores from beneath his cloak.

He slept through that day and into the next, waking only to relieve himself, share a small meal, and then return to sleep. Jobber waited, pacing the small hut until she grew too impatient. Then she joined Anard in the woods, collecting digger's root and checking the snares for rabbits.

On the following morning, Wyer rose and disappeared outside the hut. Jobber waited for him to return and was surprised when he didn't. She got up, grabbing her cloak, and went outside to find him.

He was saddling three horses, talking to the animals as he worked.

"It's time to go then, ain't it?" Jobber asked.

"I think so," Wyer answered.

"It's going to be hard to shift Shedwyn."

Jobber turned to the hut and saw Shedwyn standing in the doorway, an old blanket around her shoulders. Her hair hung in loose tresses like the rippling bark of an oak. She stepped out of the door and her face lifted to the morning light in calm wonderment. She breathed deeply, inhaling the cold air as if it were a refreshing tonic.

"It's time to go, Shedwyn," Jobber said. "They'll be waiting for us at the Ribbons."

"Oh no," Shedwyn answered firmly. "I'll not be coming with you."

"Shedwyn, you must," Jobber insisted.

"To get on a horse now would be impossible. I'd as like bleed to death before we got to the Ribbons."

"But how can we face the Queen without you?" Jobber asked, coming close to the woman.

Shedwyn took Jobber's hands in hers. "I've been thinking on that and I think I know the answer. I have this body, and the needs of any woman. I have a child growing in me like a winter plum. But this body, this flesh, is only a small part of me. Lirrel was able to bring us into the sky above Oran's cradle. She could do that because we're not just ordinary women. We're a living piece of Oran, elements in His cradle."

"We can die, like anyone," Jobber countered.

"And give birth." Shedwyn smiled. "But we are elements. Oran's earthly flesh, Oran's fire heart, Oran's blood and breath. I must remain here to give this woman's body, and my child, a chance to survive. But my elemental power will be with you always through the knot."

"Are you sure about this?" Jobber asked. She didn't want to leave Shedwyn behind, to risk losing her as she had lost everyone else; Growler and Faul. Even Lirrel, traveling somewhere along the coast.

Shedwyn embraced her, hugging her close. Jobber felt the round hardness of Shedwyn's breasts against her chest. "I will be there . . . and here," she said simply.

Jobber released her, her hand resting on Shedwyn's shoulder a moment longer. Then quickly she turned and mounted her horse.

"Ready?" Wyer asked, holding his reins up.

Jobber drew a ragged breath and nodded. "Yeah, let's go."

At the doorway to the hut, Shedwyn waved, one arm draped over Anard's shoulder for support. Wrapped in the faded woolen blanket, Shedwyn appeared the same dull color of the hut, the green of her skirts like a tattered gown of moss. Jobber smiled and waved back a farewell. *It is right,* a voice whispered in her head, and Jobber knew it was Shedwyn who had spoken. The musty scent of wet soil clung to Jobber's nostrils as the sun warmed the forest, melting away the night's frost.

Jobber looked ahead and felt an unexpected surge of eagerness. Soon, she thought happily. Soon she would be in Beldan and she would taste the city's smoke-filled air, hear the clang of the streets. Soon she would be home once more in Beldan, where she belonged.

Chapter Nineteen

Gray clouds hovered over the eastern horizon, softening the edge between sea and sky. In the brisk wind, Tayleb steered the skiff alongside Oran's rugged coastline. The waves rocked the small boat as the centerboard shuddered over the lifting ridges. Tayleb licked her salted lips and longed for a drink of fresh water. She was tired, her mind quiet except for the subtle tugging sensation of the current. She followed it, tacking the boat against the worst of the wind to follow the ambling current.

The faded cheek of the sail billowed, full of the late-afternoon wind. Tayleb glanced at the coastline, weary of its seemingly endless stretch. She realized now how small Tynor's Rock had been. She could have navigated her world in a single afternoon, but after four days on the water, the coast had remained as constant and without distinction as the horizon. Even the bays in which they had sheltered at night had seemed exactly the same; the same ragged tree line, the narrow strip of a pebbled beach surrounded by rocky headlands that tumbled into the water. When she closed her eyes Tayleb could see the white spray of water lashing against the rocks and the exposed roots of trees that continued to cling to the eroding headlands.

"Look." Alwir pointed. "We're coming to the Ribbons. There's the Plains of Beldan, just beyond the city walls."

Tayleb peered toward the shore, surprised to find it changing slowly. Trees thinned and a line of rolling hills lifted gently up from the shore. Marsh grass grew in muddy shallows and then marched in wide swaths up the dunes until it covered the hills with waving strands of pale green. The grass was pressed against the ground into spiraling patterns as the wind gusted fitfully back and forth over the hills.

"It looks like the ocean," Tayleb said.

Alwir laughed. "Feels that way when you stand in the midst of it as well. The wind moving through the grass sounds like the waves scraping the shore." He twisted around, his face growing animated as he searched for something else over the crest of the hills. "Look, over there, under those clouds—that's Beldan!"

Tayleb heard a longing in his voice as he named the approaching city.

Lirrel chuckled and withdrew her flute from the pocket of her skirt. "There's no greater love than a Beldanite's for his city," she said, smiling at Tayleb. "It's a city like a mother, at once loved and resented."

A matching smile eased the gaunt lines of Alwir's face. "Lirrel, I am as traveled as you, but surely you must agree: there is no other place in Oran like Beldan."

She laughed. "You sound like Jobber! Alwir, I am Ghazali, I have no loyalty to one city. Each town I have passed through is in its own way beautiful."

Alwir pursed his lips. "Then tell me the truth, Lirrel. What beauty was there in that scrub port of Remmerton? Nothing but dried fish and dirt road! Admit it, there is nothing in Remmerton, not even for a Ghazali. But there is everything in Beldan."

Lirrel pursed her lips as if framing a tart reply. And then she smiled and shrugged at her defeat.

Alwir was gracious enough to accept his victory without

gloating. He returned his gaze to the dense gray cloud that hung over the city, obscuring it in mist.

Tayleb exchanged worried glances with Dagar, whose face held a cautious expression. Like her, he had never seen Beldan, nor any other city besides his own village. Tayleb felt relieved at not being the only ignorant villager among them. She had heard so many tales of Beldan, but it was hard to imagine a city larger than the whole of Tynor's Rock with buildings taller than the bluffs where she had gathered tern eggs and crabs.

Tayleb sensed the current drifting from the mouth of the Hamader River and layering the top of the cold ocean waves with warm fresh water.

"There's the Ribbons," Alwir called, pointing over the bow of the skiff.

The sun appeared briefly from between the clouds and the bright gold rays slanted across the water. Long narrow strands of white sand shimmered in the sudden light like the Firefaire ribbons of a woman's bodice. The waves lapped at the bars of sand, making it seem as if they fluttered on the surface of the water.

Beyond the Ribbons Tayleb saw the harbor, opening like a huge mouth into the port of Beldan. Tall-masted ships rested in their berths, the branches of masts and riggings like a forest of leafless trees. Dories and smacks scuttled over the water between the ships. And behind the rim of the harbor wall, Beldan rose in a mountain of cut stone, wood frames, and plastered walls. Trails of cobbled streets switched back across the sprawling face of the city. Rows of huge-shouldered buildings hunched side by side. Glass windows caught the reflection of the afternoon sun and twinkled brightly in the gray sky. Smoke lifted between the buildings and was sucked by the wind into the hovering clouds.

"It's changed," Alwir said sadly. "It's smaller." He turned a perplexed face to Lirrel.

"Smaller," Tayleb repeated, shocked. "But it goes on forever!"

"The Harbor Tower." Alwir pointed along a broken seawall.

"It used to be there. And look higher up, about halfway, near that green patch we call the Hiring Field."

Tayleb leaned forward, following the direction of Alwir's outstretched hand. All she could see was a dark gutted scar.

"There used to be two Guildhouses there. A weaving house, with all glass windows that looked out to the harbor. And next to it, a cloth warehouse. On the gables of those roofs were dove cotes and in the late afternoon you could see the doves. But they're gone."

"It's like Sadar," Lirrel said. "Zorah has lost her grasp here too. Look at the Keep. The west tower is gone."

Alwir slumped in the boat, his face filled with bitter disappointment. "Are we too late?"

"Not yet," Lirrel said quietly.

"Where should I dock?" Tayleb asked wearily. It was hard enough to keep her courage as a stranger here; the sudden weight of Alwir's misery was more than she could bear.

"It doesn't matter," Alwir replied. "Head for the one there with the small shack. At least we can shelter there for the night."

Tayleb guided the small boat toward the shore, watching as the dilapidated old shack loomed closer. A curtain of torn cloth blew in and out of the open window and Tayleb wondered how much shelter a hovel like this might truly provide.

A child's head appeared at the window, holding the ragged cloth out, the better to see the approaching boat. A small, tense face watched with suspicion as Tayleb guided the boat toward the shore. As she released the sail, the sight of the child was lost behind the flapping cloth. Dagar helped Lirrel out of the boat and together they staggered through the cold water to the shore.

As Tayleb and Alwir struggled to bring the boat into shore, the child appeared at the door of the shack. He was a young boy, his black coat patched, his knobby knees visible beneath a pair of torn trousers. He shivered in the wind, his cheeks a chalky color beneath fine yellow hair. He approached sideways, like a wary mongrel. And then he stopped, seeing Lirrel's face. At once, he shed his fear with a wide grin.

"I knew I'd find you all here first," he said, puffing out his thin chest proudly. "Z'blood, I knew you'd come this way. I just knew it."

"You've done well," Alwir complimented the boy. "But we're tired and we need fresh water and some food. Do you have any stored by?"

The boy's face crumpled. "Nah. I didn't figure on that. It ain't far to Harbor Wall. I could take you all there now."

"How dangerous is it?"

The boy shrugged his bony shoulders and scratched his cheek. "Well, it ain't easy. Butcherboys is a bit thick out, on account of their numbers deserting to ships and all."

"What do you think?" Alwir asked Lirrel.

"Jobber wanted us to wait here for her."

"I could go," Dagar said quickly. "How long would it take?"

"Just you and me? Not bad at all. We'd be back before start of thirdwatch."

Dagger looked confused. "When's that?"

"After moonrise," Alwir explained. "We'll be able to hear the lighterman call the hour."

"Why do people in Beldan need to know the hour?" Tayleb asked, surprised. "Either it's day or it's not."

The boy scoffed at Tayleb's country ignorance. "How else to know when your laboring stretch is done and the drinking started? The Master tucks in his toes at secondwatch while poor cutter lads labor 'til third. But in the slip between third and first is an hour to call your own."

"Were you apprenticed to a weaving house, then?" Alwir asked the boy.

He shook his head. "Worse. Pirate cloth house. Mam sold me into it. Used to weave rugs 'til I went near blind. Met up with a weaver named Soltar who fought in the New Moon. Talked me into it, he did, though I can't say he had to work hard at it. Been one of their Flock ever since."

"I know Soltar," Alwir said, smiling at the familiar name.

"Knew him," the boy corrected. "Scaffered a few days ago in a brangle near Market Square."

Alwir was silent and the wind flapped at the torn curtains of the shack.

"What's it like in Beldan now?" Alwir asked stiffly.

The child's face hardened. "Ain't easy. But one day," he said, more to himself than Alwir, "one day, it'll all be ours again."

"What's your name?" Dagar asked. "I'm called Dagar Zegat, from the village once known as Cairns."

"Tip. From some back street of Beldan," he answered and smiled.

"And you've the old magic," Lirrel said. "I can feel it in you."

The child blushed proudly. "Yeah, I have. I'm a water element. Don't worry so much about Readers like I used to, though. Butcherboys are the real danger now."

"Is that how you knew where to meet us?" Tayleb asked, surprised to find herself having something in common with this rough street child.

"Yeah. It were something in the water." Tip held his hands up, trying to shape his reply in terms they might understand. "I knew you was coming, this way, and soon."

Tayleb nodded her head. "I was thinking of Beldan, thinking of the water and hoping there would be someone here to greet us."

Tip's face became serious. "Then it was you called to me. You're her, ain't you? The Water Queen, the fourth in the knot?"

"Aye, though not too much of a Queen," Tayleb answered shyly.

Tip grabbed her hand and squeezed it hard. In his eyes, expectation sparkled. "All those days at the loom, with the whispers going round about the new knot, I knew you'd come and that I'd not face the Readers, nor the noddy-noose."

Tayleb blushed red, flustered at the boy's outburst. Islanders were a sober people. They kept to themselves; even the holding of hands was a rare gesture of intimacy. And here was a strange child, clinging to her with cold, chapped hands. She heard the longing in his voice, the silent plea for reassurance that his dreaming had not been in vain. Whatever her own fears and misgivings, Tayleb knew she could not deny this child a word of encouragement.

"Aye, I've come," she said thickly. "And I'll do my best to see that Oran is healed."

Tip put his arms around her waist and Tayleb could feel the fragile bones beneath the old coat. He's really just a child, she realized. Terrified, but being brave. Like the rest of us.

Then Tip pulled away and gruffly pulled at his coat. His face became hard once more. "Yeah, well, let's go then." He motioned Dagar toward a long, narrow boat farther down the beach. "We'll be back with food and drink," he said.

"If you can," Alwir called after him, "tell Kai!"

"If it ain't too wicked out there," Tip replied, heading down the beach with Dagar.

Dagar waved farewell, his smile uneasy as the narrow boat rocked wildly in the water. Dagar's wave ended as he clutched the sides in alarm.

Alwir *tsk*ed in sympathy. "I should have told him about the riverboats."

"He's safe enough with Tip," Tayleb said, watching the boy expertly poling the riverboat in the rough current. "He's following an easy path. His element guides him."

Tayleb watched until she could no longer see Dagar and Tip. And then she shivered, looking up at Beldan looming over them. They had arrived, all right. They were close enough to smell the stink of the harbor and the thick smoke of tavern hearths. But here on the Ribbons they were still outcasts, waiting for the city to receive them at last. Tayleb sighed, exhausted and numbed by the days of worry and flight. In the quiet stillness of the Ribbons, her thoughts tumbled to life around her. She looked up at Alwir, his expression distant. He, too, was lost in other times, his eyes fixed on the darkening face of the city.

Suddenly Tayleb wanted to be alone. Alone in the sea.

"I need—"

"Go on," Lirrel finished. "We all need a moment's peace before it begins."

"Or at least before Jobber arrives," Alwir said with a thin smile.

Tayleb lowered her head, not wanting the trepidation to show on her face.

But Lirrel touched Tayleb on the arm. "Don't worry about Jobber. She's got a temper, but she's true at heart—and can be very funny too."

"I fear she'll find me too much of an Islander."

"Did you feel that when we tied the knot?"

"No. But she scared me a little," Tayleb replied honestly. "She's powerful."

"Just loud, really," joked Alwir.

"Remember, Tayleb," Lirrel said, "you're a water element. It's your element that balances Jobber's power. You're as strong as she is." Lirrel smiled again. "Just not as vulgar."

"Few are." Alwir laughed dryly and Tayleb joined him, not so much out of humor but relief. Then he stopped laughing and Tayleb saw him sway on his feet. He sighed and raked his fingers through his beard. "I need to sleep," Alwir said. "I feel I could sleep forever. But call me if I'm needed," he said firmly. Then he trudged with heavy footsteps through the sand to the door of the hut, turning once to wave at Tayleb and Lirrel.

"And you?" Tayleb asked Lirrel.

"I shall sit on this beach and wait for Dagar," she said. Lirrel withdrew her flute and held it up to show Tayleb. "I could use the practice."

Tayleb stripped off her clothes and laid them in a neat pile. The wind was cold on her bare skin, but she felt more at peace without the constraints of clothing.

As she waded into the water, the last rays of the sun scattered across the surface like a handful of gold coins. The gentle waves lapped at her ankles and then her thighs. She closed her eyes to the bright reflection of the sun and sank beneath the water. She exhaled the last of dry air from her lungs. Her chest tightened for an instant as she inhaled, water flowing into her lungs. On her tongue was the salty taste of kelp. She smiled and brushed away the velvety nap of bubbles along her arms.

As Tayleb swam deeper into the sea, the light faded to darkness and the distant waves were no more than a soft murmuring. She reached with her arms, gliding along the current, raising puffs of sand as she stroked the water. Then the sandy bottom dropped away and the sea floor opened into a vast black gully of rock and coral. From out of the dark a tide of luminous jellyfish appeared once more. They floated around her like white roses, lighting her way to the deep recesses of the sea.

On a small sandbar, near the mouth of the harbor, Stickit sat on an old crate and waited. She'd been waiting for three days and wasn't happy about it. She hated the constant rasping of the sea, the screech of gulls clamoring over the garbage that washed down daily from the Hamader River and came to rot in the marsh grass of the sandbars. It reminded her of the old Waterling days, when Kai had her poling the Hamader in search of floaters, people with no better sense than to get themselves drowned in the river. Stickit and Slipper would strip the bodies of any valuables, the odd ring or a well-made jacket, before sending them on their way again downstream. But the floaters never disappeared for long. Stickit shuddered, remembering how many of them returned to haunt her, their bloated carcasses half eaten by fish and eels as they languished, trapped in the slow waters of the marsh grasses.

But the Upright Man would make this wait worth it, Stickit thought. He'd give her a place of her own and that cocky bitch, the Petticoat, would be down here, rotting in the grass. If Stickit played the game right she might get some extra brass from the Upright Man so as not to have to whore anymore. She'd a little saved by, some gold rings and a few strings of copper gleaned over the years from the floaters and hidden from Kai. Never enough to get what she really wanted, but with the Upright Man giving her the room, well, she'd more than a good start.

Stickit scowled with a pang of fear. The Upright Man was sticky to deal with; never could be sure of his intentions. She tensed, thinking on the knife he'd held so close to her throat. Stickit rummaged nervously in her pocket for the honeystick she kept there. She took it out, picking off the lint, and stuck it in her mouth. Her eyes half closed, she concentrated on the sweet syrupy taste. Then she sighed and smiled. Nah, she thought confidently, she'd managed him before, she could do it again. Just had to remember to stay out of range sometimes and not get too greedy.

Her head picked up, seeing a small boat poling between the Ribbons as it headed for the harbor wall. She recognized Tip, traveling with a stranger, and her heart gave a little jump.

"Oy!" she called and waved her arms.

Tip stopped poling and waved back. Cupping his hands around his mouth he shouted back as his passenger clung to the wobbling sides of the riverboat, "Tell Kai, they're here!"

Stickit waved to let him know she had heard his message. "Right," she sneered. "I'll give out the message, but it won't be to Kai." Stickit waited until Tip and his passenger were safely out of sight before she slipped her own boat into the water. She grunted as she hoisted herself inside and began to pole toward the outer Ribbons.

Stickit wondered what story she ought to tell to convince the water girl to come with her. She wasn't even sure how she'd recognize her. She shrugged her shoulders, her face determined, as she neared the sandbar and saw the leaning shack. She'd figure it out when she got there. Best to say as little as possible.

As Stickit neared the beach she saw a woman sitting alone on the sand. She was small and dark, with a sweep of black hair over her shoulders, and she was playing a flute. Stickit grinned, noticing the woman was wearing an Islander's skirt, a pattern of black fish circling the red fabric at the hem. That'll be her, she thought, pleased that the dress had given her the information she needed without her having to ask.

She docked her boat and looked around nervously, wondering where the others were. The woman on the beach had risen and was coming to meet her.

"Are you looking for me?" she asked quizzically.

Stickit shrank back uncomfortably, frightened by the girl's moon-colored eyes.

"Yeah," she answered. "I got a message to take you to Kai."

"I thought we were to wait here."

"Nah, it's too dangerous," Stickit fumbled. Her heart fluttered nervously. The young woman looked back at the shack.

"I'll get Alwir, but I am afraid we shall have to wait for Tayleb—"

"Nah," Stickit said a little sharply, stopping the woman. "I mean, we need to go over now, but one at a time, like. It'll be too hard to slip you in all at once." Stickit congratulated herself for this piece of fantasy. It sounded reasonable, and to some extent it was true. She'd have to do a good deal more lying if she took all of them to the Upright Man. All she needed was this one. "Come on," Stickit said, jogging the woman's elbow. "We got to go. Tip will be coming back for the rest."

The woman raised her head to examine the clouds. The night sky was a deep blue in the East over the back of Beldan. A star twinkled in the remains of the Keep's tower. She shook her head as if uncertain.

"Come on," Stickit fairly whined, anxious now that the others might return at any moment.

"All right," the woman said at last and followed Stickit into the boat. Stickit pushed off and began to pole the boat rapidly. She wanted to get out of there before anyone else spotted them. The current dragged at the boat, bouncing it along the tops of small waves. Stickit swore as a wave splashed the sides and wetted her skirts. The least this water element could do was make their passage easier, she grumbled to herself. She wanted to ask, but didn't, fearful of saying the wrong thing at too important a moment. Get her to him, she told herself. Get her there and you'll never look on this frigging water again.

"There now," said Tip, cocking an ear toward the city, "hear the lighterman?"

Dagar concentrated on the faint, hoarse cry carried over the water of the harbor. It sounded sad to him. "Aye, I hear it."

"Right. It'll be safe to go ashore now," Tip said, poling the boat away from the shadowy remains of the Harbor Tower and into the river channel. "With the butcherboys changing the watch, there won't be many of them near the Harbor Wall. I wish I could have gotten you ashore sooner."

"It's all right," Dagar muttered. The rocking of the riverboat made him queasy. He was desperate to set foot on land again, and just as desperate to return to Lirrel and the others.

Tip poled the boat alongside a landing jutting out of the river wall. He tied the boat to the iron rings set into the wall.

"Come on," Tip said, giving Dagar a hand out of the boat. "It'll be quiet out now."

Dagar stepped on shore, delighted and shocked by the sudden hardness of the stone. He stumbled, unsteady on his feet, but Tip caught him before he fell. The boy led him up a narrow set of stairs carved into the stone wall and then suddenly they were standing on an empty cobbled street.

Dagar took a deep breath and stared, awed by the endless rows of tall buildings like a dense forest of stone. Tip guided him down a street and Dagar glanced up, frightened by the weight of the gabled roofs that arched across the narrow streets. Shop signs banged against the plastered walls, creaking and groaning in their rusted bolts. As Tip took him deep into the maze of streets, Dagar was seized with confusion. There were no landmarks, no hills or trees to give him his bearing. He was quickly lost, with no sense of where the sea and Lirrel waited for him. He passed darkened doorways, scurried beneath the midnight shadows of balconies or stepped across rectangles of light that fell from upper windows. Far above the evening stars glimmered between the huddled tile roofs.

Even at the late hour the streets were crowded. People passed them walking two and three abreast, often filling the street with their noisy banter and swinging arms. Dagar pressed against a wall to let pass two burly watermen and a woman, all arguing loudly as to which inn they should visit. As he watched the woman pass, he smiled, recognizing Finch's peculiar hip-swinging stride. A journeyman, his pockets full of bobbins, kicked out with sturdy legs, his eyes set straight ahead on his destination. That's like Jobber, Dagar thought; demanding and getting space on a crowded street. He realized now that Jobber was not as strange as she had first seemed to him. Many of her oddities were a normal part of Beldan, her walk and her brash speech acquired from the city's own personality.

A group of children came up to Tip, plucking at his coat and talking rapidly like a flock of chattering sparrows. Their eyes darted over Dagar but they never addressed him.

"Give off," Tip growled back and brushed them away from his sleeves. "Where's Kai and Slipper?"

"Old Mouth," replied a little girl in a dress several sizes too large for her. The bodice draped from her shoulders, the low neckline showing a thin, delicate chest.

"Right," Tip answered, tucking away the information. "Now who's got eats?"

They fell silent and backed away from Tip, unwilling to answer. Dagar was horrified that Tip might be asking these half-starved children for food for himself.

"It doesn't matter," he started to protest, but Tip stopped him.

"Don't get twisted," he said amiably. "These here is as good as any nickers you'll meet." He turned back to the quiet flock of children. "Come on, Maisy, you most of all," he coaxed. "This is important, give o'er."

The girl in the too-large dress gave a little pout and then, lifting the skirt of her dress, pulled out two loaves of bread carried in pockets that were sewn into the lining. Tip gave her bodice a brisk shake. Three sausage rolls fell out between her feet as she made a rude noise with her lips.

"Thanks, girl," Tip said, scooping up the food.

"You ain't such a digger as to be calling me a girl," Maisy pouted.

"Right then, you're a dell," he retorted, and grinned as the other children tittered with laughter.

"Frigging all to you," she snapped at them and stormed down the street, her too-long skirts dragging in the mud.

"Fine airs that one has," said Tip, handing Dagar a sausage roll.

Dagar bit into it cautiously. He chewed slowly and his eyes widened at the spicy taste. Jobber had been right. All those months of listening to her and Wyer groan about Beldan sausage rolls had been true. They were good, better than any of the stodgy, thickened stews of Sadar. Even the food of his village couldn't compare to the sharp tang of grease and spices, the bread soaked soft with meat juices. He chewed faster, swallowing big chunks as his appetite outstripped the speed of his jaws.

"Ease off now," Tip said as he handed him a second roll with a knowing grin. "Good, ain't it? Only don't choke. One of

Maisy's smarts is that she'd rather snitch from a good stall than a bad one. If you're caught and sent up to the noddy-noose, might as well be worth the last swallow.''

Dagar nodded, wanting to make some reply, but couldn't. His mouth was stuffed, his teeth grinding in an unstoppable fashion and his nostrils filled with the scent and taste of spiced meat. But Tip didn't need any words, just shoved his hands in his pockets and continued down the street, Dagar straggling behind him.

They continued walking through Beldan, winding down the endless streets and sometimes cutting through alleys where they climbed over fallen rubble. Once Tip jerked Dagar into a doorway as a squad of Guards marched down the street. Tip pushed open the door, dragging Dagar in after him. Inside was an old weaving house now abandoned by the Master and his apprentices. The floors were cluttered with the broken remains of old looms. Tip reached down and picked up a shuttle, a dusty thread still visible in its bobbin. He tossed it away and hurried through the old building to the alley behind it.

A small stream of water sluiced through the alley, carrying with it the stink of raw sewage.

''Naffy, ain't it?'' Tip said, holding his coat sleeve over his face.

Dagar was silent, his own cloak over his mouth as the sausages that had been so good going down were now beginning to turn in his stomach.

''Quick now,'' Tip urged, ''it ain't far yet.''

He led Dagar through another building and then between two old houses, their upper floors joined by a balcony. The decaying husks of the houses hid an old garden in a small square at the back. Stony paths radiated from a broken fountain that marked the center of the garden. On one wall a huge stone face, its mouth wide open, stared back at them in frozen surprise.

''We're here.''

''Where?'' Dagar asked, confused.

''Through the mouth and into the tunnels. Late as we are, I'm thinking I'd better take you to Kai and let her decide what's to be done.''

"I need to get back," Dagar protested.

"Fair enough. Stickit's probably been this way already. Kai's most likely got it worked out, so I'll just take you to her first." He tucked his feet over the tongue of the stone face and wriggled his body through the open mouth. " 'Sides," he said, just a head looking up from between the stone lips, "I ain't so sure Kai wouldn't scream at me if I didn't come here first! She's good, but Z'blood, she's a raver if you make a mistake!" Then his head disappeared through the mouth.

Standing alone in the deserted garden, Dagar hesitated. He looked around him, lost and uncertain. There was no way he could return to Lirrel on his own. He hadn't a clue where he was, and even if he did find the harbor he didn't know how to get out to the Ribbons again. Worry gripped the pit of his stomach and warred with the greasy weight of the sausage rolls.

"Come on," echoed a ghostly voice from the hollow of the stone mouth.

He had no choice but to follow. He resigned himself to the stone mouth, trying to keep the unpleasant image of being eaten alive from his mind. His feet dangled below him until Tip reached up and tugged on his ankles. Then Dagar let go of the stone lips and allowed himself to fall.

There was no light at all in the tunnel and the stale air was dank. Water droplets *ping*ed as they dripped somewhere unseen in the dark tunnel.

"I can't see!" Dagar said, holding down the rising panic in his voice.

"I know where we're going," Tip answered calmly and took Dagar by the hem of his cloak. "Follow close."

"Do you live down here?"

"Nah, but the Waterlings once did. They were Kai's Flock and she kept them down here in the old tunnels 'cause most of them had power. Later on, she brought New Moon to hide here as well. But since the quakes it's been too dangerous. Kai and Slipper still meet down here, though. Habit, I guess."

"How do you know your way without getting lost?"

"I don't really. Water tells me some, the other I figure it's

Slipper that will find me. Water down here talks to him, it does. He's never lost. Oy, look there, what'd I tell you?''

Dagar became aware of a warm light brightening in the black night of the tunnels. In another moment he could see the old mining scars on the walls of the tunnel. They rippled like tiny waves in the cavern above.

"Oy there!" called a man's voice from the mouth of a glowing tunnel. A small stream of water sparkled with light.

"Tip here!"

"Who else?"

"I picked up one from the Ribbons. Ain't Stickit been here yet with the news?" he asked impatiently.

Slipper and Kai stepped from the tunnel. As they hurried, the light from Kai's torch bounced along the curved ceilings.

"Who's come to the Ribbons?" Kai demanded, looking Dagar up and down with accusing eyes.

Dagar inhaled quickly, the uncomfortable sensation in his stomach gripping harder. Kai lifted her torch higher, the better to see his face. Her black eyes glittering like a crow's as she appraised him. Dagar could understand why Tip might have cause to fear her. Slipper, standing next to her, was an easier face to confront. Though he knitted his brow, his mouth was soft. A black lighterman's hat was pushed back on his head, revealing a curious gaze.

"I am Dagar Zegat," he answered, annoyed when his voice quavered slightly. "I've come with Lirrel—"

"Lirrel!" Kai's stern face broke into a smile as unexpected as sunlight in the tunnels.

"Aye. And Alwir and Tayleb, the fourth Queen in the knot," he finished.

"But ain't Stickit been here already?" Tip asked. "I saw her at the Ribbons, told her to come to you as I was bringing Dagar here for food and blankets. We had to wink out of sight for a while. Too many butcherboys. So I thought I'd come here first, see what was out."

"Stickit hasn't been here," Slipper answered. He took off his hat and punched a dent in the soft crown. "Ain't right. Something ain't right here. I've been feeling it ever since that day at the Petticoat's.''

"Why were you at the Petticoat's?" Kai asked sharply.

"It weren't like that, Kai," he answered firmly.

"Sorry," she muttered, her eyes downcast.

"I was thinking I'd take a drink. But I seen the Petticoat coming up the street looking like the loser in a waterman's brangle. Face greened on one side, and limping.''

"A pimp," Kai spat in disgust.

"Maybe. I got a wink of the man. Dark, bearded." Slipper's voice trailed off as he concentrated on the memory. "Stickit was there, jumped out at my elbow. She knew the pimp too. Said it was secret-like." Slipper crushed his hat between his hands in sudden alarm. "Frigging shit! Oh frigging shit," he groaned.

"What is it?" Kai demanded.

Panic swept Slipper's face. "Stickit was here, too, the day Shefek come in with the news. I didn't think on it as I was happy enough with the news. But Stickit knew that Jobber and the rest were coming.''

"So! Out with it then!" Kai yelled.

"It's the Upright Man hiding out at the Petticoat's. That face," he moaned. "I didn't think to see it there so I didn't listen to what my head was trying to tell me. No wonder the Petticoat was scared of him. But it's Stickit that's squealed. She's gone to him, not to us!''

"Z'Blood," Kai swore, "not him again. Quick!" She snapped at Tip, handing him the torch. "Get him back to the Ribbons. There may be time yet to warn them. Slipper, we're going to the Maidenhead. I'm going to scaffer that frigging bastard.''

Kai turned and sprang into the dark tunnel. Slipper dashed after her like a shadow chased from the light.

"Come on," Tip said, grabbing Dagar's hand. They began to run through the tunnels, water splashing around their ankles. Dagar wanted to cry or to scream, anything to chase away the dread that weighted his chest and made him breathless. The thin, stale air of the tunnels was unforgiving. It burned in his nostrils and scratched the side of his throat.

Even after they had left the tunnels and run through the crowded city streets, Dagar choked on his fear. Please let them be all right. He tried to concentrate on the image of Lirrel, sitting while she played her flute, her black hair draped over her shoulders. He longed for the woody scent of her perfume and the soft, low music of her voice. He glanced up and saw the full moon, and thought of her eyes.

Around him the city of Beldan closed a menacing fist. The high-gabled buildings and low balconies that had fascinated him when he arrived now threatened. They towered above, like mocking specters hiding from him the sight of the harbor and the long, thin strands of the Ribbons where Lirrel waited. His heels ached from pounding on the hard, cobbled streets, but he couldn't stop running.

A lighterman bawled the hour and Dagar nearly cried out at the sound. Hoarse and empty, it tolled away the time and hastened his driving fear.

Chapter Twenty

The wind was brisk off the harbor, bringing with it not only the dank odor of the sea but the clamoring thoughts of Beldan's citizens. Lirrel closed her mind's ear, trying not to let the din overwhelm her. She had forgotten how "loud" Beldan could be after so many months away. That's why the Ghazali travel, she thought, to have the peace of the road after the noise of city crowds. She trailed her hand in the water just to let its cold wetness distract her attention from the approaching city and relieve her of anxiety.

Anxiety, she thought sourly. She had rarely experienced it until now. Once she had had confidence in the road that lay ahead of her. Now she mistrusted her instincts, second-guessed the future. She was no longer as certain whether a thing was true or imagined. She glanced at Stickit, gnawed by worry. She thought she had sensed disquiet in the woman's speech, that there was something left unsaid. And yet, Lirrel argued with herself, she had heard nothing untrue in the answers the woman had given her . . . It *was* dangerous to make this crossing. She was to bring only one. Tip and Dagar would return. Lirrel heard those truths. But hidden within those answers was a darker shadow, a truth with a different substance altogether.

But then, that is the way with people in Beldan, Lirrel reminded herself. Life was hard for those of the Flocks and one owned precious little except for secrets. Perhaps that was it. Finch had that quality; so did Faul. Lirrel had never known their thoughts entirely, so natural was dissembling to them as a habit of survival. Only Jobber crackled noisily and without restraint in Lirrel's mind. But that was the result of their elements, entangled in the knot, and not Jobber's merely being free with her thoughts.

Lirrel watched the city rise up from the harbor as the dusk shaded into night. The lightermen had yet to light all the torches and Lirrel marked the poorer districts of Beldan by the sooty darkness of their streets; higher up on the hills, where Silean mansions sprawled, their stone-fenced gardens butting up against each other, the torchlights already shone like distant suns.

Lirrel took out her flute and placed it against her mouth. She blew, but there was no sound and, in annoyance, she lowered the flute to wet her parched lips. When she blew again the low voice of the flute was tentative. Try as she might to find a pleasing harmony in the rushing current of voices, Lirrel's flute would shape only haunting melodies.

Lirrel ceased playing and, settling the flute in her pocket, tried to interpret a reason for the somber music. The tune played muddled images in her mind: the world twirling like a leaf in the wind, and then a child's spinning top in the breathless moment before it slowed and toppled to one side. In one passage she saw the smooth white oval of an egg. It cracked, and a thin stream of blood-colored yolk stained the brittle edges. The end and the beginning, the flute sighed.

"We're here," Stickit hissed, hauling her pole into the boat. She grunted as she bent down to lash the boat to the iron rings in the river wall.

Lirrel caught the pungent scent of Stickit's body as she pushed past Lirrel and scrambled out of the boat.

She's scared, Lirrel thought. They climbed the narrow steps in the wall and stepped out onto a nearly deserted street. Lirrel tensed, alarmed to hear the tramping boots of the Guards. She has a reason to be scared, Lirrel realized as they hurried away from the sound of the approaching Sileans.

As she looked around Lirrel saw how much Beldan had changed since Firefaire. It wasn't just the destruction of buildings or the rubbled remains of street battles. Desolation hung in a clammy mist over the city. Tension gathered in the damp air like the static of approaching lightning. Lirrel sensed the faces that watched from the dark windows, heard fear mingled with rage, felt reckless daring overlaid with resignation. Beldan was being torn into fragments and its people clung to whatever emotions helped sustain them during the disintegration.

Lirrel wanted to play her flute once more, to find direction amidst so much painful confusion. She trembled, her nerves jangling with an increasing sense of panic. "Oh, no," she breathed as she sensed her mind touched by the tendrils of a vision. The thickened air swirled, bleeding away colors and flattening the buildings so that the street resembled a child's drawing, scrawled against an empty sky. The vision buzzed its angry warning in her ear, demanding to be released. No! She resisted its tugging, clutching the flute in her pocket. Not now! She could not have a vision, here in Beldan and without Dagar to protect her. She squeezed her eyes shut and blindly stumbled over a jutting cobblestone. Stickit caught her before she fell.

Lirrel gasped, hearing a blasting cry of hate. Lirrel stared at Stickit's hand on her arm, not knowing whether it was Stickit's thoughts that boomed so loudly or the vision that stung like nettles laid against her skin.

"Oy, get up," Stickit was saying, her voice urgent. "We're almost there. Look, just the other side of the street."

Lirrel stood slowly, hearing her bones crack as she did. Squabbling voices pounded in her ears, grower louder and more indistinguishable until they became the shriek of howling winds. The vision was going to happen and there was nothing to stop it. Lirrel relaxed her shoulders, opened her closed fists, and prepared to receive its onslaught.

Her gaze lifted to the smiling face of the wooden woman over the lintel of the Maidenhead. Almost at once the deafening howl

of the winds ceased. The flatness of the street diminished and
the world took on color and form again. Almost as quickly as it
had come, the vision faded. In the hushed silence Lirrel waited,
her lips parted in surprise. She listened and heard the gentle
creak of hinges as the wind pushed the sign back and forth.

Lirrel's confusion was replaced by the warming sensation of
calm. It brushed her on the lips with a welcoming kiss. Yet the
disappearance of the vision puzzled her. She had no explanation
for its sudden release. Her eyes itched with tears of frustration.
If only she had all of her power again. She needed to be able to
see clearly into the future, to know what was expected of her.
Despite the soothing calm, Lirrel felt the tremor of anxiety return.

"A strange place for Mistress Kai, isn't it?" she asked Stickit.

Stickit gave her a humorless grin. "Come on, they're waiting
for you."

Lirrel followed slowly behind Stickit. She looked about her
with a sudden hunger for details: the humped-back cobblestones,
the curved cheek of the carved woman over the lintel, the ra-
zored edge of the sky cut into shapes by the jutting rooftops. On
the door to the Maidenhead she saw the patterned grain of the
wood softened over time from the oil of a million hands. She
noticed where passing feet had eroded gentle slopes into the
stone steps and cracked the mortar between the flagstones.

Everything solid and real mattered intensely to Lirrel, even
the drabness. Her senses were flooded with the minutiae of the
world: the smell of soured ale, the sheen of Stickit's dirty dress,
the cackle of a woman's laugh, the irritating throb of a splinter
in her palm. She drifted like an unexpected breeze through the
old tavern. And as each sensation, each image rushed into her,
it faded abruptly, so that she felt at once filled with knowledge
and emptied at the same moment.

"Oy, open up!" Stickit was saying to the closed door. "I'm
here!"

The door opened and the small, battered face of a young
woman peered back.

Stickit grabbed Lirrel, her fat fingers digging into Lirrel's arm.

"Get him," she hissed to the weary eyes half hidden behind the door.

The door was opened farther and the young woman behind it was thrust brusquely into the corridor. She stumbled, catching herself before she fell. Into the gap left by the woman's rough passing Stickit shoved Lirrel.

Lirrel's head struck the door frame as she careened through the doorway. The sudden crack of pain dissolved the veneer of calm that had shielded her from fear. Shocked and dazed, she heard the door close behind her. The heel of a palm rammed into her shoulder blade, sending her sprawling along the floor. Her chin bounced against the floorboards, causing her to bite her lower lip. Her mouth was filled with the warm, salty taste of blood. She turned to look up, icy terror spreading through her veins. Betrayed! she realized with despair. Betrayed by her own blindness.

The man who loomed above her smiled coldly. Twin pricks of red light gleamed in his dark eyes as he studied her. Though he moved slowly, the air vibrated around him, agitated by his barely suppressed emotions. He smoothed his beard with one hand, the polished nails white crescents in the black hair. In his other hand he held a small knife, his thumb resting against the hilt.

"I've waited a long time for you," he said.

Lirrel was silent, her gaze traveling over the room as she searched for an escape. The man's face was familiar, but not the red horror of his eyes.

The room was tiny, only the door and the small window providing a way out. The bed was lumpy with dirty sheets; a small table was covered with the decaying remains of old meals— bones heaped on a plate and a curling rind of cheese. A silver fork with bent tines rested near the plate. Lirrel stared at it and then just as quickly averted her eyes. Maybe she could get to it, use the fork to defend herself.

"Let me introduce myself," the man said, kicking her hard with his boot.

Lirrel recoiled from the blow, a hand protecting her ribs as her body edged closer to the small table.

He bent down close to Lirrel and her eyes widened as she recognized him.

"You're Antoni Re Desturo," she said, whispering. She remembered him from the massacre at Firefaire. It was the strangeness of finding him here alone, in this filthy little room, that had confused her.

"So my reputation precedes me, even to the Islands," he said with a tight nod of his head. "I am the Silean, Re Desturo, and also Beldan's Upright Man. But soon," he said pausing, "very soon now, I shall be King of Oran."

He seized Lirrel by the wrists. She struggled one arm free and lunged away from him. But he held her captive even as she kicked him frantically, trying to find a target in his body. Her mind reeled with her ignorance and fear. She was not a fighter; she was a Ghazali, a peacekeeper.

Antoni smashed the knife handle against her temple. Pain exploded across her face, her neck, ravaging down her spine. She cried out and tried again to roll her body closer to the small table.

It was happening too fast, too fast to think, too fast for her to change from a peacekeeper to a fighter. He struck her again and she raised her arm in a vain effort to ward off the blows that followed. Her shoulder hit the table leg and the fork clattered to the floor, just out of reach. Antoni grabbed her again and jerked her toward him.

Use your element! her mind commanded. Use it to save yourself!

But how? How? she panicked. She was terrified, her wits scattering as she fought back clumsily.

Antoni laid one leg over her wriggling body. He sat on her, his weight cracking her ribs as she thrashed beneath him. He held her tightly by the wrists, the blood draining from her fingers. Then he pinned her hands to the floor, his face hovering over hers. Sweat dripped from his brow and landed on her mouth, the salt stinging her cut lip.

"Now I will take what I have waited for," he rasped.

He pressed one of her wrists beneath his knee, clamping it to the floor, and with his freed hand readied his knife.

Lirrel heaved her body, her shoulders scraping across the floor in an effort to free herself.

Antoni dragged the blade across her wrist and Lirrel cried out with the sudden sharp pain. A line of blood flowed from the slash, making a bright red bracelet. Antoni held up her arm, his black eyes shining as he watched the blood trickle down to her elbow.

Her arm throbbed as Lirrel continued to fight, trying to wrench it free from Antoni's grasp. Lirrel freed her other hand from beneath his knee and reached out wildly for the fallen fork. Her fingers groped the floor and collided with the cool metal handle. She snatched it up and prepared to strike Antoni, who was bending his lips to the wound on her arm.

Her arm trembled violently as the fork remained poised to strike. She could stab him in the neck, in the back, anywhere that might wound him enough to allow her to escape. She might even kill him.

But Lirrel hesitated, the desperate nature of her fear replaced by the cold knowledge that in that act she would no longer be Ghazali. She would succumb to the corruption of violence and she would abandon the very principle she needed most to exist. What would her life matter if she ceased being Ghazali? But Jobber, and the knot? Didn't they both need her? Didn't this moment demand action of her?

Distracted by her quarrelsome conscience, Lirrel watched distantly as Antoni placed his mouth over her slashed wrist. She gasped, sensing the tingle of magic, his power calling to the element in her. Then she understood what it was he wanted from her. He regarded her not as a woman, not as another living creature, but as an element of magic. A wellspring of power to which he had come to drink.

And so she was, Lirrel realized. More than human, much more than a helpless and frightened young woman. She was Oran's breath. It was her element that hurried the winds of Chaos.

Lirrel closed her eyes and traveled inward, seeking the core of her element. She passed through her body, hearing the slowing of her heart, seeing the warm red glow of tissue and marveling at its ingenious design. But the body, though beautiful, was a fragile vessel at best. She would not fight Antoni for its survival. She would not taint the purity of the peacekeeper's path by clinging to it. She would surrender the body and return to a pure elemental spirit.

Lirrel gathered her element from every portion of her body. It drifted through her flesh, bubbled in the blood, and seeped through the pores of her skin, released into the air in a long exhalation. Lirrel felt it snag as Antoni tried to call back her element to himself. But he had underestimated her strength. There was nothing that could hold her and she continued exhaling until she reclaimed from him all of her element that he had tried to steal.

Freed from the confines of her body, Lirrel became weightless. She felt herself expanding, spread thin and formless throughout the room. She filled the hollows of the gabled ceiling, rolled the gray dust from beneath the bed, and made the candle flames flicker and dance. And still the magic flowed from her body in a swift current. She lost a human's sense of touch, and the awareness of pain diminished rapidly as she drifted farther away from her body. A final gust withdrew the last breath of power from her abandoned husk.

She thought of a sigh and a soft breeze fluttered the old lace curtain of the room. She looked down without malice at the man crouched over her body. His mouth was clamped over her wrist and his shoulders were hunched. He pulled away from the limp arm in anger and slapped her unresponsive face. He tried again, his mouth on her wrist, and his cheeks caved in as he sucked furiously at the wound.

Then he threw down the lifeless arm in white-faced rage. Antoni lifted his head, the blood smeared over his lips and dripping through his beard. He stared wildly around the room and she knew he could sense her presence. His scattered thoughts came to her like the clattering roll of knucklebones. The red spark in his black eyes flared as he realized he had lost the gamble. He reared up his bloodied chin and howled in anguished defeat.

* * *

The Petticoat huddled near the end of the bar, a tankard of ale in her hand. Belle, the tavern mistress of the Maidenhead, had clucked in sympathy at the sight of the battered girl stumbling into the bar. She had given her the tankard on the house and then promptly ignored her in favor of paying customers. The Petticoat's gaze strayed to the stairway, imagining the closed door of her room. Being replaced was ordinary enough in a whore's life. She glanced sidelong at Stickit, who was ordering a tankard of ale, pulling out coins from her bodice. Stickit turned and, seeing her, sneered. The Petticoat chewed the inside of her cheek nervously.

She hated Stickit. Worse yet, she feared her. Not long ago she would not have thought twice about Stickit, an ugly, stupid whore. But since the Upright Man had bullied his way into her life, the Petticoat had come to fear Stickit and her strange friendship with the man. What hold did such a worthless whore have over him? The Petticoat felt her world crumbling, shearing away like the towers of the Keep the night she had invited the Upright Man into her life. She was afraid, afraid to stay and just as afraid to leave—for then he would find her and kill her.

And now this. Stickit brings another dell to the room and the Petticoat is forced out. Waiting down here, with the other aging whores.

Stickit sauntered over to the Petticoat, one hand rubbing her belly while she took a long draught from her tankard. She lowered it and showed an unpleasant smile. White foam rested on her upper lip. She came close to the Petticoat, her eyes raised to the room above them.

"Yer frigging done for," she gloated.

The Petticoat's fist gripped the handle of her tankard. "So who's the dell that'll replace me? Ain't that scrawny blind thing you dragged up there!" she scoffed.

Stickit gave a low chuckle. "You know frigging all. She ain't no ordinary dell." She leaned closer to the Petticoat and whispered. "I'll tell you, just so you know what a used-up dogsbody you really are. That dell's one of them. One of the new Queens, and by the time he's done with her, he'll be King. King of everything!" she bragged. Then her watery blue eyes narrowed maliciously. "And you'll be cocking up yer toes downriver. You never could handle him. Not the way I can!"

The Petticoat listened, her body growing rigid with Stickit's words. And then the fear in her snapped, like a branch hacked from its trunk. The Petticoat swung her tankard hard, crashing it against Stickit's temple.

The heavy woman staggered back with the force of the blow, too stunned to cry out. As Stickit tottered backward, the Petticoat struck her again. Blood appeared on Stickit's temples as she collided with tables and chairs, trying to get away from the Petticoat's frenzied blows.

The Petticoat threw down her tankard, ignoring the angry shouts of the other patrons. Skirts bunched in her hands she tore up the tavern stairs. Why had she let her fear of the Upright Man make her so stupid? Now everything would be destroyed, suckered under the thumb of that bastard. Slipper, the New Moon, everything. She had not meant to betray them. The walls rushed past her as shame and fury hurricaned in her body. On the final landing she froze, hearing the howls that echoed from her room.

She had been mortally afraid of him, but now it didn't seem to matter. There was nothing left to save, nothing left to protect—not even herself. She flung open the door, prepared to battle with nothing more than her rage and her fists.

She saw the Upright Man and screamed. His bloodied lips were pulled back in a feral snarl. His eyes were jet black, unseeing, as he howled over the remains of the woman's body. His long white hands were dyed crimson.

The Petticoat launched herself at the Upright Man. She scratched his face, digging her nails into his eyes. He roared and shoved her back, grabbing her by the arms. Then he struck her hard across the face with a closed fist. White stars flared in her eyes, but fury drove her on. No more, her mind shrieked, she would take no more.

Antoni recoiled his arm to strike her again. She snatched at a chair and swung it at him. He grunted as it hit him across the ribs, folding him in two. She swung the chair again, bringing it down over his shoulders. He bent deeper, groaning with the blow. She raised the chair a third time, but he straightened and punched her hard before she could block it. Her head snapped to the side, her jawbone giving a sharp crack. She lost her grip on the chair and it crashed to the floor.

Antoni's bloody hands closed around her throat. Her fingers scrabbled at his tightening grasp, her nails digging into his knuckles. Her eyes bulged as her throat was constricted. No breath passed her mouth. She wanted to scream, but her opened mouth could only gag. She kicked her legs, refusing to surrender. The toe of her boot slammed into his shin.

His grip loosened for an instant and she gulped at the air. His fingers, slick with blood, slipped against her skin as he struggled to regain his hold on her throat. He forced her down to her knees, bending over her.

Trapped by his stranglehold, her heart pounded, her lungs burning for want of air. She grabbed his thumbs and pulled them backward to break them at the joints. But his grip was hard, his rage outstripping hers as she suffocated. Panic was overwhelming her, but still she fought, her arms flailing weakly as she hit back. There was a roar in her ears as the last breath of air leaked away. The edges of the room began to dim as if a veil were being drawn across her sight. She stared up into the red, gleaming light of the Upright Man's eyes.

And then over his shoulder another face appeared. A woman's face, her black eyes glittering like a raven's.

Kai! It was Kai's face, leaning over the Upright Man's shoulder. It was Kai's hand grabbing a fistful of his hair and jerking back the Upright Man's head.

"This time I won't miss," Kai said.

The Petticoat saw the flicker of alarm in the Upright Man's face. And then Kai's knife was buried to the hilt beneath his chin. The hands on her throat released her, the bloodied fingers slipping away. She fell back, her head banging against the wall as she slid to the floor.

The Upright Man tried to twist away, his breathing labored as pink bubbles foamed in his mouth. Blood was everywhere, flowing down his neck, over the collar of his once-white shirt, and on the knife that continued to plunge again and again into his neck and chest.

The Upright Man collapsed to the floor and Kai followed him with her knife. Slipper finally stopped Kai's arm and freed the knife from her rigid grasp.

He bent down to the Petticoat, who hid her face behind her hands.

Slipper pulled her hands away and held them. "Are you all right?" he asked softly.

She couldn't speak, her throat swollen and raw. Tears formed in her eyes as she mouthed words of apology.

Kai knelt by Lirrel's body, her fingertips pressed against the hollow of Lirrel's throat. Kai shook her head in disbelief.

"She's dead," she whispered. "Lirrel is dead."

Silently Kai brushed the black hair away from Lirrel's face. Then she picked Lirrel up and cradled the limp body in her arms. Tears welled in Kai's dark eyes and flowed down her pale cheeks. "It's over," she cried. "We're finished."

The Petticoat closed her eyes, choking on the sobs that could not pass the swelling of her bruised throat.

Chapter Twenty-one

*D*agar banged an impatient fist on his thigh. *"Faster,"* he hurried Tip. *"Can't we go faster?"*

"Tide's against us. I'm going as fast as I can now," the boy replied through gritted teeth. He leaned hard on the pole, stroking the resistant water.

In the dusk the flat bands of the Ribbons were settled like long shadows on the water. Dagar glanced behind him, seeing the pinpricks of firelight that dotted the darkening city. He turned back to the Ribbons and imagined Lirrel waiting for him on the beach.

Dagar listed all the reasons why Lirrel would still be on the beach where he had left her. Lirrel and Tayleb were together; they would know if there was danger. Alwir was there; he wouldn't let anyone hurt them. Even if this Stickit had told the wrong people—dangerous people—Tip and he were returning in time to warn them.

But no matter how he sought to calm the panic in his heart, Dagar found that he could not look out across the harbor without fear. He hummed between his teeth, hoping that the tune might dull the edge of his worry. But he couldn't hold the notes together. Every knock and shudder of the waves beneath the thin, flat hull of the riverboat jarred his nerves and he lost the thread of the tune.

"What's that?" Tip asked, staring at the sky.

Dagar glanced up and saw a wide band of shimmering silver light extending over the water. A sudden wind frothed the surface of the waves and caressed their faces with a warm breath. Dagar inhaled and recognized the woody scent of Ghazali perfume. He felt confused and frightened as the band of gleaming light undulated toward them. Tip stopped poling and gawked, his mouth open in awe. Pale colors sifted through the light, blooming green, blue, and pink, and then faded into a sheer curtain of white light. A stream of light rained across the water and spilled into the boat, bathing Dagar in a fine white mist. The waves calmed beneath them, and the boat, trapped in the circle of light ceased its motion.

Dagar heard a flute, playing a melancholy tune.

"Lirrel," he whispered and the brilliant light cooled into blue and violet streaks as his breath filtered through it. In the showering light a ghostly image of Lirrel's face appeared, as insubstantial as starlight. Her eyes glimmered like two moons, her lips sketched by a pearl-colored dust. The dark sea flowed around her nearly transparent face like the long strands of her black hair.

"Dagar," she murmured, her voice no louder than the soft rasping of the wind through the hollow chambers of an empty shell. Her silvery face smiled at him and she reached out a glittering hand.

"Lirrel, what's happening?" he asked, watching his fingers pass through the diamond-bright light of her hand, leaving smears of blue and violet.

"There is little time to explain," she said. "Dagar, I have loved you, and I have greatly needed your strength. You alone sought a Ghazali's road to peace, when others sought vengeance. You saw, even when my vision failed me, that I was more than my own flesh and taught me."

"Lirrel, where are you?" Dagar asked. He shivered, afraid of the strange vision before him.

"I will riddle it to you," she said. "I am a house without a door."

Dagar frowned, searching for the answer. His dark eyes sparked with a flash of quicksilver light as it came to him. "I will not answer it otherwise, I am an egg!"

Lirrel laughed softly, the sound splintering with shards of mirrored light over the water. *"Ahal,"* she agreed, "it is the answer I expected from you. But for me, the answer is the tomb." The starlit face dimmed. "The girl, Lirrel, no longer lives. I exist as an element only and that will not last long before it is reclaimed by Chaos. I have come to give you what I was, so that the knot might survive."

"I don't understand—" Dagar said.

"Do not fear," she whispered and came close to his face. Dagar squinted in the blinding light. He saw the outline of her lips as she bent her face to kiss him. He leaned toward her, into the light, his mouth parted to receive the feathery brush of her lips.

Dagar closed his eyes and waited. He heard her sigh and then felt the sudden rush of air that gusted through his throat and filled his lungs. He gasped in alarm as his ribs stretched and arched, groaning with the strain of his ballooning lungs. He tried to resist the invading wind, but the air continued to fill him. He clenched his fists, terrified of the wind that forced power into the finite limits of his body. The wind howled in his ears, shrieked like the winter storms that battered the peaks of the Avadares. He choked, trying to gain a breath of his own. He heard the brittle snap of his ribs and his arms flared with pain as if they were being torn from their sockets. His jaw was forced open by the driving wind and dislocated, the joints cracking like tossed dice.

Lirrel was destroying him, tearing him into pieces with her element. He could not contain her power. *Faith*, a voice crooned in the shrill keening of the wind, *just a little more*. Though frightened, Dagar obeyed and stopped resisting. He opened his hands, palms upward, to catch the billowing wind. He had no knowledge of himself as a whole anymore. He felt smashed into pieces, his body blasted apart like the stones. Then he was loosened scree, rolling and tumbling in a landslide that was sent coursing down the mountainside. And still the wind hurried him, pounding him further until he was no more than grains of sand. A final gust of wind sucked him high into the air and exhaled him into the night sky as a sprinkling of white dust.

And then there was silence; no more the rumbling storm or the knife-edge keen of the wind. Dagar floated through the empty night among the dust motes swirling in the starlight. Lirrel appeared once more to him, her face etched in the shining dust.

"I shall be with you always, Dagar," she breathed. "I shall hold back the drain of power as long as I am able. But do not wait! Jobber must go now to Zorah."

"Lirrel!" Dagar called to the fading face. "Lirrel, what do I do?"

"Listen and find the harmony that is there," she answered weakly. Then she was gone and Dagar was alone, still drifting in the starry sky. Out of the silence he heard the low roar of approaching thunder. As he listened, perplexed, the din grew louder and louder until it pounded in his ears. A deafening multitude of voices babbled, sang, shrilled, and wept. He heard rage, joy, despair, and triumph all hammering in one incomprehensible cacophony. He cowered beneath the roar, his hands clamped over his ears. He couldn't do it! Lirrel had had time to learn, time to prepare. . . . She had told him to listen and had challenged him to find the harmony in such a chaos.

Slowly Dagar lowered his hands. He allowed his ear to follow the thread of a single thought. He strained to hear it, one voice from the many, as distinct as the insistent tapping of a drum. Then he plucked another voice out of the thundering chorus. It blared like a shrill hunting horn. Then another voice, sweet as a flute, and yet another that resonated like plucked strings. With a spark of understanding, Dagar blended the voices together into a single tune. That was the gift of the Ghazali songs, to shape harmony out of the confusion of such voices.

He could do it. He could shape the disparate voices into a song of peace. Dagar hummed, longing to feel a flute pressed against his mouth. The soft melody cast a net over the cacophony and the voices thrashed like silvery fish captured in its strands.

But the voices changed, the discord settling into phrases and then longer passages of a vibrant song. Dagar smiled, hearing in the music the steady rhythm of Oran breathing.

Light encircled him with a gleaming thread, twisted a bright ribbon around his hand. He pulled on it and saw the other length of it disappear into a knot of red, green, and blue threads. It was then that Dagar understood what Lirrel had done. Lirrel had gifted him with her element, joining him to the Queens' quarter knot. He was to take her place among the knot, bound to her three friends.

But he knew, looking into the tangled mass of colored threads, that the knot had suffered damage in Lirrel's passing. Threads were pulled and looped unevenly. Lines of white thread were untangling from the knot, slipping into the boiling mass of Chaos overhead. Frantically he closed a hand over a fading coppery thread that threatened to snap. A white thread sprouted from his fingers and entwined around the pale one. The two held together and slowly the coppery color returned to the damaged thread. Then he reached deeper into the core of the knot and held on to the other threads of green and blue that threatened to come untied. He clung to them until the gnarled twisting stopped. The knot was changed, but it was still whole.

"Dagar?" a voice called plaintively. "Z'blood, Dagar, is you scaffered?"

Tip was calling him. Dagar remembered his body, remembered it as if it were years and not seconds past that he rested on a boat. Clinging to his own thread, he let himself fall away from the knot. His vision reeled as he whirled downward through the night. As the world became solid once more, he could sense again the confined limits of his body. A thought flashed in his mind and he cast a message through the colored threads of light to the others just before he was driven into his flesh.

Gravity claimed him, and he felt the sky press like a rock against his chest. Every muscle in his body ached. Dagar groaned, and as he turned to his side the world seemed to tumble over his shoulder at the same time. He held up a limp hand, startled by its heaviness. "*Ahal*, I'm all right!" he said weakly to Tip. The boy's anxiety chirped noisily in his mind. Dagar shut it out, but not completely. "I'm all right!" he said more firmly and sat up. His head leaned forward to rest on the tops of his knees. Tip's anxious thoughts changed into sighs of relief.

"So what happened? First there was that frigging light and then you went all strange-like. I couldn't move the boat one way or the other. It just stayed here, 'til the light let us go."

Dagar rubbed his temples between his palms. His head throbbed but the pain was going away. He raised his head slowly, marveling at the startling changes in his awareness. Across the water, currents of air knitted patterns of icy lace. The worried hum of Tip's thoughts came to him as did the sudden crackle of Jobber's reply. Somewhere in Oran she had heard him. He smelled the sharp metallic reek of her hair. And then, as the wind carried it away, he caught the soft fragrance of Lirrel's woody perfume. He lifted his hand to his nose and sniffed. Lirrel's scent was on his skin and in the damp moisture of his sweat.

Then Dagar was seized with grief at the realization of his loss. Lirrel was dead. But her elemental spirit was now in him. He would carry her element, her knowledge and memories, even her scent, for as long as he lived. But he would never again see her, or hold her. He raised his hands to the wind, feeling it rush through his splayed fingers, unable to close his hands around it.

He turned a solemn face to Tip.

"Z'blood," Tip exclaimed, his hands clutching the pole to keep from falling. "Yer eyes. What happened to yer eyes? They is all blazing white!"

Dagar averted his face and stared out silently over the dark water. So, she had given him that too. Every time he looked at his reflection he would be reminded of her eyes. He swallowed, his throat tight with anguish. Touching his fingers to his pocket, he found his reed flute. He withdrew it, and as his breath blew over the hollow reeds he played an old Ghazali tune, one he had not known before.

Shedwyn tossed in her bed, her skin chilled and damp with sweat. She drew her knees up close to the rising hump of her belly and then woke with a start. The walls of the hut seemed to close in on her. She couldn't breathe and she sat up, staring about her in mounting panic. But the quiet room offered no explanation for her fear. Eneas stirred beside her in the bed and then returned to sleep. Anard lay huddled next to the hearth, the bottoms of his boots close to the powdery ashes of the fire.

Shedwyn lumbered to her feet and wrapped a second cloak around her cold shoulders. She slipped on her clogs, feeling the room swaying and tilting. She laid an arm across her belly, holding it protectively.

She flung open the door and staggered out to the dense line of trees. In her wake the ground shook, clods of dirt and stones erupting on the path. She stumbled when a tree root lifted unexpectedly from the soil. Her ankle twisted and she cried out as she was thrown down to the buckling ground. She hit the ground on her hands and elbows and then rolled onto her back. Overhead the near-leafless branches matted together, blocking the sky.

"What is it?" Shedwyn called to the trembling earth beneath her body.

In response, shaggy-headed roots tore out of the ground with a ripping sound, earth clinging to the root hairs. They reached for her, snaking over her legs. She tried to crawl away but they were faster, wrapping around her wrists, clasping her by the ankles. More roots rose from the earth and imprisoned her against the ground.

Shedwyn screamed as the thick, woody roots of the trees clambered across her thighs and the finer sprays of grass roots spread out across her belly. Forest lilies stretched their rhizomes over her arms, bulblets dangling like dirty jewels.

Shedwyn opened her senses to the forest that had once been home and now attacked her. She heard the wrenching crack of branches sheared from their trunks and the grinding of stones as they scraped against each other in the earth. And then the forest began to spin, like a world trapped in the core of a cyclone. The leafless branches rose straight into the air, shaking like spears. The small shrubs and saplings were stripped of their dried leaves and torn out of the ground. Shedwyn dug her fingers into the trembling soil as she felt the wind drag at her body. The roots held her firmly and only the smaller roots snapped and were sucked into the twisting wind. The earth shuddered, clods of dirt, stones, and smaller trees ripped away. And still the binding of roots clung to Shedwyn, held her close to the ground.

Shedwyn closed her eyes to the dizzying swirl of the forest and reached for the green thread of her element. It swayed wildly, eluding her grasp. Everything was wrong. The knot was coming untied.

She tried again frantically to reach for her thread and saw the gleam of a white hand take hers. *Lirrel*, she thought, relieved, and then gasped with surprise as the hand that touched her was strange and unfamiliar. A white thread of light bloomed and twined around Shedwyn's green thread, strengthening its place in the knot. She felt the tremors in the earth quiet and the knot looped and folded in on itself again.

But the knot was different. It lacked the symmetrical precision that had been there when Lirrel tied it and now resembled the snarled back of a child's embroidery. Shedwyn peered through the aura of white light.

Not Lirrel, she saw, but Dagar, his clumsy movements shaped by a tentative hand. Despite its ugliness, the knot held, and in the next moment Dagar fell with the streak of a falling star. Shedwyn heard the distant echo of his voice along the threads of the knot. Lirrel had died, gifting him the thread of her power. Dagar was now the fourth, the air element of the Queens' quarter knot.

Shedwyn returned to her body. Already the roots that had clung to her legs were sliding wearily back into the gouged earth. Dirt sprinkled her chest and her arms and the sap of the trees streaked her legs. As she lay on her back, she looked up at the stars that glittered coldly between the withered leaves of the remaining trees.

"Lirrel," she whispered sadly to the gleaming stars. Tears welled in her eyes as she reached out to touch the far-off light.

"Shedwyn!" Anard called her from the doorway of the hut.

"I am here," she answered and stood slowly and carefully. She rested her hand over her swollen belly.

Anard was beside her, his young face dazed by sleep. "What's happening?'' Then he swore, seeing the ravaged woods. ''Zorah,'' he spat.

''Lirrel is dead,'' Shedwyn said, ''but Dagar holds her place in the knot.''

''Dagar?'' He frowned. ''But he's not got the old magic.''

''Lirrel gifted it to him somehow, as she was dying.''

''But there's never been a man in the knot.''

Shedwyn looked again to the distant stars. ''In the knot, I think our sex makes little difference. It is the heart and the spirit that count. Dagar is generous with both.'' She slid her arm over Anard's shoulders, shivering with the cold, and drew him close to her side beneath the cloak. ''Come,'' she said, ''we must return and wait.''

Tayleb swam deeper into the black water of the sea. She had not thought to return to its depths so soon after reaching the Ribbons, but now that they were here, now that there was time to think, she needed this moment to be alone with her fears.

For the first time since they had left the island, Tayleb wondered at her place in the Queens' quarter knot. It wasn't enough, she thought, just to have the power. She had to know how to use it. But there was no one to guide her. Or to guide anyone else in the knot for that matter, she scowled.

Silvery fish, attracted by the light of the jellyfish schooled around her, were curiously nipping at her hair and feet. They darted bravely amidst the dangerous frilled tentacles of her luminous escorts.

At least Lirrel was educated, Tayleb admitted, lazily stroking her arms through the lighted path of the jellyfish. And what of Jobber and Shedwyn? Tayleb tried to recall the way they looked with their aura of colored light shining on their faces. From Shedwyn she had felt generosity. But Jobber was prickly and sharp. Tayleb didn't want to admit to Lirrel that she wasn't so sure she could handle Jobber. It would be easier, Tayleb reasoned, if she knew what she was supposed to do in the knot.

Balance, Lirrel had said. Balance the fire element with water. Tayleb kicked out her legs, swimming toward the edge of a coral-crusted reef. Sea bracken waved in the currents, fanning the small fish that darted in the unexpected light of the jellyfish. Tayleb stared at the jagged underwater terrain and imagined she was flying, soaring over the peaks of the Avadares Mountains. How like the land above was the seascape below. It must not have been so hard for the Namires to leave the land above and settle in the kelp forests and coral gardens of the sea.

From the depths of the dark water, Tayleb heard a low echo, a sound that rose like an immense bubble lifting out of the deep. The sound became a murmur that vibrated the water, churning sand and small creatures into whirlpools. The school of fish scattered, disappearing with a flick of their silvery tails. Cracks appeared in the shelved landings of coral and sections broke off and fell, scraping end over end down the sides of the reef.

Tayleb panicked and began to swim rapidly to the surface. The luminous jellyfish were gone, and she lost her bearings in the black water. Only by the subtle changes in the current could she discern that she swam upward and not down. She thought she saw the reflection of the moon pooling on the surface of the water. Was it night already above?

And then at once her senses failed. The water twirled her in a dizzying whirlpool of fish, kelp, and sand dredged from the bottom of the ocean. She was blinded by the sand and couldn't see the surface. In the churning water she no longer sensed the layers of currents. Now she could only guess, desperation guiding her in what she hoped was an upward direction.

And then her eyes widened in terror as Tayleb felt the water in her lungs harden. She began sinking like a drowned man, her lungs weighted. She thrust herself upward again, kicking wildly for the surface. The booming echo of the ocean became the booming of her heart, bursting for want of air. Her fingertips broke the surface of the water and one last kick propelled her upward until her face emerged from the thrashing waves, open-mouthed and gasping.

She coughed and gagged on seawater, sculling her hands and trying to stay afloat. Her body felt as heavy as sodden driftwood. Her feet kicked weakly and the cold water made her teeth chatter. She looked out over the horizon and saw the narrow strip of the Ribbons far off in the distance. She was adrift, alone in the sea.

As she floated on her back, gasping, the water calmed and Tayleb felt again the warm currents rise to caress her. She waited in the water, just floating quietly on her back and watching the stars wink above her.

"Lirrel is dead," a voice said above her. "But I am in her place and the knot holds."

Frightened, Tayleb stared into the night trying to find the source of those awful words. As she studied the stars it seemed that the lines drew together in a shimmering likeness of Dagar's face. She could almost imagine the eyes staring down at her and the lips of a sad smile. Thin strips of clouds stretched out overhead, obscuring the sky and Dagar's face. Tayleb rolled onto her stomach and felt herself buoyed by the water. She stroked her arms through the quiet water, her head above the waves as she swam toward the dark shore of the Ribbons.

Her hopes seemed to bleed into the water. How could they succeed without Lirrel? Tayleb asked herself. How would any of them know what to do?

The jellyfish had returned to light her journey back to shore. And though the water warmed her body, Tayleb felt a cold chill in her heart.

From deep within an exhausted sleep, Wyer heard Jobber's voice muttering angrily. Annoyed to have his sleep disturbed, he reached out, his eyes still shut, and nudged Jobber on the shoulder to quiet her. Suddenly he was awake, his hand scalded by the heat of Jobber's body.

"Jobber?" he called, sitting up and blowing cool air on his burning hand. "Jobber!"

Jobber swore loudly as she turned in her sleep. Her hair glowed a brilliant coppery red and the air was filled with its sharp metallic stink. Then she lurched upright, her eyes bright with gold flames. Smoke curled up from her clothes and her hair crackled with showers of yellow sparks.

"Jobber!" Wyer shouted as around them the dried grass withered with heat. A circle of fire erupted with shooting flames.

Wyer scrambled back, away from the fiery circle, crying out as the flames caught the wool of his cloak. He rolled on the hard ground, extinguishing the sparks in his clothing. Little wisps of foul-smelling smoke lifted from his hair and beard. He turned back to Jobber.

She was standing in the middle of the fiery circle, her head thrown back, her eyes fixed on the stars above. Her hair was a gout of flames, spread around her shoulders and head like the sun's flaming corona. Wyer had to shield his eyes from the heat and brilliance of her firelight. Her clothing ignited and then crumbled into black ash. Jobber reached toward the stars, her arms white and bare. She shrieked at the sky and around her the fire lifted higher into a solid wall of flames.

Wyer stayed low to the ground, watching helplessly as the fire engulfed Jobber. He could hear her anguished cries through the roar of the wind as it sucked through the flames. Encased by fire her body glowed like the white-hot core of the forge bed. Her hair flowed down her back like molten copper. Blue-tipped petals of flame bloomed in her hands.

Wyer's breath came in shallow heaves, starved as Jobber's fire claimed the air. Heat scorched his face, but still Wyer could not turn away from the sight of Jobber. His father had been the mastersmith at Crier's Forge and he had taught Wyer long ago that fire mattered most in the art of the forge. It was the magic that transformed old, cold ore into steel. The smith may learn of metals, and of hammers, but without the fire his work was lifeless. Wyer watched in awe and fear as Jobber was changed by her element into something at once beautiful and deadly.

It was then that Wyer realized that the fire was contained within the blazing circle of flames. She's like Zorah, he thought, standing in the Great Bonfire of Firefaire. She's controlling the fire. Jobber lowered her face and through the curtain of flames held Wyer's gaze. Her green eyes shone like emeralds against the pallor of her skin. On her cheeks tears flowed, leaving a reddish streak of cooled flesh in their wake.

The ring of fire began to wane, the flames growing weaker. Jobber's white body shimmered, and as she cooled her skin changed from an iridescent blue to a burnished copper. Her hair settled into wiry strands over her shoulders, and black ash coated the crown around her face.

"Z'blood," Jobber said and crossed her arms over her chest. The ring of fire spluttered in the wind and then gutted into gray smoke. Wyer approached cautiously, seeing the heat radiating from her shoulders. The ground around her was scorched black, and Wyer could feel its heat through the thin soles of his old boots.

"Lirrel's been scaffered," she said in a husky voice.

"Z'blood, no," Wyer answered, feeling the breath knocked from his chest.

Jobber gave a bitter smile. "She passed on her element to Dagar. He's taken her place in the knot. He told me to go now to find Zorah and forget coming to the Ribbons. There just ain't the time." Then she groaned and bowed her head. "Frigging shit, Wyer. I can't do this. The knot's a brangled mess. And Dagar." She looked up, the tears steaming on her face. "Dagar's all right, but he ain't Lirrel." Jobber's shoulders sagged. "Z'blood, seems I know more dead people than living."

"I'm still here," Wyer replied.

Jobber cocked an eyebrow at him. "If I was you, I'd turn heel."

"No you wouldn't."

"Might have once," Jobber said softly.

"Once, but not anymore."

"Yeah." Jobber nodded. "That's right. Lirrel taught me that. Not to turn away."

"Do you know what happened?" Wyer asked gently.

Jobber shook her head, her cooled hair rustling with the movement. "Not all of it. Just that she was a Ghazali, even at the end. Wouldn't fight back, 'cause she knew she'd lose that way. So she gave up her body and gave her element to Dagar." Jobber gave a weary smile. "Feels like she's out there. Watching, almost."

"And Dagar?"

Jobber brushed ash from her cheeks. "He hurts. He has her and yet he doesn't. It's the same for me," she said hoarsely.

Wyer ran his hands through his hair, his face lowered to the blackened earth. A crack splintered his resolve. The war was hard, but they had counted on the knot as the real hope for a future. And now Lirrel was dead. Wyer's head ached with fatigue. He knew the others relied upon Lirrel's knowledge to make the right decisions. Could they make those decisions without her?

"Oy, Wyer," Jobber called, shaking him out of his worry.

He glanced up and saw her sad face. There was neither anger nor bitterness in her expression. The smooth skin had softened into a graceful curve.

"I'll need the spare clothes from your bedroll. I can't exactly slip into Beldan like this," Jobber said, gesturing at her nudity.

Wyer rummaged through the saddlebags and returned with an old linen shirt and trousers that were too large for Jobber's slim frame.

She pulled on the clothes, wrapping the extra fabric around her waist. Wyer gave her a length of leather cord from the horse's bridle and she used it as a belt.

He watched her, puzzled by the change in her. There were no signs of her usual temper bubbling just beneath the surface. The grace she reserved for fighting she exhibited now in the calm movements of dressing. The muscles of her arm bunched and relaxed as she drew on the trousers and shirt. She brushed her hair from her face, exposing the clean line of her jaw.

They moved their camp to a new spot, not bothering to light a fire. The sky was already beginning to grow light over the horizon. If he stared hard enough, Wyer imagined, he could see the gates of Beldan on the other side of the Plains.

Jobber laid down beside him and reached for his hand. Her palm was warm and dry and he found it comforting in the chilly morning.

"I know what to do," she said softly. "Lirrel's death has shown me." Then she turned toward him and nudged herself between his arms. She laid her face against his chest and the coppery scent of her hair filled his nostrils. He folded his arms carefully around her, his hands flat against the planes of her back. "But I must sleep first," she said drowsily.

Wyer lay awake while Jobber slept in his arms. One of his arms became numb with Jobber's weight and he hesitated to move it for fear of disturbing her. At last he shifted her slightly, and though she murmured in her sleep as she curled her body more tightly against his, she didn't waken. Wyer winced as the blood tingled back into his deadened arm. He thought of Lirrel and what Jobber had said about feeling her still watching them. He hoped it was true.

Wyer stared at the distant twinkle of winter stars. And without meaning to, he fell asleep watching the stars fade away one by one into the dawn's light.

Chapter Twenty-two

Zorah scratched her head, irritated with the knitted cap that hid her flame-colored hair. She stood alone at the entrance to Crier's Forge. The doors, long since pried off their hinges, lay rotting in the street. The huge mouth of the ancient forge bed was filled with cold ash. Broken ceiling beams had collapsed over the shelves and tables where once tools were stored.

Zorah bent and picked up a hammer lying in the street. Its wooden handle was split near the joining to the claw. She flung it angrily through the open doorway.

"Useless," she muttered scornfully at the dreary, abandoned forge. Her scalp was hot, her hair smoldering beneath the confining cap. "Give me the Upright Man," she said to the doorway, her hand clenched in a fist.

Too late she had learned that he was the real danger. Now she had to find him before he found the others; to stop him from stealing what was rightfully hers. But so far in her nightly searches, she had found nothing but trouble. Zorah had taken to wearing the knitted cap because her red hair attracted too much of the wrong attention. She wasn't recognized as the Fire Queen, but mistaken for a woman vain enough in a time of civil war to dye her hair like a war banner. Street brats catcalled to her from windows, as if she were a common whore. The Guards bullied and insulted her, and when she pulled her sword in response, they attacked her. She had wasted too much precious time defending herself from fools.

Zorah walked away from the forge, her steps taking her down the gloomy street toward the remains of the weaving houses. She was alone now in Beldan. Three nights ago Guards had returned to the Keep with Gonmer stretched out on a board. Zorah's eyelids lowered as she recalled how the body had been hacked almost beyond recognition. The long black braid had been cut off and Zorah had later seen it hanging like a trophy on the belt of a Guard. Gonmer's young page had also disappeared.

Zorah slowed her steps, hearing ringing shouts and the clash of swords. Smoke drifted over the top of a weaving house. The roof was gone, and through the skeletal husk she could see the bright flicker of new flames from a barricade in the next street. The harsh caw of the Sileans' alarm rose over the battle cries. Zorah hid in the dark curve of a dark doorway. She had no desire to join this fight on either side.

Zorah tensed, hearing the slap of bare feet on the cobblestones and the breathy gasps of someone running. In the shadowy darkness she made out the figure of a child pelting down the street. Zorah stepped out of the doorway quickly, sticking out her leg to trip the fleeing child. A girl, her long braids flying out behind her as she fell, sprawled over the cobblestones with a terrified shout. Zorah reached down and grabbed the girl by the scruff of her too-large bodice.

The child continued to struggle, legs kicking, fists striking out in blind fury. A string of obscenities burst from the small face.

"Shut up, or you'll get us both knackered," Zorah growled.

Instantly the child quieted, but continued thrashing in Zorah's grip.

Zorah lifted the slight girl by the shoulders and slammed her against the remaining wall of the weaving house. The walls shook, wobbling noisily with the blow. "Be still!" Zorah commanded.

The girl ceased struggling and stared back at Zorah with battle-scarred eyes. "Frigging let me go!" she spat.

"The Upright Man, you know him?"

Zorah felt the shoulders bunch beneath her grasp as the girl cringed.

"Where do I find him?" Zorah demanded.

The girl's body coiled unexpectedly and then exploded with a new burst of rage. She kicked wildly, and as Zorah's attention was drawn to getting her shins out of the way, the girl bit Zorah's hand. Zorah yelped as blood erupted in a neat semicircle of teeth marks. She released the child and the girl dropped heavily into the street. She crouched, dazed, and then, gathering up her skirts, fled into the black hole of the building.

Zorah swore, shaking her wounded hand and staring angrily at the beads of blood. The girl's voice called out to her from the dark building.

"The New Moon is rising!" the voice taunted shrilly. "And if you've an eye for the Upright Man, you must go to the noddynoose. Fuck the traitorous Queen and her butcherboys. We'll scaffer them all!"

Zorah put her lips to the bite wound, tasting the warm blood. Turning smartly on her heel, she jogged down the street, away from the burning barricades and the taunting voice. The scaffolds were near Scroggles and that's where the girl had said she'd find the Upright Man.

Near Scroggles a stitch in her side forced Zorah to slow her pace and walk. The thick, pulpy smoke of the crematorium clung to her face and made it hard to breathe. Zorah stopped, seeing Antoni Re Desturo swinging from the scaffolds in the faint orange glow of the pyres.

They had hanged him upside down, by his ankles. His upper torso was naked and covered with stab wounds. Rusty stains streaked the broken white skin. His arms dangled, and taloned hands cupped palmfuls of dried blood. His eyes were open, black pools that stared back at Zorah. His lips were twisted in a grimace and a second leer gaped beneath his chin where his throat had been cut from ear to ear.

A woman's scream caused Zorah to seek the dark shelter of an alley. She leaned her shoulder into a door of an old warehouse and pushed, feeling it give under her weight. The woman's terrified screams grew louder and Zorah could hear the rapid tramping of boots. Zorah looked out from behind the door and saw a woman fleeing before three Guards, the cool white of her heels catching the light of the pyres.

But the Guards were faster. They grabbed her, their voices raised in an ugly chorus of triumphant laughter. Zorah gripped her sword on an impulse to stop the Guards.

And then she hesitated as a listless feeling drained her of motion. Her knees buckled and she crumpled to the dirty floor. Her body contracted into a fetal knot, her hands closing in a knuckled grip. Vertigo swept over her, shearing away the ground beneath her crouched body. She was sent spinning, the wind tossing and blowing her over and over. The sound of the woman's screams deepened in pitch and became the shrill keen of Chaos.

The knot was slipping, the threads becoming untied!

Though her body was tightly curled, Zorah felt as if her limbs were being pulled apart, each to a different direction of Oran's cradle. She was stretched thin, like batting twisted by the fingers of Chaos into thread. She wanted to scream like the woman on the street, but her throat denied her.

And then, gradually, Zorah became aware that the twisting wind had slowed. The vertigo left her and she opened her eyes to the dirty floor. Zorah gave a wracking cough as her chest expanded, air finding its way through bruised passages. Her body retrieved control, her hands to unclench, her legs to uncurl from the agonizing coil. Her spine cracked as she raised her head. She groaned, feeling battered and sore.

Zorah stood, trembling with a cold, arthritic pain in her limbs and hands. She listened and noted that the street beyond the door was quiet again.

Leaning on the edge of the door, she peered out and saw the woman lying on her back in the street. Her legs were splayed, her torn skirts fluttering in the wind farther down the street. Her head was tilted back, the neck cruelly arched as it lifted her bare chest to the dull orange glow of Scroggles' pyres. Black hollows shaded the eyes.

Zorah limped toward the woman, her pelvis aching with each step. She could see that even in death the woman's face was contorted in defiant rage, and her hands held clumps of hair. Zorah paused to stare at the woman and then bent to close the torn bodice over the naked breasts.

"No!" Zorah cried as she saw her hand, freckled with age and blue veins snaking over the back. She snatched her hand back and stood quickly. Then she touched her cheek, feeling where the flesh lay slack against the bone. She looked down and saw that her breasts sagged, the nipples no longer taut but rounded, lying indifferently beneath the fabric of her shirt.

She had aged again! As the knot was fumbled in their inexperienced hands she had aged once more.

Zorah began to run, shooting pains rising from her heels to her hips. There was no place safe for her except the Keep. Like this she was too vulnerable. She dared not use her element, for Chaos held her too tightly in its grip. And though she had the skills of the sword, she could not rely on them in this unaccustomed body that betrayed her with its stiffness. She must wait in the Keep, preserve her strength until the firegirl came to her.

Zorah wanted to snatch the knitted cap from her head, but she didn't dare in the harsh, forbidding streets of Beldan. She huddled in doorways, skirted through alleys to avoid meeting anyone. It was only when she reached the ancient doors that opened on the ridge of the hill behind the Keep that Zorah slowed her feet. She entered the Keep and found herself in the old corridors of crumbling frescoes. She sucked in grateful breaths of the cold, dank air as her heart rattled with fear and exhaustion.

As her breathing calmed she had time to reflect on her aged hands. She grew hot with the fury of her impotence. She yanked the cap from her head and threw it down to the granite floor. The fiery hair spilled over her shoulders, crackling with an angry static charge.

And by the light of a spluttering torch Zorah sobbed suddenly, seeing the long strands of gray in the faded rust-colored hair.

Alwir woke with a start, his legs twitching nervously. He had been dreaming, seeing in vivid repetitions his father's death. Over and over the man fell, his voice a deep rumbling moan, the knife protruding from his chest. Each time the image repeated, Alwir strained to see where the truth of the moment lay. To protect him, or the Silean? He tried to see recognition in his father's eyes, the glance that might have shown Alwir the man's motive. But it was not there to be seen. Only the clouding of pain. His body jerked in sleep as he threw himself over the side of the Silean ship.

Alwir stared up in confusion at the roof of the leaning shack. He blinked, trying to reconcile the odd angles of the beams with the images of his dream. The sound of Dagar's pipes drew him slowly out of his stupor and made him remember. He stretched out his legs, the fabric of his trousers stiff with dried saltwater. He unfurled the cloak and sat up, shaking his head.

He had slept too long. Like a dead man. He wiped his face, his eyes sticky with grime. Sighing wearily, he stood, his head throbbing slightly. He left the shack, trying to shrug off the dulling trance of sleep. Out on the beach he saw a small fire, the bright orange flames cheerful. Dagar sat with his back to Alwir, and on the other side of the fire Tayleb and Tip huddled together. Alwir frowned, seeing the taut expression on Tayleb's face.

Something had happened. Were those tears on Tayleb's cheeks or seawater? he wondered. She looked damp, her wet hair plastered to her head. Tip had drawn his knees up to his chin, his child's face anxiously studying Dagar.

Alwir hurried to join them, his concern mounting as he listened to the haunting tune of Dagar's pipes. It was not a tune that Dagar usually played. It sounded more like Lirrel.

He clasped Dagar on the shoulder, wanting the eerie music to stop. Dagar lowered the flute and turned to look up at Alwir.

"Z'blood," Alwir said and lowered himself slowly beside

Dagar. Dagar's eyes stared back at him, white as opals. "Where's Lirrel?" Alwir asked, bewildered.

"Read me," Dagar said.

"Where is Lirrel?" Alwir demanded again.

"In here," Dagar answered quietly. "Read the truth for yourself, Alwir."

Angry and confused Alwir let his gaze unfocus. Dagar's face disappeared within a wreath of pure white. Alwir gasped, recognizing in the shimmering aura Lirrel's presence. Her face seemed to peer back at him, reflected in the tiny facets of diamond light. But the image of her face shifted, never remaining long enough for him to grasp completely the sight of her features. She was there and not there.

Alwir closed his eyes to the brilliant light.

"Lirrel has been murdered," Tayleb said softly.

"But she's not dead," Alwir said, his eyes snapping open. "I can still sense her in the aura that surrounds Dagar."

"She gifted me her element before her death," Dagar said. "She is here, in me."

"And you are in the knot?" Alwir asked.

"*Ahal.*" Dagar nodded. "Though there isn't much time left." Dagar shifted his attention away from Alwir to Tip. The boy straightened in expectation. "Tip, you must go and tell Kai what has happened, that I have taken Lirrel's place and the knot holds. Tell her also that Jobber says to gather people—as many as she can—and flee Beldan. They are to wait for her on the Plains beyond the city gate."

"But they'll be out in the open. An easy target for the Sileans!" Alwir argued.

"*Ahal*, out in the open is safer than in the city, where they may easily be destroyed when Jobber and Zorah meet."

"Kai won't believe me," Tip said, shaking his head.

"She must," Dagar urged. "The safety of your people depends on it."

"I'll go with him," Alwir said stiffly.

"Good," Dagar said gratefully.

Quickly, Alwir and Tip left the fire and pushed Tip's riverboat back into the water. Tip took his place and held the boat with the pole, waiting for Alwir.

Tayleb laid her hand on Alwir's shoulder and, without a word, he embraced her. His arms circled her slim waist and he held her tightly. The skin of her neck smelled of the cold sea and was cool on his heated face.

"Come back," she whispered.

"I will." He sensed that she wanted him to change his mind, to stay. But he couldn't. He had to be there to join the New Moon on the Plains. Dream the hero's dream, Dagar had urged him once. Alwir smoothed his hand over the sleek shape of Tayleb's head. One dried curl twisted around her temple. He kissed her salted lips. "I will return, I promise," he said, his forehead resting lightly against hers.

Then he released her and joined Tip in the boat. Dagar pushed them off the sand and into the current. The boat rocked and swayed on the waves as Tip poled the boat swiftly toward the Harbor Wall. Alwir craned his head around to catch a final glimpse of Dagar and Tayleb standing on the sandy shore of the Ribbons. And then he turned back to Beldan, impatiently watching the Harbor Wall grow larger as they neared it.

"Well," Jobber said to Wyer, "this is so long, then."

"What do you mean?" he asked frowning.

They were standing on the crest of a hill overlooking the wide sweep of the Plains of Beldan. Below them at the base of the hill was the old stone wall that marked the edges of Beldan. The west gate was gone, only a few stones remaining in the blasted opening. In the gray morning light the city was barely visible beneath a bank of dense clouds.

"From here, I go on alone," Jobber explained. She searched the horizon for familiar landmarks in the city. It saddened her to discover there weren't too many left.

"Ridiculous," Wyer growled. "You need me."

"No, I don't," Jobber said. "Not to come with me, anyways. But I do need you to wait here for Kai and the rest of the New Moon. I let Dagar know last night that I wanted as many of our people out of the city as could be rounded up."

"But why?"

Jobber faced Wyer, her expression thoughtful. "The old Queen Huld thought that the only way to stop Zorah was to challenge her with the Fire Sword. But she also knew that when Zorah's Fire Sword was broken, Time would escape. Zorah's been twisting Oran round and round, like a dell with a pail of milk. And if she stops suddenly—"

"Everything spills out," Wyer finished.

"Yeah. The new Queens' quarter knot is to be a net to keep Oran, and us, from flinging off into Chaos. But Lirrel's death gave me another idea," Jobber said, her brows knitted together. "A different way to straighten things out. I just have to get close enough to Zorah, let her think she can take me."

"Can she take you?" Wyer asked.

Jobber shrugged and gave a half smile. "She fights with her body, and she's afraid of losing it. In clinging to it, she ignores her real power. That's my advantage. But," Jobber warned, "I don't know if I can slow Oran down and keep it from ripping apart anyway."

"So we wait for you on the Plains," Wyer said, understanding at last.

"Yeah, where the buildings don't drop on you, or throw you into the sky, like Sadar." Jobber pulled the sides of her cloak tighter over her shoulders. Wyer's clothes were too large and the wind whistled in the huge folds. She could feel the dampness in the air that would soon fall as snow. "Oy, one more thing," she added gruffly, freeing the sword from her belt and handing it to him. "Take this frigging thing. I don't want it getting in my way."

"But Jobber, you can't go into Beldan alone *and* unarmed," Wyer argued.

"I ain't unarmed. I got two arms right here," she said, grinning as she held up her white-knuckled fists.

Wyer clapped her on the shoulder and when she leaned willingly into his grasp he slid his hands over her back and held her close. She laid her cheek against his solid chest, smiling at the steady thump of his heart, beating like a forge bellows. He smelled of iron and wet wool. He tipped her chin back, his eyes searching her face. Jobber was calm when he lowered his mouth to hers, his lips unexpectedly soft.

He released her and Jobber's shy smile stretched into a grin. "Not so bad," she said.

Wyer's sober face broke with laughter and the sound of it echoed over the Plains. Jobber joined him, glad for a moment of happiness.

"I'm off, then," Jobber said in the quiet that followed their laughter. She nodded quickly at Wyer and then set her face toward Beldan. As she trudged down the hill toward the old gate, fat snowflakes began to drift in the air. But even the wet lick of snow on her cheeks could not dampen her feverish excitement. She was returning to Beldan, and what was left undone at Firecircle would now be settled.

Beldan huddled cold beneath the falling snow. Jobber started to jog, the snow hissing on the fiery hair that billowed around her face.

She opened her senses to her city, letting the heat of her desire and her fiercely held hope spark the empty grates. Fire kindled and burned in every hearth where there was wood, and even where there was none.

Beldan's fire was home, at last.

Chapter Twenty-three

*T*he snow was falling in a thick white curtain as Jobber reached the old city gate. She scrambled over the stones, alert for the black-and-gray uniforms of the Guards. Crouched low, she ran down the snow-covered road that opened to a small square. The square was empty of people, the dark fronts of the buildings surrounding it scarcely visible through the dense snowfall. Jobber straightened cautiously and then entered the square. As soon as the soles of her feet felt the hard cobblestones, Jobber smiled. After the dirt roads of the West and Avadares Mountain paths, the pebbled surface of Beldan's streets gave her the distinct sensation of home.

On the corner where the square angled into Drover's Road Jobber passed an inn with sooty black windows called the Crow's Wing. Jobber remembered it as an easy place for the snitch. So close to the West gate, it housed many a traveler and farmer unused to the ways of Beldan. Jobber fingered a loose coin in her pocket. Her tongue clucked thirstily at the thought of Beldan ale, its cream-colored froth spilling over the top of the tankard. She peered in the window, seeing the fire that beckoned warmly in the hearth. The steam of her breath clouded the glass, and on an impulse she went in.

Tattlebells over the door jingled as she entered. Standing in the common room, Jobber shook the snow from her head and shoulders and then faced the bar with an expectant smile. Behind the bar the innkeeper stared back in alarm, his eyes locked on the flame of her red hair. Jobber's smile faltered and she touched her head in memory. Z'blood, she swore, her hair! She had almost forgotten that in Beldan such a color was dangerous.

"Ale," she ordered.

The man moved quickly, his hands shaking as he poured a tankard of ale from a brown pitcher. Wordlessly he set it before Jobber, his eyes never leaving her face.

Jobber grabbed the tankard greedily and put it to her lips. She sighed at the scent of malt and yeast, the taste at once bitter and sweet on the tongue. She drank slowly but steadily, and when she reached the bottom she set the tankard down reluctantly on the bar. Jobber withdrew a coin and set it on the bar beside the staring innkeeper.

"Thanks," she said.

He nodded.

At the door of the inn, Jobber suddenly turned back to the silent man. "Oy, do yerself some good," she said briskly. "Get out to the Plains as soon as you can."

"What for?" the man stuttered.

"May be the best way to make it through the day without getting scaffered." Jobber wrenched the door open and the tattlebells jingled again.

"Wait!" the innkeeper called. He picked up the coin with a nervous smile. He came out from behind the protection of the bar and Jobber saw the heavy sword he'd hidden beneath his apron. He took her hand and placed the coin in her palm. "Come back," he said, "later, and the Crow's Wing will welcome you home properly."

Jobber grinned. "I will," she said, folding her hand around the gold coin stamped with the profile of the Fire Queen.

Outside, Jobber covered her head with her cloak, not so much to hide her hair as to prevent the cold, wet snow from trickling down her neck. The ale was warm and nourishing in her stomach. Jobber felt her body as well as her spirits renewed. She had received an unexpected welcome home and it was enough to give her encouragement.

Jobber walked briskly down the street, staying close to the protective shelter of the buildings. She swore, seeing how the old street had been changed, the workhouses of the Guild District now mostly in ruins. The tiny gardens that had once squeezed between the alleys were filled with stones, fallen beams, and broken glass.

The sudden hoarse cry of a lighterman jarred her, bringing Jobber fully home to Beldan. Despite their beggared appearance, the streets sparked with memories. She saw clearly the route of each street as it twisted through the maze of the Guild District. She knew the side streets and the alleys that joined the backs of the workhouses like connecting bars of thread in lace.

The lighterman's voice bawled the hour again and Jobber frowned. She looked up into the cloud-covered sky. The snow had abated, only a few flakes drifting from the rooftops with the wind. And though the sky was a dove gray, she was certain it was still morning; too early to call the watch change. Why was he crying the hour now?

Standing in an alley, Jobber edged her way through a partially open door, knowing by the acidic smell of the steam that it was a dyers' workhouse. The huge room was empty, but in big-bellied vats blue and green skeins of wool churned in the slow-boiling dye. Jobber wove her way through the skeins of hanging wet yarn draped over a narrow gutter.

Where had they all gone? Jobber wondered. The fires beneath the heated vats had been stoked, mortars and pestles for grinding the dyeballs were sitting as if recently abandoned. Even the stickboys with their long sticks for stirring the wool were nowhere to be seen. Ahead of her in the open street the lighterman still gave out his raspy cry.

Jobber stuck her head cautiously between the front doors that looked out onto the High Street. In the swirling snow she glimpsed the black coattails of the lighterman farther up the street.

"Frigging shit," she swore as he turned, his torch pole disappearing around the corner. Jobber bolted down the stoop, clinging to a bent railing so as not to slip on the snow-covered stairs. She ran to catch up with the lighterman. At the corner, she stopped abruptly in the silence. Huddled against a wall, she peered around the building into the alley. The lighterman was there, surrounded by the dyers. They had thrown on jackets over their stained shirts and aprons. Blue-dyed hands clutched weapons as they gathered around the lighterman, murmuring and nodding. The stickboys were there too, their sticks scraping excited patterns in the snow. Within moments they had finished talking, calling hasty farewells as they scattered in different directions.

An older boy ran past Jobber, his pale face shining with sweat. His jacket flapped in the wind, and his long hands and bony wrists, dyed a greenish blue, stuck out from the too-short sleeves. He looked up, seeing Jobber waiting by the corner. Jobber pulled the cloak tighter around her face to keep her hair from spilling out.

"Oy," he said, taking in the sight of her old clothes and thin boots. "Word is out. To the Plains and make short work of it."

"Where you going then?" Jobber asked as the boy continued in the opposite direction.

"To warn them at Cloth House. Whole city is clearing out. Won't be none of us left in Beldan after the lighterman finishes calling his hour." Then he hurried away, intent on his errand.

Jobber smiled and let the cloak fall from her head. Dagar had done it. The word was out on the street and Wyer would soon find himself in good company, Jobber thought with a smile. She began to walk again, her pace steady as her long-legged Beldan stride returned. She watched, satisfied, as people began to gather in the streets, their arms loaded with blankets, tools, and the few precious items not to be left behind. Shouldered close together, they flowed down the streets toward the western gate. On the arms of their black coats the men wore blue ribbons as symbols of the New Moon. The young men and apprentices walked on the outer edges of the stream, clubs and long-handled pikes in their hands as their eyes watched for Silean Guards. In

the center the women walked, children on their backs or clinging
to their hands. Their skirts brushed against the cobblestones and
their clogs beat a muddied trail through the new snow. Jobber
slipped into a deserted alley to avoid the crowds and make her
way more quickly.

Around her, Jobber heard the city become as silent as the
softly drifting snow. She peeked into taverns, pleased by their
emptiness and the fires that burned gaily in the grates. On Finnia's Alley, Jobber hid behind the abandoned remains of a barricade as a squad of Guards marched past. Nervously they
scanned the quiet streets, muttering oaths between them.

"What's frigging going on?" a young captain in a new uniform asked his sergeant. He knocked the snow from his polished
black boots.

The sergeant was an older man, the elbows of his worn uniform threadbare. He coughed and spat into the snow. "They're
fleeing the city."

"Like rats," said the captain glumly.

"Makes one want to get off the ship, doesn't it?" the sergeant
said quietly.

The captain clamped his hand on the hilt of his sword, his
face flushed red and white. "I will not tolerate desertion," he
snapped.

"Nor common sense," rasped the sergeant, drawing his
sword. Cold steam issued from his white nostrils. "There's
nothing in this frigging place worth getting killed for. We're
going home."

The captain fumbled for the alarm whistle around his neck.

Stupid fool, Jobber thought, knowing the futility of the captain's position. It ended quickly as two Guards overpowered the
young man, knocking him to the ground before he'd put the
whistle to his lips. The sergeant thrust his sword into the captain
as he lay sprawling in the snow. Then he withdrew his sword
and wiped the blade clean on the dying captain's sleeve.

"To the ship," the sergeant said.

"Which one?" asked another Guard.

"I'll tell you that when we're there, lest any of you have a
mind to murder me and steal my passage," he said, brandishing

his sword. The Guards glanced sideways at each other but held quiet.

The sergeant grunted his approval and sheathed his sword. "This way," he ordered and the others followed him as he headed quickly down a side street.

Jobber left her hiding place and came to look down at the slain captain. She shook her head at the beardless face, sprinkled with snow. He wasn't much older than herself. Warm blood melted the snow and oozed around the base of the cobblestones, separating them like islands in a red sea.

Jobber left him and continued on her way down the High Street, her gaze trained on the skeletal remains of the West Tower. Zorah was there, waiting for her. Jobber could sense her presence; could hear Zorah's heartbeat as a faint echo of her own. She imagined the cool white face and green eyes brightened by flames. In the damp air, Jobber caught the stinging scent of burning copper.

The usually bustling High Street was subdued. A woman bundled against the snow passed Jobber carrying a crying baby. And after that a cavalryman rode by, his horse's hooves kicking up clods of snow. Anxious faces appeared at shop windows in glassy circles rubbed clean of mist. Gone were the snitches lounging on the corners, the barrowboys who hawked their wares from the backs of wagons, bakeryboys with trays of bread for the inns, and girls selling ribbons. There were no Ghazali tents, no music from their flutes and drums. Even the taverns that could be counted on for spilling a brawl out into the High Street were quiet, their doors standing open to reveal emptied common rooms. On the storefront of one shop with smashed windows, a huge crescent moon had been painted in defiance of the burnt-out ceiling.

The High Street ended at the entrance to Beldan's Keep. A huge courtyard lined with barracks and an armory guarded the entrance to the Keep. Jobber noticed with disgust that the two marble sentry posts, mounted like a pair of fangs at the gate, remained intact.

Jobber's legs ached with fatigue from the long walk to the Keep across the city. She lowered herself unseen in a doorway and, huddled on its cold stoop, watched the Keep. She needed to rest and to think through her next move.

She sighed wearily. The black-and-gray uniforms covered the courtyard like a flock of ravens. Too many going in and out. There was a sudden flurry as Silean noblemen rode up to the gates on horseback and loudly demanded to see the Regent. The Guards restrained them with drawn swords, turning them away. More rats, Jobber thought, trying to flee.

"You'll not get in that way," said a quiet voice close behind her.

Jobber tensed, but she kept her eyes on the Keep's gate. "How then?" she asked.

A girl squatted beside her and in a sidelong glance, Jobber saw her profile. She looked almost like Faul. As Faul might have looked when young, Jobber thought. The same short black hair cropped at her jawline, cool gray eyes, and the slight mocking smile. Beneath her black cloak Jobber saw the long scabbard of a good Oran sword and a smaller dagger at her waist.

"You're the firegirl, ain't you?" the girl asked, nodding at the strands of red hair that had escaped the cloak. "I've been waiting, figuring you'd show up here soon enough."

"And you're page to the Knackerman I'll wager," Jobber said, pointing to the fire emblem stitched on the collar of the girl's cloak.

"I *am* Firstwatch now," the girl replied bitterly. "Last one got herself scaffered in a brangle with the Guards." A determined look filled the cold gray eyes. "My name's Lais, and if you'll have me, I'll serve you."

"Why me?" Jobber asked.

"Zorah doesn't need me."

"Neither do I," retorted Jobber. She didn't trust the girl. She was too edgy.

"Ah, but you do, because you've never been in there before," Lais said, gesturing toward the Keep. "You wouldn't know how to get in unseen, or even where to go once inside. But I do," she said with a confident smile. "I'll take you."

"What's yer price?" Jobber asked, her eyes narrowing.

"I hate the Queen."

"Vengeance, then?"

Lais nodded, her lips pressed tightly together.

I trust her even less, Jobber thought. She had her own score to settle. Jobber didn't want this girl's anger getting in her way. There was too much at stake. A slight tremor shook the stoop where Jobber and Lais crouched. A few cobblestones heaved and popped out of their muddied sockets. They rolled down the street toward the open courtyard. Lais's face paled, her gray eyes open wide. She clutched the shaking stair as if to stop it from moving. Jobber swore under her breath. There wasn't enough time to argue. She had to rely on the girl's knowledge to get inside.

"Right, then. Let's go," Jobber said, deciding quickly. The ground settled uneasily and the jiggling cobblestones stilled.

Lais released the breath she had held during the tremor. "This way," she said and motioned Jobber up a winding side street nearly hidden between two old shops whose windows showed the remains of boots.

Along the street small shops clustered like barnacles clinging to the rising slope of the hill. The snow began to fall again, making it impossible to see exactly when the slope flattened along the ridge of the hill. Jobber felt the angle change as her aching knees straightened and her cramped stride grew long again. The snow penetrated the hood of her cloak and dripped down between her shoulder blades.

"Frigging snow," she snorted in a cloud of white steam.

"Look," Lais said, "over there."

A stone wall blocked the end of the street. Looking back through the snow, Jobber realized that the side street had circled around the flank of the Keep toward the back where the Keep dug into the hill for protection. The stone wall at the end of the street had once enclosed the private gardens of the ancient Queens. Jagged gaps in the wall revealed the old courtyard within. Snow covered everything with a blanket of white, softening the harshness of its decline. Lais and Jobber scrabbled over the fallen rubble and entered a garden of stones.

"Gonmer sent me out here for guard duty after the New Moon used this door once to get into the Keep," Lais explained. "No one else knows about it."

The old wooden door was left partly ajar, snow drifting inside through the narrow crack. Lais pulled on the door, but it wouldn't open, the damp wood swollen stuck. Jobber helped her, both pairs of hands wrapped around the warped wood, tugging. The door groaned and then scraped along the stone threshold, opening at last.

Lais slipped in and Jobber came close behind her. In the darkness of the corridor Jobber shook herself free of the clinging snow. Her nose wrinkled at the musty odor. Moldy plaster crumbled as Jobber laid a hand on the wall to steady herself in the dark.

"Come on," Lais urged in a harsh whisper. "We've a ways yet to go."

Jobber trailed a hand along the ancient wall to keep from stumbling. Sometimes her hand touched the unexpected coolness of granite, moist with humidity. Jobber could hear loud voices and the hard tramp of boots. Farther down the dark corridor she saw a line of light shining from beneath a closed door.

At the door, Lais stopped, putting her ear to its wooden back. "Wait," she hissed, "they're changing over the Guards."

The even tramp of boots on the stone floors trailed away at last into silence. Slowly, Lais opened the door, cursing at the sudden creak of its hinges.

Jobber followed her, casting a quick glance around for the Guards. But in the middle of the hallway she stopped, struck by the cold beauty of the Keep, the one place in Beldan she had never thought she would see. Beneath her boots was a floor of pink-and-gray Avadares granite, tiny flecks of mica glinting in the torchlight. A huge staircase of polished white marble imported two centuries ago from Silea filled one end of the hallway, gracefully arching out of sight as it ascended to the second floor. Along the walls, carved in stone, were scenes of the Queen at the Great Bonfire of Firefaire. Tall flames frozen in stone by the sculptor's hand encircled Zorah. Jobber was chilled as Zorah's stone face stared down at her.

"Come on," Lais snapped, "or we'll be seen!"

Jobber averted her eyes from the cold gaze of the Queen and followed Lais past the huge stairway into another, smaller hallway. A door opened to a narrow wooden staircase that spiraled upward in the dark.

"Servants' stairs," Lais muttered.

As her foot touched the stairs, Jobber was reminded of Sadar's Keep with its similar set of stairs circling the old tower to where Faul had kept her private chambers. Higher up, tiny windows studded the dark column of stairs with squares of pale daylight. Suddenly Jobber knew exactly where to find Zorah; knew as if it were Faul guiding her and not Lais. Faul was a creature of habit, of discipline. Jobber guessed that at Sadar's Keep Faul would have quartered herself in the room most familiar to her.

Lais stopped on the final landing, panting heavily as she waited outside another door. She edged the door open slowly and reached for the dagger in her belt. She opened the door farther and grabbed at the back of a Guard. She stabbed the man in the throat before he could do more than choke with surprise. Then she laid the limp body in the stairway and gestured to Jobber to follow her.

Jobber's skin prickled and her ears were filled with an angry buzzing. Her scalp grew hot, her hair charged with static.

"Get out now," Jobber ordered Lais.

Lais turned in surprise. "You've no frigging idea where you are."

"I do," Jobber said. "I know exactly where I am. Now go."

"No," Lais said vehemently. "I won't be turned out. I want to see her die."

Jobber's cheeks flushed bright red, her hair hissing as the last of the wet snow melted to steam. "Then stay out of my way," she commanded.

Lais pressed her lips tightly together but she backed up to let Jobber pass before her.

Jobber walked down the corridor, counting the doors as her boots clicked quietly on the stone floor. Faul's room had been behind the fifth door. Jobber stopped in front of a wooden door banded with bars of brass; exactly the same as the four doors preceding it. There was nothing to suggest that behind its simple facade the Fire Queen might have kept her chambers. Yet Jobber knew with utter certainty that she was right. Her heart quickened as she tried the door and found it unlocked.

Jobber passed from the dark corridor into a well-lit circular room. Windows on all sides of the circular wall opened to the gray cloud-filled sky. There were no corners that might cast shadows, no vaults in the domed ceiling to trap darkness. Jobber stared in wonder at the fresco painted on the ceiling showing the sun eating away at the dark night. Along the floors the smooth polished wood flowed like poured honey.

In this room shaped like a circle Jobber saw the emptiness of Zorah's life. It was a closed world without beginning and without end, its hollowed core stagnant and lifeless.

Zorah stood erect at a window, her back to Jobber as she faced the harbor. She was dressed in black wool trousers and a white linen shirt. Her hair draped over her shoulders, its once copper color subdued by streaks of gray. One white hand rested on the window ledge and the other held the Fire Sword at her side.

Jobber's mouth was dry, her face flushed with excitement.

"So," Zorah said, "you've come."

"Yeah," Jobber answered, annoyed at the coarse sound of her voice amid the richness of the Fire Queen's chambers.

"I would thank my sister Huld for bringing you to me if it weren't for all the trouble she caused me." Zorah turned to look at Jobber.

Jobber drew a startled breath between her parted lips. At Firefaire they had been like sisters, a mirrored image of the other. But a flaw in the perfect circle had changed her features since then. Zorah was still beautiful, her expression proud, her green eyes opaque. But she was older, much older than last time. Fine lines crossed her forehead and pulled at the corners of her full mouth. Along her throat the white skin was creased like the folds of a crushed lily. She no longer appeared like a sister, but wore the disapproving face of an unforgiving mother.

Jobber's confidence stumbled. It wasn't at all what she had expected. She felt humbled, shamed beneath Zorah's scornful expression. Her tattered clothes were dirty, her boots left puddles of muddy water on the polished floor. She was again a filthy street snitch, trapped by the bright glare of the Fire Queen.

Zorah stepped forward, her thumb pressed against the guard of her sword. She hesitated, her eyes narrowed to slits.

"No Fire Sword?" she asked, incredulous. "Have you come to me unarmed?"

Jobber opened her hands to show they were empty. Her nails were black with dirt and hard yellow calluses dotted her palms.

Zorah reared back her head and laughed. She shook her head and gave Jobber a withering stare. "Too easy," she said, withdrawing the slim blade from the scabbard. She raised the sword in a mocking salute. "I've worried on nothing."

The Fire Sword shimmered, a pattern of red waves scrolled along its cutting edge. Its red-gold light sparkled in the flames of Zorah's eyes and colored the gray hair a tarnished gold.

The power of the Fire Sword hummed in the circular room. Its angered voice pricked the surface of Jobber's skin and clawed along her spine, lifting the hairs of her neck. Her hands closed into tight fists. She bristled against the invading barbs, resisting its invitation to battle. But as she stared at it, the blood-red waves of the Fire Sword ignited Jobber's temper. Too many dead because of its seduction. A world enslaved beneath its shaft.

"Frigging sword," Jobber said as her fury burned away her shame. "Come on," she goaded Zorah, "try!"

Though her heart quickened its pulse, Jobber allowed her shoulders to relax. Lightly she shook out the cramps in her clenched fists, her arms poised to block or to strike. Jobber intended to defer to Zorah's strikes, flow with the direction of the attack. She would let Zorah get in, close enough to inspire her confidence in winning, but not close enough to kill.

With a swift, graceful motion Zorah slashed the Fire Sword upward toward Jobber's face. The air hissed and the searing heat of the blade struck Jobber's cheek as she shifted back and out of the way. Zorah flexed her wrist inward and the blade turned, the Fire Sword falling with a gleaming trail of red light. Jobber darted sideways, her kneecaps cracking as she quickly bent out of the path of Zorah's sword. Momentum drove her body toward the polished floor, so she flowed with it, tucking her shoulder protectively as she collided with the floor and rolled beyond the reach of Zorah's sword.

Jobber scrambled to her feet again, zigzagging as Zorah attacked with a flurry of strikes. Zorah's face was as hard as the stone carvings, her green eyes expressionless except for the flickering of yellow flames. But the Fire Sword gleamed red, its handle white hot with the heat of Zorah's attacks. A metallic stench peppered the air. Jobber ducked a sideways slash, the blade cutting through the curved stone wall with a grinding screech.

The sword, slowed by the dense stone, gave Jobber the opening she wanted. She straight-punched Zorah hard in the face. Zorah absorbed the blow with an angry gasp, her chin rolling to the side beneath Jobber's fist and deflecting the worst of its impact. A thin trickle of blood started at the corner of Zorah's mouth.

"Frigging shit," Jobber swore and grabbed Zorah's hands, which were still locked on the handle of her Fire Sword. Jobber cried out as her hands felt the surge of power in Zorah's sword. She remembered the cleansing rage when she had drawn the Fire Sword at Sadar's Keep and destroyed everything in her fiery path. The rose of fire opened in her heart, responding to the command of the Fire Sword. Jobber bit down hard on her lower lip and the sharp, sudden pain dimmed the enticing power of the sword. Gripping Zorah's wrists harder, Jobber slammed Zorah's hands repeatedly into the wall. The skin of Zorah's knuckles grazed the stones, leaving spattered dots of blood. Though Zorah fought to free herself from Jobber's grip, Jobber held on tenaciously. Each time Zorah's hands smashed into the wall and the blade of the Fire Sword scraped against the stones a blast of outraged pain quaked through Jobber's body.

"Let go! Let go of the frigging sword!" Jobber shouted. Again and again she beat Zorah's hands into the wall, waiting for the clenched grip to loosen.

Zorah screamed as her bloodied fingers opened at last, letting go of the handle. The Fire Sword fell with a noisy clatter. Jobber kicked it and the sword skittered across the room.

Then Zorah fell on Jobber, shrieking and clawing at Jobber's face. Graying strands of hair lashed the air. Eyes squeezed shut, Jobber reached in and grabbed Zorah by the collar of her shirt. She bent her knees, dropping her weight backward toward the floor, and pulled Zorah, screaming, down with her. At the last moment, Jobber twisted her hips so that Zorah landed with a heavy thud on the floor beside her. The boards peeled and warped with the heat of their bodies. Locked in a furious embrace, Jobber and Zorah rolled over the wooden floor, a shower of flaming sparks scattering as they struggled.

Zorah broke free from Jobber's hold and, reaching wildly, closed a hand around Jobber's throat, digging her thumb into Jobber's windpipe. Jobber punched back hard, hitting Zorah in the side of her temple. Her green eyes went white, rolling to the back of her head, and she shook her head, dazed by the blow. Exhaling hard through her sore throat, Jobber grabbed one of Zorah's hands and twisted it at the wrist. The joints locked from the wrist to the elbow. Zorah howled and struggled to free her arm. But each time she tried to pull away, Jobber tightened the twist, immobilizing her further. Zorah lay panting on her back, Jobber's knee, pressed into her armpit, keeping her pinned to the ground. For the first time Jobber saw fear in Zorah's eyes. She swallowed thickly, her own breath coming in short painful gasps.

"It's over, Zorah," Jobber said.

"I can still burn you," Zorah replied. Gold flames flared in Zorah's eyes and a red flush stained her whitened cheeks.

Jobber gritted her teeth and held on to Zorah, the scorching heat of her body soaking like rain through sand on Jobber's palms. Steam-filled blisters erupted along Jobber's arms and across her chest. The rose of fire in her heart strained to open but Jobber resisted.

She realized she was afraid. Afraid that she would not be able to contain Zorah's power.

Jobber stared down at Zorah's face, the green eyes bright with furious flame. Zorah's body rippled with heat waves, her skin glowing like a shining bar of hot iron.

"To surrender to the moment is to give it life," Shefek had once told Jobber during training. Then it had made no sense to her. But Lirrel's death had shown Jobber the wisdom in Shefek's words. Lirrel had surrendered to the moment and in doing so transformed the bitter defeat of her death. Resistance was no longer a choice for Jobber or the Oran people. Their future would be decided in this moment and no other. Jobber closed her eyes and, breathing deeply, surrendered to the weight of Zorah's power. The rose of fire crackled with a sigh and its blue-tipped petals opened to reveal its white core.

Zorah's fire swallowed Jobber, surrounding her with eager flames. Fire flowed into the white core of her heart, its copper sheen bright as new blood. Jobber felt herself disintegrate in the crucible of Zorah's power, her flesh dissolving into a stream of molten iron.

But there was too much of Jobber, and her fire was too intense to be contained within Zorah's grasp. Cracks opened in Zorah's crucible as Jobber's fire continued to flow without stopping. It reached the scarred rim of Zorah's crucible and poured down over the sides, splattering away into Chaos. The cracks widened and Zorah cried out as the relentless flow of Jobber's fire squeezed through the cracks, forcing her apart.

Frantically, Zorah tried to retreat to the hollow safety of her whirlpool. The twisting wall of the whirlpool sucked at both of them as Zorah withdrew to its center. Splashes of molten copper swirled like heavy raindrops in the spinning column.

Jobber fought against the violent stream, stopping the flow of her element from following Zorah into it. She banked the white core of her fiery heart and the blue-tipped petals folded protectively. As Jobber released her hold on Zorah, the Queen curled her body into a terrified knot. Jobber reached down and held Zorah's face between her hands.

"Let go, Zorah. Don't be afraid," Jobber said.

Zorah stared back like a frightened child terrified of a darkened room. "I can't die," she said stubbornly. "It may not happen to me."

"It must happen to you," Jobber said, the coppery strands of her fire hair casting a sunset over Zorah's frightened face. "Let your element join with me. I will be with you in the fire. You won't be alone."

"But my body," Zorah cried. "It will decay . . ."

"No, no." Jobber hushed her quickly. "You will be like the Great Bonfire, beautiful and pure," Jobber soothed.

Zorah's face relaxed, her lips softened. "I'm tired," she breathed.

Hope eased over Jobber like a cool breeze on her heated face. Zorah would not fight her. Jobber would absorb her element, bring the fire back into the balance of the Queens' quarter knot. Together they would slowly stop Zorah's whirlpool without tearing open Time.

"Come to me, Zorah. It'll be all right," Jobber said to her softly. She embraced the Queen, folding her arms around the trembling shoulders. With a deep sigh, Jobber returned her senses to her fiery heart. The rose of fire bloomed again, the blue-tipped petals reaching out to the edges of her form. She sensed the flow of Zorah's fire, tentative at first and then more swift as Zorah gradually relinquished her burden. Jobber imagined the circle of Zorah's prison opening and stretching into a thread of gleaming red light.

At the edge of her vision, Jobber caught the sudden dart of motion. Lais's white face appeared, hovered over Zorah's Fire Sword. "No!" Jobber shouted as Lais picked up the Fire Sword. But Lais didn't listen, her cold eyes set on Zorah. Jobber struggled to move, but the flowing of Zorah's power made her body sluggish and heavy. Jobber twisted away to protect Zorah from the sword, but she was too slow. Lais drove the Fire Sword into Zorah's back and Jobber screamed as the tip of the blade pushed through between Zorah's breasts. Zorah's hands gripped Jobber's shoulders and her head arched back. The exposed tip of the Fire Sword nicked a bloody line down Jobber's breastbone as Zorah fell heavily against her.

"Frigging idiot!" Jobber shouted as the pain wracked through her limbs.

Then Zorah pushed away from Jobber and staggered to her feet, a hand closed around the blade between her breasts. Blood seeped between the closed fingers of her fist and soaked the white linen shirt.

Jobber stumbled, shocked at the resonating pain in her chest.

Zorah looked at Jobber, realization chasing away the astonished expression. She let go of the Fire Sword and reached a bloodied hand out to Jobber.

Jobber went to take it, hoping it was still possible to prevent the release of Time. But as she touched Zorah's fingers a blast flung her back, slamming her into the curved walls. She heard Lais's ragged scream and stared out at the stars snapping before her eyes.

Zorah's body was disappearing in a spreading flash of brilliant light. It filled the room like a sun rising from beneath the floor to take its position in the sky. Zorah's face faded as the light washed the rounded corners of the room. Only her hard green eyes remained, like two black tears on the sun's face. The blazing red of her hair fanned into the orange flames of the sun's rays. A hot and cold wind circled over Jobber before it was sucked into the flaming corona of sunlight.

Within the core of gold light Jobber saw the faint black outlines of the Fire Sword. Then its form broke apart, scattering into a fine ash. The brilliant light dimmed and fiery tongues licked the charred floors as the flames retreated.

In the once-golden center Zorah's face reappeared. Her features had withered, the skin drawn tight over her skull, her hair gray as old linen thread. The pale lids closed over the hard green stone of her eyes. Zorah's skin blackened and peeled back from a frame of delicate bones. And then the bones burst into a powdery dust.

The roaring winds quieted as the fiery sun shuddered. The flames gutted in thick clouds of smoke and black soot darkened the dome of the once shadowless room.

Jobber touched her ear fearfully as a dense, impenetrable silence followed. The Fire Sword was destroyed. For two hundred years it had stored Time in its blade and now, in a single moment, Time would be unleashed across Oran. Jobber bowed her head to the floor, waiting for the world to tear apart.

She felt it first tug sharply on her hands and then her feet, stretching and pulling in opposite directions. The room canted sideways, wobbling like a slowing top. Jobber resisted the increasing tug. She clenched her body into a knot, her knees pressed to her nose, the curtain of fiery hair draped over her shoulders.

Time poured out lashing waves of conflicting currents; the present dashed between the past and future, and the future rushed headlong to meet history. Fragments of Chaos trapped in the foaming waves of Time spilled aimlessly over Oran's cradle.

Oran trembled violently as Time and Chaos snapped the threads of its sustaining cradle. In the midst of winter, snow melted into streaming rivers. Along the banks of swelling rivers the yellow flags of iris unfurled briefly and then curled into hard brown stalks. New trees sprang to life, changing from saplings to maturity in the span of a single breath. And as they branched, a canopy of green leaves spreading over the bare brown landscape, they also began to rot. Trunks still shimmering with splashes of green toppled and disappeared.

In the shrill keening of Chaos, Jobber heard a dry whisper.

"To rest at last," said a voice no louder than the rustle of pine needles.

Jobber smelled the sharp fragrance of pitch, the sticky sap on her fingers as somewhere, in another place and moment in Time, a hand, dry as wood, touched her on the cheek. Huld, Jobber thought, and saw her face whorled with the lines of a tree's life. The brown lips smiled and the face faded into the burled trunk. The tree shook beneath the fierce breath of Chaos. Pine needles were torn into the wind and the trunk blackened. The branches withered into a powdery, red-colored dirt. The trunk resisted and Jobber caught a glimpse of Huld, her head bowed beneath her shoulders, as she sat resting her arms over her thighs. Then she folded over, her head into her chest, her chest into her lap, until all that remained was a rotted stump. On it, pale pink orchids lifted the bright bowl of their flowers to the wind, and shivered, and died.

The ground heaved as Time reached down and scooped handfuls of soil, raising mountains and then eroding them. It drew forth sweet grass from the barren Plains of Sadar and then withered them brown again as the winds swept across. It clawed at Oran's headlands, sending boulders tumbling into the sea; in the same moment, it lifted new islands out of the ocean, water sluicing from deep gulleys of wet, sandy soil. Stiff coral branches cracked in the dry air and silvery fish thrashed on the unexpected land; anenomes folded their white arms and shriveled in the howling winds; crabs and starfish scuttled down the ravines, returning to the safety of the sea.

Jobber was startled by the sound of voices. In the blackened room ghostly images from other times appeared before her. She saw Huld sitting at a table, her thick, black hair draped over her back and her eyes gray as the Avadares granite. Jobber guessed the other two were Laile and Fenni, once sisters in Zorah's knot. They talked in low, worried voices. Then Zorah entered, sharp with the edge of youth, the Fire Sword dripping flames in her hand. Before Jobber could cry a warning to the vision long past, it was swept away, replaced by another. Men and women cloaked in robes of simple brown leaned over the parapets of a Keep and transformed into Kirians. They lifted noisily into the air, their chorus of shrieks as loud as the keening winds of Chaos. And then Ghazali women circled Jobber, their long black dresses studded with shards of mirrored glass that glimmered like stars. Arms linked, they danced to slow and somber songs, as if long ago they sensed the arrival of this moment and sang to ease the violence of the wind. But the soft shushing of their bare feet and the gentle harmony of their voices was not enough to calm the Chaos.

Night descended in the room and the visions changed again. Jobber gasped, seeing herself as an old woman, her skin oat-colored, her shoulders slightly stooped. Her rusted hair was braided, errant strands stroking the sides of a wrinkled cheek. She laughed, inclining her head toward a man with leather-brown skin. Wind burns starred his cheeks, but his eyes glowed with a soft pearl sheen.

And then Chaos snatched away the vision, filling the room with a choking black smoke and dust from exploding plaster. The Keep rumbled, tremors shaking its foundation.

Oran groaned in the shifting stones, and ribs of earth splintered under the pounding weight of Time. Limbs were cracked and eroded. Along the slopes of Avadares, walls of rock slid away, and in the western Plains gullies wounded the fields. The threads of the Queens' quarter knot were being sawed away by the sharp edges of Chaos. Throughout Beldan hearth fires gutted as Oran's pulse weakened.

"No!" Jobber shouted at the driving winds. "I won't let go!"

Jobber closed her eyes and reached for the thread of her power. At once it dragged her into the night sky, sending her snapping like a whip around a fraying universe.

Dagar was there, struggling to hold together the threads of the knot that were coming undone before the wind. But each time he grasped the threads and tried to bind them anew in a semblance of Oran's cradle as Lirrel had done they faded in his hands, or blew away.

Shedwyn winked into the sky, her vivid green light brightest across her round belly. Leafing tendrils of green light held secure the shape of the curled child within her.

Then suddenly Tayleb appeared beside her, shimmering like a sapphire star.

Two more threads twisted and snapped.

"You must make the knot whole," Jobber screamed to Dagar in the howling winds.

"I don't know how!" Dagar shouted back. "Lirrel's knot won't work this time. Oran has changed. The cradle no longer holds!"

Jobber's thoughts leapt before her, trying to find a new direction. They would no longer be served by the past alone. Jobber remembered the fleeting image of her and Dagar grown old. A future was possible. Even in the strangeness of Chaos, Jobber had seen the bond of intimacy in that brief moment between her and Dagar, a bond of friendship carried through long years. She heard the sweet voice of a flute, a short refrain that sounded clear in the shattered night sky. At once a way to survive occurred to Jobber. In spite of her fear she smiled. Lirrel would have appreciated her plan, she thought, wondering if Lirrel had not come to her in the fragment of flute song.

"We must leave our bodies and become our elemental threads," Jobber shouted.

"Like Lirrel?" Dagar asked, his eyes glowing bright.

"Yeah," Jobber answered, drawing in a deep breath. "And

then we must become each other, in order to join into a single thread. A knot that is tied from within each thread.''

"I don't understand," Shedwyn cried.

"But you do!" Jobber exclaimed. "It was you that said it first. We're elements of Oran and not just flesh. So I will travel through you, and you through me.''

Around them Chaos closed its fist; the howl of the winds was deafening. Another thread snapped and was sucked into the mass of violet clouds.

Jobber reached for the wilted bloom of her fiery heart. The rose responded, opening petals that had deepened into the red glow of dying embers. She plunged herself into the core of her heart, abandoning the thin sheath of skin. She let go of the bones, the muscle and sinew that had shaped her as a human girl. She felt transparent as she released herself, uncurling like a frond of yellow flame through the threads of the knot.

Jobber was drawn through the twisting strands of the knot and then slowed, meeting resistance in Shedwyn's hesitation. She waited, the fire warming the threads. And then at once, Shedwyn's body opened to her and Jobber passed through.

The heat of her fire changed, tempered by the green coolness of the earth, the damp of the wet stones. Jobber exhaled, her flaming thread blazing brighter with the shocked sensation of another's body. It was almost like the first time, when Lirrel had tied the knot and Jobber had experienced the sudden sharp awareness of the others. But then they had held something back, clinging to their four separate identities.

Jobber's element filled the curved, hollowed shape of Shedwyn's body. She marveled at the density of her flesh, the broad shoulders and muscled arms. She gasped, short of breath, and felt the rounded bulge of a baby beneath her ribs. Jobber rested her hands beneath the swollen breasts, amazed that they could feel so heavy.

Her fire element adapted easily to Shedwyn's element. Black ore melted in her hands and cooled into hardened palmfuls of shining metal. Wood crackled with flames and changed to blackened ash. Out of the enriched soil, the faint green stems of flowers appeared, mingled with spears of cream-colored wheat.

Through the red thread of her element, Jobber saw a thin line of green light twisting like a vine.

The winds of Chaos howled and shifted, driving Jobber out of Shedwyn. There was a flash of white light and then she was hurtled into Dagar's empty body.

As she filled out his waiting form she burst out laughing in shocked surprise. Her voice sounded deeper, a lump in her throat bobbing up and down as she laughed. Jobber had always believed that with her hipless torso and her flat breasts she was closer to being male than female; but now, shaped by arms that angled strangely from wide shoulders and a waist that arrowed into a narrowed pelvis, she realized how unrealistic that notion had been. She sensed Dagar's equal surprise in the white shimmering light. *Wait 'til he reaches Shedwyn,* she thought as warm currents of air rose from the heat of her fire. A flute played its song, its voice reaching into the sky, bringing them closer to distant stars. Jobber's fire gentled and fine white light streaked through the red and green of her thread.

But her awe was shortened as the winds of Chaos intensified and fanned the flames of her element. She had passed through Dagar but she was caught now in the backdraft of churning air. Flames shot out around her, reaching down to the scarred earth below. Jobber was burning out of control. The winds of Chaos had transformed her into a twisting column of fire, and Oran shuddered under the lash of a second Burning.

Jobber shouted in protest, trying to rein in the exploding column of fire, but the winds were too strong and she careened over the land leaving a trail of blackened earth.

Jobber's thread burned coppery red, the green and the white fading beneath the raging fire. She was growing thin as sunlight, vaporous as waves of heat.

And then a tidal wall of cold saltwater splashed over her. An exalted cry was torn from Jobber's lips as the column of flames was violently quenched. Drenched in the ocean, Jobber felt like a new sword, its heated blade plunged into cold water. Steam hissed in her ears as her core solidified in the cooling waves.

Once again Jobber could sense Shedwyn and Dagar as the threads of their elements annealed into resilient steel threads.

Tayleb held the threads of light together, like a fisherman's daughter tying the knots of a new net.

She looked up with a shy smile and waited for Jobber.

Inhaling a steaming mist, Jobber passed through Tayleb's body. Jobber sighed as she shrugged into Tayleb's form. Now Jobber found herself small and neat, her hands cool and smelling of fish. The length of her legs had shortened, her fingers become nimble. Cold water splashed over her thighs and spumes of white foam settled on her shining arms. Along Jobber's thread, a line of sky blue blended with the others.

Jobber tumbled free again into the sky, startled by its huge black expanse. She wore her own shape and stretched her arms out gratefully in the peaceful quiet. She looked at Shedwyn, Dagar, and Tayleb and they sparkled like stars set into a new constellation. Between their drifting forms the auras of Oran children glittered like coins, carrying the old power and brightening the empty spaces. As Jobber watched, tiny threads reached out from the children to where the four elements of the knot anchored the new constellation in the sky. Oran drifted in the colored light of a newly spun cocoon.

Shedwyn started to laugh. She laughed until tears poured down her cheeks, green as flowing emeralds. Leaves unfurled around her face and fire-tipped flowers bloomed in her hair.

Her joy was infectious and Jobber found herself laughing too.

"Z'blood, you're bigger than I thought, farmergirl!" Jobber blurted out and Shedwyn, who had nearly calmed herself, erupted in a new fit of laughing.

"At least she was another woman," Dagar said, screwing up his face. His black hair stuck up from his forehead, blue droplets of sweat clinging to the ends. He touched himself curiously, as if to reassure himself that in the frantic tying of the knot he had not lost some portion of himself.

"Yeah, it was naffy all right," Jobber admitted. She turned to Tayleb, who had been quiet throughout the laughter. In Tayleb's blue eyes small flames flickered warmly. "I'm glad you were here. I didn't know how to stop."

Tayleb broke into a smile. "It was Lirrel who said that water balanced fire."

Jobber's face grew sober, thinking of Lirrel. Lirrel who should have been here.

Dagar sighed, his breath like the faint mist of starlight. "I wish she was here too."

"We must return to Oran," Shedwyn said, her urgency ringing through the threads of the knot. "The land is badly damaged."

"We've done it, then," Jobber said wearily.

"*Ahal,*" Dagar agreed. "We have tied a new knot, one that is secure and strong." He cast one more longing glance into the night sky and Jobber felt his sorrow.

Jobber watched the other three wink out of the sky, one by one, taking with them the bright aura of their element. But they remained within her, their senses mingled in the threads of the knot. She looked up and saw the winds of Chaos churning far above the shining web of the knot. The shrill keening was gone, and for the moment Oran floated peacefully amid the net of new stars.

Chapter Twenty-four

*J*obber *waited impatiently on the ruins of the Harbor Wall. She* shielded her eyes from the morning sun as she stared out at the brightly spangled water. In the orange glow of the sun the waves flickered like flames. Beyond the Harbor Wall she could just make out the long sandy islands of the Ribbons. "Where are they?" she demanded.

"They'll be here soon," Shedwyn said, sitting down on an old crate. She opened her shawl, her face turned up to catch the warmth of the sun. "After the last five days, it feels good just to sit here and rest."

Jobber sighed heavily, brushing the windblown hair out of her eyes. She sat down next to Shedwyn and forced herself to relax. Shedwyn was right, she decided. In these last days she had scarcely given herself time to think, let alone sit in the sun and rest.

Beldan had suffered deep wounds in the aftermath of Zorah's death. Whole sections of the city had been destroyed and lay in rubbled heaps of stone, torn beams, and broken glass. There had been no fresh water, a scarcity of food, and fires burned out of control. Some Sileans had chosen to be stubborn and to fight even in the burnt-out remains of the city. It had taken three days to convince them their cause was lost. Jobber figured it wasn't so much the superior fighting skills of the New Moon that changed their minds as it was the utter poverty and desolation of the city they sought to hold.

Treys had arrived two days ago with the army from the North. The Sileans there had surrendered to the New Moon. Their commanders were dead and they had lived through the terror of witnessing Oran's upheaval in the spilling of Time. The soldiers saw no reason to sacrifice their lives in such a fruitless battle. All they hoped for now was passage home. But even that had taken time, for the harbor was cluttered with wrecked ships, their hulls smashed against the harbor walls or beached along the remains of the Harbor Tower. The ocean currents had been rough and unpredictable, and only recently had Tayleb been able to calm the sea enough to allow the ships that could sail to depart, their holds laden with the fleeing survivors.

But not all the Sileans had chosen to leave. Eneas's army of Sileans and Orans had offered a glimmer of hope to those Sileans still in Beldan who saw no chance of returning to Silea. Jobber gnawed her fingernail, remembering the raw emotions of the first few days. The joy of imminent victory went hand in hand with the thirst for vengeance. She had called a hasty council of Guildsmen and New Moon leaders to insist on an end to the slaughter of Sileans and Readers in the city. Reprisals would serve nothing toward establishing a future peace. Slipper and Kai were quick to put out the word among the street Flocks, and the Guildsmen, though they dragged their feet, finally accepted the condition. A fragile truce held, and though the Sileans and the Readers were forced to share their lodgings, their food, and surrender their wealth, Jobber considered it a fair trade for their lives.

Shedwyn, Eneas, and Anard had come five days ago. Wyer had sent an escort to fetch them from the woods and bring them to Beldan. Jobber had hoped that Dagar and Tayleb could have come as quickly from the Ribbons. She wanted to see Dagar, talk to him about Lirrel. But the rough seas had prevented the riverboats from navigating the harbor and they had had to wait until the water calmed.

"Do you see them?" Alwir called to Jobber as he hurried over the broken cobblestone road. Behind him Wyer helped Eneas, who hobbled slowly on a crutch.

"Not yet," Jobber answered. Her impatience returned and she scowled at the near-empty harbor.

"There!" Shedwyn cried, standing up and pointing to a small, narrow shadow that bounced over the tops of the waves.

Jobber's heart jumped as she saw Tip standing in the prow of his boat, his arms pumping as he poled it toward the Harbor Wall. Two passengers rode behind him, and Jobber grinned as she saw Dagar clutching at the sides of the rocking boat and felt his queasiness through the knot.

She waved her hand furiously in the air and her grin spread wider as she saw him wave back. "They're coming," she called to Alwir.

"Can you see her?" he asked, his breath shortened as he hurried to join them.

Jobber and Shedwyn exchanged a quick smile. "Yeah, I see *her*," Jobber answered. "Seems like she's looking out for you too," she teased.

The riverboat was bumping into the sides of the Harbor Wall by the time Wyer and Eneas arrived. Jobber had clambered down to the landing and was steadying the boat as Tip tied it to a mooring. Alwir was the first to offer Tayleb his hand and help her from the boat. Jobber whistled low between her teeth when Alwir embraced her tightly in his arms, only her small hands visible on his long, lanky back.

She turned to help Dagar and paused, stunned by the unexpected sight of his moonlit eyes. She recovered quickly, hearing him groan with seasickness. His face was pale and sweating.

"Come on," she said thickly, pulling him up, "let me get you out of there."

"I want the hard road," he moaned, "not this riding on the back of a serpent."

"It weren't that bad," muttered Tip. "A bit dippy in places, but mostly fair, I'd say."

"Welcome, Dagar," Shedwyn said, coming slowly down the narrow stairway to greet them. "It's good to see you again." She embraced him warmly and then stood back to examine his face. Tears welled in her eyes but she didn't cry. "So like Lirrel," she whispered and stroked his cheek. "And yet you are very different," she added, smiling.

"Can't call us a Queens' quarter knot anymore," Jobber said. "Just Oran's knot, I guess." Then, slowly, Jobber retrieved a bone flute from her vest pocket and handed it to Dagar. "You should have this," she said gruffly. "By rights it's yours."

Dagar's lips parted in surprise and he stared at the familiar flute resting in his hands. "Lirrel's flute," he breathed and touched the flute to his mouth. He blew one note and then stopped. "Where is the body?" he asked, his eyes still lowered to the flute in his hands.

"Fairuz's tent claimed it. They took her north along with my Fire Sword to bury in the Kirian forges at Myer's Cave," Jobber answered and her voice grew tight.

Dagar nodded. "Seems right," he said softly.

"Do you really have her memories?" Jobber asked, curious.

"All of them." Dagar sighed heavily and looked up at them.

"She loved you very much," Tayleb said to Jobber. "She often spoke of you." The wind ruffled her curly hair and the sky was reflected in her bright blue eyes.

"Yeah?" Jobber sniffed hard and then forced a pained smile. "Well, then. Only one thing to do."

"And what's that?" asked Shedwyn, the shadow of a smile beginning to cross her face.

Jobber hesitated. "It's off to the Crow's Wing. We'll drink a round to our dead. And then we'll drink to our future, now that we got one."

On the street again, Jobber linked arms with Wyer and Dagar. Behind her, Alwir and Tayleb held hands, Alwir pointing out the remaining sights of Beldan. Farther back Shedwyn and Eneas walked more slowly, conversing quietly together, while Tip scampered ahead to warn the innkeeper at the Crow's Wing of their arrival.

"And what's that?" Tayleb kept asking as more and more of

the city came into view. Alwir and Jobber argued over who had the better answer until Tayleb grew completely confused.

"Beldanites," Shedwyn mumbled to Eneas and they shook their heads.

On the High Street they were joined by a lively crowd of street children who had busied themselves collecting cobblestones. They trailed along chattering excitedly. A boy at Finnia's Arms ran to tell Slipper and Kai that they were headed for the Crow's Wing. As they walked through the Guild District, Jobber shouted greetings to the opened doors of the workhouses. Inside, Masters and apprentices were clearing rubble and setting up their trades again. Weavers left their broken looms and came to the steps, waving their blue neck scarves. A ragged gang of cutterlads and stickboys joined the growing stream of people headed for the Crow's Wing. At Crier's Forge the smiths turned out into the street, bringing with them the sharp odor of smoke and heated iron.

Someone pressed a fiddle into Alwir's hands and he played a fast tune that quickened their steps. At Blessing Street Alwir found himself accompanied by a waterman with a concertina. The old squeezebox huffed out its asthmatic tune like a badly winded singer. Two ribbon sellers handed out blue and orange ribbons. The whores from Blessing Street and even respectable women from the Guildhouses tied them on their bodices and apron strings.

On Drover's Road Jobber turned to look at the noisy crowd that filled the street behind her. They were mostly young, and on their expectant faces Jobber saw the future of Oran come alive. She would never again be free of responsibility, Jobber realized wistfully. She and the rest of the knot would be needed for a long time to come, entangled in the lives of every Oran.

But it seemed to Jobber a reasonable price for the privilege of standing on a Beldan street beneath a bright winter sun and amid such a jubilant celebration. And as a reckless joy filled her, Jobber threw back her head, the fiery hair shining like copper sunlight, and let her laughter ring out over the streets she loved.